the COMPANY of GLASS

the COMPANY of GLASS

Everien
~ BOOK ONE ~

VALERY LEITH

BANTAM BOOKS
NEW YORK   TORONTO   LONDON
SYDNEY   AUCKLAND

THE COMPANY OF GLASS

A Bantam Spectra Book / July 1999

SPECTRA and the portrayal of a boxed "s" are trademarks of
Bantam Books, a division of Random House, Inc.

Book design by Casey Hampton.
Map by James Sinclair.

Library of Congress Cataloging-in-Publication Data

Leith, Valery, 1968–
The company of glass / Valery Leith.
p.   cm. — (Everien ; bk. 1)
ISBN 0-553-37938-0
I. Title.   II. Series: Leith, Valery, 1968– Everien ; bk. 1.
PS3562.E4622C66   1999
813'.54—dc21   98-56460
CIP

Published simultaneously in the United States and Canada

Bantam Books are published by Bantam Books, a division of Random House, Inc. Its
trademark, consisting of the words "Bantam Books" and the portrayal of a rooster, is
Registered in U.S. Patent and Trademark Office and in other countries. Marca
Registrada. Bantam Books, 1540 Broadway, New York, New York 10036.

PRINTED IN THE UNITED STATES OF AMERICA

FFG   10   9   8   7   6   5   4   3   2   1

FOR THE ANIMALS OF BOURNE HILL
THE TAME ONES AND THE WILD ONES
AND ESPECIALLY
THE ONE CALLED STEVE MORRIS

CONTENTS

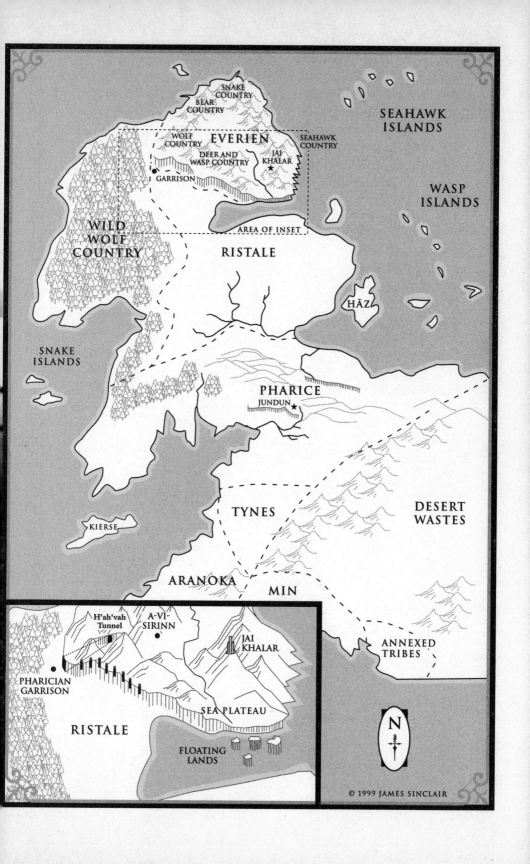

SNAKE
COUNTRY
BEAR
COUNTRY

SEAHAWK
ISLANDS

WOLF
COUNTRY   EVERIEN
DEER AND
WASP COUNTRY   JAI
KHALAR   SEAHAWK
COUNTRY
GARRISON

WASP
ISLANDS

WILD
WOLF
COUNTRY

RISTALE

AREA OF INSET

HĀZ

SNAKE
ISLANDS

PHARICE
JUNDUN

TYNES

DESERT
WASTES

KIERSE

ARANOKA
MIN

ANNEXED
TRIBES

H'ah'vah
Tunnel   A-VI-
SIRINN

JAI
KHALAR

PHARICIAN
GARRISON

SEA PLATEAU

RISTALE

FLOATING
LANDS

N

© 1999 JAMES SINCLAIR

Rose
oh, the pure contradiction
delight
of being no one's sleep
under so many lids.

—RAINER MARIA RILKE

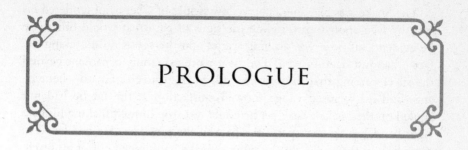

PROLOGUE

Men are animals. It is no slander to say so, for only by skillful application of all his faculties can a mere human evoke that creature within whose senses are sharper than his, whose heart is truer, whose mind is wiser. A Clan warrior at the height of his powers is never more than a handsbreadth from his own animal nature—it is from this proximity to his primal spirit that he derives a joy unknown to others.

Yet it was not joy that polished the bare skins of the Snake and the Bear who faced each other in the ring—it was hard sweat. By the time Queen Ysse entered the training ground, the two combatants had whipped each other up into a froth of hatred that aroused their animal natures to savage violence. The metamorphosis was not magical—there were no scales or tails. It was chemical. Transfigured by emotion, the contenders moved in communion with the wild creatures whose fighting skills their ancestral traditions had taught them to emulate. They had become more than human.

Ysse smiled. The Company were too absorbed in watching the test match to notice the old woman come limping in, but Quintar the Captain of the Guard picked up her movement in his peripheral vision and glanced in her direction. A tall, rather homely man with claws of Seahawk paint decorating his face, he was lounging against the far wall of the arena, apart from his charges. He might have been handsome once, but his countenance had known so many fights it was impossible to be sure what features he had been born with. As Ysse made her way toward him, he acknowledged her arrival with a slight wave, but his gaze never left the ring.

The Snake was bleeding. The yellow stripes of Clan paint rendered his swarthy face anonymous, hiding the signs of pain that would otherwise be evident; his nose was gushing scarlet and there was no mistaking the fact it had just been broken. The Bear wore no family ornament beyond the silver earring that showed his rank in the Queen's Guard—lieutenant—and his exposed visage showed satisfaction at the hit he had just landed on the Snake's face; yet he could not stop himself shaking his bare right hand, trying to disperse the pain in the knuckles. He had failed to capitalize on the strike, for the injured Snake had slipped out of his reach, leaving red footprints on the bleached white wood of the arena. Both men were stripped for the fight, and the Bear's ribs heaved; his relentless pursuit of the elusive Snake had winded him.

"Come on, Vorse!" called the Company from the perimeter, clapping their hands in encouragement for the injured Snake. The Snake was lean and sinuous as befitted his family name, and he had managed to stay just out of range of his heavier opponent until the Bear had countertimed his feint and scored the lucky hook. Ysse's body twisted slightly as she followed the Snake's movement. Even through the frailty of her illness she could feel what it was like to be the Snake. She could feel the fight coming alive in him. Mouth open, red-toothed and angry, the Snake now wove back and forth before the larger man, who aimed a series of kicks at him, attempting to compound the damage he'd inflicted already.

Ysse tensed as the Bear went in. But the attack was too slow, and the Snake slipped into the gap in his opponent's timing and wound himself around the Bear like a snare drawn suddenly taut, destroying the Bear's balance and dragging him to the ground. A shout went up from the observers as the Bear managed to twist on the way down and land on top of the Snake.

"Stay cool, Vorse," said the Captain of the Guard as the scramble continued on the ground. "It's only a nose. We'll get Hanji to knit you another one."

He edged along the wall, head tilted as he watched the opponents wrestle. The floor of the ring shuddered when they slammed against each other. As Ysse reached his side, Quintar murmured, "They're fighting for the twelfth place in the Company, the one left by Ajiko when he broke his leg."

"Why not take them both and have thirteen?" Ysse asked.

"Because that would be a compromise. It's better for them to fight for it. I'm going to take them to clear the Sekk out of Bear Country next month, and this contest will motivate the whole Company. Yesterday they all climbed the North Face. I made Vorse and Lerien race ten miles this morning before the fight. They hate my guts."

Ysse warmed with affection for him: she could see the bonds between Quintar and his men as if there were lines drawn in the air between them. He had handpicked the members of the Company from across Everien, then spent eight years teaching them to destroy the monsters that the Sekk called down from the mountain wilds on the Clan villages. He spared no effort with them: elite bands like the Company were Everien's best hope of survival against the Sekk scourge, which could appear any-where and at any time—from beneath the hills themselves, sometimes. He had pushed his men to their limits until their limits stretched and broke, and they got better than they'd thought themselves capable—and none of them could ever have been called modest. The men of the Company were a strong-willed bunch, each a warrior of note within his original animal Clan, conditioned from birth to fight. Left to their own devices, they would have fought each other: no Clan warrior needed an excuse to challenge a man of another Clan. Yet Quintar managed them with a mysterious blend of intelligence and coercion that kept him always one step ahead of them. They hated him for his harshness and occasional brutality, but they also learned to trust each other, until the esprit de corps of the Company overcame their Clan rivalries. All became tougher and smarter and faster, and Quintar's reputation grew. Only Ysse knew how he fretted over his charges like a grandmother, losing sleep over their failures and endlessly searching for ways to get more out of each of them. Only Ysse could see how every one of their triumphs and failures was felt doubly by Quintar, who affected aloofness for the sake of maintaining authority. Yes, the men hated Quintar, but she suspected that by now they also adored him. For his part, Quintar had come to have no exis-tence independent of the warriors he led to victory over victory.

She knew how he felt, for she was the monarch of a country that she had struggled to build against heavy opposition from Clan chieftains who would as soon kill one another as unite against the Sekk; a fragile country built on the ruins of ancient Everien; a country that had never known a king, much less a queen. Her existence was the very definition of soli-tude. She only ever felt slightly less alone when she was with Quintar, her protégé. She wondered if he knew this and decided that he probably didn't: he was too self-contained, utterly focused on the work at hand. Like all her subjects, Quintar could not help but view the queen through the legends that had grown around her. Ysse sometimes wished it could be otherwise. She shifted her weight unobtrusively to her right hip, for the pain in her legs made it hard to stand, though she tried not to show it.

The Bear and the Snake were tangled on the floor, breathing hard. It did not look good for the Snake. The Bear was sitting on his chest and beating at his head with huge fists; the Snake covered what was left of his face with his elbows and forearms. Blood flew like flower petals in a wind.

"Just say when you've had enough!" roared the Bear, enjoying himself. The rest of the Company screamed encouragement, some to Vorse, some to Lerien, who rode on top.

A lifetime of fighting the Sekk had left Ysse no stranger to violence, but now she began to cast reproachful looks in Quintar's direction. He ought to stop the fight. It was clear that the Bear was dominating, and what was to be gained by letting him rip the Snake to pieces? Both men had lost all self-control.

Quintar had moved off to get a better look at the action. Angrily the queen dragged herself to his side. "Stop the match," she whispered.

He didn't look at her. "Who will be there to stop the fight when a Sekk monster is trying to eat them? Will it be fair when their own brothers attack them, consumed with madness under the Slaving of the Sekk?"

"This is *training*," Ysse snapped, grabbing his arm. "You abuse Vorse. He'll be killed."

The Snake was virtually invisible beneath the mass of the Bear. He appeared limp, possibly lifeless. Ysse drew breath to command a halt, but some premonition checked her. Her nails bit into Quintar's forearm as the Snake made his move. Seemingly boneless, he writhed, pressed his right shoulder against the ground, and with a lightning jerk that seemed to ripple through his entire body, suddenly upended the Bear, wrapped his left leg over the Bear's shoulder, and snapped his pelvis up to trap the neck between his thigh. In the same fluid movement he caught a wrist and locked the arm at the elbow. The Bear screamed. The joint snapped audibly, and then before the crowd could react, the Bear was choking in the grasp of the Snake's legs and the Snake, throwing all of his slight weight into the movement, levered the Bear's back off the ground, almost breaking it at the neck.

Quintar had already leaped in to intervene, and now the surrounding Company fell on the pair, separating them. Spitting teeth, Vorse stood up and was enveloped in a buffeting of congratulatory slaps. Quintar emerged from the crowd and beckoned his comrades to attend the defeated Bear, who got to his feet more slowly, head down, broken arm dangling.

"He'll be all right," Quintar told her, clicking his tongue as he swung his head from side to side in disparagement. He reminded Ysse of an auntie fretting over a pair of recalcitrant children. "Stubborn! Lerien should have conceded quicker. Vorse might have gotten carried away and broken his neck."

Ysse sighed. Quintar was still young—and like all the young, he didn't know what that meant. Standing beside him, the queen felt weary, and she remembered now why she had come down here. She drew herself erect and said: "The White Road has opened. Jai Pendu draws nigh. Are your men ready?"

Quintar reacted as one well accustomed to Ysse's style of leadership; he had learned long ago that when she had something of moment to say, she always said it casually, without warning or preamble. He was startled, and for a second his brown eyes fixed on her face; then he shrugged. He gestured toward the sand arena at the far end of the training ground. "My archers are practicing target-shooting right now. Do they look ready to you?"

Four black horses flowed across the sand each in a different rhythm, changing direction suddenly at invisible signals from their riders' legs, for the Wasp archers rode without aid of rein. On the ground among them was a small man wearing only a loincloth and elaborate Wasp Clan tattoos. Unarmed, he was engaged in evading the arrows of the four Wasps who ferociously attacked him.

"What can you be thinking?" the queen rebuked Quintar, and forgetting the pain in her ankles she took several long strides closer to the fence. A stray arrow flew by her, which she ignored. She snapped, "Get Chyko out of there before he's killed."

Chyko darted and changed direction like a crazed fly. When one of the horses braked suddenly he disappeared into the white arc of sand that spat from its hooves. He reappeared momentarily, then slipped beneath one of the other horses. There was a flash of metal in his hand before he whirled away from the slashing hooves, waving his arms and shouting taunts at the riders, the nearest of whom toppled when the saddle slid off his mount: the girth had been cut.

"I can't control Chyko," Quintar said, admiration coloring his tone. "Maybe he'll listen to you. He likes women."

"If you can't control him, you shouldn't have him in your Company," Ysse reproached, unsettled by the display. "You have worked too hard on these men to spoil their discipline with a wild creature such as this."

Quintar said, "He brings up their ability. And he's worth twenty of the rest. Look!"

Chyko, surrounded by the snorting horses and cocked bows of his fellow Wasp Clansmen, stuck out a hand and caught an arrow. He ducked another shot, spinning at the same time and sliding onto the back of the loose horse, to which he clung like a flea. The horse took two strides, jumped the fence, and roared past Quintar and the queen like a hurricane.

Stunned, she said, "That one cannot be a man. He must be something else."

"To answer your question," Quintar said, smiling, "they are ready. We will set Vorse's nose in a splint; the discomfort will help him to concentrate. Maybe he'll make fewer mistakes the next time he takes a bigger opponent to the ground."

"What about the Bear who lost the match? Lerien? He fought well."

"His arm is broken. I leave him to you. You will need someone to command the Guard while I am gone."

Those words hurt. For a moment she had been caught up in watching the Company train, and she had forgotten that they would ride away without her. They would ride off to Jai Pendu as she had once done, when she was as young as Quintar was now. Even from far away she swore she could feel the floating city approaching on the tide; she could feel the pull of its Knowledge and she wanted badly to go with them, to witness Jai Pendu's wonders once again. She ached for the glory of holding the Fire of Glass in her bare hands and knowing that she, Ysse, a mortal creature, had touched a transcendent Artifact of the ancient Everiens.

But her time was past. This was Quintar's age, and Ysse must stand aside. Her hand was on the sword she carried—even in Jai Khalar, her own castle; even in her illness and age. She drew the blade. Quintar stepped back a pace, his eyes holding hers with the empty quality that meant he still took her seriously as a fighter; he was prepared for the possibility that she would attack him. Lowering her blade, she slid off her sword belt and extended the scabbard to him. He looked surprised for only the briefest instant; then he took the scabbard and ran his hands over the incisions that were Ysse's personal signs. Years ago, when she had gone to Jai Pendu, she had acquired the three symbols she had worn on her blade ever since. She had never discussed them with anyone, much less explained them. Emotion made her throat tight as she now passed on to Quintar the scabbard bearing the signs of the Eye, the Sun, and the Rose. Her voice was hoarse.

"I will not see you again before you go. Hanji will bring you my standard and help you find the White Road. Go tonight."

Quintar nodded assent, his usually sober face lighting with anticipation. Yes, he was young. She reached out and touched his shoulder, aware that the gesture was too weak, too feminine, for such a martial occasion.

Yet when she thought of Jai Pendu, she could not bring herself to pretend she felt powerful.

"Farewell," she said, and turned away, trying not to hunch with the ache in her spine as she reached for the door. The clash of weapons answered her but she didn't look back at the men in whose prowess she placed all her hope. These were men who loved the fight above all. They lived for it. Her heart swelled with pride and she began to laugh. They would succeed at Jai Pendu. She could feel it.

The door closed behind her. It was the last she would ever see of the Company.

EIGHTEEN YEARS LATER

The clatter of fast-flying hooves on stone jarred the youngest blacksmith of the Deer Clan at A-vi-Khalar from exhausted sleep. A thin, runny light intimated the place where dawn would crack the northern sky; the time couldn't be much more than an hour past midnight. The blacksmith rolled over, groping for his wife. As the hoofbeats passed by his window, a voice bellowed in an army accent. "A horse! Bring out the king's horse!"

Another messenger. He moaned softly. He ached all over. Yesterday he had worked a brutal double shift in the Fire Houses forging weapons for the defenders in the mountains; he needed more sleep, a reprieve for both mind and muscles. But it was not to be. Duty to one's Clan always came first, and he was the youngest; he would have to go down to the stables and get the royal courier horse ready . . . in his mind he was rolling out of bed, gliding outside to open the stall, checking the hooves, and—

The rider passed again going the other way, still shouting for a horse at the top of his lungs. The blacksmith started from his dreamlet and groaned.

"Dzani, get up before the whole Clan's disturbed," his wife chided sleepily, shoving him. The blacksmith grabbed his shirt and staggered into the street. The brightly colored tiles that paved the road were dulled with fine ash from the Fire Houses, which had burned all night for months: the cones of the ancient structures could be seen presiding over the village, their blackened shapes resisting the onset of dawn. Geese were running to and fro in the gray light, flapping their wings and generally adding to the cacophony.

From the noise being made, the blacksmith had expected a restive horse, prancing and rearing, and a royal messenger wearing red and sporting elaborate face-paint showing both Clan affiliation and rank within King Lerien's house at Jai Khalar. But the coat of the black horse was soaked with lather and sending up clouds of steam, the harness and saddle skirts were mud-caked, and the animal's head sagged toward the ground in weariness. The rider was dressed in scarred leather battle gear and the hood of his stained green cloak was cast back so that the dew settled on ragged, uncombed brown hair. He was not young. His beard had grown at least three days, and when he dismounted, he stumbled before catching the reins and steadying himself.

"I'm sorry to wake you." His soldier's accent was even more pronounced when he wasn't shouting. "I need your fastest horse, and"—his mount strained toward the blacksmith's trough, and the stranger swayed and almost lost his balance again—"and please fetch your boy to walk this one until she is cool. I hope I have not misused her."

Dzani had begun unsaddling the horse even as the stranger spoke; now he gave a sharp whistle. His older daughter scurried out of the house barefoot to pry the reins from the soldier's fingers. Before the man was aware of it, she had looped a rope around the animal's neck and led it away. The blacksmith hoisted the warm, damp saddle onto his shoulder and motioned for the stranger to follow him to the stable. He took a good look at the saddle. The king's crest was embossed on the leather, but he could see no similar mark on the man's clothing. He wore no Clan paint at all, nor any ornament that would identify him. Dzani noticed the messenger's bloodshot eyes and his pallor. The blacksmith paused outside the kitchen door.

"Go inside and get something to eat while I tack the horse. It won't hold you up but a minute."

"The mare—she's been going hard," said the stranger weakly, looking guilty. "She must be walked for a time and if you crack an egg in her mash—"

"My daughter will take care of her," Dzani interrupted, amused. Before the other could protest, he added caustically, "Now, get some breakfast. Fine lot of good will be done if the mount arrives at the Citadel bearing a dead man."

He half expected the stranger to take offense—the king's men could be very touchy about being tendered respect—but the man laughed hoarsely and said, "Thanks, friend—you're right."

Dzani entered the dim stable, whose occupants were still dozing. "Wake up, you lazy sods," he called, and emitted a huge yawn.

IN THE KITCHEN, the blacksmith's wife had quickly heated soup and carved the stale crusts from yesterday's bread. The messenger came in, bowed to her, and sank onto the bench. When she turned from the oven, he had fallen asleep with his face on the table. She finished preparing the food and set it on the boards, but he didn't stir. She hesitated, unsure whether she should wake him—and then the scabbard of his sword caught her eye. It bore no Clan marking. It was dark blue, and the insignia was an eye, a stylized sun, and a rose. Recognizing it, she felt herself flush and stood there frozen for a moment—then, without making a conscious decision, she quickly reached out and shook his shoulder. He sat bolt upright; the soup slopped on the table. He favored her with a broken-toothed smile and a nod of thanks before falling to. The blacksmith's wife hovered.

"Please . . . sir . . ." she ventured, clasping her hands behind her back because suddenly she didn't know what to do with them. She deliberately averted her eyes from the scabbard. "These tidings you carry to the king . . . is battle to come even here?"

He drained the soup bowl and set it down. He stared at the wood, and it seemed as though he was gripped in some inner struggle. Suddenly he slammed his palm down on the table; crumbs leaped into the air. She jumped in her skin.

"My message can only be given to the king himself."

She had already slid back fearfully, bumping into the hot stove and then recoiling. "I see. Of course. I'm sorry—"

He was shaking himself like a wet dog, blinking rapidly as he brushed disheveled locks back from his face. His gaze fixed on her and he seemed to take her measure for a moment. His eyes were bloodshot. She relaxed slightly as she realized he had only slapped the table in an effort to wake himself. Emboldened, she searched his face, expecting to find tragedy there—but she saw only exhaustion.

"Are you all right?" she whispered. "Do you want me to brew some *sita* for you?"

Still looking at her, he reached for a handful of bread and cheese and surged to his feet. "*I* am sorry," he said as he passed her on the way out. "Battle is coming to this whole land, even to the Citadel. Prepare yourselves!"

•   •   •

BY THE TIME Dzani had a fresh horse ready, a handful of children and old women had straggled into the courtyard to see the messenger. They looked small and dull among the soaring, brightly frescoed Everien houses, and their hands were work-reddened. The blacksmith thought, not for the first time, that more of the Deer Clan's men ought to have stayed behind, for there would be little for the soldiers to come home to at the rate things were going. Sometimes he even thought of leading his family off into the western hills, where they might eat only berries and rabbits, but where the Sekk might not find them to Enslave and torture them. Not that the graybeards of the Deer Clan would ever accede to such a plan. They still dreamed of Everien as one great country ruled from Jai Khalar, its ancient cities bright with jeweled flame as of old. He wondered if the Knowledge that the elders wrought in the Fire Houses had turned their minds.

Dzani gave the messenger a leg up, fearing that otherwise he would be too weak to mount the tall gray gelding—an older animal, but the best horse this branch of the Clan possessed.

"The bridge four miles from here was washed out last month," he offered. "In case you're new in these parts. You don't look like the king's messengers we usually see."

Still chewing voraciously, the stranger gathered the reins and looked down on the blacksmith. A flash of humor crossed his tired face as he swallowed.

"I'm not the king's messenger, nor even one of his subjects," he replied, and expertly turned the animal toward the street. "But his horses will have to suffice me in my need. Thanks for your hospitality."

The gray horse dipped its head slightly and shot off like a yearling. There were a number of protests and startled cries, and Dzani fell back a pace, dismayed. The faces of his people turned to him for explanation.

"Did you just give the king's horse to some brigand?" someone called.

"If I did, so did Geiri at the next station up the line," Dzani said defensively. "That's a royal horse he rode in on."

"What Clan was he, then, eh? He's not of the Deer Clan, that's certain."

An argument began, with several children running down the street after the horse and the old women speculating colorfully as to Dzani's fate when his mistake was discovered.

Then the blacksmith's wife laughed.

"You're all fools. Did you not see the sword he carried? Did you not see the scabbard?"

They looked at her as if she were mad.
"He wears the sign of the Eye, the Sun, and the Rose."
In the growing daylight she saw their faces change.
"That was Tarquin the Free."
She flushed again when she said it.

JAI KHALAR

$\mathcal{H}e$ $\mathfrak{had}$ $\mathfrak{been}$ riding forever; his legs, his tailbone, his back would never forgive him. Days without sleep becoming nights of the winding road pale as a river under moonlight, and always the horse's gait like a second heartbeat—they wove into a continuity that flattened and dimmed his perceptions and his thoughts. The excitement of the first day's ride from the mountains above Ristale was long gone, and since then he had done all he could to keep his spirits up. He'd rehearsed his speech to King Lerien a thousand times; he had strategized and considered every angle on the news he brought, every tactical and political consequence. These ruminations led his mind back eighteen years, to a time when he himself had been at the center of the war against the Sekk, and the doings of Jai Khalar had meant everything to him. The decisions he had made in those days seemed now dim and somehow misguided. Flashes of regret and despair and most of all confusion, all vestiges of a long-abandoned self, had ridden with him day after day toward the Citadel.

Now, as the sun blazed free of the peaks and rose toward noon and the road unraveled through the last fields below the walls of the Citadel of Jai Khalar, there seemed to be nothing left in his mind. He passed one caravan bringing goods commandeered from the farms; a handful of fresh soldiers marching away from the Citadel to their postings in the hills; and the dead returning in slow carts driven by old men. Otherwise the road was deserted. He was too tired to initiate greetings and unaware of the gray, resolute lines carving his own face that discouraged approach from any but the boldest. He was half dreaming in the saddle, and the landscape took on an indistinct, surreal quality. He might well have been traveling back in time: eighteen years of self-imposed exile were wiped away as the familiar features of the mountains rose to either side like the legacy of another lifetime.

The topography had changed during the course of his journey south. Even in the north whence he had traveled, the mountains that bounded Everien stood dramatic and steep-sided. At the southern end of Everien their angles intensified and the valley became a tapering canyon. Sheer white cliffs rose to either side of the road, which followed the course of a small river upstream, traversing a strip of flat farmland only a few miles wide. The very depths of the valley would be untouched by light in the depths of winter, a lake of shadowed snow passable only by sled; but it was high summer and the shores of the river burgeoned with ripening grain. The canyon deepened as its floor sank toward sea level, until the cliffs rose many thousands of feet to either side, finally converging to frame a natural gate through which was revealed a hazy view of the tidal plain to the south. The main road led this way, over the border of Everien and into the flatlands beyond, coming eventually to the Floating Lands and the sea itself; but Tarquin had no wish to go that way, not ever again. Not in this lifetime.

It was a strange thing, though, how he could not keep his head from turning that way. Even as he took the fork in the road that followed the river to its source in the foot of the cliffs beneath Jai Khalar, he found himself glancing to the right, where a snatch of softness marked the termination of Everien in a gauzy mist of sea light. Between the stark cliffs the gates of Everien left a gap like a milky gem polished to dream smoothness. He shivered and made himself think of swords rending flesh. It was the only way to clear his mind.

Often he had imagined how easy it would be for an army to sweep in from the plains and take the entire land of Everien, which was otherwise protected by natural barriers. It seemed ironic that the safest part of the land should be here, at this apparently open door on the very edge of the wild country. The rest of Everien, though sheltered by mountains, contended with attack by the Sekk and their minions—human and otherwise—almost daily. Yet here where the valley was most vulnerable, no troops or garrison were to be seen. Queen Ysse had laid claim to this part of the valley in Tarquin's youth, beating back the ghostly Sekk and awakening the Knowledge that had opened Jai Khalar, which had become the shelter of her people. For it was the Citadel that defended Everien against enemies old and new—the Citadel hidden up in the white cliffs, standing guard over the passage to the sea.

The invisible Citadel.

Tarquin had acquired the ability to see Jai Khalar, but only at a great price. To everyone else it was undetectable from outside. Though the Clans had lived under its protection for many years now, the Citadel and much of the Knowledge it contained remained mysterious to them. Carved from the mountain's flanks by the art of the vanished Everiens, Jai Khalar could be perceived only via a subtle enchantment that could steal into the very bones and render the impossible real. Each tower and wall, each window and crenellation and rooftop of the Citadel had been artfully constructed to mimic the appearance of natural stone . . . most of the time. As a rule Jai Khalar was indistinguishable from the mountain itself. Yet every so often as if at random the Citadel would release a glimpse, an image of itself in all its staggering glory: layer upon layer of walls receding toward the sky; towers, seemingly unsupported, jutting out into thin air; buildings of strange geometrical design, with triangular and even round windows, some of them winking with colored glass. The impression would last only long enough to print itself on Tarquin's eye, as if to remind him of its great power held in check; then the craggy and lumpy mountainside would reassert itself and the road would appear to lead to a simple cave at the bottom of a great cliff.

As Jai Khalar's architecture began to resolve out of the pale stone, its strange lines and uncanny surfaces brought him too many memories; they added to the burden of dark tidings carried a great distance in haste. He was unready for this. He had always known he would have to return someday—had known it with the kind of dreadful certainty that came from the marrow of his bones—but eighteen years wasn't long enough to be gone from a place that he associated with the breaking of his own mind.

For nothing here would ever be straightforward. Already he could feel the Knowledge of Jai Khalar preying on him. Maybe it was simple exhaustion, but gray areas were starting to appear in his vision, and since this morning he had been hearing music coming from somewhere over his left shoulder. How he would cope with telling enchantment from reality once he was inside the Citadel was anybody's guess.

He rode on doggedly toward the cave.

The modest notch in the white face of the cliffs had grown as he drew near; now it was a high, arching entrance wide enough to accommodate fifty horses abreast. To Tarquin's right, the river flowed fast and deep from a second aperture in the stone: he could hear the water singing as it issued from the darkness. As the horse and rider passed inside, daylight yellowed and dimmed. Currents of air whirled and danced around the horse's legs. After only a short distance, the road grew smooth and the hooves ceased to echo. The path began to descend, curving and sinking until light and sound were somewhere far above. Darkness pressed close. The animal must be depending on sense of smell alone, for he slowed and finally stopped. Tarquin gently encouraged him with a slight shift of weight. The gelding's head dropped and the muscles of his forequarters loosened as the descent grew steeper. He twisted sharply around a corner and then another and another until Tarquin lost all sense of direction. The floor leveled, and faint gray illumination began to appear. The horse continued forward, bearing Tarquin into a large chamber. Light flared from a great rectangular aperture in the floor; he dismounted and looked down into the hole. There was nothing but vacant blue.

The horse was not bothered, but Tarquin's stomach pitched. He closed his eyes, took a deep breath, and led the horse down into the sky.

BUT DOWN WAS not down: it was up—far up. And the sky, of course, was not sky but the white city of Jai Khalar.

Through some means Tarquin would never understand, with a single stride they had come to be standing on a broad promenade that overlooked the valley floor. The road that led to the cave had shrunk to a narrow dun band, partially obscured by the guard wall that provided some relief from the vertigo Tarquin felt when he emerged onto this exposed shelf. The atmosphere was curiously still, for despite its height the Citadel was positioned in a sheltered aspect from the worst of the mountain winds—in fact, it would not have been difficult to believe that the view of the farmlands beneath was simply a mural, so distant did it appear.

He turned away from the parapet and toward the bulk of the city, most of it still tiered above him. It looked plausible enough, but he knew better. He swayed slightly and fixed his attention on his immediate surroundings. There was a wide flight of steps leading up from the promenade to the main avenue of the first level. A gold-covered gate had been placed between the promenade and the stairs, cutting off the outer wall from the rest of the city. A man stood on the other side of the gate, a mantle made of feathers covering him from shoulders to ankles; he was wearing silver beneath. There was a sword at his side and a leopard at his feet. The guard stepped up to the gate and eagerly asked, "Have you brought tidings from Wolf Country?"

Tarquin did a double take. "Wolf Country? No, I have come from the slopes above Ristale."

As if he had suddenly caught himself and realized he'd shown too much emotion, the guard's face now stiffened to become a mask, and he said formally, "That is one of the king's horses. What is your rank, and why are you alone?"

Tarquin halted, biting back an angry response when he realized it was only fatigue that made him resent the question. If he had been allowed to get this far, he had already been identified as a friend. Everything else was formality.

"I'm called Tarquin," he said shortly. "The king knows me."

The guard was barely more than a boy, Tarquin noticed now, seeing past the costume. At the mention of his name, three successive thoughts transisted across the guard's face as clearly as if they had been written in words: (1) *Tarquin* must mean Tarquin the Free, returned from exile; (2) but what has become of the great hero? he looks like a goatherd; (3) this must be some other Tarquin, therefore—

"You have not answered my questions, sir. You have been admitted because you ride one of our horses, and we know you are not Sekk, for the Sekk are beautiful. However, you are in the king's home in a time of war—you will have to give more than your name. You wear the garb of a warrior, so I ask again: What is your rank? And who gave you permission to take a messenger horse?" The young man's lips were set in a taut line.

"I have no rank in your army. I'm not a member of it. I wore these leathers in battle years ago, when I had the honor to serve Queen Ysse. As for the horse: there are convenient message posts in a dozen villages between here and Ristale, so I have been riding nothing but the best for several days." Here the guard began to temporize, and Tarquin held out a hand. "I would not be so impertinent, except for the urgency of my message. I must see the king immediately. It will not go well for you if he finds I have been kept cooling my heels outside the first level."

The young guard did not look impressed, and the leopard's tail lashed from side to side. "I will have to ask permission for you to go up. Wait here."

There was little else he could do, other than climbing over the parapet and jumping to his death. He turned his face away from the moodily staring cat and leaned against the horse, who was already dozing in the sun. Above them, wall upon wall climbed toward the sky, towers and fortifications designed to repel what kind of enemy Tarquin had never understood. Even assuming one could see it from outside (which was assuming a lot), Jai Khalar was all but inaccessible: the thought of an army trying to swarm up the cliffs with ropes and grappling hooks was ridiculous, and even a siege would be difficult, given the vast storage caves behind and below the Citadel. Yet the builders, unsatisfied with astonishing heights and impregnable outer walls, had been driven on by some architectural frenzy to create a fortress that baffled and astonished the eye at every turn. Jai Khalar had been constructed on a grand scale, and it could easily have held twenty times the number of people who actually lived there now, rattling around the place like children in a giant's playhouse. While Tarquin waited, he pictured the guard traveling up through the first level, across bridges, up and down flights of stairs, along winding avenues, and through buildings until he found some lieutenant or captain who could advise him, and then the two making their tortuous descent through tunnels and parlors, places where the light changed and distant laughter followed them. . . .

The gate shrieked open, startling Tarquin awake. The guard was returning, and behind him came not a senior officer, but a scrawny, grayhaired man in blue robes leaning on a stick.

"Hanji?" Tarquin hadn't expected to see anyone he knew, not so soon—not looking so much the same, as if eighteen years meant nothing. . . .

"Aye," Hanji said to the young guard. "That's him. Better let him in before he makes trouble."

The guard unlocked the gate and Tarquin walked in leading the horse, which shied when it passed the leopard. Hanji took the reins from him and cast a critical eye over Tarquin.

"You look like hell," he said. "Have you been living under a rock?"

Hanji began to lead the horse along the avenue; Tarquin sagged against his mount as they went. Focusing his bleary eyes on the older man's face, he opened his mouth to make a rejoinder but instead of words, a thin croak issued from his throat.

"I'd always suspected you were truly of the Frog Clan," Hanji remarked amiably. "That skin, those eyes . . ."

Tarquin cleared his throat and said nothing, aware that his mind was too numb to cope with Hanji. Radiating the air of someone who shouldn't have to be doing this sort of thing, the old man brought the horse to a small guard house and surrendered it to a boy there; then he turned to Tarquin and wrinkled his nose fastidiously.

"Don't even start!" Tarquin said, holding up a hand palm outward. "I have no time for your bathhouses. I've been riding day and night and I need to see the king at once."

Hanji fixed him with a deceptively mild eye. "Are you feeling fit enough to climb the approximately two thousand steps to his audience chamber?"

"No, I'm not." Tarquin stumbled to the nearest wall and slid down it until he was sitting on the pavement. "I'm going to sit here and wait for him."

Hanji rapped his stick impatiently on the wall. "Quintar, this has gone far enough. Your timing is atrocious. We are beset by problems with the Eyes that no one can fathom, and Jai Khalar is acting as tetchy as a pregnant ferret. What makes you think you can swagger in here after eighteen years' absence and demand an immediate audience?"

Tarquin spoke slowly, afraid that he would slur or skip words otherwise. "There is a Pharician army massing on the plain at Ristale. I have seen them with my own eyes. They march south toward our borders. No, old man, I don't think I'll be climbing any steps. I think I'll sit here and wait for the king to come down personally and speak with me, and after that he can send the most beautiful women to come and treat my saddle sores."

Hanji said nothing at first, thinking. "How many troops?"

Tarquin snorted. "More than I could count. They covered the plain from the west road to the hills and a mile to the north. Like flies on rotting fruit."

"How many days ago?"

"Four. I was in the mountains when I saw them."

"*Four* days from the plain of Ristale? How many horses did you kill to get here?"

Tarquin didn't feel obliged to answer; he again felt sleep like a vise closing on him. . . .

"Get up. Come on—do I have to carry you? Quintar!"

"That's not my name," he snarled.

"*Tarquin,* then. Get the hell up."

Tarquin struggled to his feet, dimly aware that people were staring at him as they passed. Hanji crossed beneath an arch and stood beside a doorway.

"Where are you going?" Tarquin demanded. "That passage leads to the armory."

"The armory? You are in Jai Khalar now, and eighteen years have passed. Jai Pendu draws near at the other end of the White Road. Things change here almost every day."

Tarquin passed under the arch and followed the old man into a room he didn't remember. It was small, windowless, and made of blood red stone. A large egg sat in the middle of the floor. Hanji stooped and picked it up, and the flagstone where the egg had been turned black.

"Follow me," Hanji said, and stepped down into the black stone as if it were a hole, disappearing from view by degrees.

"I despise these enchantments," Tarquin muttered, reluctantly lowering a foot into the darkness, which flung itself up at him and wrapped him like a soft velvet curtain. He thrashed it to one side and found himself entering the already crowded Council antechamber, which he knew very well was nowhere near the gates of the first level. He stood there dazed until Hanji dragged him forward, recruiting attendants to help. The old man took one of the yellow-robed Council secretaries aside and they spoke quietly together.

"Drink this. It's *sita*." A young woman put a steaming cup in his hand. He swallowed the bitter drink and handed her the cup for a refill. After three cups, his head began to clear. He blinked slowly. The place looked as he had remembered—and yet different. For one thing, there were small trees in white and yellow bloom all around the perimeter of the room, and pink birds moved in their branches but did not sing. The trees seemed to grow directly out of the stone.

"I will take you inside in a moment," Hanji said. He and the secretary were standing at a stone plinth, poring over the contents of a large ledger. "As it happens, the king is in closed conference, hearing testimony on other war matters, but they will open the doors to allow one group to exit and the next to enter. It is almost time for the next hearing."

Tarquin looked at the people assembled in the antechamber. There were a number of young soldiers, including a woman in battle gear—an Honorary, presumably—in addition to the clerks, whom Tarquin automatically discounted as useless appurtenances. Some stared at him, although the Honorary and two of her companions had their heads together and seemed oblivious to whatever else was going on in the room. Revived temporarily by the strong *sita,* he sat tapping his foot anxiously and looking at the chamber doors.

"What was that you said about the Eyes, Hanji?" he said. "What problems?"

He was met with a blank look. "Did I say that? I don't remember saying that."

Tarquin sighed. "I see your memory has not improved over the years. In fact, if—" The words died in his throat. A flight of stairs had appeared where before only a blank wall had been. In a weak tone he asked, "Where did those stairs come from, Hanji?"

"You're hallucinating. How long since you slept?"

"I don't recall. You must talk to me so that I can stay alert."

"All right. Pick a topic. My herb garden, for example. Shall we discuss calendula versus comfrey, or—"

"How goes the war? On my way here I saw dead soldiers but few living. Every village has been drained of men and lives in fear of the Sekk and their monsters. Yet the king sits in council and his girls brew *sita.* Why are the border posts unmanned? There should be guards posted in the hills above Ristale, no matter how great you think your friendship with Pharice. How can you monitor the Sekk without men on watch?"

"All this and more can be done from the Eye Tower," Hanji said absently. He had concertinaed his spindly bones into the seat beside Tarquin. "Or so it has been until recently. What do you think is the point of having the Water of Glass, if not to use it to connect all the Eyes?"

"Do not speak to me of the Water of Glass," Tarquin said. The Water of Glass was the Artifact he had brought back from Jai Pendu, alone and broken in spirit after all his men were lost. It had awakened the translucent lumps of crystal left behind in the abandoned monitor towers of the Everiens, so that visions appeared in them; but compared to the Fire of Glass, it seemed a mere toy. At the time Tarquin renounced his original name and Clan and turned his back on Everien, the Water of Glass had remained mysterious. It had not, as Ysse once hoped, helped the Clans exterminate the Sekk once and for all—or at least drive them so far back into the wild heights that they would never haunt Everien again. He well remembered how he had felt when he realized all his Company were lost for the sake of an object that had no martial value, but merely offered visions of Everien—and those only to the Scholars who understood how to use it.

Tarquin had no use for visions or the Knowledge that imparted them. His eyes had taken in more than enough in Jai Pendu; in fact he would have happily gone blind after that.

"You may wish to forget your part in bringing the Water of Glass here, but you would be a fool to deny its power. Over the years we have located several large, fixed Eyes scattered throughout the remains of the ancient Everien structures, and there are many more smaller ones that can be carried from place to place. We think that each of these was once a part of the Water of Glass, which is a sort of Mother Eye. All of the lesser Eyes offer up their sight to her, so that we can See all across Everien from the Eye Tower."

"It all sounds like damned nonsense." Tarquin shifted impatiently. "Is that how you knew I was coming?"

Hanji gave a little start and squirmed visibly in his blue robes.

"No," he said curtly. "I did not know you were coming."

"Then what bloody good are these Eyes of yours? I might have been an enemy." He swung his head from side to side, cursing under his breath, too worried and exhausted to even attempt to curb his temper. "This whole land lives under a curse of foolishness and vain hope. I never should have come back. Everything I try to do goes afoul."

"You were wrong to leave," Hanji retorted sharply. "Your sacrifice—the sacrifice of your men—it was not in vain. We have held on to Everien, and only thanks to you. The Water of Glass is crucial to our defense, and without your effort we would not possess it."

"But have you the Knowledge to really use it? You are not the Everiens, and I fear their Artifacts can only give you an illusion of safety."

From across the room, the Honorary was staring at him intently; her gaze was neither hostile nor friendly, but there was something about her that made him uncomfortable. She must have overheard. He was about to go over and speak to her when the doors to the king's audience chamber opened and a knot of people slipped out; the old man shut up abruptly and hustled Tarquin inside ahead of the next group, and before he knew it he was back in the room where he had sat sobbing at the feet of Queen Ysse, confessing the loss of his Company and vowing to leave Jai Khalar forever. But the queen was dead, and forever is a long time. He lurched after Hanji to a seat in the back row of chairs, hidden from the sunlight that spilled over the king and his councillors.

CODDLE THE MESSENGER

"*Wait a little* while and I will introduce you when I see an opportunity," Hanji murmured in his ear. "It will be better to handle this quietly. The king's secretary is telling him an emergency messenger is here, but I thought it wise not to give your name. Yet."

The room was circular, so although they were in the back row, Tarquin and Hanji had a side view of the proceedings. The king was seated at an oval stone table, surrounded by various advisers, some of whom Tarquin recognized. Lerien himself had lost condition but retained his bulk, which made him look older than he was. Instead of Bear Clan colors he wore the black of Clanlessness, and he had cut his blond hair to a short bristle. He had generous features and large hands, which now pawed slowly through documents on the table before him. The half sphere of the room behind Lerien had the look of having been appropriated for all-night meetings and hasty meals: the Council sat rather informally in armchairs and at desks, some of them writing or conferring quietly but paying no attention to the citizens in the rows of seats. Ajiko was there looking like a small mountain, talking informally with a couple of young officers, and Tarquin saw that he wore the rank of general now. The yellow-robed secretary bent down beside the king and whispered to him, and the ruler gave a brief nod. Lerien did not look old enough to be king, Tarquin thought, and calculated his age from memory. It did not please or reassure him to arrive at the conclusion that Lerien was older, now, than Tarquin had been when he had led his Company to Jai Pendu. He sagged in his seat, feeling geriatric.

A Snake Clan soldier was speaking.

"There were fifty of us. We were guarding the high lands on the border of Snake Country east of here, where people had been disappearing and stock had been mysteriously dying without a mark on them. The thing . . . it came on us in the night. I never saw it. I simply woke up and five of my comrades were advancing on me with their weapons already blooded. I didn't know what was happening. Krestar came running—to help me, I thought, but he shot at me! The others had begun to get up and fight. Then Taniki engaged the five Enslaved with the sword and they simply cut him down where he stood. I . . . I know it is dishonorable, but I could see no chance against so many, so I ran. The last time I looked back, even more had joined the mob and Ruarel was trying to fight but he was surrounded." His voice broke and he halted, looking at the floor.

Ajiko had been listening with the attitude of a dormant volcano. "What did you do next, soldier? Did you run straight home to mother?"

Ashamed and distressed, the Snake did not meet the general's gaze. He swallowed repeatedly, attempting to master his expression. "I got out of bowshot and found a vantage point above them. I watched them. Of fifty there were now only about thirty-five alive, and they were packing up the camp and getting ready to move."

"Do not lie to us, boy!" Ajiko growled. "The smallest child knows that the Enslaved do not behave rationally. Packing up camp! And thirty-five alive of fifty! If they had been Enslaved, they would have murdered each other down to the last man."

Lerien snapped his fingers at Ajiko to silence him. He addressed the Snake.

"Epse, tell us of the Sekk. What did it look like, and what was it doing?"

The Snake's voice was a whisper. "I did not see the Sekk."

"Then how can you say they were Enslaved?" Ajiko mocked.

"I know of no other explanation," murmured Epse. "There was another man among them when I saw them in the morning"—

Probably a Pharician, thought Tarquin. *There is treachery afoot.*

—"a Wolf Clan chieftain. He seemed to be in charge. King Lerien, General Ajiko, truly I do not know more than this. I only know what I have told you, and I am not lying." His voice shook. "I would swear it was a Sekk. The way they acted when they attacked their fellows, I would swear they had been Enslaved by a Sekk. But perhaps the spell wore off later."

Ajiko said, "Who was your commander? Urutar?"

"Sir, it was Jenji."

The general's left hand was clenching a scroll; it crackled in his fist. "You have all been trained in the methods to escape the Slaving spells. How is it that your fellows could have succumbed so easily?"

The Snake hung his head. "I cannot say."

"What did you do after you got away?"

"I followed them on the heights until I could see that they were heading deeper into the hills, traveling west. I could do no more: I had fled with no provisions. I came here as quickly as I could, but all told it has been three weeks since this incident."

"And the locals?" said Ajiko. "Did they witness any of this?"

"The people of the Snake Clan refused even to approach the bodies, and they are abandoning their steadings. There will be more refugees in Jai Khalar come a week's time."

"Yanise, you heard that. You will have to confer with Hanji about where to put them." Lerien looked at the Snake soldier. "You may go, but inform Yanise of the names of the dead so that their Clans may be notified. Ajiko, there is already too much doubt about the positioning of the commanders in the Wolf Country. I begin to think we should pull our men out of there before we lose control of their movements. Have your horsemen not reached them yet?"

Ajiko said, "I am still waiting for their reports. Mhani was to maintain contact with their Carry Eye; is she not here to tell you?"

"Mhani is in the Eye Tower," Lerien said. "I want to hear reports from the ground. Vallitar, did you have any success with the birds?"

A pimply Seahawk teenager near the back of the room stood and shook his head. "They will not fly so far inland, my lord, and there are few Animal Magicians now who can use them well. The art of Flight was lost with Eteltar."

Yanise leaned forward and said something in the king's ear. Lerien passed a weary hand across his eyes. "Yes, we will discuss this in private, Ajiko. We need to change our tactics in the distant mountain regions."

There was a brief, unhappy pause. Tarquin was thinking that it was cruelty on the part of Hanji to expect him to sit through this; the formality of these proceedings would put anyone to sleep. He wondered what sort of treachery was going on in Wolf Country and why Ajiko was acting so uptight. He felt sorry for Epse the Snake Clan soldier. Tarquin knew all too well how it felt, trying to explain the inexplicable to people who were bereft of imagination. His lip curled. Ajiko could be such a pile of bricks.

Then the king's secretary shuffled documents and announced, "The king will now hear the matter of Lieutenant Kassien, the Scholar Xiriel,

Honorary Lieutenant Istar, and Pallo the Pharician. Please come forward."

The armored woman and her coterie walked up the aisle and knelt before the king. Tarquin's old instincts for evaluating men flashed into operation. The lieutenant looked reasonably sharp. He was of no great size, yet well-knit as Bear fighters were wont to be. He was brown-haired and handsome bordering on pretty, and he moved without fuss or swagger while still managing to convey an air of warning that he should not be touched. The one called Xiriel was much taller, darker, and clad in the robes of a Scholar instead of battle costume; yet of the four this was the one Tarquin would have chosen for a warrior. There was something unexpected in his eye, a hardness that suggested he was capable of ruthless intent. By contrast the other, the Pharician, was a blond slip of a boy, probably completely incompetent at arms to judge by the delicacy of his wrists and forearms. Nervously the Pharician scanned all the faces, his glance slipping past Tarquin without recognition.

"Be at ease," the king said to the little group. "You may state your business."

At first Tarquin had been annoyed that he had to wait behind these neophytes, but as he focused his tired eyes on the Honorary, he found himself studying her face perplexedly. There *was* something about her. She was familiar; yet there was no way he could have seen her before—not in Everien.

She was no more than twenty by his guess, but sported a battle scar from right temple to jaw. Her skin was olive and well tanned, and her features sat in her face uneasily, as though jostled from their proper places and proportions. She wore her black hair in several dozen small, neat braids, decorated by beads in the Seahawk Clan's colors: orange, dark green, and silver. Her prominent, hooked nose bore a bone ring with a sapphire inset, and her forehead had been painted with four parallel waves in silver indicating her rank. She looked formidable: although she was not tall, her physique was broad and her large hands capable. The scabbard at her side was battered and scratched, and her leather uniform was almost as journey-worn as his own. When she spoke she laid her palm heel unconsciously on the pommel of her sword, and her dark eyes scanned the room assertively, resting on each of the assembled in turn with a confidential air. Even her body language was familiar, but Tarquin couldn't imagine how he had met her. The Seahawk Clan had been his own, long ago when he had been called Quintar and was bound body and blood to his people; but she would have been an infant then. And yet . . .

"I have no brothers," she was saying in a husky contralto. "I was my parents' firstborn, and my father was killed in the war against the Sekk while my sisters and I were still young."

It was a familiar story, and her tone was matter-of-fact, not seeking pity.

"This is why I wear the costume of a man, and why I know how to use this sword—because I am responsible for the honor and even the very survival of my family. I have served in the army for four years, and in that time I have fought Sekk slaves and monsters, and once I fought and killed a Sekk Master. My lord, I am battle-hardened. As for my comrades . . . Kassien's name is well-known here as the commander who repelled the H'ah'vah invasion of the tunnels at A-bo-Manik last year. Xiriel is a Seer, a specialist in the history of the Knowledge and student of my mother, Mhani, these past ten years—"

Now the rough wind of memory tumbled against Tarquin: memory, and grief. Mhani he knew well: she had been the mate of his best friend, Chyko, lost under Tarquin's command at Jai Pendu. Their daughters would now be grown: this was Istar, the eldest. Only a week or two before the Company's ride to Jai Pendu, she had been named into the Seahawk Clan by Quintar's protection. Under laws that traced back to the time when the Clans had been at constant war with one another over the scarce resources of the wild country, the offspring of marriages between two different Clans could belong to neither—preventing such alliances was a way of protecting the autonomy of the Clans and keeping any one Clan from gaining too much power by means other than martial. It also kept the bloodlines pure for the practice of the Animal Magic. Mhani was Deer, and Chyko was Wasp. They had asked Tarquin to take their children into his own Clan, which he had done gladly, having no offspring of his own. But soon afterward he had renounced the Seahawk Clan when he renounced everything, so he knew his foster child not at all.

Now that he knew who she was, he could see nothing but Chyko in Istar's face. The resemblance was striking: they shared the same fierce nose, almost the same coloring, the same wide mouth and flashing white teeth. Why had he not seen it immediately? Tarquin remembered Chyko's mouth laughing as he danced drunkenly by firelight; he remembered that same mouth with its lips curled in agony, the head thrown back, and the tendons of the neck standing out like trees. Tarquin's hands clenched the arms of his chair and he held his breath, fighting his emotions as the memory swept over him like a wave. Perhaps he had not recognized Chyko in the young woman's face because it hurt too much to recall his friend. He forced himself to listen to what Chyko's daughter was saying. Something about an expedition . . .

"—because it's clear that Jai Pendu holds the key to the Everien Arti-facts. Xiriel can explain this better than I can, but when the Everiens fled from the Sekk they probably used Jai Pendu in some way. Perhaps they sailed away in it; for the few references we have discovered all suggest it is like a great ship, a ship the size of a city. Each of the two Glasses that was brought back has proven to be a great boon to us, and each has dismayed the Sekk. Yet all you have to do is look around you"—she gestured to the building at large with a broad sweep of her hand—"to realize that we have penetrated only a tiny fraction of Everien Knowledge. Imagine what we could do if we had more! The Scholars have calculated that Jai Pendu is due to pass through the Floating Lands this very summer. It is an opportunity that comes only once in nine years. King Lerien, my com-rades and I are here to petition you for aid in mounting an expedition to Jai Pendu."

There was a rustle of feet shifting; murmured commentary; a collec-tive sense of everyone who had been holding their breath letting it out. Tarquin didn't move. He was too dazed—yet he no longer wished to stay awake. It was better to think of all this as a bad dream.

Ajiko stood up and said, "Kassien, Istar, you are both old enough to remember the most recent pass of Jai Pendu nine years ago. Since Quintar returned without the Company, the White Road has been lost to us; Ysse believed it closed forever. Why she believed this is unknown to me, but I do know that the Pharicians attempted to cross the Floating Lands anyway, and came to grief there."

Lieutenant Kassien spoke up. "Yes, their land forces were killed and their fleet was displaced and scattered wide across the sea. But we might learn from their tactical mistakes."

Istar raised her voice above Kassien's. "Xiriel has studied the Floating Lands extensively. He can find a way through that does not depend on the White Road." She gestured to Xiriel the Scholar—no, *Seer* they had called him, Tarquin recalled. The tall, brooding young man cleared his throat and said, "It is clear that the Floating Lands once connected Jai Pendu to the mainland, and though damaged, even now they are joined by bridges like stepping-stones out into the sea. In the past, Jai Pendu has come within spitting distance of the last island."

"No one—not even Ysse—has ever crossed the Floating Lands to reach Jai Pendu. They are more than dangerous—they are impossible!" Ajiko was exercised at the very suggestion, but the Seer answered him calmly.

"I agree that the White Road is the only sensible way through the Liminal that divides Jai Khalar from its sister city Jai Pendu. But the Floating Lands were once connected to Jai Pendu. We believe they were damaged in the collapse of Everien in ages past, and their structure is fault-ridden now. They intersect the Liminal, but they are also a part of our world, much like Jai Khalar only less organized—"

A loud guffaw exploded from Ajiko's direction. "How much less organized could you get?"

Xiriel continued as if he hadn't spoken, addressing his words to Lerien. "We have accounts of those who have tried to cross the Floating Lands before, as well as images from the Eyes that have recorded fragments of Everien history. There are systems of codes, a kind of language the Everiens used in managing the Knowledge, and they seem to control the bridges and passageways among the Floating Lands. These symbols are not unlike Pharician musical notation, which appears as marks on paper but to the mind of the musician signifies sound. The Everien codes have the same power to—"

"You're talking nonsense," Ajiko interrupted. Lerien glanced up, frowning.

"Yes, it does make me cross-eyed," agreed the king. "What is the final meaning of all this, Xiriel?"

The Seer took a patient breath. "It means that we may not be able to call the White Road up and walk easily to Jai Pendu by magic, but that doesn't prevent us from crossing the Floating Lands. We know more than the Pharicians do, as Kassien said."

Eagerly, Istar added, "We only need ten or twelve swords to support us. Kassien and I are both tried and tested in facing the creatures that the Sekk call down from the heights and up from the depths. We are not faint of heart."

Tarquin was on his feet.

"Are there no lessons in history?" he said in a clear voice. "Istar, if you had seen what happened to your father at Jai Pendu, you would not attempt such a stunt now. Lerien, do not make the same mistake Queen Ysse made eighteen years ago, or these young people will throw their lives away."

Istar's sword was out and she was plowing toward him, pushing aside chairs, small tables, and people as she went. "Who dares use the king's bare name, or disrupt this Council? Come, answer for your disrespect!"

She had a clean eye and the fine energy of a sword fighter, so she had done well by the Seahawk Clan. Her blade wove hypnotically as it came toward him, but Tarquin forced himself to stand still. Beyond Istar, he saw Lerien rise and lean across the table, gaping.

"*Quintar?* Istar, stay your hand. Why did no one tell me Quintar was here?"

The secretary had conveniently vanished, but Hanji sported a faint smirk. Ignoring Istar's sword, Tarquin bowed to the king.

"I bring news, Lerien, but not, I think, for the ears of the entire Council—not yet. I have been riding hard from the borders, and I hope I am in time to do some good."

The king passed a hand over his forehead. "Yes, I see. Istar, Kassien—I will have Yanise send for you as soon as I have time, but for now I must dismiss you." He extended an arm across the room. "All of you, actually. I will see Quin—forgive me—Tarquin—alone, in my rooms. Thank you all—we will reconvene as soon as may be." The assembly began to pick themselves up, muttering and casting curious glances at Tarquin. Istar put away her sword but kept watching him; he couldn't read her expression.

"We should talk," he said to her. "There are so many things—"

"Tarquin, *now!*" Hanji tugged his sleeve and he turned away from Chyko's daughter blearily, aware of her eyes on him as he followed the king.

ON THE WAY to Lerien's chamber they passed through two sunset windows and across a courtyard quilted in midnight sky. They traversed galleries tiled with maps of lands Tarquin had never heard of. They disturbed a squadron of pale green doves that descended suddenly from above only to disappear into an ornate piece of grillwork in the corridor floor. Tarquin was not pleased. His carefully prepared speeches were being evaporated by the Knowledge that seemed to emanate from Jai Khalar's very stones like a smell, compounding his fatigue with confusion. Yet the urgency of the message meant that even in his delirium he kept trying to tell Lerien his news. He knew he was saying a great deal inside his head, but he was not certain which of his words were making it out.

For example, he was thinking: *Lerien, you should have seen the Pharician army. All of them wear exactly the same armor and carry the same weapons and they are organized in groups of identical size and disposition. Their numbers are obscene. What country sends men to war as if they were cattle when it is well-known among the Clans that a well-trained warrior can stand for an entire village, even if he fights a winged monster or other large predator? I do not understand the Pharicians and I never will.*

Whereas what he heard himself actually say was "They remind me of bugs."

He must have been making some sense, though, because after a while Lerien began to direct replies at him.

"Surely when you said the plains of Ristale you simply meant the garrison to the north, where the Pharicians are in the habit of training their men to patrol the wild country and protect their herds. Perhaps there is a larger force than usual stationed there for exercises. For I know nothing unusual has been Seen—"

"No," Tarquin interrupted. "Not a garrison. They were marching. Supply trains. Thousands. Herd animals."

He swayed; Lerien took his arm and he lost track of things for a little while. He remembered climbing stairs and panting. Then Lerien brought him to a map painted on the wall of some vast hallway. The colors were far too bright. Tarquin tried to point out the positioning of the Pharician force, but when he put his finger on the place, the entire map broke up and became a cloud of butterflies. He began to sneeze. Hanji appeared then, emerging from a nearby tapestry with a large book clutched to his chest. He cast a skeptical glance over Tarquin.

"Details," he said, and snapped his fingers. "When. Where. How many. And what under the belly of the Great Nesting Toad have you been doing all these years that you return to us in this condition? Lerien, let's bring him into your rooms before he faints."

"I'm trying to *find* my rooms," Lerien responded in a slightly petulant tone.

Hanji snorted and opened a door Tarquin would have sworn wasn't there a moment ago. The old seneschal ushered them both into Lerien's private apartments, which were as spacious as Ysse's had been but more cluttered—mostly with books and papers, which Tarquin thought was odd, since Lerien had never been known to read anything in his youth. Tarquin yawned and rubbed his eyes. His head was slightly clearer now, and he no longer wanted to collapse. He was shown to a comfortable chair but perched himself on the edge of it in an effort to hold his alertness.

"I'm going back to my kitchen," Hanji announced, and he slipped away through a green glass window. They were left with Yanise, who provided more *sita* and made himself inconspicuous among what seemed to Tarquin an inordinate amount of documents. Lerien nodded to him and sat down at a table covered in papers. He steepled his hands beneath his chin.

"Tarquin, tell me exactly what happened. Start at the beginning."

Tarquin had begun to tremble a little from the stimulant he was drinking. "As you may know," he said, "for some years after I left Jai Khalar I was not entirely in my right mind. I left Everien and traveled in the far reaches of Pharice and beyond. For years I roamed without purpose, until I wandered in the Wild Lands and lived among the barbarian Clanspeople in the cold wastes of the north, where our distant kinsmen who never descended to Everien scoff at our foolishness in plundering the Knowledge of the ancient Everiens. They say we have stirred up trouble that should have been left to lie beneath the hills, for the Sekk prey even on them sometimes and the wild people blame us. They are rough folk and not easy to know, but in time they became my friends.

"This spring, Freeze Wasps were raiding the herds of the wild Wolf Clan beyond Everien's borders, and I set off into the hills to see what I could do. I suspected that a Sekk was behind the Freeze Wasps, which would normally never come down off the heights in summer."

He paused, sipped.

"I was looking for Sekk and I found Pharicians. I stumbled upon a reconnaissance patrol of fifteen of them in the hills above the plain of northern Ristale. They were not interested in exchanging news with me."

"They attacked you? But you are not identified as Clan. Perhaps they thought you a bandit."

"Is this an excuse for fifteen to attack one?"

"What happened?"

Tarquin looked at the king from beneath heavy lids. There was a silence.

"You killed them *all*?"

The yellow robes emitted a squeak, and the king scowled briefly at his secretary. Tarquin said: "I traced their trail back to the plain and saw the army from the height. Their formation was the standard Pharician Imperial march. I have seen the Pharicians use this style across their empire. By their standards the army is not the greatest of forces, but it will mean serious trouble for Everien. I have given some thought as to how to deal with the Pharicians. Fortunately, they will never function effectively in the mountains. If you can't cut them off at the gates to the sea plateau, you can still retreat to the high country and force them to fight you on your own terrain. . . ." He broke off, yawning.

The king said, "Yanise, send for Mhani! This whole situation in Wolf Country has gotten out of control. I want to know how an army of any size could have escaped our Sight. Also, bring Sendrigel. He's supposed to be on top of doings in Pharice."

"Mhani is locked in the Eye Tower," Yanise replied. "The Seers will refuse to disturb her, because—"

"Shut up. No excuses—get her down here now."

Yanise bowed twice and backed away. Lerien shuffled papers. He muttered, "That schemer Hezene; what's he up to?"

Until this moment, Tarquin had been singularly unconvinced by Lerien. What kind of a king suffered himself to be managed by clerks and old men, or spent his days sitting on his hindbones and talking when swords were being wielded throughout his land and fires set? What kind of a king said so little and was so weak of eye as to take advice from anyone who offered it? This sudden display of temperament was overdue on Lerien's part, Tarquin thought. For he measured everyone's character according to Ysse's, and Ysse had snarled at people like a wildcat.

Now the king leaped to his feet, throwing papers over his shoulder. He prowled the chamber, weaving among the furnishings with more precision than his bulk would have suggested him capable. "Hezene is supposed to be our friend and trading partner. How many shipments have I sent him from our Fire Houses, craftwork the like of which his country could never produce in a thousand years? And how many of his damned musicians have I housed, raised their bastard children that seem to pop up everywhere in every shade of color, entertained his traders and sent them home with full purses? Do our treaties mean nothing to him?" He halted suddenly and drummed his fingers on the sill of one large window, gazing out into the vague green of Everien. "Could there be some misunderstanding? Maybe he is mustering troops to go to Jai Pendu."

He turned to look at Tarquin when he did not reply right away; the need to cling to this one hope was naked on the king's face.

Tarquin said, "Perhaps—but why would he send his men across the vast plain of Ristale and then down our borders, when they could go directly from Jundun down the Sajaz River to the Floating Lands?"

Lerien turned away abruptly, as if by doing so he could dismiss the remark. *Why all this delay?* Tarquin thought irritably. By now he could have had twenty messengers out to rally their forces. He could have had a defense plan knocked together. Hell, he could have had the whole country set in motion if the Eyes did what Hanji claimed they did. But Lerien wanted to weigh and consider and confabulate.

"And what happened to your border guard?" Tarquin added. "The lands between here and Ristale are empty. Where are all your forces if not protecting the hills from Sekk-controlled monsters?"

"That is another matter," Lerien said. "Don't confuse the issue."

"It's not another matter," Tarquin retorted. "You've been in Jai Khalar too long, Lerien. You're out of touch with reality." He yawned again, spoiling his point.

Yanise slid into the room. Lerien waved him away, saying, "Double the guard on the Pharician envoy." Then he frowned at Tarquin. "I'm not saying it couldn't happen. Pharician politics are complex, and their center of power is far away. Yet Pharice is our ally, and we depend on them for trade. I truly thought Hezene's word was good."

Tarquin sighed at this display of naïveté. "Then maybe they are only coming to help bring in the hay."

Lerien's rebuttal was preempted by the arrival of food. When it was set before him, Tarquin hesitated. His stomach was making extraordinary sounds. "If I eat, I won't be able to stay awake."

"If you don't eat, you'll be gnawing the legs off the furniture soon," Lerien scoffed. "Anyway, you've done your duty by bringing me the intelligence. Eat, and Yanise will find a bed for you, and after you're rested we'll speak again. I'll organize a team to go out to the borders immediately with a Carry Eye, so we can see what's happening for ourselves. If only you had had one with you, you might have saved yourself a brutal journey."

"I mistrust the Water of Glass," Tarquin said with his mouth full. "Tell me why these precious Eyes of yours didn't See the army or detect signs of trouble in Pharice."

"If what you say is true, the Eyes have indeed failed us," said a woman's voice from the doorway. "But we have yet to understand why, my lord."

Tarquin swallowed and got to his feet as Mhani entered the room. She looked at him levelly, and he couldn't tell what she was feeling. There were streaks of gray in her dark hair, and she was heavier, but her calm, round face was the same. He felt like a barbarian and a miscreant. He had never forgiven himself for Chyko's death, and he'd barely been able to speak to Mhani when he'd returned from Jai Pendu, alone, with the news of her mate's loss among Tarquin's doomed Company. Today he had criticized the Knowledge openly, barged in on her daughter's petition to the Council, and now cast doubt on her competence—for if she was the foremost Seer in Jai Khalar, it was she who should have detected the Pharician army.

The king glanced from Mhani to Tarquin before saying, "Mhani, is it possible the Sekk have some power to interfere with the Eye?"

"If they do, then the presence of a large army on our border is not the worst news of the day," she replied cautiously. "I would not like to think what the Sekk might do if they could command the Eye of Jai Khalar to see things that are not there."

They exchanged glances over his head; Tarquin, having dispatched most of the food within minutes, was now blinking slowly because his eyes burned too much to stay open. Every time he closed them they seemed to glue themselves shut, and his train of thought went swirling off into dream. Rather belatedly, he realized that Mhani's statement could be taken to imply that it was *he* who had seen what wasn't there.

"Sleep, Tarquin. You've done your part," Lerien was saying. "Yanise, give us a hand."

Yanise gripped Tarquin's shoulder to help him up.

"Come on, then, Tarquin the Free. Your bed is waiting for you."

Tarquin groaned, finding sentences too demanding. "You don't believe. Rather trust Everien Knowledge than an ordinary man."

"I would scarcely call you an ordinary man," Mhani said dryly. "I don't want to believe what you've said, Tarquin, but if you can provide evidence for it, I will accept it."

"No time." Yanise was leading him out into an empty white hallway with windows that looked out onto nothing but clouds. Tarquin's head lolled from side to side. Just before the door closed behind them he heard the king say, "Call up the Council. I want an emergency meeting in two hours. Make sure the Pharician representative knows nothing about it. Now, where's that Sendrigel—"

A DITCH TO SLEEP IN

"If they're in there much longer I'm going to scream."

Kassien flipped his wrist back and released a dart with a little too much thrust: it went high of the mark. The octagonal tower room was full of smoke and sunlight, stale crusts, spilled beer, and bits of discarded uniform. Xiriel had folded his long form into the window ledge, where he pored over a translucent blue stone the size of an apple. Pallo was blowing smoke rings and idly polishing his bow, and Istar was beating Kassien at darts.

"I'm surprised at you, Kassien," said Pallo in his Pharician lilt. "Times like this, don't you soldiers sing songs and slap each other around to combat boredom?"

"You want to be slapped around? Come here."

"Civilians," Istar remarked, ignoring their banter, "can never do anything quickly. If an arrow's coming at a civilian he has to stop and discuss the situation with his neighbors before deciding whether to dodge right or left."

"You don't dodge my arrows," Pallo said. "You don't hear them or see them coming."

"That's easy to explain. You never shoot anything." Kassien flung another dart and hissed when it scored badly again. He scowled. "What's it been? Five hours? Weeks of preparation, days of Istar polishing her speech, we get all decked out in full dress uniform—for what? Tarquin the Free barging in like something someone found in a ditch . . . I'm going to get reassigned. I know it."

"Don't be so hasty, young man," Pallo answered in a high voice.

"That's the trouble with today's young people, always in a hurry to—*oh!* Good shot, Istar."

Kassien tossed his last dart and flopped into a chair. "You win, Star. I can't concentrate. Just give me something to swing at, eh? Give me a tent in a field somewhere and a wall to scale. But I can't take this strange *place.*"

Xiriel stirred and spoke in a deep voice, still scrutinizing the orb. "You really don't like Jai Khalar, do you?"

"Do *you*? Well, I guess you do—you spend all your time here with your nose in old records and your hair standing on end from looking into the Eyes. I keep getting the feeling I'm going to open a door and walk into a room that isn't there. Like the place could just disintegrate at any second and leave you falling half a mile to earth." His finely shaped body gave an exaggerated shudder, and Istar's eyes lingered on him. When he glanced at her, she looked away.

"Mhani says that the Knowledge is more real than the Earth itself," Xiriel replied softly—almost absentmindedly—and rubbed his thumb over the blue surface.

"Yet she can't find the troops, or the White Road . . . meaning no disrespect, Istar."

"How did Ysse do it?" Istar asked suddenly, ignoring Kassien's remark about her mother.

"Do what?"

"Find the White Road? If Jai Khalar didn't exist then, how did she get across the Liminal?"

"Eteltar called the White Road for her."

"Taretel," Istar corrected automatically.

"Whatever you call him, he was a gifted Animal Magician," Xiriel said. "He summoned the White Road for Ysse. When she came back from Jai Pendu, the end of the White Road opened onto Jai Khalar and that's how we penetrated this place. Until then, no one knew it was here. No one could see it."

"What about Quintar? Who called the White Road for him? Ysse?"

"Hanji."

"Hanji?"

"He and Jai Khalar have always had a sort of *understanding.*"

"But he can't find it now," Kassien said.

Suddenly Xiriel let out an exclamation. The others stared at him in surprise.

"Tarquin has told the king that Pharice is attacking us!"

"Who?" Pallo squawked.

"Your countrymen, fool. The king's trying to confirm it with Mhani."

Apparently Tarquin has seen a huge Pharician army at Ristale but the Eyes haven't picked anything up."

"That's crazy," Kassien put in. "We just had Hezene's court musicians here last month. They were full of praise for our hospitality and brought gifts by the cartload. Sendrigel was just telling me the other day how—"

"Shh!" Xiriel said. Soft lights reflected from the stone flickered across his excited face. "Here, see for yourselves. It's not the clearest image, but it's better than nothing."

The others crowded around. In the stone, represented in miniature, were the king, Mhani, Ajiko, Yanise, and Sendrigel. The setting was the Eye Tower.

"Relax. Let yourself be drawn into the Eye," Xiriel advised. "If you're very still, you'll be able to hear everything they're saying."

The others obeyed, but not before Kassien made a feeble protest. "Oh, just give me a ditch to sleep in and flatbread to eat, but not this. . . ."

It was generally believed that the Eye Chamber was located in the highest point of the highest tower of Jai Khalar, but because the structure of the Citadel itself was mysterious and subject to change, no one had ever objectively mapped the place. Only the Seers knew how to find the trick doors that led to the Eye Chamber. Anyone who didn't know the way would quickly become lost among countless flights of stairs and imperceptibly curving hallways; so those who were not Seers had to take it on faith that the Eye Tower was the very pinnacle of the Citadel.

Wherever it was, the Tower boasted a phenomenal view. The windows opened unobstructed in every direction, even across the eastern mountains that abutted the Citadel. The Eye Chamber was the only room in the Tower whose shape was subtly elliptical. A ledge about a yard wide ran along the inside circumference of the walls; the rest of the floor was drowned in water whose depths probably reached the very foundations of Jai Khalar. This was the Water in its active form, which Quintar had recovered from Jai Pendu as an Artifact made of Glass. Above the Water, Eyes were suspended on wires from the ceiling as globes of varying sizes and colors.

Sendrigel, the minister of trade with Pharice, hovered near the archway that was the only way into the chamber, appearing ill at ease; Yanise stood a little apart from him, watching Lerien. Mhani stood diametrically across from Lerien and Ajiko on the ledge, facing them over the Water. Light played across the obsidian hair of her bent head, and her face was smooth with concentration.

Lerien said, "Can you See the army that Tarquin speaks of?"

Mhani tilted her head toward a nacreous globe in the ceiling. The color of its surface flared and shifted like a flame when some reactive element is added.

"I can see no army," she said in a monotone. "I will show you what I can see."

The others gazed down into the Water, and a moving image appeared, reflected upon the surface of the pool beneath the globe. Dun grassland, without hill or flower, stretched out beneath the view, which moved as if the Seer were flying. Mhani moved the vision from the edge of the mountains into the plain, scanning from side to side. There were herds of deer and flights of birds, but no people, and surely no army.

Sendrigel let out an audible sigh.

"Ah, what's that?" Lerien exclaimed.

The Eye had steadied on a gray horse with black fetlocks and a white mane. It bore a woman with red hair and white skin, her every gesture graceful as a dancer's.

"We will not look in her face," Mhani said in a tight voice. "For we cannot be certain she will not Enslave us, even at a distance. Lerien, this is the only person within a week's ride of the place Tarquin spoke of. As you can see, the Sekk do not interfere with the Eye, or we would not be able to See this one."

"What makes you think she is Sekk?" Lerien asked. "We can't see her face."

"I don't know." The Seer's tone had changed; she sounded confused. "I don't know why I said that. The horse is Pharician, to be sure."

"She is either Sekk or Deer Clan," Sendrigel said, hitching his thumbs in his belt and rocking back on his heels. "She may be in Ristale, and she may ride a Pharician horse but she is too pale to be Pharician."

"Pale like Pallo," Lerien jested. "The boy does not look Pharician, either, but his mother is certainly Iano, and the Pharician musician she claims is his father acknowledged him."

"She never should have sent him to Pharice," Mhani said.

"She saw he would never make a fighter," Ajiko said. "Better that he should live in a Pharician city like Jundun where they have use of such delicate creatures as Pallo, than to watch him fail at every weapon he tries."

Istar laid a consoling hand on Pallo's arm, but he shook it off.

"Never mind that. What is a lone woman doing on a Pharician battle horse in the middle of nowhere?" Lerien said. "It is not sensible. Show me the rest of the border. Show me the route from Jundun to the Floating Lands."

Mhani frowned. "I cannot. We have no Eye in that region."

"Then how can you see Ristale?" Lerien asked impatiently.

Mhani sighed with the air of one who has had to explain her art to the uninitiated one time too many.

"There is an Eye among the old Everien buildings on the mountain overlooking A-vi-Sirinn on one side and Ristale in Pharice on the other. We have tuned it to the Water here. However, there are no Everien remnants in Pharice, so there are no Eyes, which is why we cannot See. In any case, Lerien, there is no army. Tarquin was wrong."

She turned her gaze away from the Eye and the surface of the Water cleared.

Lerien sighed. "He was a great man. Maybe he still is. How can I judge his tidings?"

Mhani said nothing.

"Don't be stupid, Lerien—Tarquin's wrong," whispered Istar, and was hushed by Xiriel.

"Sendrigel, I want none of this to reach Hezene. Not a whisper. Go about your business as if nothing is happening."

"Can I release the Knowledge-lights from the Fire Houses for trade?" Sendrigel asked hopefully. "For Ajiko has ordered more horses from Pharice, and we must have a way to pay for them."

"I suppose it's all right. Knowledge-lights can hardly pose a threat to us in the hands of the Pharicians. But be vigilant for anything unusual. Yanise, tell Hanji we need a week's marching rations for eight men and horses. Ajiko, organize the six best fighters you have in Jai Khalar at the moment."

Kassien inhaled sharply—a high, delighted sound. "Ajiko's going to give us his best men!"

Xiriel elbowed him into silence.

Ajiko said, "The Eyes fail us in Wolf Country even now. For three weeks I have had no contact with my commanders through their Carry Eyes, and the Eyes that stand in the ruins are not able to See among the mountains."

"The Carry Eyes are not being used," Mhani said. "I cannot See through them if your commanders have decided not to report. That is a problem between you and your men. Perhaps they did not agree with your orders and decided to leave their positions for reasons of their own."

Ajiko was apopleptic. "You insult my men and my methods if you think that such indiscipline—" he began.

"They are Clansmen," Mhani said mildly. "They have minds of their own."

"Do not try to blame me for your failures, Mhani!"

"Enough!" Lerien spread his hands. "We will never solve this problem if the two of you cannot learn to work together. Ajiko, like it or not, the Knowledge is here to stay. Mhani, you must admit that strange things have been happening in Jai Khalar lately. We cannot rule out the possibility that the Eyes are at fault in Wolf Country—how could we? I'm lucky to find my bed at night the way things are going this summer."

"That is due to the coming of Jai Pendu," Mhani replied. "The White Road cannot be far."

Lerien turned to Ajiko as if she had not spoken.

"See how he fears the thought of going to Jai Pendu?" Istar whispered. "He's afraid of the White Road. He doesn't want Mhani to find it."

"I will prepare the men you asked for," the general said, and left in a tightly controlled rage.

Sendrigel said, "I will try to find out more about affairs in Pharice. There is a dissident faction in their government which has itself set on recovering the Everien Knowledge that remains in Jai Pendu. They call themselves the Circle, and they operate by stealth—Hezene will not tolerate overt opposition to his policies. I am not sure of their strength on land but they have some support in the Imperial Navy."

"Have they not learned from Hezene's failure to intercept Jai Pendu by sea?" Lerien guffawed. "The Floating Lands sank six of Pharice's best galleons."

"If there were a Pharician force traveling down the western range, they might be doing so to get to Jai Pendu without being detected by Jundun. They might be renegades."

"I don't understand why the Pharicians want any part of the Knowledge," Mhani said peevishly. "The Sekk do not trouble them, and they lack the Eyes and the other remains of Everien civilization which support the Knowledge."

"They are a culture obsessed with possessing things," Sendrigel answered. "Information has value to them, and the Knowledge is a kind of information."

"Speaking of information," Lerien said, "get me more about this faction called the Circle. Call in your informers and prepare reports. Bring your findings to Mhani in my absence."

Sendrigel bowed, and Lerien dismissed both him and Yanise with a gesture. Then the king turned to Mhani, his posture slackening. In a completely informal tone, he said, "I can feel you thinking something unpleasant. Say it."

"I have been looking for Ajiko's armies in the Eyes for days and days. They are not where he says they are. I have Seen the entire land of Everien and all its borders, and if there is no Pharician army in the Eye, there is also no great force of ours, unless it is dispersed in the Wilds. Ajiko orders Pharician horses and holds meetings and makes maps, but it doesn't add up. We ought to have armies not far from A-vi-Sirinn on the border of the Wolf Country, but I cannot See them and they will not call me. You blame the Eyes but you should consider Ajiko!"

Lerien's voice was kind, as if to make up for the words he was speaking. "I know he is hard on you. He is Clan, Mhani. He has not the scope to appreciate the Knowledge and that is why he dismisses it. But he is a seasoned warrior and he has devoted his life to the defense of Everien."

"He is a bully," Mhani said.

But Lerien was pacing along the ledge, head down. "It troubles me to see Tarquin again, especially so close to the coming of Jai Pendu. I know you wish me to approve Istar's petition. But Ysse was clear on this point; even on her deathbed, she was adamant that the White Road should be allowed to lie. That we were to strengthen our material applications of the Knowledge, and avoid the Liminal. I am sure she knew something we do not—as does Tarquin.''

"That is what I am spending night and day trying to discover for you, Lerien. So that you will not be dependent on the legacy of Ysse—or the testimony of a madman. So that you will be able to determine your own destiny.''

Lerien laughed. "Or so that you will be able to make my destiny for me, Mhani? No, do not frown. I like it well that you are strong. I will consider your words while I ride.''

"Ride?''

"Have I any choice? I must find my troops in the Wolf Country and lead them down to guard the gates to Everien. Even if there is no Pharician army on our border, I must have command of my men. I cannot rely on the Eyes exclusively— not now, not in a summer when Jai Pendu comes and mysteries abound. And I would be a fool to ignore Tarquin.''

"He is a hero in the eyes of many,'' Mhani said expressionlessly. "Yet you might send men without going yourself. Send Ajiko!''

"I must go. According to our traditions, the Clans do not live by the Knowledge. Today Tarquin accused me of losing touch with my people, locked away high up in this castle—and I am willing to suffer these accusations because I believe the Knowledge is essential to our survival. Have I not always supported your work, Mhani?''

"You have.''

"But if I place all my faith in the Knowledge, I betray my origins. My own senses must be the judge. I will ride to Ristale tomorrow. I hope Tarquin is deluded. But if he is right, there will be no time for heroism at Jai Pendu. We will have to prepare to repel Pharice—somehow.''

Mhani did not appear convinced.

"Who will command in your absence?''

"Ajiko, I suppose, can handle military matters. No, do not fret: the Eyes will always be yours—you know I don't understand them.'' Mhani smiled at Lerien when he said this. "Hanji can manage the rest. I will give you my decision about Istar when I have seen what there is to see at Ristale. One thing is clear: the Pharician Pallo must be watched closely. I like it not that he moves about so freely.''

"He's just a boy,'' Mhani protested.

"I'll not send him to Jai Pendu, and you should—''

PALLO GAVE AN inarticulate cry and jolted the Eye.

"Don't do that! I've lost the image now, and if Mhani guesses I've been spying . . .'' Xiriel hurried to conceal the Eye in his robes.

"Tarquin!" Istar uttered savagely. "For one man's whim, all our plans gone to ruin."

The others backed away from her. She paced the room, her face closed and angry.

"Pallo, are you a Pharician spy?" she snapped sarcastically.

"No," answered Pallo, his voice cracking.

Istar threw up her hands. "What is happening around this place? Pharician spy, my toenail." She halted at the window and stood there silently. "Duty," she whispered. "How I hate it. Yet what am I without it?"

"Don't take personal insult," Kassien admonished. "The king has to consider all his subjects, and we are only—"

Istar gave him a look so dark he bit off his own words. She took a deep breath.

"Humor me in this. Stay away from Mhani and the king—especially you, Pallo! That shouldn't be too hard. In fact, endeavor to speak to no one. We will meet back here at midnight, after we've all thought this through. Agreed?"

The others nodded dumbly. After she left, Kassien seemed to shake himself awake. He looked at Pallo and mused, "I wonder whether they'll kill you as a traitor. And how. Hanging? Beheading? Throw you off the Eye Tower? What do you think, Xiriel?"

VALIANT OR CRAZED

Tarquin had fallen asleep on a white pallet in a room full of vines and silkspiders, but when he woke everything was red except the sky overhead, which was black. There was a soft glow coming from the red fabric of the circular bed where he lay, and from the carpets and their shimmering designs that moved like oil on water, and from the tapestried walls. The color was so pervasive that the room reminded him of a hand through which a bright light had been shone, illuminating its blood so that all was crimson but the dark bones.

He leaped up and ripped the door open, expecting to find the corridor and its wide windows. Instead he stepped into the enormous vault of the training arena. He stopped in his tracks. At first he couldn't believe it; he was amazed to find himself back in the place where he'd spent so much of his time of old amid the cacophony of mock battles and endurance drills. Now the place was empty. The ropes and nets had been removed; the quicksand pit had been filled in; the diving pool was decorated with ornamental plants. The school that had once been used to train horses had been replaced by a bare section of stone floor painted with lines that Tarquin guessed were meant to act as positional markers for soldiers. He wandered across the smoothly raked sand to the fighting ring where he'd conducted the test matches and stepped up onto its raised floor. Most of the bloodstains on the aged wood were familiar. Remembering how the place used to reek of men and horses and dogs, he sniffed; now it seemed sterile. Tears pressed the backs of his eyes.

Tarquin swore and kicked at the scuffed wood. He missed Ysse. She had been a bitch and a half but at least you always knew where you stood with her. Same with Chyko—you could trust Chyko. Maybe not in a card game, granted, but in the important things he had always been sound. Shit, you could trust Chyko, and Chyko had been a criminal.

He laughed, recollecting. Those days when he was training the Company for Ysse—they had been the best of his life. He shuffled over to the wall where all the weapons had once been stored: spears and crossbows, swords, fighting sticks of all description, axes, flails, dart guns and flying knives, partisans, glaives, whips, now all replaced by practice swords. Alongside there was a duty roster posted in neat handwriting composed of ruler-straight lines. He turned away, momentarily depressed; then he laughed again, thinking what Chyko would have made of Ajiko's duty rosters.

Quintar had heard rumors of Chyko for years without ever actually encountering him. In the spring of the year that he began recruiting for Ysse's special Company, he would have said that every Clan warrior of note must have passed through this training ground. Word had gone out that Quintar was looking for the twelve best fighters in the land, irrespective of Clan, rank, or standing of any kind, for "special training." Ysse had insisted on the unification of the Clans under Jai Khalar, but this had never been easy to accomplish, and the Clans tended to retain the strongest of their fighters for themselves, sending only their younger sons to Ysse's Guard at Jai Khalar. By appealing to Clan pride and a sense of elitism, Ysse hoped to smoke out the real warriors so that Quintar could teach them how better to destroy Sekk—with the promise that the warriors would then return to their home territories capable of serving their Clans better than before.

Yet the ultimate purpose of the Company was to form a cadre of warriors who could fight across all Clan territories, systematically eliminating the threat of the Sekk and their monsters while eroding the hostilities between Clans at the same time. It would mean bitter enemies fighting side by side, so that a Bear Clan fighter confronted with members of his own family Enslaved by the Sekk would not succumb to pity, nor face the dishonor of killing his own kindred—but would rely on his Wasp Clan comrade to slay honorably the relative that he could not. It would mean each warrior's placing his life in the service of others outside his Clan, against an enemy none of them really understood. Only the most valiant of Clan warriors would wish to take on such a task—or the most crazed, depending on how one chose to look at it.

At that time, Quintar was the most renowned swordsman in Everien, and he enjoyed Ysse's favor, which was not lightly bestowed. Members of the Guard jockeyed for position in Quintar's esteem, but he had not been interested in them so much as in the outlanders, civilian Clansmen from whom he hoped to draw new, wild blood. Clan tradition said that the warrior should make himself separate from society, autonomous and free. Life in Jai Khalar could dampen that spirit, and he suspected his own Guard had become too caught up in the military culture—had come too far from their origins—to retain the individual courage that would make them exceptional. He wanted men who had blood—not merely in their veins, but on their weapons—and, even better, on their teeth. To test their mettle he decided to fight them each himself: this would be part of his own training.

Warriors of every stripe began to show up at Jai Khalar, enticed by the challenge. Most of them were untrained beyond their Clan weapons of preference, which posed a problem because Quintar needed swords and bows above all. A gifted Snake, even one who could wrestle a buffalo into submission, would still die when confronted with the clumsiest of Wolf axes or Seahawk swords: metal, after all, would always cut flesh. Yet he tested them all, and picked the ones he deemed able to learn new weapons. Most of these men had reputations in their own lands or within Ysse's army. All of them were seasoned fighters who had faced the monsters that the Sekk could draw down from the hills to prey on humans. None of them could beat Quintar in a mock fight, though a few pushed him harder than he'd liked to admit.

One day, Quintar had just arrived back in Jai Khalar after a trip to the Fire Houses to inspect some new shield designs that had been highly touted by the blacksmiths. Hanji greeted him at the gate with a curious expression on his face.

"I think there's something you should see."

"Is it food? I'm starving."

"A prisoner has escaped from the dungeon and is causing havoc in the aviary."

"Havoc in the aviary, eh?" Quintar snorted. "Find Lyetar and ask him to help you. And get me something to eat, please."

"You can have cakes and beer after you've seen what's happening in the aviary," drawled Hanji, plucking at Quintar's sleeve with a bony hand. "You will only accuse Lyetar of lying when he tells you what he's seen."

Skeptically, Quintar followed the seneschal to the wire enclosure where the fighting birds were kept. It had been the pride of Ysse's reign to construct the aviary, where birds of prey were trained to hunt and kill. Only the young birds were restrained in this way, while they were learning their manners and their moves; the mature killing falcons went free and were called at need.

The place was indeed in an uproar. The prisoner was loose among the birds, and the guards seemed unable to catch him. A falcon-girl was standing at the gate, peering anxiously up at her disturbed charges.

"Who is he? What are his crimes?" said Quintar to the falcon-girl. She gave him a red-lipped smile as she gripped the wires with delicate hands.

"He's called Chyko, and he lost at gambling—badly—against Zedese. When he was asked for the money, this scoundrel fled and stole Zedese's chariot, which happened to contain his wife and his wife's sister. By the time Zedese and his friends finally caught up with him, the wife didn't want to come back! It was too much for Zedese. He decided to have a go at this bandit and got a poison dart in his, uh"—she smirked and looked down, so that Tarquin would be quite sure which part of Zedese's anatomy had been attacked—"which numbed it. Apparently he couldn't use it for days. . . ." She broke off again, giggling, and then was seen to forcibly control herself. "I heard it took a dozen men to bring this reprobate in, and he kept saying he only surrendered because of the women. Zedese's wife, and the sister. He was afraid they'd be hurt; they kept throwing themselves between him and the soldiers to protect him! They have been visiting him every night in jail, trying to bribe the wardens and chanting and begging: 'Release Chyko, free Chyko.' Then this afternoon, he knocked down the guards, stole back his weapons, and the wardens have chased him halfway across the Citadel."

As he listened to her story, Quintar was watching the action inside the aviary. The escaped prisoner was hanging upside down from the wire ceiling, firing his bow, and then scurrying across the wires to the next tree, to hide once again from his avian attackers. The men on the ground had been forced to retreat, hit one too many times in the buttocks or calves with bolts or darts or arrows from what seemed an endless supply. Birds had been sent in to harass Chyko; but the prisoner did not spare these from torment: instead, he was making a sport of shooting them.

Quintar was disgusted, although he had to admire the inventiveness of the method. The Wasp did not shoot the birds to kill them; rather, he waited until their wings were extended and then systematically shot off their primary wing feathers in such a way that they could not fly straight, and were reduced to spiraling and veering around the cage. He did this to three seahawks in succession before the guards wisely called off the birds.

Quintar stepped out in the open and said, "You have dishonored my Clan. You fight like a Pharician tree ape and a coward."

"Have me killed, then, O Captain of the Queen's Guard," laughed the small, dark man with the white teeth.

"I have a better idea. Come down from the ceiling, monkey, and let's see you fight like a man."

"I could kill you where you stand." Chyko brought a blowgun to his lips.

"Maybe. But you would then deny me the pleasure of thrashing you with my sword."

"Ah, so you will have a sword and I will have nothing," sang Chyko. "Yes, that is honorable, queen's man."

"Give him a sword," said Quintar to the guards. They obeyed him, already beginning to look pleased at the prospect of watching their captain teach this outlander a lesson.

The prisoner came down from the ceiling of the aviary to take the sword that was placed on the ground for him. Quintar was aware that he had acquired quite an audience, but tried to ignore it. He used all his senses to assess the Wasp prisoner: the way he moved, how he used his eyes, what his weaknesses might be. On the surface of it, Chyko didn't look like much. He was small and wiry, with very little muscle on his bones. Picking up the weapon as if it were unfamiliar, the offender tossed it from hand to hand, made a few rather awkward practice strokes, and nodded at Tarquin that he was ready.

It was over in seconds. Quintar remembered making a test pass or two at the archer, who fell back and parried clumsily. He was thinking that despite the stranger's crimes and flagrant disrespect, it would be a shame to dishonor him by humiliating him publicly because he was not allowed to use his weapon of choice. He had shown masterful skill with dart and bow, and ought not to be thrashed now.

Then again, the stranger had humiliated some of his best guards and insulted him as well. Best to sort him out and teach him a lesson. Quintar spotted an opportunity and acted on it.

The next thing he knew, his own sword was flying through the air end over end even as his legs were being taken out from under him. He ended up on his back with the point of his opponent's sword snuggling into his throat. He looked up the blade into Chyko's laughing eyes.

"Ah, Quintar!" called Ysse, applauding—for she had a way of sniffing out trouble in Jai Khalar and appearing on the scene without warning. "Well done. I see you have found a friend at last."

The word "friend" was the farthest thing from Quintar's mind at that moment; but Ysse, as was her irritating wont, turned out to be correct in the long run. Chyko joined the Company, and his mere presence among the other men was enough not only to entertain and electrify but to raise the collective standard of proficiency. For Chyko alone held himself to be Tarquin's equal. For the other men, Quintar felt the affection of a father for his sons or a master for his hounds; and they, for their part, spent hour after hour speculating about him, exchanging stories about him; inventing nicknames and looking for ways to break through his exterior without ever succeeding, for Quintar's bond with his men depended on him holding himself apart, keeping them in fear of him. Yet Chyko was different. He stood out even among the individualists of Quintar's Company. He did not need to be declared Free by anybody: he had declared himself Free, and spent most of his time getting in and out of trouble of one kind or another. Over him Quintar had no authority.

Quintar soon lost count of how many times Chyko had angered him almost to the point of violence. Yet it had been impossible to hold a grudge against someone who had so much zest for life. Chyko had taken such pleasure in battle as Quintar had never seen. Some of it had rubbed off on the Company and Quintar himself; but all of that was before Jai Pendu, in times of honest battles using flesh and steel. They had been the greatest days of Quintar's life, and they would never come again.

A door slammed somewhere nearby and he whirled, following the echo to its source. Ajiko had come out of the office carrying his crossbow and several large scrolls.

What, Tarquin wondered, was the preoccupation with paper in Jai Khalar of late? If a man couldn't remember everything he needed to know without writing it down, he probably knew too much for his own good.

Tarquin swung down from the ring and went toward the general. Ajiko had been an outstanding fighter in his time. He had missed going to Jai Pendu with the Company only because he had been injured just before Ysse dispatched them on their fateful mission. He had also been the foremost archer in Everien until Chyko came along and changed all the standards.

Ajiko saw him and halted.

"What have you got there?" Tarquin asked, gesturing to the scrolls.

Ajiko shifted restlessly for a moment before squaring himself to face Tarquin, as if this were a conversation he did not wish to have. He slid his crossbow onto his back and Tarquin noted that it was charred and scratched with long use. The symbols of his Clan had been carved along its length, unintelligible to Tarquin but probably telling something of his family history and boasting of battle prowess. The general himself was built like a small bull, with black hair going gray and a rugged face whose nose was displaced half an inch to one side after having been broken one time too many. He grimaced slightly as he withdrew a scroll case from his leather coat. He used large, blunt teeth to open the knot binding it, then spread out the map on the pavement, weighting it with raw lumps of glass. The drawing had been painstakingly labeled in his small, neat hand, with lines and arrows indicating troop and supply movement in contrasting colors, and enemy positions with dates written beside them. The whole thing was coded according to what seemed an incredibly complex system of signs. It was a far cry from Tarquin's recollection of sketches drawn in sand with the occasional use of a boot to indicate a warship.

"Are these your troop numbers?" Tarquin said incredulously. "Where have you found so many?"

"My army uses men of all ages, in different capacities. We use women behind the lines. And there is a whole generation grown to adulthood since you left."

"But so many all together? It reminds me of Pharice." He had not meant it as a compliment, but Ajiko took it that way.

"Pharice has a highly effective system," Ajiko said proudly. "Our forces are highly disciplined, tightly organized, and swiftly coordinated. Despite what you heard in the Council today, the majority of Everien is safe from the Sekk under this regime—and it would be safer still if the king would only let go of Mhani and the Knowledge that she has made us all dependent on."

Looking at the complicated map, Tarquin felt slightly out of his depth. If what was needed in a warrior today was book learning and map-making, then better that he had stayed in the Wild Lands.

"But Everien seems so empty," he murmured. "I thought the war must be going very badly."

"Everien is one country," Ajiko said, as though reciting a well-practiced speech. "We cannot afford to sit in our Clan holdings bickering like a nest of seahawks while the Sekk prey on us. We must unite against a common enemy. As Ysse believed, so do I."

"Maybe there is a chance against Pharice after all," Tarquin acknowledged awkwardly. "I had never seen so many arms together as made up the Pharician force. But if all is as you say, it may be that the enemy can be cut apart and repelled. Are your elite fighters to hand? Can you reach them through the Eyes, or bring them here?"

"We do not rely on elite warriors as of old," Ajiko answered. "Again, you are thinking in terms that no longer apply. It is dangerous, very dangerous, to allow a powerful fighter to engage with the Sekk. For if he is turned and Enslaved, not only have we lost his strength, but it can be used against us."

"This is news to me," Tarquin said. "In our Company we had the best men in Everien, and not one of them was ever Enslaved."

Ajiko gazed at him and his face was like a wall. "We live in swiftly changing times," he said.

Tarquin, thinking of the implications of Ajiko's policy, became agitated. "But the Pharicians treat their soldiers as sheep, or worse. Often the Pharician soldier is merely a prisoner from one of their conquered lands, without rights or land of his own. Why would you wish to model Clan warfare on Pharician ways? I would say that by building these big armies, you are making the Clansmen into servants, little better than Slaves. The Clan warrior must uphold family honor and tradition, but the way in which he expresses these legacies is his own to choose. He lays his life down for his people; therefore he is not meant to be bound by the same rules as others. All our great warriors were men of strong will and strong imagination. To march in formation this way, to be made to subvert their instincts in favor of the Knowledge gained by the Artifacts—this would be intolerable to such a man."

"Such a man as you describe," Ajiko said carefully, "would soon find himself to be an officer in my system. Much as you were an officer under Ysse. A great leader can take men anywhere, do anything with them."

"Ysse was such a leader," Tarquin agreed. "She was barely mortal in the eyes of her subjects. But we never fought as you ask your men to fight, Ajiko. Ysse always inspired the man, the group, but the strength came from within. If there is no desire within, no fighting spirit, then all the discipline in the world cannot put it there by artificial means. They will only ever fight out of sheer terror, and this will make them vulnerable to Slaving. No administrative technique, however clever, will make your men heroes if it takes away their self-will."

"Heroes?" Ajiko said bitterly. "I have no hopes that they would be heroes. The heroes of Everien are long dead. I must work with what is left over, and these men do not have the talent to be the kind of warrior you led in your day."

"Nonsense! What about the younger generation?"

"They have no experience of a world without the Knowledge. They believe in the Artifacts. They don't wish it to be any other way. We have had eighteen years of relative peace now, thanks to the Water of Glass."

Tarquin noted the clumsy flattery and felt like ripping Ajiko up with his teeth. "Show me your men, then. I would like to look on this army for myself."

"Most of our forces are deployed high in the western hills, in Wolf Country and in Snake Country. The east is patrolled but has gotten off lightly of late, so we have diverted most of these men to support the west." He indicated the trend on the map.

Tarquin frowned. He had seen no evidence of a large force anywhere in the northwestern mountains through which he'd passed in recent days on his way from Pharice; so this must mean that Ajiko's troops were farther south, closer to the sea plateau. He pointed to the area on the map and said, "So they are somewhere around here now?"

Ajiko's face gave away nothing. Indicating the map, Tarquin said, "If we could mobilize our forces in these hills, we might make a stand on the sea plateau at the mouth of Everien. We could fight them from a superior position on the edge of the sea plateau, among the waterfalls and rockslides. If this fails, we'll draw the Pharicians into the mountain gates and so contain their assault." He was getting into the spirit of things now, and he added excitedly, "They'll get bottlenecked in these hills, and we can rain fire down from above with our Wasp archers. I suggest you move half of these troops to the sea plateau and occupy the high ground. The other half should wait in the mountains above the gates. If we can establish a supply train, we might hold them off indefinitely. At the same time, we must determine their supply lines and attack them. An army this size cannot be easy to feed. What is going on in Jundun, the capital?"

The general's famously dispassionate countenance allowed a flat smile. "You are ahead of yourself. We need to see this Pharician army before we can move troops. And as of yet the Eyes do not show it."

"The Eyes this, the Eyes that! What good are they?" He didn't attempt to disguise his annoyance. He was not surprised that the hardheaded general should be uncooperative, but it seemed incredible to him that Ajiko had become so reliant on the Knowledge—ironically, on the very Knowledge that Tarquin had brought to Everien personally in the form of the Water of Glass.

"The Eyes would be extremely useful if the Seers who use them would pay more attention to their military applications. Eyes help us to monitor the high country, where the Sekk are most likely to move in and Enslave people. I have to protect people from themselves, and that's never easy with the Clans competing with each other to see who can be more proud, more self-sufficient, more indifferent to suffering. It calls for subtlety of method."

Taken aback, Tarquin said nothing for a moment. The pragmatic Ajiko had always impressed him as having about as much imagination as a cheese, yet now he sounded like a Seer. He couldn't think how to respond to this unexpectedly philosophical analysis; then he shook himself a little. "But the high country is practically empty. If they're not in the mountains, then where are all your *men*?"

He kicked sand at the map and saw Ajiko throttle his anger.

"I have much to do," Ajiko said. He bent and collected his map. "You should be satisfied: the king rides to Wolf Country in the morning to gather up our forces. He will attempt to verify your claims through the monitor towers on the way, and if the Pharicians are behaving as you say, he will make a stand by the sea gates."

"It's not an answer, Ajiko," Tarquin called after him as he left. "What is the matter with you people? None of you can deal with confrontation. No wonder you hide in Jai Khalar. You can't even answer a straight question."

But Ajiko was gone.

Eighteen years. Tarquin sent his gaze around the silent training ground. Again he pictured his men—valiant or crazed, it hadn't mattered in those days.

A LIGHT SNACK
BETWEEN MEALS

𝔒t took hours before Istar located the entrance to the Eye Tower lurking under a large potted fern. When she made her way inside, she found her mother kneeling on the brink of the Water, eyes closed, one finger touching its mirrory surface.

"I know Xiriel spied on us," Mhani said by way of greeting. "He is a devil when it comes to shortcuts and tricks in the Knowledge."

"I don't believe this is happening," Istar replied, not bothering to apologize. She certainly wasn't sorry.

Mhani murmured, "Connectivity. The Water of Glass connects that which is separate. The connection is broken, but what can break water?"

Istar stamped her foot. "Mother! This is no time for Philosophy. Where is Tarquin?"

"He is sleeping," Mhani said tonelessly. "Leave him be. He's exhausted."

"Not you, too. Why is everyone on his side?"

"Once," Mhani said, "Chyko was caught by a Sekk. It was a powerful Master, and it enthralled Chyko and he could not escape."

"My father, Enslaved? That's impossible." Istar was revulsed at the thought.

"Quintar broke the spell."

"Always Quintar!" Istar snarled. "Saving Chyko; saving Everien; Ysse's favorite—always fucking Quintar!"

Mhani didn't seem to be listening.

"Chyko must have been lying if he told you that," Istar went on. "Or drunk. It can't be a true story. I'm sick of hearing about the past, anyway. Tarquin's crazy, I'm telling you."

"They thought Ysse was crazy to seek the Artifacts of Jai Pendu. Before that, she was a mere girl, an Honorary with less status than yourself."

Istar looked at her mother as if she'd blasphemed. Mhani added, "Oh, she was better than many, a valued fighter—but an Honorary nevertheless, and no match for the best men. Until she got it in her head to ride the White Road to Jai Pendu. Then the Fire of Glass changed everything. She had tapped into the Knowledge and she returned . . . different. Better. She was still an Honorary, but none could bend her will."

Yearningly, Istar said, "That's why I have to go to Jai Pendu. My father was Chyko! If anyone was ever born to fight, it's me."

"Istar, it's never the same problem or the same solution. Ysse's time was different. The Sekk have changed us. Always we warred among ourselves. Always we honored the fighter. But the Clans were untame people in the years before we came to Everien. The Knowledge gave us a taste of something we never tasted. It refined our ways, civilized us. So that when the Sekk came to take the family of a Clan warrior, it was a battle unlike any he had ever known. It was a seduction, and every man of every Clan had to learn to resist it. Every man stood alone. Every one was a dedicated warrior, bound body and blood to his Clan and territory, but Free in his heart. He trained only in hope of remaining free. In the hope that the day he encountered not merely one of its monsters, but a Sekk Master itself, he might stand his ground, resist the Slaving. And if he was worthy, he hoped to destroy the Sekk. For if he failed, his will would be taken, and he would go mad, slay his own family and stock, and ultimately kill himself under the domination of the Sekk. There was no army to speak of before Ysse came, and the Sekk were a terrible scourge in those days—far worse than anything you have seen, Istar."

"I find that difficult to believe."

"I hope you never have to pay the price of underestimating them. Their beauty is haunting and irresistible."

"I have resisted it," Istar boasted. "I killed one, Mhani. No one seems to remember that when they deal with me."

Mhani shook her head. "Stop being such a child! You know next to nothing, Istar. Ysse would have had you for a light snack between meals."

Istar went quiet at the name of the queen. Mhani's cheeks were pink with indignation as she continued. "It is recorded that when Ysse returned from Jai Pendu with the Fire of Glass, this entire valley lay under sway of the Sekk. Our people had been driven up into the mountains but for a small band of us who held the Fire Houses, where we made our swords. We had lost all our territory, but what Clan warrior would relinquish a weapon in favor of mere grass, of mere sunlight? We held the Fire Houses until Ysse came with the Artifact and awakened the Fire Knowledge, opened Jai Khalar, and ushered in the beginning of our present age. Nothing has been the same since."

"Mother, if you don't believe Pharice is attacking us, why don't you convince Lerien he's foolish to leave Jai Khalar?"

Mhani looked at her sharply. "Men seldom do things for the reasons they give," she said. "You might have learned that much by now."

"Better to be like Chyko," Istar murmured, "and never give any reasons at all."

"Stay out of trouble, Istar," her mother advised. "Keep your head down and wait—perhaps we will find the White Road after all, and Lerien can ride to Jai Pendu."

"But we know a way through the Floating Lands! The White Road is not needed, Mother, and you exhaust yourself looking for it."

Mhani bristled. "I am not exhausted! Calm yourself, daughter. Self-restraint is called for here. Now, go get Pallo and bring him here for safeguarding, before Lerien decides to throw him in prison."

Istar wished she could slam the door behind her, but today there was no door out of the Eye Chamber. She passed through an arch into an overgrown, weedy garden where the noon sun beat down even though she knew it was almost night. The only way out was a broken gate that led to a flight of steps climbing hundreds of feet.

"Kassien, you're right," she said to the air. "Give me a ditch."

She climbed until she could climb no farther. At the top of the stairs she found herself on the battlements two levels above the main dining hall. She turned left and walked to the end of the wall, where she could look out across Everien. She wanted to be alone with the birds and the wind and, with the passing relief of night coming on, the stars.

There was a whirlpool turning in the pit of her stomach, and at the center of it was Tarquin the Free. She had heard so many stories about Quintar the Captain of the Guard, but of Tarquin the Free no one ever seemed to speak a whisper. He had been right to change his name, she reflected. The man she had seen this afternoon was not the hero of the stories. This man had killed Quintar and replaced him with something bitter, rough, and crude.

For years she had fantasized about meeting him. She would be traveling somewhere far away, at a strange inn on a desolate road, and she would be thrashing the entire clientele at darts, and a tall stranger with keen eyes would challenge her. They would engage in a hotly contested match that would end with Istar throwing the winning dart from behind her back. And then he would reveal his identity and she hers, and they would drink together and Tarquin would tell her that he had been watching her from afar for years. He would talk of Chyko and how Chyko's death had destroyed him. And she would befriend him and he would teach her all his best tricks and together they would ride out and make an end to the Sekk . . . or something like that. In any case she had expected him to be better-looking. And she had expected him to make some overture of kinship to her, for he had after all left her unsupported in the Seahawk Clan, all but forcing her to become an Honorary in order to stand for her sisters.

She certainly had not expected him to arrive out of the blue and swipe aside her years of careful planning with a few words—ruin her hard-won audience with the king, disrupt all her goals—and then merely say, "We should talk."

She was fuming. The sky ambered in the south over the sea, and the mountains seemed to grow larger in the falling light. A soft wind blew sheep calls from the valley far below. Istar felt murderous.

Footsteps sounded behind her. She turned. "I thought you were asleep," Istar said coldly. "I thought you were exhausted from your journey."

Tarquin came to a halt just out of sword range. "I am tired. But I find it difficult to sleep many hours in Jai Khalar. And every hour spent sleeping here is another hour for the Pharician army to advance."

Istar said nothing. She didn't want to give him the satisfaction of knowing how agitated she felt.

"I regret my interruption of your petition," he said after a minute. "It was unfair. Poor timing on my part."

She put her elbows on the parapet. She couldn't see his face clearly. Behind him the moon was coming up in a bright wedge over the mountains.

"Then support me with the king," she urged. "Ajiko's strategy is doomed to fail. Surely you can see how he has turned into a poor imitation of a Pharician. He denies the Clan ways and makes everyone march to a pattern. We could do so much better."

"Ajiko was never what you could call a great thinker," Tarquin agreed. "It disturbs me now to see him with so much power."

"We were only asking for ten swords, Tarquin—the men won't even be missed. Tell me ten swords could do anything against an army such as you tell of! We have a good strategy, and—"

"It has nothing to do with the Pharician army," Tarquin cut in. "You're out of your mind to wish to go to Jai Pendu. For one thing, you'll never get through the Floating Lands. The bridges no longer connect them to each other, or to Jai Pendu. You'd be stranded."

"Xiriel knows a way."

"He's wrong. There is no way, I tell you," he said vehemently.

"I don't see how you could know, Tarquin. You took the White Road. How can you be so sure?" She watched him carefully. It was as if he didn't want for there to be a way.

"I am sure. It is a fact. No one can cross the Floating Lands."

"You can't know that."

"It's true! Don't argue with me."

She slid back half a pace, wondering why he was so emotional. He looked older all of a sudden, and bleak.

"You'd be throwing your lives away and you don't even know it."

"No, I don't know it," Istar said bitterly. "You're the only one who knows, because you're the only one to come back alive. Even Queen Ysse is dead. She would have agreed with me—I know she would have. She went to Jai Pendu herself."

Tarquin's rough profile smiled. "Queen Ysse would not have stood here and argued with the likes of me," he said. "She would have taken her men and gone by now, and cut to pieces anyone who stood in the way. But those were different times."

Thinking of Ysse made Istar hot with ambition. Ysse had been the only Honorary to actually lead men at a high level. By assembling her small group of dissidents, Istar hoped to do the same. Certainly she hoped to escape Ajiko's system of discipline, which irritated her beyond speech.

"Chyko was a brilliant fighter, and my best friend," Tarquin said, disturbing her nascent thoughts of putting Ajiko's smug, order-loving officers in their places. "I miss him still."

Istar supposed this was the closest she was going to get to an apology. She could think of nothing to say in return. What *could* she say to this strange man, who knew nothing of her or her goals?

There was only one real question. "What happened to my father at Jai Pendu?"

His gaze swerved away from her scrutiny. "I can't say."

She frowned. "What do you mean, you can't say? Is it true what I heard, that Ysse forbade you to speak?"

He was silent. She forced herself to wait for his answer, but what she wanted to do was hurl her fists against him. His lined face, his shadowed eyes, his unruly hair—she wished to see it all smeared with his blood when she smashed his teeth. How could a man so many times renowned be so resigned, so full of doom—and so deficient in the hauteur required of a Clan warrior?

"I met a terrible foe," he said at last. "One beyond my scope, and I failed, and their deaths are on me, and it drove me out of my mind. You would not understand the details."

"Try me."

He shook his head. "Leave it, Istar."

"I won't leave it! Why did you come back, then? How dare you face me and refuse me what you owe?" She was spitting with emotion.

Kassien was calling her from somewhere below.

"Istar! Istar, come quickly!"

She did not react. She was staring at Tarquin, trying to read his face— demanding an answer with her eyes and body.

"Your friend calls you," he said woodenly.

She spun on her heel and ran toward the sound of Kassien's voice.

"Move your legs, Istar! They want to put a guard on Pallo. Istar!"

She came around a corner in the parapet and nearly bumped into him; he grabbed her arm and started to drag her into a doorway. She resisted him, craning her head around the corner to see back the way she had just come. Tarquin was no longer there.

"Quick, Istar. It took forever to find you, and Xiriel says the way might change at any moment. This damned castle is doing my head in, I swear."

He was tugging her into the passage.

"Where's Pallo now?"

"With Xiriel. Hanji's on the trail, though, so it won't be long before we're discovered. We've got to make a decision."

They were running through galleries and down stairs.

"There's no decision to be made from my point of view. What about you, Kassien? You'd be directly disobeying the king, abandoning your duty, and ruining your good name forever."

Kassien stopped suddenly, flattened himself against the wall, and put a finger to his lips. They were nearing the barracks that housed such soldiers as yet remained in Jai Khalar. Pierse the Captain of the Guard could be heard droning at one of the cadet squads.

"I don't care if you're sleeping! I'll give inspections anytime I like. This is a war, you little midgebites. Your boots are a disgrace, Liese. Let me see your kit. What a mess. What's this for?"

"It's a hunting knife, Captain."

"Did you ask permission to carry a hunting knife?"

"I've always carried it, ever since—"

"Not anymore. Thank you, Liese. Close your mouth."

Every muscle in Kassien's body had gone taut. Now it was Istar's turn to do the tugging.

"Kass, don't! Come on. Don't listen to him."

Istar cursed under her breath. Just the sound of Pierse's voice was enough to blind Kassien with rage; for years he had been avoiding Jai Khalar, not only because of the Knowledge, but to avoid running into Pierse and having to refrain from killing him.

"Star." His teeth were clenched. His hand was on his sword. She didn't know whether he wanted her to stop him, or just to hold down Pierse while Kassien disemboweled the captain.

"No, Kassien. Come on."

She knew he had to be thinking about Bennen. Kassien's younger brother had been her only friend in her early years training for Ajiko's army, and he had fallen afoul of Captain Pierse, whom Istar privately believed was a sadist. Istar, an Honorary, had been almost as ill suited to the group as Bennen, and the two had clung together as outcastes will. At first they had been ignored by Pierse as the ineffectual usually are; then Bennen invented a bird out of wax and paper and wood, and they had flown it from the Eye Tower on a string until it was caught on a sudden gust and shot in a window, where it frightened some women spinning. Word had gotten back to Captain Pierse, who confiscated the toy and interrogated both cadets.

"How did you do this? Explain how it works!"

Bennen shrugged dumbly. He affected an idiotic expression whenever he didn't want to answer something; this occurred frequently under Pierse's authority, with the result that Pierse thought Bennen a simpleton.

"Are you ill, boy?" he snapped.

"My friend is an Impressionist," Istar said, and Pierse reacted as though she'd said, "My friend eats babies."

Pierse put them both on punishment for no good reason, but Bennen was undeterred. Bennen was always making things. They used to build fire-propelled boats and race them on the lake outside the training grounds. Pierse got wind of this, too, and took the boats away. He was unpleasant to everyone but downright vicious to Bennen, who admittedly was not much of a soldier. Bennen had a tendency toward sleepwalking, and sometimes he would say things in a language no one could understand. Pierse thought he was playing games and criticized him for being the weak link in the chain.

He'd sneer at Bennen. "Everyone else is looking over *here*. Why are *you* looking over *there*?" Bennen would give a secretive little smile and comply with directions, but later he confessed to Istar that he'd been watching some people no one else could see.

Pierse was obviously embarrassed to have such a weird boy under his command, but Bennen might have made a decent fighter had he been left to his own Clan for informal instruction. He was big and an apt wrestler, even if he was less interested in swordplay and not interested at all in military discipline. Where Kassien had thrived on the strict environment of Jai Khalar's military school with its romance of strength and status, Bennen's very nature made it impossible for him to fit in to the ranks. Istar remembered how Kassien always stuck up for his little brother, until eventually it was understood that if you harassed the freak with fainting spells you would receive a severe whacking from Kassien. It was something Istar had always liked about Kassien, especially because she knew Kassien himself was afraid of Bennen's Impressions. Most everyone was: there was a deep suspicion among the Clans when it came to the Everien Knowledge speaking through the mouths of their own children. Even now, mere mention of the Knowledge made Kassien uncomfortable.

Things had begun to go badly for Bennen after Kassien was placed under Taro and went to Wolf Country to fight the H'ah'vah in the tunnels under the northwest cliffs of Everien. While he was away, Bennen was assigned to the less dangerous Deer territory, where the typical Sekk, instead of calling monsters to serve it, tended to pass itself off as human and attempt to Enslave a villager who would then turn on others in unseeing rage. If the Sekk got a warrior, a whole village might be wiped out when that man went berserk.

Istar had been with Bennen when he engaged with just such a Sekk in Deer Country, but it had escaped before it could be killed. Recalled to Jai Khalar for placement in one of Ajiko's new armies, the group had been subjected to immediate inspection by Ajiko. She would never forget it. Bennen fell into a trance in the training ground and began inscribing symbols and diagrams in the sand. Ajiko claimed he must be Enslaved, and Pierse took Bennen's sword away and cut him down with it on the spot. Afterward they said that the Sekk Bennen had encountered in Deer Country must have put a Slaving spell on him. There was no arguing with such a claim, for paranoia about the Sekk had reached new heights in the past five years or so. Anyway, what was done was done: Bennen was dead.

Kassien never spoke about his brother. As far as Istar knew, he had always been the perfect soldier. He never stepped out of line, and on the field he displayed daring and excellence, fighting with a cold intensity held barely in check. But Istar suspected he was only biding his time, waiting for an opportunity to bring down Ajiko and Pierse. Recently, when Istar made the rounds of the young officers, seeking support for an expedition crossing the Floating Lands, most of them had shrugged her off. But Kassien had listened to her ideas and to her surprise agreed to sign on. He had not interfered with her leadership in organizing the group or gathering information, and he had even let her speak before Lerien. And until now he had shown a level disposition, for all that he seemed to hate and love the army in equal measures. She was not prepared for the way he reacted to the mere sound of Pierse's voice: he was shaking with rage.

"This is not the time or the place, Kassien," Istar said in his ear, and dragged him away from the doorway. "Where's Xiriel? Let's get out of the Citadel before you do something you regret."

He shook himself a little and let her draw him away. Then he seemed to pull himself together, and he led her to a round room containing a sculpture of a running horse.

"Xiriel's waiting for us, but we have to get through that statue," he said. He shuddered. "Nothing here is ever simple, is it? Why can't it just be a fucking door?"

"Shh. Let's go."

Kassien hesitated.

"Wait, Star. Think what we're doing. Is it really worth it to have Pallo with us? He's probably safer here in prison, even if he has done nothing wrong."

"I told him he could come, and I intend to keep my word. No one has ever given Pallo a chance."

"Istar." His serious tone made her look at him, and she felt herself weakening under his gaze. She knew he was thinking that she was letting her sympathy for Pallo color her judgment. That Pallo could easily be killed.

She argued automatically. "Any of us could die on this mission. It's his choice. If he wants to come, we can't afford to turn him away. We're dissidents; we're not going to get ten swords from Lerien, and we have no future with Ajiko. Do we?"

Now it was Kassien's turn to look away. "No," he answered grimly. "There's no question in my mind about that. I don't want to stay here. But Pallo could be a handicap for us. At least Xiriel knows how to use the axes. At least he has a head on his shoulders."

"I'll be responsible for Pallo," Istar said. "Come on, let's argue about this somewhere else. I thought you said there wasn't much time."

"There isn't." Kassien went up to the statue and studied its eerie shape in the moonlight. "Xiriel got me through here, but I don't know how to get back. Jai Khalar is starting to make me sick, I swear it."

"I remember this statue," Istar said. "It goes to a staircase. You have to mount the horse to get inside it."

Kassien put out a cautious hand as if afraid to touch the statue. Then he let out a sigh and remarked over his shoulder, "All right, we'll take Pallo. It would be cruel to leave him in a place like this."

He took a deep breath, scrambled up the side of the stone horse, and was gone.

WINGS

In defiance of anybody's idea of what a castle was or how it should behave, Jai Khalar was rearranging itself around itself. The hourglasses quickened in some rooms and slowed in others, to the chagrin of the clerks. Corridors became shafts and windows became rooms; children learned mathematical tricks in their sleep. Things went missing.

Jai Khalar was preparing to disgorge its king into the world. In one night emergency plans were drafted, supplies were organized, objectives altered. Messages sped all over Everien through the Eyes, and were returned. A general flapping and frenzy animated the Citadel from root to crown. Tarquin knew nothing of this; he had gone to sleep after he left Istar, flat on his back on a small section of roof where he'd found himself when he finally grew too tired to move another inch. The stars were hidden by cloud, and at some point he was drizzled on, for he woke shivering and damp to the sound of Hanji's voice.

"Pancakes, they say, but the flour shipments are delayed and Ajiko's Pharician horses eat twice as many oats as our little mountain ponies. Tarquin, I said wake up. Where I'm going to put these refugees I can't begin to guess. We have plenty of space if only I could *find* some of it."

"What time is it?" said Tarquin.

"The king's party is almost ready to go. Your horse will be saddled by now. Come, get up."

"It's a terrible idea," Tarquin said, rising stiffly and feeling sorry for himself at the prospect of spending another day in the saddle. He was feeling his age this morning. He crawled through the window into a small, anonymous room where Hanji was waiting to bustle him on his way.

"You should have come back a long time ago," Hanji remonstrated. "There have been lots of terrible ideas going around this place, but what would you know? You've been off being Free and all that."

"You make it sound like a holiday," Tarquin said. "Do I look like I have been enjoying myself for eighteen years?"

Hanji sighed. "No, you look like a mean old dog."

Tarquin followed the senseschal through ever-shifting rooms. Unperturbed by moving floors, disappearing windows, and changing levels, Hanji nevertheless occasionally paused to adjust a picture frame or move a table a few inches to one side. He stopped before a small gray door left slightly ajar. It looked as though it led to a closet. Hanji planted his hands on his hips.

"Who's left this open?" he muttered. "Don't they know this door leads right out of Jai Khalar? If someone could sneak out, then someone could sneak *in*."

Tarquin yawned. Hanji sighed and rubbed his forehead. "I suppose you'll be wanting breakfast. That way is the gate; I will bring you some food to eat in the saddle."

He had turned toward the small gray door Hanji indicated when the old man suddenly remarked, "Aye, it was a morning just like this when you came back from Jai Pendu with the bad news, wasn't it?"

Tarquin turned and gawped at Hanji, who had achieved new heights of insensitivity, he thought. Hanji continued dreamily, "I'll never forget how the White Road came. I was in the middle of disciplining that little pip of a chimney sweep Fausen when the whole wall above the crèche gave way. There were children running about and women screaming. It was like an avalanche, all white and roaring. . . ." He spread his hands, evoking the explosion. "And the White Road opened. We heard hoofbeats coming through a storm of light and sound. And then there you were: on foot, bleeding, pale as ash. Ah, you looked terrible, you did. Fausen escaped in the confusion, damn him. Come to think of it, I never saw him after that. Maybe something on the White Road ate him."

"Is there a point to this story?"

"I was just thinking aloud, that's all. Thinking that the White Road never showed itself after you returned, but now that you're back, maybe it will open again."

"No! Don't say such things. Jai Pendu must not be disturbed. I left . . . *things* . . . behind there that you would not wish to meet."

"Things, what *things*? Your silence on this matter grows tiresome, Tarquin."

"It is not my purpose to entertain you. Go back to your kitchens and supervise something!"

Hanji sniffed. "If you're going to be so obstinate, I will. Go on, you're late already." He pushed Tarquin through the door and locked it behind him.

Tarquin was inside a storage cupboard. There was a door at the far end. He opened it and stepped into a small white alley. A tabby cat was trapped there, mewling pathetically. It was surrounded by a dozen dead mice, some half-eaten.

"How long have you been stuck in here?" Tarquin asked it, and was treated to a long, complaining howl. He opened the door at the far end of the alley and the cat shot through as though chased by fire. "I know how you feel," he called after it. "I hate this place, too."

He followed the cat to the gates of the Citadel by a tortuous route that led through storage rooms and over bridges, emerging at last into the entrance cave without quite knowing how he could have descended so far. The cat shot away into the dark recesses of the cave and he found himself caught up in a bustle of activity and drawn outside. There seemed to be an inordinate number of anxious clerks and grooms about, but the warriors Ajiko had chosen for Lerien numbered only six. They stood still and almost silent to one side. When Tarquin approached they glanced at him and then made themselves busy with their gear after the manner of people who don't wish to be caught staring. One stepped forward to greet him, a Wolf Clan captain with gray hair and sagging jowls.

"You don't remember me," he stated. Tarquin looked at the man more closely as he gripped his proffered hand. The face had seen some years, but he recognized the broad-shouldered body and the stiff-jointed way of moving that disguised the speed of the man's footwork.

"*Stavel?*"

The Wolf laughed. "Bet you didn't think I'd live this long," he said. "I got lucky. More than once. You always said my stubbornness would get me killed."

"You still refuse to wear the sword," Tarquin observed, indicating the twin axes in his belt, the traditional Wolf weapons. He remembered Stavel as an arrogant young Wolf fighter who had refused to even train with the sword on the grounds that he would betray his family honor. His attitude made him unpopular with Ysse, who insisted on unity among the Clans despite their long history of war. The Wolves had come from the forests to the southwest of Everien and had access to metals for their axes through trade with the Pharician Empire in the far south, so they were powerful by comparison with the Bear Clan, who had always been impoverished mountain nomads obliged to fight bare-handed.

When the Wolves, lured by the Knowledge of the vanished Everiens, began to encroach on the Everien highlands, they had immediately tyrannized the Bear Clan who occupied the same territory in the northwest. Oppressed by the axes of the invaders, the Bears by needs developed a sophisticated and crafty weaponless martial style; yet when Ysse came along offering swords to any who would learn to use them, they were quick to capitalize. The Bears had been the first to cooperate in the unification of Everien under Ysse, much to the displeasure of the Wolves, who now found their axes outmatched by the superior Seahawk weapon. Tarquin smiled, recalling some of the grudge matches between Bear and Wolf that had taken place in his training ground, for though obliged to join against the Sekk and fight as comrades, the two families had never completely let go of the old hate.

The proud Wolves retained as much of their autonomy as they could get away with, but Stavel had been the only one to decline to handle the sword, even in training. "The axes are my Clan legacy," he had once said to Quintar. "I will not betray them for another weapon. All my skill goes into these." At the time, Quintar had been monumentally annoyed. Yet now it was good to see that not all of the old animal spirit had been quashed by the formalism of Lerien's rule.

"This is Taro," said the Wolf, indicating a stocky young archer with black hair and dark skin. "And Kivi the Seer, Miro, Jakse, and Ketar."

The others nodded greetings, and Tarquin's attention focused on Ketar, who was big and blond, leonine in appearance. He looked uncomfortable, probably because he didn't know whether to address Tarquin as kin or not.

"How is Mintar?" Tarquin asked him, trying to be friendly.

"She died last year," Ketar said. "Peacefully, in her sleep—but it hit Santar and Jietar hard. They went off to join Ajiko's army with darkness in their hearts."

Tarquin didn't say anything. He had often thought of his mother but had never gone to see her after the destruction at Jai Pendu. Now she was dead. He adjusted his sword belt. What a morning.

"Where the hell's Ajiko?" he asked suddenly, casting about himself. "And where's the king? Are we going or not?"

A young groom put reins in his hands, and he looked up at a tall black horse decked out in battle gear. "So many Pharician horses," he muttered. "I hardly feel I am in Everien. I hope it's not a prophecy of what's to come."

Finally Lerien emerged from the cave into daylight, accompanied by Mhani. When the king mounted she stood at his stirrup, listening to his final instructions. Her hand reached up to touch his knee, and Tarquin's eyes froze on the gesture and the intimacy it implied. Lerien's face was turned away, and Mhani turned and left after a moment, but the exchange left Tarquin wondering what was going on between them. Mhani was soon lost among the advisers, who scurried from horse to horse, their colored robes fluttering in the dawn breeze, their voices sounding high and childlike above the noise of the stream flowing from the entrance cavern. Tarquin realized he didn't know Mhani anymore. Maybe he didn't know any of them.

The air was heavy with the smell of cattle and dew. There was a fell light in the southeast where the sun would be when it had cleared the peaks, but the rest of the sky was robed with muddy gray clouds running under a high wind. It was the kind of day that reflected back to Tarquin his own inner sense of desolation and gave him a perverse satisfaction by doing so. He pulled the stirrups down and prepared to mount.

Hanji appeared out of the knot of people and hobbled exaggeratedly toward Tarquin. "We old men must stick together," he said in a quavering voice, as if reading Tarquin's mind. "See you don't strain yourself."

Tarquin got into the saddle with an effort. He gathered the reins and frowned down on Hanji, who thrust a cloth-wrapped packet at him. "What is Lerien thinking of?" Tarquin demanded, opening the cloth with his teeth. He frowned at the mixture of hard-boiled egg and rice. "Riding off and leaving his castle to a bunch of clerks, and Ajiko! The Pharicians will seek to attack here first."

"And what would you have him do?" Hanji countered. "All his troops are hidden somewhere in Wolf Country and must be gathered. The Eyes cannot save his people, and you've said yourself that Jai Pendu is unreasonably perilous. He must go and see this army with his own eyes."

"What good will that do? If he believes my account he should take whatever fighters he's got and ride immediately to intercept the Pharicians before they reach the sea gates, while sending messengers to bring the rest of his forces. And he should order his people to flee to the hills until it is all over. If he doesn't believe me, then he should—"

"What?" Hanji whispered. "Kick you out of Jai Khalar and risk you riding around the countryside telling everyone what you saw? If Tarquin the Free were to ride into any town or farm in this valley, he would be listened to, and believed. And then who would rule Everien?"

The party had begun to move. Tarquin had taken a bite of his breakfast and now had to swallow in a hurry.

"But I don't want to be—"

"I know." Hanji raised his staff in farewell.

"—king," Tarquin murmured to himself.

• • •

THERE WAS A confusion of hooves as the riders picked up speed, and the party moved off at a good clip for the first few miles: a dramatic exit for Lerien, Tarquin thought. The king soon slowed the pace and Tarquin found himself riding alongside Kivi the Seer, who was casting curious glances in his direction.

"What?" grunted Tarquin. "Speak."

Kivi was small-boned and brown-skinned, and he had a nervous air about him like all his family; the Deer Clan were too damn sensitive for their own good, Tarquin had always thought. Kivi said, "You don't look like I expected."

"What did you expect?"

"I don't know. But you don't look like it."

"Are you supposed to be a Scholar?" Tarquin scoffed. "If that's the extent of your analysis, you can't be too bright."

"I can't put my finger on it," Kivi continued, unperturbed by the insult. "It's something in the air about you. I can't decide whether or not I like it."

Tarquin gave an uneasy laugh but Kivi didn't seem to notice for he kept talking. "I'm glad to see you all the same. I was to have gone with Lerien to Jai Pendu, and I was afraid. A part of me is relieved that we cannot find the White Road."

"You should not even be looking for it."

"But we need another Artifact! The Knowledge is the only way we can possibly fight the Sekk, and anyway how else are we to obtain trade goods from Pharice if not by the arts that depend on the Knowledge? It is our wealth."

Tarquin yawned. The sun was getting hot already; at this time of year it seemed always to be in the sky. Sleep had become a myth.

"But it's madness," he said at last, rousing himself. "The Everiens couldn't withstand the Sekk—they fled, didn't they? What makes you think that their Knowledge will let you do what they could not?"

"We cannot be certain why the Everiens fled," Kivi said timidly.

"It seems obvious to me," Tarquin argued. "The more powerful that Everien Knowledge became, the more it attracted the Sekk, like insects to sugar. Is it not true that after each Glass we recovered from Jai Pendu, instead of defeating the Sekk we found ourselves harder pressed than ever? They crave the Knowledge, I tell you. Why else are there no Sekk in the Wild Lands, or Pharice, or the islands? They are drawn to Everien."

"Maybe," Kivi said. "There is a logic to what you say. But when we look back in time, we do not see Sekk in Everien."

"What is this about looking back in time? Does Mhani now gaze on visions of ancient Everien? How can you trust visions that you cannot verify?"

"We have gained much Knowledge by looking back," Kivi said defensively. "If there were not so much prejudice against them, we might even use the Impressionists."

"You must live in the here and now, Kivi," Tarquin scolded. He gestured to the landscape. They were riding across flat country filled with ripening wheat; Everien wind towers whirred almost inaudibly to either side of the road. "Look how rich this land is! And the ease of lifestyle that the wind towers can give you. That's what you should use the Everien remains for, not visions of a time long gone by."

"The wind towers are one of the great boons of Everien, but we don't have enough people to bring in the harvest," Kivi said. "There will be famine this winter if we do not get our soldiers back soon."

"Ah, the Knowledge," Tarquin groaned. "It's a cruel trick. It always promises a better life, but matters only ever get worse."

Kivi didn't answer. Tarquin knew he must be thinking that it was tedious to talk to such a cynical old man.

"I'm going to go spread gloom over Lerien," Tarquin said, and urged his horse forward. When he glanced back at the Seer to gauge the effects of his words, he saw to his surprise that Kivi was smiling.

Riding at the head of the group, Lerien appeared to be enjoying himself, as if unused to fresh air and physical activity. Tarquin brought his horse alongside and remarked, "Ajiko has changed."

"He finds it hard to balance the Knowledge with the Clan ways," replied Lerien carefully.

"What's that got to do with the simple need to maintain a strong corps of warriors?"

Lerien snorted. "And what would you have him use for talent? You saw Istar. Shall I make an army of girls?"

"I'd take her at my side before Ajiko. At least her mind is clear."

"Her mind is clear because she is young," Lerien retorted. "When Ysse lay on her deathbed and gave me the kingship, mine was equally clear. Yet I was saddled with a people dependent on the Knowledge. I don't claim to understand it. Do you think me at home in Jai Khalar? I would rather go back to my Clan, take up some handicraft, and quarrel with my neighbors, like in the old days you always used to talk about."

Tarquin brushed wind-tears from his eyes. Lerien was too young to remember those times. He realized with a sudden pang that he wanted to be talking now to Ysse, but he would never see her again. He said, "There are lands to the east, between the mountains and the sea. My Clan settled there when they first were driven from the islands by the Wasps. You might retreat to that region. It is harsh country, but the Sekk have never come there."

The king was studying him keenly. "And neither will I, if it means the Pharicians and the Sekk cut up the cake of Everien between them. We cannot go back to Clan times, Tarquin. And you can't be Free. Not anymore. If you are going to be in Everien, you must support me in this."

Lerien reined in his horse to a walk, and as Tarquin did the same, he noticed that they had pulled ahead of the other riders by some hundred yards or more. He realized Lerien was waiting for an answer, and remembered Hanji's final words. "I have no desire to lead anyone," he told the king. "If my legs would carry me better, I wouldn't even take charge over this horse."

He dropped the reins to illustrate his point, but the Pharician stallion was too thoroughly trained to misbehave. He kept on beside his neighbor at the same pace, and Lerien began to laugh. From behind them, Taro gave a hoarse shout of alarm.

Tarquin turned in the saddle to see Taro pointing at a huge shadowy thing hurtling out of the sky. There was no time to take in more than a flash of great scintillating wings. Then the horse swerved and bolted, the bit in his teeth.

A Sheep's Bladder in a Kicking Game

The panicking horses scattered the party as the gigantic avian pulled out of its dive and glided overhead, darkening the ground. Fast on its tail, others appeared in the sky, growing rapidly larger as they dropped from a great height. Each was as large as a Pharician family's traveling tent, and as insubstantial; wings made of translucent webbing that stretched over delicate fingers of cartilage supported limbless snake bodies with diamond-shaped heads. A whirring sound accompanied them, and a dazzle of sunlight reflected off their bodies.

"What are they?" Miro shouted in dismay, craning his head back while he reached for an arrow. Instead of fighting his running mount for the bit, Tarquin ripped off his cloak and leaned low over his horse's neck, slinging the fabric across the animal's eyes. The horse slowed and then halted in confusion and turned in a circle.

"Don't fight them!" Tarquin exhorted. "They aren't attacking, they're just curious."

"Curious?" screamed Ketar, roughly curbing his rearing horse with one hand and drawing his sword. "I take no chances with curious!"

"Stop! Sailsnakes are ferocious when aroused. Cover the horses and try to soothe them." Tarquin had managed to fix the wrapped cloak such that it acted to block his mount's view above him and to the rear, and the horse calmed. The sailsnakes swooped and turned almost on their tails, passing overhead with a rush of noise and color.

Lerien had quickly adopted Tarquin's strategy, and his horse also steadied. Kivi had been dumped on the ground and Taro was struggling to nock an arrow even while his horse was bolting; he would already be out of bowshot of the sailsnakes, Tarquin realized gratefully.

"Do not shoot!" Lerien shouted, ducking in the saddle as one swept over just a few feet above his head. "Try to ignore them."

Stavel and Ketar looked incredulous but obeyed. The sailsnakes whipped through the air, their heads darting from side to side, their tongues flickering and their gleaming black eyes roving to examine the party. The horses were still nervous, but once their eyes were covered they could be controlled. Kivi's was half a mile away and still running.

"What is a sailsnake doing so far inland?" Lerien said to Tarquin while overhead the creatures turned their wings inside-out and rose in acrobatic spirals, light and free as ash released from a flame. Tarquin shrugged and clamped his legs hard against his mount's ribs, for Jakse's horse was still acting up and its fear was contagious. Ketar reached out and caught hold of the horse's bridle while Jakse clung like a burr to its back as it bucked.

Then, as quickly as they had come, the sailsnakes rose and fled on the wind. Taro set off after Kivi's horse, and the others reassembled.

"What *were* those things?" Jakse asked, obviously shaken.

"They normally live on the sea," Lerien replied, shading his eyes and looking after the disappearing sailsnakes. "They are equally at home underwater or in the air, but they don't eat large prey or they'd be too weighed down."

"I've never even heard of them," Stavel said.

"There are records referring to them in Jai Khalar. I have never actually seen one, either. I would not have identified them if it were not for Tarquin."

Tarquin said, "I've seen them before, in the outer islands. They appear offshore at sunset, if at all. It's very strange that they should be here, now."

"Ride on," Lerien said. "We have a long journey ahead of us, and no time to spare."

They rode gently during the heat of the day, Kivi and the king side by side, talking. The road passed through a forest that had reclaimed the once-cultivated fields of Deer Country. At odd intervals, Everien towers punctuated the landscape, rising over the tallest trees like paintbrushes turned on end. Tarquin observed that they no longer held sentries as they would have done in Ysse's time.

"We have placed monitor Eyes in some of these watchtowers," Lerien said. "Let's stop here and check this one."

They rode to the base of the tower, and Lerien ascended with Kivi while the others rested and ate. Sunlight filtered through the leaves of the trees and the naked scaffolding of the metal tower.

"Why doesn't Kivi just use his Carry Eye?" Taro asked. "That's what it's for, isn't it?"

Stavel shrugged. "Perhaps, after what's been happening in Wolf Country, the king doesn't want to take any chances. And Mhani should have some news from Wolf Country today. I hope."

"Mhani won't find anything," Ketar said, overhearing. "She's probably not even looking. She doesn't care about the army, only about the White Road."

Tarquin chewed his lunch without comment. Stavel settled in the curve of a tree's roots and closed his eyes. "I wouldn't say that in the king's earshot," he said mildly.

"I wonder if the Pharicians are really planning to annex us," Taro said. "I always wanted to go to their land. They say the sky changes color over Pharice. At night their cities turn the sky red and gray and wipe out the stars. In the day a yellow light lies in the west, over the Khynahi Mountains. They say in the far south the sky is gold all the time, for it reflects the sands which are greater than any ocean."

Tarquin chuckled at this romantic description. Miro glanced at him expectantly. "You have been there, Tarquin. Tell us."

Tarquin frowned, considering. "They are a strange people, the Pharicians. They have given over their roaming rights and their land to the emperor, and in exchange they have got roads and all manner of fine goods acquired in trade or by craft. And they have got order. Things happen on the day they are supposed to happen, and men place themselves in order with each other, and records are kept of everything that occurs, even the smallest transaction. At first I was fascinated but after a while I saw that the whole thing is a trap. None of them had freedom and their voices all sounded the same. No man had his own speech. They just passed the words back and forth like a sheep's bladder in a kicking game."

"Give me a good Clan fire and some dancing girls any day," said Ketar. Out of the corner of his eye Tarquin saw him flexing his biceps. Ketar was a golden boy if he'd ever seen one: he'd probably never had a day of bad luck in his life. Tarquin didn't think much of the training that had brought about this attitude, for Ketar was the type to wilt at the first sign of adversity, having never experienced failure. He was spoiled. Tarquin resisted the urge to unspoil him and went on with his narrative. "In Pharice they are seldom cold and never hungry, and they are all bound to each other visibly and invisibly. It is a wonder anybody can move at all. They have a rule for everything and so no matter what you do you are either breaking a rule or obeying it, but you can never live to one side of the rules. They are always there and men judge you by your adherence to them, even if you only obey or violate a rule by accident."

"The Clans have rules as well," Taro put in. "You could say much the same thing about many of our laws."

"Yet the Clans also have the provision of freedom, do they not? So I have declared myself exempt from Clan law, and it does not apply to me."

"True," the archer acknowledged. "Go on, then. Say, do they have the Knowledge in Pharice, also? I have heard their Scholars know things that ours do not."

"They have no Artifacts that I have ever heard of," Tarquin said. "They have learning of a kind: how to build machinery, how to calculate numbers of things, how to measure. Their architecture is simple by comparison to Everien buildings, but though I say that, the Clans could not duplicate Pharician buildings. We do not have the art of it; nor would our people bend their backs together the way the Pharicians do. They have complicated codes of behavior that I never could remember. They line up in rows and act on command. You see this in their armies, too. Each man fights by rote; none has the space for his own style. They deny their fear and comply with their commander. This I will never understand. Whenever I have ever fought, I have used my fear to build defiance for the enemy—or anyone who stood in my way. If I had to fight like a Pharician . . . I could not do it. That's why Ajiko's maps and charts disturb me so. They remind me of Pharice, and I would not see the Clans emulate the Pharicians. A hawk does not seek to emulate a pigeon."

While he was talking, Lerien and Kivi had descended. Lerien announced, "There is smoke in the hills half a day's ride away, and the troop that is supposed to be responsible for this section isn't in position."

"What does Mhani say of Wolf Country?" asked Stavel, and was ignored.

"We don't have time to investigate the incident," Lerien said brusquely. "But keep your eyes open as we ride. We will make straight for the monitor tower above A-vel-Jasse. Let's go."

They hurriedly packed up and set off at a trot on the pitted road. Tarquin noticed that Kivi held his Carry Eye in one hand as he rode, glancing at it from time to time.

"Should you risk dropping it from the saddle?" he asked the Seer.

Kivi put the Eye away with a furtive air. He said, "It's acting up a bit, and I was checking it, that's all."

"Ah," said Tarquin. "This is why Lerien stopped at the monitor tower, yes?"

"Yes," Kivi admitted. He drew his horse closer to Tarquin's and glanced around to see that they couldn't be overheard. "But I could not See Mhani from there, either. Don't tell the others! Lerien is worried."

"Why don't the Eyes work?" Tarquin said. "Is this usual?"

"No, but it's not—"

"Yet he persists in riding to the border when he could take my word that the Pharicians are marching on him."

Kivi said, "Tarquin, lower your voice. There is nothing wrong with the Carry Eye, or the monitor tower we just left. It's that Mhani is engaged in work and not responding to us, which is very surprising given that she knows this Eye is being used by the king." He started to say more, but Lerien and Ketar had slowed, ahead of them. Kivi clammed up.

"Hmm," said Tarquin. "Well, your use of these Eyes is a mystery to me. If you told me that the Knowledge only worked when the wind blew a certain way, I would have no way of knowing whether you spoke the truth."

"But the Eyes are simple," Kivi said. "It's where they come from that is hard to understand. We are taught that the Knowledge is just a few principles from Outside the world, bent and shaped into many different forms; but that if you were truly Outside—if you could be Outside which no one can be, not even great Scholars—but if you could, then everything would be of the stuff of the Knowledge and all that we see and know and do would be nothing more than a bit of dirt smudging the Glass of that world."

"Do you really believe that?" Ketar said, turning in the saddle and looking irritated.

"It's the basis of my studies."

"Do you believe it, my lord?"

Lerien shook his blond head. "I don't know. No one can go Outside and return, so it seems pointless to me to speculate."

"No one can go Outside and return," Kivi repeated under his breath. He was scrutinizing Tarquin, who scowled and reached down to tighten his horse's girth, even though it had not begun to slip.

"What are you looking at?"

"Nothing," said Kivi.

IMPRESSIONS

Mhani came to a halt in a swirl of red robes, her hand flying to her throat as she inhaled with a sudden, strangled scream. Two inches beyond her toes the floor simply disappeared. She stood there in shock while below bats spiraled against a background of dim stars. Shaking all over, she backed away from the edge. She had been sprinting along the passage, eager to get back to the Eye Tower, when the floor in front of her had suddenly dissolved.

"Hanji," she whispered, fear giving way to anger. "This has got to stop."

She crept along the passage wall, seeking something to hang on to even though she knew perfectly well that if the Citadel wanted to trap her inside its very walls, it probably could. It was a miracle, she thought, that there hadn't been a tragedy already, given the way this castle was behaving. She made her way back to the gate, where Ceralse the guard was so preoccupied in looking over the parapet at the departure of Lerien and his riders that he didn't notice the way Ires the leopard was hunched at the end of his silver tether, lashing his tail and making high-pitched squeaking noises. Around him, just outside the circumference of the rope, were gathered about a dozen mice. If Mhani hadn't known better she might have believed they were taunting the big cat.

"Mice!" Mhani cried, and kicked at them to disperse the creatures. Ires strained at his rope, gazing at her appealingly. "Why are we inundated with mice lately?"

Ceralse turned and saluted her.

"Where is old Hanji? The first avenue isn't safe."

"He's gone to the stables. I think he's trying to fix—"

. She didn't stay long enough to listen to Ceralse's explanation. She descended to the undercaves again and made her way to the outermost chambers, the ones that bordered the fields below Jai Khalar on the far side of the stream. The crowd around the entrance cave had cleared; the riders were gone. She swallowed against the lump in her throat and entered the dim stables, wrinkling her nose. She could hear Hanji's voice.

"*Please* return the kitchens to the lower annex," he implored. Mhani hurried toward his voice, past girls at work grooming the animals in their stalls, noticing with annoyance that there were too many mice here as well. In one of the largest boxes she found Hanji, blue robes fastidiously held a few inches off the dirty cobbles, addressing a blood-bay mare. The horse stood without an inch of tack on her sleek body, eyes focused somewhere over Hanji's head in apparent boredom.

"It's only yourself you're harming," he said to the mare. "How are you to get your grass or your exercise if you persist on displacing the First Level? I'll have you confined to your stall. And don't even *think* about displacing yourself."

The horse sighed gustily and shifted her weight. Her eyelids lowered.

"What's going on?" Mhani said, and Hanji started at the sound of her voice.

"It's this damn horse. She has some of Ice's blood in her, don't you, you wicked thing? She has the Animal Magic and she senses Jai Pendu approaching at the other end of the White Road—and you don't like it much, do you, my love?"

Mhani put her hands on her hips and shook her head skeptically. "How can you possibly blame the horse for rooms gone missing?"

"It's a good sign," he said. "For there are horses on the White Road such as you cannot find anywhere in this world. Perhaps they're calling her. Perhaps the White Road is not so far away after all."

"Horses on the White Road? How do you know that?"

"My grandfather taught me. Anyway, you can hear the hoofbeats." Hanji stroked the animal's shoulder and made cooing noises. "You're going to have to go if this doesn't stop," he murmured. "We'll turn you out. Rokko, where are you?"

"Coming!"

A boy of about ten came feeling his way along the outside of the stalls, head tilted up at an odd angle. Mhani stared for a moment before she realized the boy was blind.

"Rokko, take care of this princess of darkness, will you?"

The blind boy greeted the mare nose to nose and then wriggled onto her back. "I'll take her out to pasture," he said confidently. "She's a very nice horse. She can't help it if she has demon blood."

"There are no such thing as demons in Everien," Mhani said to Hanji in a tone of reprimand.

"The horse comes from Pharice," Hanji answered.

"*Ah . . .*"

The mare responded perfectly to the boy's aids and they left the stables. Hanji opened a stall door and ushered Mhani into a long corridor with no windows and a door at the far end.

"This is starting to get to me," she said. "There's a gaping pit in the middle of the First Avenue. Can't you do something?"

"I'm trying, but I'm only the seneschal, after all. . . ."

She looked at him sidelong. The passage they'd entered seemed endless. "Where are we? I have to get back to the Eye Tower."

"It's not far," Hanji said absently. "Mhani, you must be careful. Ajiko is in charge now."

"Only of the army, and that doesn't concern me. He can't very well invade the Eye Tower."

"If we do not find the White Road soon, we will lose our chance to reach Jai Pendu during this passage. That means another nine years at least before we have another Artifact. Do you think we can stand against Ajiko and his kind for that long? Do you think we can stand against Pharice? For whether or not they are attacking us now, sooner or later they will decide to include Everien in their empire."

"I have enough to do without worrying about politics," Mhani dismissed.

"You have no choice," Hanji said, scratching his head and patting himself down. "I thought I had a ledger with me when I came down here."

"My alliance is to the Knowledge itself," she said repressively. "All I do is dedicated to understanding it. It is not for me to concern myself with power games; not while Everien is in such peril. I could try to open the White Road, but as of now I cannot find it. Perhaps you should ask your horse to help you!"

"No, she is too capricious," Hanji muttered, the sarcasm lost on him. "Mhani, I don't think you're really trying."

"I *am* trying, but there are all these problems in Wolf Country, and Ajiko's looking over my shoulder all the time. Remember, my job is to watch the borders and manage communications. Now let me get back to the Eyes." She started to walk faster.

"The Eyes are made to be more than mere monitors," Hanji replied, worry making his words rapid and light. "That application is for those who walk on the shores of the Knowledge and comb the sands for whatever it casts up. I'm talking about the ones who swim for their lives. I'm talking about the Impressions."

She walked faster still but the corridor just kept getting longer and longer and she couldn't seem to reach the door at its end.

"I don't know what you mean. Only children can have Impressions, and they can't control them."

"I'm old, Mhani, not stupid."

She threw herself forward but the corridor continued to lengthen.

"Mhani, if we don't find the White Road, all you have worked for will fall into disfavor and be abandoned. Hear my words."

She had no choice but to hear his words; she couldn't get to the door. Furious, she turned, nearly in tears. "I hear you," she shrieked at his figure, now reduced in the distance. "You wretched old man, I hear you. Now let me go."

Two steps brought her abruptly to the door, which opened on the stairway to the Eye Tower. As she passed through she heard him call after her, "The White Road, Mhani. It can't be far. These damn mice are coming from somewhere!"

She picked up her skirts as another couple of mice hurried by and disappeared in a crack between risers. Near the top of the stairs there was a hidden door that led to a small chamber that Mhani had appropriated for her personal use, and she sought out its refuge now. She closed the secret door behind herself, jammed knuckles against her eyes to prevent herself from crying, and at last sank onto the couch. She sat there for half a minute or so before leaping up, pouring water into a basin, and splashing it over her face, slapping herself in the process.

She was already so full of *sita* she felt sick. She hadn't slept in days, trying to find Ajiko's cursed army. She ought to keep moving if she was to stay awake, but her joints ached. She pivoted slowly on one foot, taking in the small room, which she kept sparsely furnished just as she kept her mind free of clutter—so she had been taught. Now she felt cornered. She didn't want the damned Impressions. She wasn't some child freak, at the mercy of fits and seizures: she was a Scholar—a Seer, no less, and she was meant to be in command of herself. What Hanji was suggesting was repellent. She had spent all her life mastering herself even as she mastered the Eyes. To deliberately seek out the Impressions, and to use the Eyes to facilitate their possession of her . . . no, she couldn't do it. Hanji didn't understand.

When she was a child, the Impressions had come unbidden; her family had amassed a small fortune on the strength of her inventions before the

Clan elders had objected to the way she swooned and spoke in tongues and fashioned miniature aircraft out of paper and wire. "She's a spooky thing," they told her parents. "Send her to that Taretel the wizard." Her parents, unwilling to suffer the loss of income that Mhani's departure would cause, instead sent her to a local Scholar called Palavi, who showed her how to manage the flow of her mind just as the Everien farmers had managed their rivers. Palavi set her to doing research on ancient Everien, telling her the discipline would keep back the Impressions, which would cease to trouble her once she had passed puberty.

He had been proven correct, and Mhani had become engrossed in scholarship. It was not until the Water of Glass united the Eyes of Everien that Mhani's sensitivity to the Impressions had been roused from its slumber. Through her use of Tarquin's Artifact she had come to Know things she could not know. She had Seen the distant past, or so she believed. She had Seen it and also *felt* it, so that she was able to put an interpretation on the visions offered by the Eyes where other Seers could not. Her facility with the Eyes had been the making of Mhani, but in truth she did not have the technical skill even of young Xiriel. What she had was a kind of knack of drawing Impressions through the Eyes and into her body. She hadn't asked for it and she didn't want it—the ability represented a dangerous lack of control. She fought to repress the talent. Daily she groomed her mind for the use of the Eyes, for it had to be kept immaculate and free of foolish influences. A strong mind, a logical mind, was required to use the Eyes in tandem, for they were only as good as the human eyes that interpreted them.

That was why she told no one she had retained vestiges of Impressionism. She had worked too hard for her status as keeper of the Water of Glass and the Eyes to risk controversy over her mental soundness. Mhani might be soft of body and voice, and she might live high in the protective stronghold of the Citadel, but she was the ultimate defender of Everien.

This was what had her so worried. Ajiko's troops had dropped from her sight. Pharice, Tarquin claimed, was invading—but she had seen nothing but a woman on a horse. If Tarquin was right, then she had failed to detect the enemy. Uncertainty now gnawed her. Could she trust the Eyes? Could she trust herself? The very fabric of Jai Khalar was coming apart and reknitting, despite the best efforts of Hanji to keep track of all its parts; and now the seneschal himself seemed able to read her mind if he knew she could still do Impressions. He was advising her to use the talent, which would destroy the very mental composure that enabled her to wield the Eyes at all. Opening herself to the Impressions could very well be her downfall as a Seer.

How the hell did Hanji perceive these things, anyway? And if he knew so much, why didn't he do something?

Suddenly she stopped pacing. "Quit analyzing," she said to herself. "Just do what you know you're going to do in the end."

She opened the secret door and dragged herself up the last steps to the Eye Tower.

THE SEERS DEVRI and Soren were there. She dismissed Soren immediately and turned to Devri, whom she judged to be the more talented of the two. A contemporary of Xiriel's, he had practically been brought up in the Eye Tower and was conversant with the workings of all of the various monitor Eyes, major Eyes, and Carry Eyes throughout Everien. He had just started his watch period a few hours ago, but he did not seem surprised to see her here now.

"Any progress?" she asked, walking past him and glancing into the water. A collage of images colored its surface, and she took them in automatically, listening to Devri with a fraction of her attention.

"No White Road. And nothing new from Wolf Country. I've scanned all the villages that are still inhabited there, but it's quiet. There was one odd thing, though."

"Hmm?"

"It's that H'ah'vah tunnel on the heights in the southwest corner of Wolf Country. Have you noticed it?"

"No, I don't think so." She was checking the Eye that showed the plains of Ristale again, but the land was as empty as it had been yesterday. Tarquin had to be mad to have seen an army there.

"It's just that H'ah'vah don't usually descend into human-occupied territories, and yet this tunnel entrance is several weeks old, which means it was dug before all those villagers were evacuated by Ajiko's order. I wonder whether some of his men might have not got into trouble with the H'ah'vah, or if they even could be hiding in those tunnels. That would explain why we can't See them."

"Interesting," Mhani said. "Do me a favor, though. Don't mention your hypothesis to Ajiko until I've had a chance to look into it. H'ah'vah are quite dangerous, aren't they?"

"Yes," Devri said. "They kill people like we kill flies. That's why I was concerned. If the Sekk—"

"I take your point," Mhani said firmly, and ushered him out the door. "I'll take over from here."

"I'll be downstairs," he said as he went. "Call me if you need me."

She scrubbed her hands over her face. She looked around the Tower, swung her arms, paced. She thought of a thousand things she would rather be doing than this. Then she knelt by the pool and gazed at the Water of Glass.

"Show me the White Road. Please. Where is the White Road?" Mhani moved her lips without making a sound; composed her mind, preparing to enter the Liminal.

The White Road was a particular kind of ordering within the Liminal, which people pretended was a place so as to feel less baffled by it. She thought of it as the place between places, the intersection of planes in the mystical geomancy of Everien logic. It was where the rooms and windows went when they couldn't be found; it was the repository of the missing pieces; it was the lost time on the clocks that ran backward. It was an inferred reality, untouchable, unmeasurable. Like sleep, without location; like fire, without substance.

And yet she could go there. If she let the Impressions take her while she was using the Water of Glass, she could tread the high wire of paradox. All it took was nerve and concentration—and a subtle kind of surrender. For the Liminal felt like a hand gripping her, swinging and shaking her mind for its own purposes, just as a warrior swings a sword. The sword she had ordered forged for Chyko had been her way of expressing herself to him, for she knew how the sword felt. When she was in the Liminal, Mhani was the sword held by something unseen. Her mind, polished to a dazzle with daily practice, was a tool. It was a weapon. She did not know who or what was her user.

That was why she was afraid.

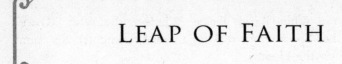

LEAP OF FAITH

"Xiriel, I swear you have bat's blood in you," Pallo whispered into the darkness as he groped nervously around a sharp curve in the passage. He caught his breath when his foot swung out over nothingness before finding purchase on a ledge to the right. He tightened his grip on the Seer's cloak and scrambled after him. "How do you know where you're going?"

"Practice," replied Xiriel, halting. Pallo walked into his back. "This part of the Citadel tolerates no light. We learn to navigate by memory, and by feeling the air currents. Stop breathing on me."

Pallo could be heard shifting his weight from foot to foot.

"We must be deep within the caves in the cliffside."

"No. We are a hundred feet above the gate to the First Level, suspended over the fields. I'm looking for one of the alternate exits. We don't want to get mixed up with the king's party."

Istar said, "Whatever you do, make sure you take us to the upper reaches of the cliffs. I don't want to set foot in the valley if I can help it."

She'd not slept that night and her metabolism ought to be at a low ebb, but she'd nevertheless broken out in a nervous sweat. Tarquin's words about Queen Ysse cutting her opponents to pieces had not entirely overcome Istar's natural caution. If she defied Lerien, she must do it with absolute swiftness and secrecy. Yet already they had spent two hours wending among the circuitry of Jai Khalar's inner workings. They had walked under arches of colored metal that sang out resonances when they passed; between the walls of shafts so deep their lines curved and converged into a distance filled with unknown light; through lattices of gems that stung their fingers when touched. The sound of rushing water followed them and went silent again. At whiles they could see the moon through some high window, but it was never the same moon twice. Now night was turning toward dawn; in summer, fewer than four hours of weak darkness blotted the sky above Everien, and three of these were now gone.

"Faster," she said.

"Could the Everiens not have drawn some maps?" Pallo asked plaintively. "I can't tell up from down anymore."

Kassien reached past Istar; she felt him shove Pallo.

"That way is down," he said. Istar almost tripped over the fallen archer.

"Kassien, will you behave?" she said. She hoped he didn't intend to prove to her that bringing Pallo was a mistake. Pallo had enough problems without having to cope with Kassien's sense of humor.

"Here we are," Xiriel announced, and opened a door, blasting the others with gray light and wind. "Now, if you'll come to the edge and look out, you'll see that we're standing on the very seam between the Citadel and the mountain. At the moment, this particular exit leads out into thin air. We're high up, just as you wanted, Istar. So, if you lot can make a good clean jump, we'll be on our way."

"Jump?"

Xiriel stood aside and the others saw the wind-sculpted cliff face that would be white in sunlight, but was now shadowed with rose and blue in the grainy light of morning. The only possible purchase was a long ledge a couple of yards below, which ran around the curve of the cliff and led, in a vague and not particularly convincing way, to a series of almost-invisible handholds probably carved by falling water. To hit the ledge would require a long jump of some twelve feet in addition to the drop itself. It could be done; but the fact that there were no more ledges between this one and the cliff base several hundred feet below did not bolster anybody's confidence. Pallo, in fact, had begun to chuckle nervously. He kept looking down, and laughing—and looking away, and looking down again, and laughing. . . . Finally, Kassien shoved him back into the passage and addressed Istar.

"We should throw our packs first," he said. "They'll only slow us down and upset our balance in the air."

She nodded and shrugged out of her pack. Standing on the edge of the doorway, she hefted it, bracing herself against the wind's buffeting. It would be impossible to grow up in Jai Khalar afraid of heights; still, she did not want to do this jump.

She threw the pack; they could all see the wind catch and drag it in the wrong direction. It bounced once on the outcropping and tumbled almost to the edge. Pallo started giggling again.

"All right," Istar said. "Everybody get out of the way."

"No." Kassien blocked her. "It's not going to be easy in this wind. I'll do it. If I can make it to the ledge and drive in a piton, I can throw you a rope. Then, if any of you miss the ledge, you'll be stopped."

"I said get out of the way."

Pallo sneered, "Who died and made you—"

"Fine," Kassien said coolly, standing back. "Let her do it. Go on, Istar."

Her insides froze; but she had gotten herself into this. She ground her teeth, balled her fists, and charged. She was still kicking when she reached the farthest point of her flight and began to drop, smashing face-first into the cliff and slithering down. Her feet hit the ledge so hard her knees went out from under her. She got up, exhilarated, only to be caught by the wind, which nearly threw her over the edge.

Clinging to the rock, she regained her footing and turned around more judiciously this time. She couldn't see the Citadel. There was only the valley below, as though she had fallen from the sky itself.

But she could hear Pallo cheering.

She got a piton from her pack, drove it in, tied a secure knot, and threw the rope back toward the Citadel. It took three tries before they caught it; then out of nothingness Kassien came sailing toward her, landing well-balanced on the balls of his feet, his knees flexing to take the jarring as if he had done this a thousand times. He untied the safety line from around his waist and grinned at her.

"You have blood on your face," he said.

THE ASSIMILATOR

After the others had slid down the rope and out of Jai Khalar, Istar let Kassien take the lead in picking a way across and up the cliff until they had reached a kind of diagonal shaft that permitted them to climb not only away from the roar of the wind, but also where the stones were rougher and provided more handholds. They were all bleary and faint with hunger by the time they reached more level ground near the top. The wind numbed their senses, and the march of clouds across the sky cast heavy shadows over the farmland. On the road below, they could see the king's horses moving away from Jai Khalar in a slow, straggling group.

But they turned the other way, up into the gentler slopes of the mountains, where the white stone yielded by degrees to moss and alpine flowers, and the arching flights of birds gave shape to the wind.

The mountains were to become their home for the first phase of their journey, and they spent days tramping through the bogs that lay on the heights. They had reached a plateau in the range and had to cross a large, relatively flat section before the extremities of the Everien Range confronted them with their snowy cliffs. In winter, these heights would be all snow and ice; but the summer sun awakened life, and stench, in the standing water that couldn't escape the furrows and clefts of the plateau. Their legs ached from the effort of walking through water, and their boots began to rot and fray. This was nobody's idea of high adventure. Tempers shortened.

It was the third day since leaving Jai Khalar. Kassien and Istar had been bickering most of the morning over frivolous things in a contest to determine who was the real leader. When they stopped to rest at midday, Xiriel told them both to be quiet.

"We're all nervous," he said. "But I for one don't need to listen to the two of you take it out on each other."

So Istar polished her sword to ease her mind. Pallo hovered nearby watching, mesmerized.

"Are you practicing your lunges?" she asked without looking up.

"What, now?"

"If not now, when? We walk all day."

"I know," he groaned. "I'm tired. How can I train my swordplay when I can barely move my legs? No—" He raised a hand to prevent her chastising him. "I'm going. I'm going to practice them right now."

Istar turned her gaze back to the blade. "It was to have been my father's sword," she said suddenly.

Pallo, sensing a possible reprieve, hesitated. She knew that his fascination with the Seahawk weapon was not lessened by the fact that he seemed to have no natural ability whatsoever. Any talk about swords and swordfighting automatically interested him.

"But Chyko was an archer," he said in surprise.

"Chyko," Istar said dramatically, and swung the sword whistling in a figure eight, "was anything he damn well pleased. Mhani had this sword made for him in the Fire Houses at A-vi-Khalar, and he would have been outstanding with it if he had had the chance to use it."

She traced the incisions on the blade: a swarm of wasps, gossamers, stingpicks, mantises.

"He was small and light." She snorted. "Unlike me. It was easy to underestimate him. But he put in three attacks where others made one at best, and he could come at you from angles you didn't even know existed. I wish I could have seen it." She paused while Pallo drew his own sword and began to get into the spirit of things, trying a lunge or two, awkwardly. "I think Mhani had this made so he would be inspired to challenge Quintar. She liked it not that Chyko was unranked and Quintar was Captain of the Guard. She liked it not one whit."

"But why was it so?" asked Pallo. "If Chyko could defeat Quintar, why was he not ranked higher?"

"Because he was a lawless man," Kassien put in from across the camp.

"And that's something my mother could never understand," Istar said. She gave the sword a final wipe. "It is easy to kill with one of these. I wonder how many my father killed, over a woman or an unwise word spoken while drinking."

"Ah, but how many did he save?" Kassien countered. "How many Sekk came to grief?"

"None with this sword," Istar said. "I have counted the deaths on it with my own hand. There were no others. I got it straight from its forging."

"Let's eat," Kassien said. "You are all too thoughtful today. We have a long walk ahead of us this evening, up *that*." He indicated a steep ravine winding into the heights, and then bent to take food from their bags. Pallo groaned and immediately sat down on a flat boulder, while Istar passed food from Kassien to Xiriel.

"We must be almost at the top of the range now," she said. "The hard part will be getting over that saddle. I don't like the look of it."

Istar turned to offer Pallo a handful of dried fruit, only to discover that he wore a face that she had never seen before. His eyes were crossed, and he had sucked in his cheeks with exaggerated horror.

"It's all right," she reassured him. "Your lunges aren't that bad."

But his expression remained oddly frozen.

"They're getting slightly better, actually," she added encouragingly. "Here, do you want some raisins?"

"I can't get up," he whispered. "I'm . . . stuck."

Kassien laughed. Xiriel looked up from his Carry Eye and frowned.

"Pallo, I think the altitude has gone to your brain," Istar scolded. "Come on, take the raisins."

"I'm not joking." Pallo seemed to be straining to pronounce the words. "My hands are stuck to the rock. I can't move."

Kassien walked over, grabbed Pallo's bicep, and gave a jerk to dislodge his arm. Pallo screamed and his hand stayed in place. Kassien exclaimed in surprise and was about to place his hand on Pallo's when Xiriel let out a yell.

"Don't touch him! Back off at once, Kassien. An Assimilator's got him."

"A which?" Kassien was still smiling as he turned.

"Pallo, don't try to move. See the stone by his hand, Kassien? See how shiny it is?"

"Ye-es, I suppose. What's happening? What's an assill . . . ?"

"Assimilator. It's a very nasty thing that lives in the mountains and eats things. We've got to find its mouth and try to choke it somehow."

Kassien and Istar looked at one another, sharing their bemusement. Istar forgot about being annoyed with him.

"I don't see anything, Xiriel. How can it have a mouth?"

"I really need to move now," Pallo announced. "I'm not happy about this. Help. Help."

"Shh. Stay still, Pallo, while we think this through."

"Think? *Think?* Get me out of here! Think some other time. Istar!"

"Kassien, did you see that?" Istar whispered. Where Pallo's right shoulder had been there appeared a flash of light, like sea foam, perhaps. Then it was a shoulder again.

"Uh-oh," said Xiriel. He turned and began casting about among the rocks.

Pallo's face wrenched itself as he tried and failed to speak.

"What does the mouth look like?" Istar called. "How will we know where it is? How big is this thing? Xiriel!"

"The mouth will be an area where there's a timeslip. So if I walk around and talk constantly without ever stopping or pausing I just continue to talk and I want you to listen for a break in my voice and notice where I'm standing when that happens okay do you follow me Istar are you listening anything yet all right I'll just go over here and maybe—"

"Stop!" Istar cried. She and Kassien exchanged glances. "Did you hear that?"

Kassien nodded. "Your voice dropped away for a second. Right *there*." He pointed with his sword.

"Now how do we choke it?" Istar asked.

Xiriel marked the place and moved away from it.

"They like complicated things. Animals, people, musical instruments, Artifacts, Eyes . . ."

"Your Carry Eye!"

Xiriel hesitated. Pallo's throat bulged as he screamed without opening his mouth. A swarm of bright lights appeared where his left leg had been.

"Surely Pallo is worth more than a piece of Everien glass."

"All my information is stored in it. Also, it's the only way we have to communicate with Mhani."

"I don't want to communicate with Mhani," Istar said immediately. "Let me think."

"There's no time to fucking think," Kassien snapped. He took two strides and seized the Carry Eye from Xiriel's hands before the Seer could react. He edged toward the spot they had marked as the mouth and held the Carry Eye out at arm's length, then dropped it.

Pallo shrieked and propelled himself up and away from the rock, landing in Istar's arms, unabashed at his own fear.

"Let's go!" he cried. "Let's go let's go let's go. Let's get out of here!"

No one argued. They scurried away, running among the rocks and bushes of the plateau until they came to a scree slope, which they slid down unceremoniously.

●   ●   ●

AT THE BOTTOM, Xiriel hung back slightly. The others waited for him, coughing in the dust they'd kicked up from the scree.

"Forget your damn Carry Eye," Kassien called back, obviously feeling guilty and making up for it by acting hostile. Xiriel met his eyes without emotion.

"It troubles me that we have encountered a creature from the Floating Lands so close to Jai Khalar. I did not expect this."

But the others didn't want to talk. All they wanted to do was scramble as quick as they could away from the danger zone. Xiriel picked up his pace and caught up with the rest of the group, but he was still preoccupied.

Xiriel knew they were afraid, and it was not that he was unafraid, in theory anyway; it was simply that he was puzzled. Sighing for the loss of the Carry Eye, he now ransacked his own memory in hope of recalling some of the symbols and memory-images that he had recorded there. It was an old habit of his, storing images for later reflection, and although the Carry Eye was a good tool, Xiriel's mind itself had been highly trained. The Seer's mind was never idle; even when he was silent and removed, he was looking over images that he remembered and trying to make sense of them. Some of the memory-images were very old, recorded automatically by the Eyes in Jai Khalar in the days before the Water of Glass had been activated. It was a great piece of luck that Xiriel had found among all these dormant images a vision of one of Ysse's conferences not long before the White Road came for Quintar and his Company. It was this memory that he now found himself studying even as he hastily departed the territory of the Assimilator.

The most accomplished of Everien's Scholars had gathered in one of the large halls of Jai Khalar to discuss a suitable route to Jai Pendu. The Scholars had been exotic creatures in those days, and no one had dared speak to them personally because they were so greatly revered. But Hanji had been there, also; Quintar and Chyko had come, bringing the restless air of warriors in their prime; and the Scholars themselves made the air electric with their intelligence, or so it seemed to Xiriel, looking on thanks to the Eye that was mounted high in the stonework. Yet none of the current crop of political leaders had been present, not even Lerien or Ajiko, and Mhani had stood in the background, shy, crow-haired, the only female in a room full of men.

And then there was Ysse. Tall and lean, shaven-headed and armor-clad, Ysse resembled neither man nor woman in bearing. The queen stalked the room, eyes steady and cool, presiding over all with an unconscious air of authority. Xiriel knew that she must have been ill by this time with the wasting sickness that had killed her, but in the vision shown by the Eye that recorded the event, she showed no sign of infirmity.

They spoke of many things Xiriel did not understand, but he had attentively taken notes when the Scholars drew maps in the air with their Knowledge, making the Fire of Glass flicker. But none of the maps were of Jai Pendu, and when Ysse perceived that the Scholars were trying to distract her from the fact that they didn't know the shape of Jai Pendu, her temper flared.

"This is a waste of time. How can we understand the configuration of the Floating Lands when we cannot see them from above? And Jai Pendu itself? It is impossible not to get lost in the strange pathways of that city, and yet if only we could see it laid out before us, we might come to trace a safe path. Why can you show me nothing? What good are you?"

"Maybe once it would have been possible," said Enzetar. "There are stories in my Clan of Seahawk Masters flying far out to sea and seeing many lands, although none of them spoke of seeing Jai Pendu on its course. At any rate, it could not be done now. The animal bonds are not strong enough anymore. In my lifetime there has only ever been one great Sky Master remaining, and that is Eteltar, who is now Taretel the Free. He would be old now, and no one has seen him in years. He had become so close to the birds that none could find him on the heights."

"He is dead, surely," Ysse said sharply.

"Probably."

"Ay, surely it must be so," Ysse said, nodding and turning to the window. Xiriel thought she looked tense and sad. "He was not a young man when he taught me sword. I was his last student. He was going to give up the ways of men altogether."

"His time had passed," Enzetar said. "He sensed that. He could not withstand the Knowledge."

Ysse bristled. "He was not interested in the Knowledge. That is all. Do not speak of one you do not understand."

"Did you understand him, my queen?" Enzetar said with a faint air of challenge.

"No. That is why I never speak of him." The hint of a smile flared the corner of her lip; then she turned her back on the room. There was a long, uncertain silence. Ysse turned around, making a sharp gesture toward her eyes. "I need to *See*. The Fire of Glass is tremendously powerful, but except for its use in the Fire Houses, it is undirected. You call yourselves Scholars but you cannot See. My memory serves me better than all your advice."

No one said anything. Ysse's anger could be felt like a wave in the air. Finally in a slip of a voice Mhani said, "There are globes of Glass here in Jai Khalar that sometimes reveal visions. But we have not been able to control them."

"That," said Ysse, pouncing on this revelation, "should be your objective. I have awakened the Knowledge for you. You must find a way to use it, or all my efforts are for nothing."

The Scholars looked uncomfortable. Ysse turned to Quintar and Chyko. "I must send you blind into Jai Pendu. For that I'm sorry. I can't prepare you for what you will find. I remember every moment of my time there; but it will be different for you."

THIS VISION HAD been so real to Xiriel that it seemed to him that the queen had spoken these words directly to him. Strangely, he was not afraid; not yet, anyway. For he had made maps of his own, compiled from the accounts of Impressionists and failed assailants on the Floating Lands and diagrams found in hidden parts of Jai Khalar, and from recovered documents from the tunnels beneath the Fire Houses at A-vi-Khalar, which had once been a great town. His maps were incomplete, but they were better than anything anybody had ever had. And Xiriel was not easily spooked. Unlike the others, he appreciated that the Knowledge was as much about mathematics and physical principles as it was about spirits, no matter how unnerving it might be when an Impressionist started spouting off in the Everien tongue. Xiriel was not afraid of math. He did not particularly think it was significant that he was not afraid of anything, that he did not even know what fear really was.

"No one has ever crossed the Floating Lands," Istar stated suddenly, breaking his concentration and recalling him to the present.

"This is true." He wondered whether she possessed the ability to read minds, that she now guessed what he had been thinking about.

"They all died or disappeared," she added after a minute.

"Not all," he corrected. "Some were able to return from the first few islands. Without their accounts we would not have any diagrams at all."

"True," she said. "But none ever went all the way to Jai Pendu that way. They all used the White Road. Even my father."

Xiriel didn't know how to respond to this. Istar's obsession with Chyko did her a mixture of harm and good, but he didn't know how to tell her to forget Chyko and concentrate on her own life. He found people confusing and difficult, and he had no idea how to talk to them about things like feelings. The Knowledge he could find words for, but the emotions that gripped others so powerfully and made them act against themselves and their own interests seemed to find no echo in him. He simply didn't understand.

"We are going the right way," Xiriel said at last. "The White Road is unpredictable. It should have appeared by now."

"But what will we find in the Floating Lands? More monsters? Trickery like that of Jai Khalar? How can you guide us through a place you have never been? Are there Eyes in the Floating Lands?"

"No, but there are codes. And there are things in the Liminal that help me to understand how the Knowledge perhaps functions in the Floating Lands."

"The Liminal is dangerous," Istar said, repeating what she'd always heard. "Even Mhani does not go there. Has she told you about it? She doesn't tell me anything, but I know it scares her."

"It is not frightening if you don't get emotional about it."

"You've been there? In the Liminal?"

"No, but I'm going to be."

"Stop talking riddles, Xiriel."

"Istar. Listen. I am not talking riddles. The Floating Lands were once one place, attached to Jai Pendu and attached to this world. They were shattered by the Liminal and now it penetrates their structure in myriad ways."

"But . . . what's the Liminal, then? I don't understand."

"Neither do I. That's why I want to see Jai Pendu for myself."

"Are there Everiens in Jai Pendu? Did they flee into the Liminal? And would they help us?"

"I don't know. But I've read all the accounts of the Floating Lands that the Scholars have ever recorded by those who tried to cross them. I don't know how accurate their memories were, but apparently there was a system of underground passages within the islands themselves. Some even believed the islands were connected underwater. I have copied the symbols and the diagrams they drew of mechanisms our ancestors encountered in the Floating Lands. I have studied these things, and tried to replicate some of them for myself, and I have decoded some of the Everien language. If we have to go underground, we won't be completely unprepared."

All this time, Pallo had said nothing. He had a troubled look on his face. Xiriel observed Istar fall into step with him, probably concerned about falling morale. She said, "Don't worry. Xiriel has studied this problem for years. He'll find a way."

Pallo looked startled. "What? I'm sorry, I wasn't listening."

"If you weren't listening, why ever were you looking so miserable just now?"

"I have a stone in my shoe."

Istar rolled her eyes and kept walking.

IN THE LIMINAL

Mhani was falling. Her question echoed about her: *Where is the White Road?* Here everything was white, and she was passing through a succession of doors windows parlors awnings bridges corridors rooftops and stairs. She couldn't control her own movement or her own sight, and terror rushed over her. With a great effort of will, she forced herself to turn and look behind her. And then she saw everything from a great distance, through a foreign self.

It was no different from being a child and watching her own hands craft a device she in no way understood, as if she were merely being used. Only now she inhabited the mind that showed her this vision.

This vision of the White Road.

I could See where the road ribboned over the sea. It was real, solid—yet unsupported by any mechanism. The shadows of birds fell on it. Waves splashed and rolled beneath it. The White Road led back toward Everien, past the Floating Lands like predatory teeth soaring from out of the deep, and finally to earth, where it disappeared in the mist of the sea plateau below the mountains of Everien.

Coming toward me up the road's soft arc was a small group of horsemen.

I did not know the Company then like I know them now. They came into Jai Pendu, and eschewing the Tower called the Way of the Sun that Ysse had already explored, they searched on until they came to the hall that is shaped like a bell, in the Tower called the Way of the Eye. I looked down on them, watched their faces stretch and gawp as they tried to understand the structure of the jewel that is Jai Pendu. A sense of the builder's personality becomes imbued in any structure, and Jai Pendu should have been no different—yet no person could have created such a place. In all their Clan legends there are no animal protectors who could have conceived of this architecture, and even the Pharician gods would surely have been baffled by the stairs that deliquesced to become ramps and the doors that opened three ways in the space of two.

Their leader was a tall man with a skeptical face. In my Eye I perceived his thoughts. He was thinking that he had stepped out of the world, into a place bigger than itself. He was thinking, *I feel like a piece of dust.*

They were looking for me, though they did not know it. When they came to the place of Three Doors, I drew them through my door and into my Way. Through halls and palaces and across bridges lit by some unknown means I brought the Company; through passages all curved and polished after the Everien manner: never the same twice, and always ever so slightly impossible. They came to the Way of the Eye, the place of the Water that connects the worlds, and they began to climb the Tower's ramp that is like a river, their horses pushing their breasts against its silvery tongues and driving upward with their great furred hooves that were not made for such surfaces.

I had never seen beings such as these before. All this time I was watching the Company through my Eyes in the Water, watching them from the Place I was Before. They charmed me utterly. They reached a hall with a black polished floor. The floor shone like calm lake water but echoed like metal when the horses stepped on it. The space was huge and the light came through it at impossible angles, refracted by the setting sun without; yet the leader was not dismayed to be so dwarfed. He urged his horse forward and behind him in a phalanx of muscle and will were twelve weapons at the ready.

I could see them from every angle, for my Eyes were everywhere.

They wanted to fight but there were no enemies for them. There was only me, safe in the Place I was Before, looking through the Water. They came over to the Water and looking in saw the Glass lying at its heart. It was the treasure they sought.

The leader turned to the others and said, "Be wary. This is almost too easy." They rattled their swords and looked dangerous; they wanted to fight. They felt only half-alive unless they were fighting: I could pick this up off them like a scent.

There was one among them who was wilder than the rest; he had rattles and vials of poison about his bare torso, and he carried a bow on his back. He looked into the Water cross-eyed, as a challenge. His hand came out toward me.

"Chyko, no!" cried the leader; but it was too late.

Never had I felt anything like what I felt when the one called Chyko touched the Water. I decided to take this one. I wanted to See his spirit. I began to stir. Jai Pendu took a long, slow, deep breath as I invoked its power. I made opponents to test the Company. They drew their weapons and fought me, though they could not see me.

It was beautiful. The way they moved; their emotions; the simple purity of their desires. There was much pleasure for me in the Sight of it, even from the great distance across the gulf of the worlds.

But while I was preoccupied with this, the leader had entered the Water. He reached in and broke the calm; like any animal will he brought the Sun into my Eye where I watched and I was dazzled and almost destroyed; I was blinded and forced out of my Place. We seized each other inside the Water and he stole my Eyes. I was drawn into his world blind, and now it was he who could See. He Saw the battle that I was waging outside the Water. He was enraptured with the many things he felt in himself and in his Company as they fought me; but he had already made his doom and theirs.

I could not stay in the Water. I was meant to be only Seeing from the other Place but now I was here—I was involved. I was desperate. He had foolishly disturbed me and now I was beyond the aid of my own kind, and my memories of what I am slipped away from me like sand. I could not See except indirectly through the Glass, and the leader held it like a weapon. I tried to get the Glass from him but I could not, and his Company were still fighting me. They had to be neutralized.

I remember calling them. I remember how I emerged from the Water and tried to gather the scattered images from the Eyes that this man could not control, he who held the Glass. I remember spreading my arms, and brightness like spidersilk shot from my fingertips. The strands branched and extended like tree limbs, each one arrowing to a target in the form of a Clan warrior. The one called Lyetar was struck by one string of light and he doubled over. I ate his pain, which was better than much music. The translucent strands wrapped his body, wound around his legs, covered his eyes and mouth, and he began to shrink until he was a bright parcel no bigger than a hand. I drew him home to me with my silken light. That is how I captured them.

Chyko was the last to go. He fought the light, wriggling almost free, clawing at the bonds, his body seeming to climb out of itself in an effort to escape. Humanity left his face, which took on the quality of some primordial living thing blindly straining away from death. One by one the radiant strands covered his throat, his forehead, his cheekbones and nose and eyes, and finally they covered the gasping mouth.

How I do love Chyko.

I turned to the leader but I could not catch him in this way, for he had the Water of Glass.

Now I held a great light in my cupped hands. With all the power of those trapped warriors, I summoned back to me the Water of Glass that had been stolen. But it did not come. Instead, the light slowly dimmed and settled in my hands. I held a piece of sculpture: three men on horseback, all merged at the base as if rising from the sea, their weapons angled forward to meet the charge.

I had made the men into a Glass.

I blundered toward their leader. It was his turn. I had to go home; but he was preventing me, for he held the Water. I could not See the Way.

"Give it back," I said.

"Give back my men," he answered.

"Come," I said, "and I will take you to them."

And we burst out of the Water. I tried to take him as I had taken the others, for I liked him best of all; but he cut the bonds with his sword that bore the sign of the Eye and the Sun and the Rose. He attacked me, but when he saw that he could not hit me with his sword he did not know what to do. I stepped back always half a pace out of sword range, and no matter how quickly he changed direction or how far he lunged, he found that the target was not there when his weapon extended.

"Coward!" he accused me. "Stand and defend against Quintar, servant of Ysse."

But I slid away; I didn't want to fight on his terms.

"Declare yourself!" he said. "What name are you?"

"I do not have a name," I answered.

"Every thing has a name," he taunted.

"Very well," I said. "I am Night."

And I brought my darkness down on him like the blow of a sword.

So he fled from me. Down through the long halls of my blindness I pursued him; down into the twilight and to the White Road where it gleamed like a moonpath on the sea, his only hope of salvation. He ran upon it but when I tried to follow I was prevented. There was an Animal on the White Road, and it hated me. The White Road curled up on itself and I could not set foot on it. I could not escape Jai Pendu; not that way. And the tide was changing.

I could feel the hollow space where my Eyes had been, like a soldier feels phantom pains in an arm that has been long amputated. I had to regain my Sight: without it I would be stranded in this world where I did not belong. I must not stay in Jai Pendu, for it was about to sail.

I was weak and my sense of what I am drained from me like blood. I decided to find a way to Everien through the cracks and ruins that are bent and turned on their sides, through the warped islands that float on the sea; and I became lost within them. I passed deep into the earth, and the last thing I remember of this is how I returned to my elemental darkness, darkness my little familiar, and let it smother me with its warm fur, and for a while I believed myself dead.

"Mhani! Mhani! Stop! Come back!" Devri was sitting on her chest and prying her eyelids apart. She shuddered and pulled away, teeth chattering. She couldn't feel her hands or feet.

"You mustn't," he said. "You'll kill yourself."

Devri stood up, and she saw that two apprentices were standing nearby with blankets and steaming vessels.

"Get them out of here!" she commanded, but her words were a whisper. "You stupid boy."

Devri ordered the apprentices to leave the items. "You haven't been here," he said sternly. "You haven't seen this. Understood?"

The youths nodded solemnly and scurried away. Mhani tried to sit up. Devri wrapped her up in the blankets and poured hot liquor into a bowl. He had to unfold her fingers so she could hold it. They were blue. She could not stop the shaking that seemed to come from the very pit of her stomach, and to her dismay tears threatened to overcome her. Devri was an idiot to allow apprentices into the Eye Tower while she was working. And then for them to see her in this condition . . . if Ajiko got wind of it, he'd probably have her locked up.

"Where's Xiriel?" she gulped. "Bring him at once."

Devri pretended not to hear her, continuing to fuss and hover. "You are doing everything you have always warned us against doing, Mhani! If I didn't know better I'd say you were playing Impressionist. It's crazy at your age. I'll tell Hanji if you don't stop. Now, before your toes fall off from the cold—*drink*!"

She managed a tiny sip. The concoction was almost pure alcohol.

"Devri, where's Xiriel?"

He looked down evasively. "I don't know. He didn't turn up the day that Lerien left. The castle's acting so strange, I suppose he could be anywhere."

"Istar, then." The tears trembled in her eyes now. "Yes, I must see my daughter."

Again Devri didn't answer.

"Fetch her, please. Send for her. Devri!"

"Mhani . . . I'm sorry. They have all gone missing. Kassien, Pallo, Xiriel, and Istar. No one has seen any of them for days."

"Days? What do you mean, *days*?"

"Mhani, please, you must come down and rest. Don't you realize how long you've been in the Liminal?"

"Where is Istar?" She was on the verge of tears.

"They've gone, Mhani. Ajiko's had a search out for Pallo on Lerien's command. His soldiers have turned the place inside out."

Mhani made a greater effort to drink. She *would not* collapse. She put a weak hand to her lips. Her fingers had begun to ache as they warmed up. "What have I done? How could I *encourage* her? And why, *why* did not Tarquin tell us?"

"What have you Seen?" Devri begged. "Have you found the army? They aren't . . . are they . . . they aren't dead?"

Through tightly clenched teeth she said, "Leave me, Devri. Lock the Eye Tower and do not let anyone up."

"I can't do that. You're in danger as it is. Mhani, let me help you. Ajiko's been pestering me for your reports."

"What have you said?"

"I . . . I've been making them up. But it's dangerous, Mhani! What if there's an enemy or a crisis and we fail to See it? What about the king?"

"I'm going to call him now."

"You mustn't. You're too tired. Please, I mean no disrespect but your judgment cannot be sound if you propose continuing. You've had no rest."

"It doesn't matter. It's got to be done."

"I'll get the others, I'll get Hanji. . . ."

"No! Hanji has his hands full, and anyway he's not a Seer. And if you open the Tower, I'll have Ajiko all over me like a rash. No, you must obey me, Devri. Look at me."

He did. Devri was not much older than Xiriel. He happened to be a cousin of Mhani's by marriage. He had long brown hair and soft eyes and he was tremendously receptive to the Knowledge, but she was sure he would never have the will to become a great Seer. Now all his worry and fear for her were writ large on his face, and his eyes on her were searching.

"You can see that I am possessed of my faculties," Mhani said steadily, sniffing and clearing her throat. "You can see that I am not insane. You must do as I say. You are a good Seer, Devri, and you must help me now. This is serious. Do as I've told you. Lock the Eye Tower and let no one in. If Ajiko makes a fuss, tell him you lost the door and cannot find it. I must not be disturbed. Do you understand?"

He was nodding, accepting the responsibility she forced on him. "What about Hanji?"

"If Hanji wants to find me, he will always be able to. As for you, Devri, keep your mouth shut no matter what. I don't trust Ajiko, and neither should you."

"Mhani, please, I'll do as you say, I swear, only tell me: Is there truly a Pharician army on our borders?"

"Pharice is the least of our worries at the moment," Mhani said. "All the same, don't put Sendrigel at your back, either. I will call for you when I need you. Now go!"

After he was gone she wrapped herself deeper in the blankets and sipped the hot liquid until she was very warm and fairly drunk. Then she returned her attention to the Water of Glass.

SHE LOOKED FOR Lerien but his Carry Eye was not in use. If they had been gone for days, probably he had tried to contact her, but she had been deep in the Impressions. She had a feeling of dangerous slippage; she was losing control of the whole system. If she let Devri in he could quickly check and record the activity on all the Eyes, saving her the trouble; but she didn't wish to break her concentration, lest she be unable to recover it. With an effort, she performed her breathing exercises and then disciplined herself to make a sweep of the entire country.

She found Lerien's party in the Deer Country, making good progress. She noted their position and continued on with her sweep. When she scanned the area where Tarquin claimed to have seen the Pharician army, it was as empty as before.

Or rather, it was empty—but not unchanged.

The ground was trampled and torn in a strip a quarter mile wide for mile after mile down the Pharician side of the Everien Range. Then the grassland resumed, undisturbed. It looked just as if a large force had passed—but where had they gone? Into the sky?

While she watched, she could see the churned ground growing slowly southward. She blinked, turned the Eye this way and that to be sure she had not imagined the movement, and turned it back. The torn earth was increasing.

"They are *invisible*?" As far as Mhani knew, even the Everiens hadn't known how to make themselves invisible. How could the Pharicians, with their primitive mechanical understanding and their worship of bone-dry bureaucracy, succeed where the Everiens had failed? It was all impossible. First she had Seen a woman on horseback; now a road that made itself out of the grassland, the earth tearing itself without benefit of weather or worm.

What did it mean?

She leaped up, stumbling down the stairs. Her voice was a shriek.

"Devri! Devri! I've changed my mind. Fetch Hanji instantly!"

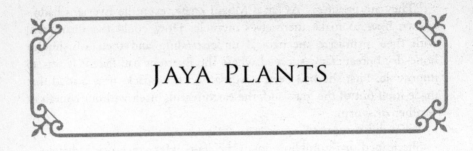

JAYA PLANTS

Two days passed while Lerien and his men rode northwest along the valley floor toward Wolf Country. On the second day they passed a company led by Inise of the Snake Clan on their way home from a successful offensive in the hills, and several groups of stragglers asked for news of the troops they'd been separated from. Smoke could be seen intermittently in the hills, and one night an eerie glow lit the sky above a highland lake. They stopped only to change horses, eat standing up, and sleep during the brief darkness.

As the shadows of evening fingered the land on the third day, they reached A-vi-Sirinn. One of the largest of the ancient Everien settlements, it had always been impeccably managed by the Deer Clan. Unlike the other Clans, the Deer were only too happy to use as much of the Knowledge as they could, and to prevent its destruction or erasure they protected the remains of the old town even if it meant they could not shelter underground in the winter. The underground city had long since been closed by the Clan Elders to prevent plunder of its Knowledge, so that except for the community of Scholars who worked to decipher the contents of the ruins, all of the townspeople lived aboveground year-round. Even so, it was plain on first sight that A-vi-Sirinn had never been built by any Clan.

The settlement draped the hillside in a series of curving terraces, down which flowed a wide stream in a series of waterfalls, bisecting the town neatly. In winter these terraces would throw elaborate shadows and the waterfalls would freeze into shaggy beards, but in summer the town's blue stone baked under the sun in sharp relief to the patches of snow that would never melt at this height. Where the stone had been quarried was anybody's guess: it was deep and true as lapis and it fitted into the natural contours of the mountainside as if set there by a jeweler. Like all Everien settlements, A-vi-Sirinn possessed no fortifications, but because it abutted the base of a cliff on its highest side, it was easily protected against attacks from above by two Clan-built watchtowers set on the top of the cliff behind the town. A simple stone escarpment had been added to the lowest terrace to create a barrier against invasion from the valley, but it appeared now unguarded.

There should be watchmen on the walls, Tarquin thought. *There should be bird-scouts.* He had passed through here coming the other way on his hasty mission from Ristale; Tarquin remembered the town as a blur of guttering torches illumining empty streets, where a woman dressed in men's garb had brought him a fresh horse and provisions. The men were all at war. Tonight, as the king's party walked their horses through the gates, it appeared that a dogged industry prevailed despite the reduced population, for some effort had been made to prepare for Lerien's visit. Kivi had contacted the town Seer with his Carry Eye to warn of their approach, so the houses were all lit and a great many children came out to greet them as they walked through the town toward its central hall.

All of the buildings were dome-shaped and hewn from the same blue stone, which possessed the sleekness of polished marble. By day the walls, inside and out, were dark blue and opaque; by night they were semitransparent and their color was that of a clear autumn sky. Light poured from the walls themselves, spilling out into the streets and revealing the contents of the interiors at the same time. No lamps were needed in such houses; yet some of the Deer occupants had deliberately covered the walls to darken them, then added ordinary lights that were traditional. They had done all they could to make the dwellings more homelike: they had put up partitions to divide the circular spaces; they had brought in wooden and leather furniture to clutter up the austerity. And they had constructed shopfronts, chicken pens, dove houses, watering troughs, and storage sheds in between the hivelike Everien buildings. The formal Everien gardens had been replaced by vegetable patches and orchards, and deer grazed around the town's central fountain.

"There may be something to be said for the Eyes after all," Ketar said to Kivi, who smiled. Fires had been lit in the central square, where spits holding game were being turned.

The woman who cared for the horses recognized Tarquin at once and scolded him because the animal he had ridden a few days ago was now lame and could not work. He apologized and offered to help her feed and water the king's beasts, which had many days of hard going ahead of them. In truth he wanted to avoid socializing, but the woman took his hanging back to mean something different, and while they were watering the horses he found himself on the receiving end of an offer that was difficult to refuse. He had his hands inside her clothes and matters were looking promising when her five-year-old child appeared outside the stall, dragging a doll by one leg and crying over a nightmare. So much for that.

When at last he wandered into the central hall where the king's reception was being held, he was ravenous and the others were drunk. The hall was of a size to comfortably hold two hundred. Its inside walls had been painted in dark colors to keep them from shining all night, and the imposing space was partitioned to create a feeling of security and intimacy at the expense of grand design. Several smaller rooms had been created by wood and stone blocks, between which were stretched "walls" of deeply colored hide cut into geometrical patterns and stitched together. One section had been devoted entirely to the display of food, arrayed on trestles and platters that rested on vats of wine and Deer Clan spirits. Small heatstones had been placed in burners scattered liberally on beams and shelves cut in the walls: they glowed with rich colors even as they alleviated the chill that came to the mountains even on a summer night.

The women of A-vi-Sirinn were dressed in the dyed linen cultivated by their lowland Clan sisters who had mastered the Everien style of spinning and weaving. Their manner of dress was simple, and they favored dim colors and long, flowing lines: few in the Deer Clan dressed to get attention. Even so, the king's arrival had prompted the donning of the silver and copper jewelry mined in these hills, and Tarquin saw more than one woman in full face paint that must have taken hours to effect, for Deer Clan paint was intricate and subtle. Yet the majority of the faces were brown from sunlight and possessed of a weariness and perhaps even an uneasiness that one night of good cheer could not completely banish.

Of the men, he saw only Elders in their white robes and a cripple. Even the boys were absent: none seemed older than ten or eleven, and Tarquin remembered how Ajiko had spoken of using women and boys behind the lines. There were a group of Scholars set apart by their red robes and hushed voices. They carried weapons but by the look of them, if the Scholars were responsible for the guardianship of the town, A-vi-Sirinn had better rely on its walls.

Lerien had given his men strict orders not to overindulge, but the townspeople were keen to make merry. The place was full of inebriated women and adolescents who couldn't hold their liquor. Tarquin worked his way toward the food, trying to be unobtrusive. A gang of oldsters had gathered around the visitors and were toasting the old days, each other, and Ysse; Lerien was barely visible in a corner with Kivi, apparently conferring over the Eye.

Tarquin took as much food as he could carry and leaned against a pillar, listening to the talk and watching the local girls circulate among the visitors, one of them going so far as to pretend to have forgotten that the top four fastenings of her dress were undone. He made idle bets with himself as to which one of Lerien's men would get her, and then, as he watched her more, revised this to a question of how many of them she would allow.

The town's elderly governor, Wodhi, was drinking freely and in between toasts addressing the group with a series of rambling anecdotes about horses; everyone was looking bored. "In Ysse's heyday, the Deer Clan bred such horses as you children have never seen. Now we have warhorses, which we derive from the draft stock, but in those times my Clan had pastures and to spare. They'd have made your Pharician beasts look like donkeys. Our horses were more fleet than the arrows from young Taro's bow."

The Wasp smiled, but the other young ones exchanged "not another one of those before-the-Sekk-came stories" glances.

Tarquin heard himself say, "I remember a horse called Ice."

"Ice! Don't say his name to me!" cried the old man, his grizzled jowls flapping. Tarquin smiled and ignored him.

"My brother took me to see the races," Tarquin said. "I remember how we spent ten days walking on the way to the meet, and ten days coming back, and by the time we got home our mother was like a ghost with fear for us, for she'd heard the news of what the Sekk were doing to people they found in the hills. Anyway, Ice was the name on everyone's lips. Nothing on four feet could outrun him."

"He was a fell beast with a black heart. His ancestors came from the cruel deserts south of Pharice. They are cannibal horses, did you know that?"

Tarquin laughed.

"It's true, you young fool! That horse never grew old and it never took the bridle. Unnatural demon-thing, born in a Fire House probably . . ." Someone refilled Wodhi's mug and he swayed, forgetting what he was saying.

They all laughed; Taro and Jakse were drinking too much and received a second warning from their leader, which was met with good-natured protests. A girl was called on to sing and everyone gathered around; Tarquin found himself standing just outside the circle, beside the drunken old man who called himself Wodhi.

"You've lost nearly all your men," he said in a low voice. "Where have they been sent?"

Wodhi shrugged and glanced toward the king. "If only we knew. I put together a battalion and sent them down the valley to join the army. That was eight months ago, and no news yet. I must content myself with the fact that the Sekk have not reached us here."

This was a pitiful excuse for contentment, Tarquin thought.

"Jai Pendu is on the way," the old man added. "Are you not riding in the wrong direction, Tarquin the Free?"

Long seconds passed. Tarquin could think of no answer. He coughed.

"Give me some of that," he said, and a mug of strong malt was placed in his hand. He tilted his head back and drank. A Deer girl had taken a stool and a polished red lute. She was paper white with auburn hair and gray eyes, and her throat trembled when she sang. She was exquisite, Tarquin thought, but for the savage X that scarred her cheek. How had her father felt, he wondered, when he took the burning knife to his daughter's perfect face, to brand her as human lest she be mistaken for Sekk? And how would men treat her, who would be both drawn to her fragile looks and repelled by the beauty that made her look like a Sekk?

> *Through summer long I'll wait for you*
> *Our vows still on my lips*
> *No night shall break your courage true*
> *No moon my love eclipse*

Her eyes were shining with emotion. He finished the whiskey and found himself filled with the wild hope that he had been wrong about the Pharician army. Maybe he had been seeing things; maybe there was no enemy marching on Everien. Perhaps it had all been simply another vision, another episode in eighteen years of sporadic insanity.

A curvy young blonde was standing beside him, her lips swollen and blurry and her hair in disarray. She took the cup away and handed it back to him full.

Better, he thought, drinking, that he should be insane and his people persist. For he had dedicated his life to Everien—this was the only thing that gave his existence what little meaning it had. In this matter he had taken his cue from Ysse. She had accepted her role as head of state not because she wanted to be queen, but because it was what had to be done, and Ysse never shrank from doing the things others feared. She had abhorred statecraft: he had never seen a crown on her head, and even in private she dressed as a warrior. In her last years, despite the debilitating illness that wasted her body, she had ridden every day, kept falcons, and was a frequent visitor to the garrison where she was in the habit of overseeing the training of the young. He had himself conducted weapons training sessions in which Ysse hobbled in with the aid of a stick, spoke to him for a quarter of an hour of inconsequential things without seeming to inspect the men, and left. Later she would summon him to her office and offer a detailed analysis of each warrior's individual strengths and failings. Sometimes her suggestions were radical.

"That one," she might say, pointing to a particularly clumsy student, "he would do better to fight without the shield."

"He's too slow to survive without a shield," Quintar would protest, incredulous. "He'd be cut to pieces."

They would argue back and forth for a while, and Quintar would go away annoyed that she passed judgment too rapidly, without bothering to spend more time with his pupils. Then, a week or two later, her words would work on him and eventually, no matter how he fought the idea, he would tell the student to work without the shield. While Quintar waited to be proven right, his slowest, most ponderous student would suddenly metamorphose and become more agile, more powerful, and more alert. Quintar would curse Ysse in private, and her eyes would laugh at him whenever the man in question was mentioned. This kind of thing happened many times. It drove him crazy; but Ysse never rubbed his nose in it, and she seldom interfered with his work unless he asked for her advice. If she had been a man, he thought, there would have been nothing she couldn't do.

As it was, she had died with her work unfinished, for the Sekk still plagued Everien. The last time he'd seen her, she had received him in her private chambers. She was dressed in a dark red robe that hid some of the effects of the disease. When she rose to greet him, she moved with the old surety, and only her gray-streaked hair in its braids hinted at her age. The black eyes were as bright and clear as ever, and her smoky skin had few lines, for emaciation had pulled it taut across her cheekbones. Yet there was now a softness in her demeanor that was uncharacteristic of the Ysse he had served all his adult life, and it gave him pause.

It was not long after the slaughter at Jai Pendu. He had already made up his mind to leave Everien. Everything had to change, because he wasn't the same and couldn't pretend he was. The only way he could get through the days was to shut down every feeling he owned, and he had walked around like a zombie as he made preparations to depart. He had delivered his renunciation to his Clan, who didn't take it seriously at first, even the day before he planned to ride. He'd made all the preparations, but everyone expected him to snap out of it; those who dared invade his privacy and speak to him told him earnestly that he was a hero. He heeded no one. He became like iron, and almost forgot that life had ever been any other way. When Ysse summoned him, he approached the audience as a mere formality, forgetting her uncanny ability to see into people.

She took his hands. The way she said his name brought his heart into his throat. He turned her hands over in his and looked at them: here could her true history be seen, in the thick veins, the scars, and the crooked fingers broken and mended and broken again. Her skin was warm and dry. She looked up at him and said simply, "Don't go."

He was nonplussed. "Do you order me to stay?"

"I forfeited the right to give you orders the day I sent you to Jai Pendu." Her eyes were steady against his, their pressure as certain as if she put her hands on some deep place in him and swung it open.

He swallowed and looked away. He let go of her hands; her disappointment rippled in the air between them.

"It is hard, Quintar." Her voice was so soft that he had to look at her. It was the second time she had used his Clan-given name.

"I'm not called that anymore."

"Why do you look this way at me?" she said. "Why the shame? Why?"

It should be obvious, he thought. The only "why" was why she taunted him. But he said nothing.

"You think I deserve this?" she said, and he glanced at her sharply as she gestured to the walls and battlements around them. "You think I am special because I was the one who blundered into Jai Pendu and captured the Fire of Glass? Are you really like the rest of them, even now?"

He hadn't bargained for this, and fleetingly wished himself anywhere but in the line of her scrutiny. "You are the queen," he answered stiffly. "That is how I think of you."

She released his gaze then. Sighed, looked out across her land. "That is all you will allow yourself, so that is all you will get."

He didn't know what this meant. Ysse was silent for a long moment.

"When death comes it should be sudden, so that our lives need not change to accommodate it. So that we need not back down from what we are. So that there will be no time for fear." She paused for breath, and he saw the quaver in the loose skin of her throat before she continued. "I will not have a sudden death. I watch my life unravel. Everything I have ever done I have charged at full speed. They thought me courageous, but I was only fearless, and that is not the same thing. I was never afraid to die in battle. I am afraid to die in bed. It is the one battle I can't fight. All I can do is stand still and watch it happen."

His hands were gripping his own knees. He was thinking of his men, and how he had been able to do nothing to save them. "I know," he said roughly.

"Tarquin," she said. "I sent you to Jai Pendu. Their deaths are on my head. Not yours. I want you—" She caught the skeptical look on his face and sighed. "I want you to go free."

"That's impossible."

"Is it? Now, maybe, it seems that way. It is all too fresh, too raw, and you are like me. You must act. You can't bear to stand still. So you will go off and think that by running you can change what's happened—"

"I know I can't change it," he contradicted her, unable to attenuate the bitterness in his voice. "I know it will never change. I know there's nothing I can do. I'm not running because of guilt. I'm running to save myself. Ah . . . I can't explain." He looked around the room as if the walls themselves would pounce on him. Everything in Jai Khalar reminded him of Jai Pendu. It made him feel sick.

"You're right, of course," she said. "I have no right to behave as if I understand."

He looked at her again, knowing she did somehow understand, wanting to plead for help. But she was not offering him authority, guidance, mentorship. The equality, the sense of being in her confidence that she held out to him now did not flatter him as it would once have done; it unsettled him.

"Come and see my flowers," she said, and led him out onto a terrace he had never even known was there. It had rained and the sky was still overcast; all of Jai Khalar was white and gleaming, but the plants Ysse was growing in stone containers on the terrace bore brilliant flowers among dark green foliage. The intensity of the wet colors was almost painful. Their petals fluttered in the wind, reminding Tarquin of the world below, of dirt and ordinary things that were so remote from this height. Ysse poured wine from a flagon and offered it to him.

"These are jaya plants from Pharice. They can live to be a hundred years old. I started growing them when I got back from Jai Pendu. They require much attention and care, and I found the pastime soothing. For years after my trip to Jai Pendu, I had difficulties. In my mind, I mean."

"You?"

She nodded. "I didn't tell anyone. I was afraid I would lose face, that my authority would suffer, if I admitted anything was wrong. But also . . . also I felt somehow that the things I had seen were secret, and that it would be wrong to speak of them to anyone else."

She didn't look at him as she spoke, but rather at the plants, moving her fingers in the soil and idly caressing their leaves. He had never seen Ysse like this, didn't know how to read her manner, and felt like he was caught in quicksand. Instinctively he went very still as she continued.

"If I could have," she said, "I would have left Jai Khalar as you are doing. I would have gone far away, started over, lived as a woman. But I could not. My duty was here, and I had started something that I needed to see through. I let them make me queen—someone had to do something!" She laughed, and for a flash there was the old Ysse, tough as nails, practical. "So to cope with the visions, I began cultivating these flowers. You probably think it sounds pitiful, but they are the closest thing I will ever have to children."

"It is not pitiful," he protested feebly. The idea of Ysse as a mother of children had set his mind reeling, but he didn't want to show it. "I mean, I understand."

"You need something like these plants. If you must go, then go. But do as I would have done. Make something for yourself. Don't give yourself over to the past, or to the labyrinth."

His breath caught. She knew. "Labyrinth?"

"Jai Pendu, and the maze it can make of you. It will trap you inside yourself if you let it."

He had started to shiver as if about to enter combat. She put her hand on his.

"I can't talk about it," he said, hating himself for his weakness. He had idolized Ysse for years, just as everyone did. To find himself now on such intimate terms with her, and to behave like a sick or wounded animal instead of a man—this should have burned deep. Yet she showed no acknowledgment of his shame.

Her hand went to his cheek. He didn't look at her face. She poured more wine and he downed the cup in two long swallows. Ysse moved away, looking out over her land, and the moment faded.

Suddenly a mischievous look came over her and she said, "Do you remember that time in the border skirmishes of the Bear Clan?"

He reached for the flask and helped himself to yet more wine. It splashed when he poured it. "If you're going to talk about that," he replied with a nervous laugh, "I'm going to have to get really drunk."

She smiled. "Why? You were delightful."

Abashed, he looked at his boots. "I'm surprised you remember it."

"Don't you?"

He let loose another embarrassed laugh and avoided her gaze. Her eyes were black and bright all at once.

"Well, obviously. I mean, how could I forget? It was all I could do to keep my mouth shut about it." He moved to stand beside her while the shadows on the white cliff deepened to blue and purple with dusk. She had been his commander, but that night in a ditch waiting for a Bear Clan messenger who never showed up, she had not been in control. What the twenty-year-old Tarquin would have given to be able to say to his cronies, "I had the queen last night"—or rather, "I had the queen last night, *in a ditch*."

"You were very young," she said. "But I knew you would be discreet. It was one of several points in your favor."

She turned and put her hands on his chest.

"Ysse," he began, troubled. But before he could frame words, she had pressed her hands against him firmly.

"No. It's too late for that, I know it. You must go. I'm dying. Nothing is going to happen here tonight, except that I'm going to say to you once again, please go free. Jai Pendu will destroy you if you let it. Quickly or slowly, the Knowledge you have witnessed will ruin you unless you find something to fix you to the physical world. Go and live, Tarquin. Live as I have not done." She paused. "It's what Chyko would do if he were in your place."

"Chyko was not like me," Tarquin railed. "He always laughed, and he didn't believe in anything, and he was never afraid. He should be the one here now, not I."

Ysse said nothing.

"I must go now," he said, a note of formality creeping into his voice. "There are things I have to do before the morning."

"Go then, Tarquin the Free." She kissed him once, and her lips were dry. "Be free of the labyrinth. Escape Jai Pendu, and never return."

Her voice was steady, but her eyes begged him with a thousand questions. He hesitated. Never had he entertained the hope of unburdening himself to anyone; yet here was Ysse, willing and able to understand some of what he had endured at Jai Pendu. She would not shrink from the horror, he knew that much.

Something held him back. He bowed his head and turned, stepping indoors where the rooms were now lamplit with the coming of night; this manifestation of the Knowledge made his lip curl, and he paused. She called after him from the terrace. "Quintar. Tell me. Please."

He only shook his head, and fled from her.

The next day, as he was riding away, he caught the last glimpse of Ysse he was ever to have. She was in the training field at the foot of Jai Khalar, flying her falcons. A coterie of young soldiers surrounded her, birds on their wrists, listening intently to her advice. He couldn't hear what she was saying, but the wind blew him her laugh, a scratchy, playful sound. She tossed the bird into the air and held her arm aloft for a long moment as her eyes followed its flight. Tarquin turned his horse and left with the impression of her stance stamped into his mind, the motion frozen for-ever half-finished.

IN THE HALF-EMPTY hill town of the Deer Clan, the singer had begun a jig and the blonde slithered against him, breathing beer fumes and running her hands down his chest. He jerked away, startled. The room was suddenly too close, too loud, too full of people he didn't know and didn't want to. He pushed his way through the crowd and went to sleep with his horse.

DARIO'S STORY

When Ketar shook Tarquin awake, it was almost midday. He had a headache and a terrible thirst.

"There you are," Ketar grunted, and offered him a hand. "It's a wonder you weren't trampled in the night."

As he rose from the straw, Tarquin thought that Ketar did not look particularly hale himself. The others were saddling their horses in relative silence; he inferred that all had drunk too much, except possibly Lerien, who seemed bright-eyed and in good spirits. They moved out of the village to the cheers of small children, a spectacle the others seemed to enjoy.

"I miss my sons," Taro said.

"And I my grandchildren," added Stavel.

"It has been months since I have been to my home," Jakse remarked. "If it were not for the Eyes, I doubt I would remember what my family look like."

Tarquin could think of nothing to add to this, as he had no relatives anymore and had lost even the right to mourn his own mother. He held himself a little apart from the others, conscious of his difference.

It was midafternoon before they reached the other side of the valley and began to climb. Up in Wasp Country, farmland gave way to forest, paved roads to rutted tracks. They had come some distance from any original Everien buildings, leaving behind the Fire Houses and the wind towers and the glass domes whose purpose no one knew. All of the villages in the hills had been built with Wasp hands, and compared with the towns near Jai Khalar, they had a rough and unfinished look about

them. They were also fewer and farther between than the valley dwellings, and for hours at a time the riders met no one on the road. Hawks
glided overhead, and Tarquin saw a vulture circling. The horses trotted
up the steep switchback trail, their riders leaning forward to ease the
weight in the stirrups. Diverted from its proper course, a stream crossed
the way at one point, turning the path to mud and slowing their progress
momentarily.

"There is a village just above us," Stavel said from the rear of the party.
"Is it not time for lunch?"

"Don't talk to me about food," Taro groaned.

Kivi the Seer was riding in front. When he crossed the water and
reached the next bend in the road, he halted, turned in the saddle, and
said, "Do not let the horses drink from the stream. It's fouled above."

Tarquin had seen the blood go out of Kivi's face and guessed what was
the matter. It was all too familiar. He pressed his horse ahead, calling over
his shoulder for Lerien to stay behind. Kivi's mount was fighting with
him and rolling its eyes, refusing to go forward. Tarquin passed Kivi and
went around the bend.

The stream was full of bodies. It had been lined with white stones to
form a sluice that ran down the steep slope; now the water spilled over
the banks and snaked between the roots of trees, sweeping green beards
of moss in its currents. Water swept over an old man's wide-eyed face, his
outflung arm, the blur of his features, and the ragged wound in his neck;
the skirts of women; the blond curls of a child—Tarquin looked away.
Swallowing, he drew his sword and guided his horse up the hill.

There were flies everywhere. Crows went up like smoke as he rode
past the mill wheel and between the houses. Nothing human moved.
The bodies in the streets had been cut down as they fled; one house had
been torched but the fire had not spread, though it still smoldered. Tarquin's horse danced agitatedly in place. He wheeled the animal around
and rode back.

"The Sekk have been here," he shouted to Lerien. "We should fan
out through the forest and do a sweep. They have taken the village just
this morning from the look of it."

Lerien gave signals and the riders dispersed, weapons at the ready.
Tarquin found himself left with Kivi, who appeared uncertain about what
to do.

"Dismount," Tarquin said curtly, doing so himself. "You can recognize a Slave by his speechlessness and his aggression. If you see a Sekk,
you must neither look at it nor listen to its voice. Be careful!"

Kivi took out his fighting sticks and moved away from Tarquin. Tarquin drew his sword and glided stealthily from tree to tree in a zigzag search pattern up and down the slope. He had learned to sharpen all his senses like an animal, and he slipped into this mode now, thinking of nothing—only reacting.

He found more bodies, all of them female or infant, indicating a typical Sekk Slaving raid. Somewhere on this mountain were the men of the village, caught under the Sekk spell. Even if they could be found, they would be out of their senses, possessed of an unreasoning violence. If a Sekk were killed and its spell broken, the Slaves might be freed: but what freedom was there in knowing your own hands had murdered your family?

After an hour, he circled back toward the starting point, taking in one last loop of high ground on the way. Here he encountered Kivi, who looked pale and shaken.

"I have found no Sekk or Slaves. They must already be far away."

"We'll see what the others have found," Tarquin said. "Come on."

They took a shortcut through a section of old forest where the undergrowth was thin; it was the only area in the radius Tarquin had set out that he hadn't yet searched, mostly because there was so little ground cover to hide anyone. But as they passed among the trees, a rain of stones greeted them. The branches overhead shook. Tarquin got a glimpse of a face and a hand; then he had to duck as another rock fell toward him with disturbing accuracy. He dived for cover and signaled Kivi not to shoot. The Seer, crouching behind a boulder, gave him a puzzled glance, for Tarquin had actually begun to smile. He addressed the trees above. "We aren't here to hurt you," he called. "We ride with the king from Jai Khalar, and we can help you. Do you understand?"

Silence. Tarquin relaxed: he could wait. But Kivi, having caught on to what was happening, chose this moment to step out from cover. He showed his empty hands. "People of the village," he announced. "I am going to walk toward you. I am unarmed. Don't be afraid. The Sekk are gone from here. You can see I'm not Sekk."

An arrow flew from behind a nearby tree and grazed his leg. Kivi threw himself on the ground as more stones came down.

"You'll never get us," cried a shrill voice from the trees. "Go back where you came from!"

Kivi and Tarquin looked at each other.

"Children," Kivi mouthed. But Tarquin was sure the archer was no child: the bow shot had been too powerful, if not particularly accurate. The archer would have to be taken out first. He darted uphill and positioned himself behind another tree, which rustled when he touched it:

someone was up there. He made a second dash and heard an arrow whiz past his shoulder, but he was level with the hidden archer now. He nodded at Kivi, who stood up again, clutching his bleeding thigh.

"Please," Kivi begged convincingly in the direction of the archer. "Don't shoot me."

Tarquin sprang out from behind his tree and leaped on the archer from behind; they both landed hard in last year's leaves. He quickly asserted control, twisting the bow from sweating fingers and grabbing the long braid to restrain the head. From above there were screams and imprecations. He sat on the back of his prisoner, who was still facedown and spitting dirt.

"Call them off. They're going to fall and get hurt, and there's no need for it. We're not your enemies."

The archer was breathing hard but ceased to struggle. Kivi had been forced to retreat behind a gnarled oak as a seemingly endless supply of missiles was hurled on him from above.

"I'm going to let you up," Tarquin said. "I won't hurt you. Just tell the kids to come down quietly. All right?"

Taking silence for assent, he removed his weight and released the braid. The archer turned over. He realized she was a woman right around the time her knee drove into his groin and delivered him into wide-eyed agony. She sprang up, a flash of triumph outshining the fear on her face. Tarquin flung himself at her legs and, gasping with pain, brought her down again. He used his weight to get supremacy. Now her body was filled with the kind of concentrated terror that hears no reassurance—and he had none to give, being unable to speak after that blow. She scratched him and spat in his face and bit his hands while he tried to find a way to subdue her without causing injury.

He found his voice and shouted for Kivi. With his peripheral vision he could see children dropping out of the trees and coming toward him with stones in their hands.

"Let her go," Kivi yelled, running toward him. "You're only making it worse. Let her go!"

Tarquin saw the wisdom in this and released her, drawing back out of the range of her feet. Two stones missed him, and he saw Kivi wrest a third out of the hand of a boy of nine and fling it aside. But the woman didn't move. She lay propped on her elbows in the leaves, staring fixedly at him and breathing hard. Her jaw trembled and her eyes filled with tears. Kivi stopped in his tracks.

"Dario?" queried one of the children. "Mother, are you hurt?"

The woman inhaled on a high note and let out a sob.

Tarquin flushed and looked away. "Do something, Kivi."

In a soothing voice Kivi said, "Dario. Is that your name? I'm Kivi. You shot me in the leg, remember?" He hopped on one foot and grimaced. As Dario looked up at Kivi, a mixture of embarrassment and gratitude magically replaced the fear on her tear-streaked face. He held out a hand to help her up and she took it, collapsing against his shoulder and wrapping her arms around his neck in relief. The children began to sidle over to be introduced; apparently they were all hers, and they were laughing now as Kivi expressed exaggerated awe at their skill in the trees. Tarquin, preoccupied with the continued throbbing in his right testicle, got slowly to his feet. He slapped the Seer on the shoulder as he shuffled past. "Good, Kivi," he croaked.

ONLY TWO OTHER villagers were found alive. Lerien decided that Stavel and Taro would bring them to the nearest settlement; some horses had been found wandering loose, and these were saddled to carry the refugees.

While Taro amused her children, Dario was pouring her heart out to Kivi. "Kenzo, my mate, joined Ajiko's army a year ago when they passed through this village demanding all men of fighting age. But Kenzo and two others returned with a Wolf Clan soldier they'd befriended. They had a H'ah'vah egg they found in the tunnels in Wolf Country, so they slipped away with it. They were going to trade it to the Scholars of the Deer Clan."

Kivi raised an eyebrow. "The Seers would pay much for that! We can distill medicines of tremendous potency from the albumen of a H'ah'vah egg."

"Then riders came through asking for news of the troops that had been sent to Wolf Country, and by this time six more of our Clan had returned to us. They did not like army life! We hid our men and told the riders that all had gone to war."

"How long ago was this?" Lerien asked crisply.

"Last month, my lord." She said it steadily, with no apology for her family's insubordination to his policy. The Wasp Clan was notorious for its reliance on prevarication and deception in its dealings. "Kenzo went off with the egg to A-vi-Sirinn, leaving us well guarded by the other warriors. Or so we thought." She gulped back tears. "Excuse me. Yesterday a lone man came down from the hills, bleeding, weak. He could not speak and he seemed very ill. We hoped for news of our kinsmen who are still with the army there, so we cared for him."

"What Clan was he?" queried Stavel. "You are not far from the borders of my country."

"He had no Clan paint, and he wore Ajiko's uniform."

"Where is he now?" Tarquin snapped, alarmed. "Is he alive? Did he escape?"

"I suppose he must have escaped." Dario's eyes were bleak. It was a warm day, but she pulled Kivi's cloak closer about her shoulders. She said, "No one suspected him! He seemed perfectly sane, and he did not look like a Sekk, and he was dressed as a soldier. And he was wounded! I still can't understand how he could have been under a Sekk spell." She took a shuddering breath. "The men had all been given swords while in the army. When they . . . when it began . . . the rest of us had no defense. If Kenzo had been here—"

"Don't think about it," Kivi said. "There is hope he has made it to A-vi-Sirinn. And your children have survived."

She nodded, looking at the ground. "I know. I am lucky. My parents. My sisters, my aunt . . . all gone."

Taro came toward them, leading the horses. "We should ride now," he said. "Unless there are things you wish to collect . . ." He turned to Dario. She shook her head and stood, trying to smile at her children. "Which of you wants to share a horse with me?" she asked brightly. Kivi looked stricken.

"We will wait for you in the fields above," Lerien said to Taro. "Be wary of riding at night; pay attention to how the horses behave. We will camp close to the road. You should be able to reach us by dawn."

When they had left, the rest of the group continued on heavy-hearted. No one asked who would bury the dead. The king didn't make them ride far; as he'd told Stavel and Taro, he pitched camp on a cleared hillside fenced from the road by a low stone wall.

"What have you seen in the Carry Eye today?" Tarquin heard Lerien ask Kivi in a low voice. The others were busy gathering wood and tending the horses, and apparently Lerien did not realize he was in earshot.

"Mhani has shut herself away from our Sight again," Kivi said. "She is too deep in her work to notice my projection to her. I have tried half a dozen different ways to reach her, but none of them work."

Lerien frowned and kicked the dirt like a boy. "We will have to go to the monitor tower above A-vel-Jasse. Even if *that* Eye is broken, we can see Ristale from there as well as Wolf Country, so we can determine what Tarquin witnessed. Then we'll continue on to whatever positions in Wolf Country our new information indicates." He sighed. "What can Mhani be doing that absorbs her so? This has never happened, just as the Eyes have never gone wrong before. It feels like some kind of curse."

Yes, Tarquin thought. *That is what the Knowledge always amounts to.* But he did not say it aloud, and he asked no questions when Lerien announced his plan over their evening meal, which they took with the sun still hovering in the sky. They lit fires against the highland cold and ate the fresh food they'd been given at A-vi-Sirinn. Ketar brought out a flute and began to play a sad air.

Stavel said, "Before the Sekk came, Everien was a land of peace and plenty. There were no empires in those days, and no armies. The Seahawk histories say Everien was not a warlike culture."

Ketar took the flute away from his lips. "Everyone has wars," he said in a tone that suggested he was ready to fight one over the point.

"Not in ancient times," Lerien corrected. "The men of Everien competed, Ketar, to be sure; but they did not fight over land and women like the Clans. They settled their disputes in other ways. They were a race of astonishing ingenuity."

Ketar shrugged and resumed playing the lamentation.

Miro added, "In my Clan it's said that the Everiens first came from a country beneath the sea, and that they returned there when driven away by the Sekk."

"Who knows?" Lerien said. "Who knows where they came from or how long they lived in this high valley, isolated from all others? Perhaps they sought out this land hoping the Sekk would not find them here. Perhaps they didn't fight among themselves because they had a greater enemy in the Sekk, who might have been hunting them down the long years. No one knows where the Sekk come from or what their purpose is, but they must have moved among the Everiens like a legion of ghosts. Perhaps the Everiens fled such a hunter."

"And now it is hunting us," Taro said, shuddering.

"The Sekk should hunt the Pharicians!" Ketar exclaimed. "They conquer every people they meet. It is time someone checked their advance."

"And we have not succeeded in destroying the Sekk with swords," Lerien went on as if Ketar hadn't spoken. "They use our weapons against us, and hurl fell beasts at us. The only refuge for us has lain in the Knowledge, for it shelters us in Jai Khalar and the Fire Houses where the Sekk will not come. For they hate and fear the Knowledge."

"Or crave it," said Tarquin. "Do not be so sure of your own rhetoric, which has never been tested."

Kivi had been growing increasingly fidgety during the discussion. "The Sekk are the very embodiment of all that is evil," he burst out. "By their association with monsters we would have reason enough to hate them, but it's more than that, isn't it? What can they possibly gain by using men as tools for killing? That Sekk back there, it destroyed the minds of Dario's kinsmen; they in turn destroyed their families, and by now they will have probably suicided, unless they've found another village to prey on. And for what? The Sekk disappears again and it hasn't stolen gold, or horses, or women. Why? Tarquin, why?"

Tarquin said nothing. After a while Jakse pulled out a flask and offered it to Kivi, who shook his head, stood up, and walked away. The others began talking quietly of the weather.

Lerien was stirring the embers of the fire with a stick, pretending not to watch Tarquin. "Would you go back to Jai Pendu," the king asked softly, "after what you saw today?"

Tarquin felt the weight of unexpressed emotions dragging at the muscles of his face. "No."

"And you will not say what happened there? Even to Istar, you would not say?"

"Even to Ysse I would not say."

"Ysse is dead."

"I know," Tarquin said, looking her successor in the eye. "Every day I regret it."

Anger filled Lerien's face, but he didn't remonstrate. Suddenly unable to contain himself, Tarquin rose and left the fire. He crossed the open hillside and wandered through a band of trees until he had emerged into the field beyond. The shadows were long, but night refused to come. A wind crept through the field from the south. No crop was growing, nor had done for some time, as was evidenced by a birch sapling springing crookedly from the grass in the center of the open space. Tarquin found himself walking slowly toward it. He had become too accustomed to being alone, if he could no longer sit at a fire and be civil to a man who was no enemy of his. Yet he was deeply troubled by this talk of a man who might have been a Sekk, or might have been Enslaved by a Sekk while somehow remaining in possession of his wits. It didn't ring true. He began to wish he'd questioned Dario further.

He reached the sapling and stopped, extending a hand absently to touch its leaves.

And something happened.

He was somewhere else, lying on the edge of sleep in surroundings he didn't quite perceive. A woman leaned over him in the half light, her russet hair flooding over her shoulders, her breasts soft and heavy, areolas dark with motherhood. The curve of her lips was familiar. He experienced a rush of relief; it was the inverse of what usually happened to him on waking, when for a moment of blissful forgetfulness he came to awareness thinking everything was all right, only to remember that nothing would ever be all right as long as his lost men weighed on his conscience. Yet the feeling, now, in the presence of this woman he knew and did not know, was one of wholly unexpected joy. He stretched toward it like a plant toward sun—and it all disappeared.

"Tarquin." It was the voice of Kivi, who, Tarquin gradually realized, had been saying his name repeatedly for some time. "Do you hear me now?"

"What is it?" He sat up, his hand going reflexively to his sword. The birch sapling cut the sky into sections above his head. "What happened?"

Kivi backed away quickly. "Put the sword down. Tarquin! Put the sword down. You're acting like a Slave."

Tarquin lurched to his feet, sword still out. "Don't be a fool! What are you doing, sneaking up on me?"

"I went for a walk to clear my mind," Kivi said. "I didn't wish to speak with anyone, so when I saw you coming I crouched in the grass. You came here and stood for a long time. Then suddenly you fell over. When I called, you didn't answer me. I thought you might have been taken. After the village today—"

"Yes, I know. You're a bundle of nerves, aren't you, Kivi?" He put the sword away. "Well, leave me now. I am fine. I was meditating."

The Seer hesitated.

"If I *had* been taken," Tarquin roared in the tone of a sergeant to a raw boy, "I would have had you, too, lurking around calling my name as if you're looking for a lost puppy. Where are your weapons? If I'm a Slave, you're dead already."

"I simply—"

"Go! I want to be alone."

He watched the Seer pick his way back across the field; by then, he had realized he was shouting because he was frightened, and wondered if Kivi knew it, too. The episode made him think of the Sekk themselves, in that it had been comforting, almost seductive. . . . What was happening to him?

He stepped away from the imprint his own body had made in the grass and began to swear at himself in every Clan dialect he knew.

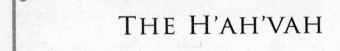

THE H'AH'VAH

In the interests of stealth, Kassien and Istar had chosen a route that led over the mountains and ultimately emerged above the sea plateau, which was a flat plain stretching all the way to the cliffs that marked the edge of the continent. The Floating Lands were arrayed on the water beyond, far below their current position and as yet blocked by the jagged white teeth of the eastern spur of the Everien Range.

Kassien was in his element, passing out ropes and hooks and pulleys that the others knew how to use only dimly, if at all. Pallo made a lasso of his assigned rope and managed to capture a large boulder before being called to task by Istar.

Kassien squinted into the glare that was coming from the clouded sky and pointed to the first goal of their ascent, a ledge some twenty man-lengths above. It did not look too difficult, but when they approached the base of the climb through a field of boulders, they found a symmetrical black opening in the stone. The edges of the aperture were smooth and rounded as though water had run over them for hundreds of years.

"This tunnel must be ancient," Kassien said. "It's been dug by Li'ah'vah, most likely; it's too big to be a H'ah'vah tunnel."

"Li'ah'vah are extinct," Xiriel observed. "Maybe we could use the tunnel to pass underneath this mountain instead of climbing over."

"It's a thought," Istar agreed, glancing at Kassien for his reaction.

Xiriel added, "There used to be lots of H'ah'vah in the hills where my Clan live, and if you know the tunnels, you can take all kinds of short-cuts."

Kassien didn't say anything. Istar reckoned he would be disappointed if he didn't get to use his ropes and grappling equipment. He walked a little ahead of the others, climbing until he stood in the mouth of the tunnel. It was pitch black, but as he turned to report, the sun came through the clouds and lit the outlines of his figure. Istar's breath caught in her throat. For a second she forgot who Kassien was or what was happening, and it seemed to her that she looked on a Clan warrior from legend. Kassien was now wearing none of the regalia of Ajiko's army but rather a bear-skin cloak and a dark red tunic over leather trousers and long furred boots. The colors of his clothes and hair were heated by the sun, and his drawn blade flared.

He gave her a puzzled glance and she grimaced, caught staring. Then she realized that he was listening. She tried to tune in to what he was hearing, but Xiriel was giving Pallo a little lecture about H'ah'vah.

"The more it digs, the bigger the H'ah'vah gets. They start off as thin slips of creatures that carve razor-thin passages, but the more they carve the larger they grow, until they are huge and can cut great tunnels. There is a legend in the Snake Clan about a chieftain who kept one as a pet and got it to dig him an entire palace underground."

"Would they dig you a bathing pool?" asked Pallo.

Istar heard it now. The sound was pitched so low that her teeth felt it more than her ears. She saw Kassien's legs flex and he began to creep to his left, away from the opening of the tunnel.

But the sound did not come from Kassien's direction. It came from below them, along the slope they had just climbed. The ground shuddered. Pallo gave a sudden squawk and was silent. No one moved. Istar's guts clenched.

Fifty feet below them the rock exploded into powder, revealing a black, shining snakelike body that rippled as it rose above the surface of the ground like a whale breaching. A cone-shaped head on a flexible stalk flowed up and roved to and fro, its white eyes devoid of pupils and glistening with mucus. If it were possible, Istar would have said that the creature's body was made of metal, for it had that sort of sheen; yet when it moved the H'ah'vah was supple as water. The whole affair was the size of a cottage.

The eyes fixed on them, and the mouth opened slow and deliberate as a drawbridge. The teeth were clear and its throat was full of light. It began to plow toward them, disintegrating the rock where it passed.

"I thought you said the big ones were extinct!" Pallo shouted at Xiriel, and started running.

"Shut up," Xiriel answered. "Just shut *up*. You little Pharician nose-bleed."

Kassien waved them into the old tunnel, where they stumbled into darkness with the pursuing crunch and shake of rock in their ears. Istar was just getting around to thinking that running from a H'ah'vah inside one of its own tunnels had to be the most categorically stupid idea Kassien had ever had when light greeted them ahead and they emerged into a bowl-shaped formation in the mountain. The noise of the H'ah'vah had subsided, but they had only moved deeper into its territory: more tunnels were visible among the rubble of displaced rock. Kassien burst out of the tunnel last and herded them up one side of the crater.

"It can be very difficult to lose them once they've scented you," said Kassien. He leaped upon a pile of boulders and shaded his eyes, surveying the area where the H'ah'vah had last appeared.

"How can they smell you through the rock?" Pallo whispered.

Istar didn't know so she didn't answer. The sight of the sinuous black body had excited her and filled her with awe. There was no way a human opponent could ever arouse this kind of emotion in her. The H'ah'vah was too big, too alien, to be treated as a mere enemy. It was a manifestation of all that was strange and unknowable in the world.

Yet to fight it you had to try to understand it. Istar could feel herself recoiling from that realization, and she knew this was exactly the means by which most Sekk monsters made their kills. A cocktail of fear and paralysis and ignorance stopped people from fighting intelligently. Istar struggled to quell these feelings in herself.

Kassien said, "We must be near its home tunnel."

"Let's get higher up, where there's more light," Istar responded, for the bowl was surrounded by high walls and much of it lay in shadow.

Kassien nodded in agreement. "H'ah'vah dislike sunlight. In fact, it's unusual to encounter them by day, especially in summer."

"What of the Sekk?" Xiriel said. "Are H'ah'vah not familiars to Sekk Masters?"

"One problem at a time," Istar told him, noticing that Pallo was looking ill. He needed something to do. "Hurry up, Pallo. After Kassien. And get ready to shoot. I don't want that thing near me—better if you kill it from a distance."

Pallo swallowed and nocked an arrow. Kassien led them up the side of the bowl and over a shoulder of rock. They found themselves in a fold of land climbing a transverse line between cliffs, bare of vegetation beyond a few wizened, dead trees that stuck out of cracks like claws.

"This way doesn't look too good," Kassien gasped, turning back toward the others. "But I'm afraid we're stuck with it. That face down there is too difficult and we can't go back the way we came without risking meeting the H'ah'vah. So let's get up as quick as we can."

Xiriel said something under his breath about what good was it having

maps if you weren't going to stay within their borders? But he set off after
Kassien at a good pace. His long limbs and lean body made the climbing
easy for him; Istar was jealous. Her pack was heavy with medical equipment and several days' food, and she took two strides to every one of
Xiriel's. By the time they reached the top of the scree field she was
breathing hard and spitting. When she had a firm foothold she looked
back.

"No sign," said Kassien, and consulted the map.

The others shifted their weight and swigged water, mopped their
brows. Flakes of rock stood upright all around them like ornamental
trees, wrested from the crack by what force Istar couldn't guess.

"I don't like this place," Pallo complained.

Istar checked Kassien's expression and saw that he was in doubt about
having led them up here. The fold had channeled them into a narrow
space where sheer buttresses walled them in and the only way ahead was
now through this forest of upturned stone. She was beginning to think
they would have been better off fighting the H'ah'vah where they first
stood, rather than wearing themselves out trying to elude a creature that
Kassien himself had admitted was almost impossible to escape if it decided
it wanted you. It could appear without warning from almost anywhere.
And there was no shelter nearby if someone got hurt; no view of the rest
of the mountain; no knowledge of where they would end up if they kept
climbing. All this flashed through her head in a second or two.

"There's no point going back now," she said. "Let's get through this
next part and hope the H'ah'vah has lost interest in us."

She hadn't much hope in this; she only knew that they mustn't start
second-guessing themselves, or they'd be wandering in circles.

They picked their way through a desolation of huge stone blades and
columns, many stained with bird droppings—although where the birds
could be now was anybody's guess, so silent and still was the air. Pallo was
chewing a lock of his own hair and squeezing the grip of his bow com-
pulsively, and every so often he jumped for no reason. Xiriel kept his
head down and glided behind the others, most likely enjoying a good
think. Kassien led, glancing around occasionally as if he expected the
H'ah'vah to break out of the ground at any second. The stones cast
spindly shadows, and it was easy for the eye to believe that it caught a
metallic glint from within the darkness, the coiled form of the H'ah'vah
preparing to attack.

At last the rocks to either side opened up to form a bowl, at the
bottom of which was a jagged rift where the mountain had been split, its
parts uprooted and turned on their sides, forming a sharp spine and a
dark cleft below it.

"Has the H'ah'vah eaten all the birds?" Pallo asked. "It's so still here."

"I think this must be its home," Kassien said. "If we were bold, we would look for eggs."

"We aren't bold," Istar said. "We want to live. What's that opening at the far end of the cutting?"

"It's symmetrical. Probably one of its main access tunnels. Maybe we can use it to cross over out of this gap in the mountains." Xiriel's eyes were turned slightly skyward, an expression they all recognized as the one he used when recalling sight of maps and texts.

"Maybe it could get us eaten," Pallo added.

"Look," Kassien reasoned, "the H'ah'vah could be right beneath us where we stand now."

Pallo jumped to one side and then apologized. Kassien ignored him.

"It can cut through stone to get us anywhere it wants to, so no matter what we do, we aren't safe. We might as well see if we can use its tunnel to get us across this ridge."

"All right." Pallo sighed. "But all this darkness can't be good for the complexion."

"Istar, shut up your idiot-boy before I make his complexion black and blue," Kassien said with a mock snarl.

They used Xiriel's Knowledge-light, which was weak but sufficient, as the tunnel was smooth if not level or straight. It took a wormlike course through the rock, sometimes following some mineral vein in à straight line for a while before suddenly plunging. Sometimes it rose so steeply it was all but impossible to climb, but on the whole the tunnel seemed to lead down. This worried Istar; it gave her the feeling of being trapped far away from light and air. She went from worried to scared when the vibrations started to build.

"It's digging," Kassien said. "Not too close yet, but we'd better hurry. It may have forgotten about us, and then again it may not."

"It may be playing with us," Xiriel observed ominously. "They are like cats that way, are they not?"

"Shh!" Istar said, punching his arm. "I don't need to hear forecasts of doom."

The vibrations grew louder. They moved as quickly as they could, now down a long slope; Xiriel's Knowledge-light flickered and bobbed like a firefly, barely showing enough of the way to prevent them from running into a wall.

Pieces of loose stone began to flake off the ceiling. The H'ah'vah was getting closer.

Ahead, the tunnel turned a right angle into a gray suggestion of light. It became straight and smooth—almost as if it had been carved by people and not the monster that pursued them and made the mountain pulse. As they ran skidding and slipping along the main passage toward the light that was their only hope, Pallo suddenly turned to fire an arrow at the H'ah'vah.

"You stupid Pharician!" Kassien screamed. "You can't hurt it with an arrow. *Run!*"

Pallo obeyed and promptly fell down a hole.

Istar stopped. "Pallo!" she screamed, dropping to her hands and knees beside the hole.

"Istar, come *on!*" Xiriel and Kassien halted, silhouetted against the illumination coming from outside.

"Come down, Istar, you can see the—"

Kassien and Xiriel came back and started pulling on her just as the H'ah'vah appeared in the tunnel behind them. There was nowhere to go. Dragging the others with her, Istar dove into the hole.

The H'ah'vah roared by overhead, leaving smoke and an alien smell. Istar bounced off a couple of ledges and landed in a tangle of limbs with the others. Pallo's voice came up. "We can get out this way," he said. "Hurry up!"

They must have reached the edge of some cliff or other, for this passage, too, led outside. They could still hear the H'ah'vah rumbling somewhere nearby. They gathered themselves and made a final push toward the light, tripping and gasping and crashing along the twisting route and into the curtain of falling water that blocked their way.

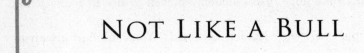

NOT LIKE A BULL

Istar had too much momentum going to stop now. She plunged through the waterfall and into a storm. It was evening and the light was dim, and while they had been underground the sky had opened to release hail, wind, and water. No one cared: they were delighted to be out from beneath the mountain. A gully surrounded them; it caught the waterfall and the runoff from the surrounding rock. There were no obvious H'ah'vah signs down here, other than the pile of small digested stones that sat in the pool of the waterfall, spilled from above. They splashed across the pool and looked back at the cliffside nervously, wondering where the monster was.

"Look!" Xiriel said, pointing to an aperture in the cliff above them. There was a square exit tunnel that gave out over a fifty-foot drop, and no real handholds. "We would have fallen down that had we kept running."

Kassien grabbed Pallo's head and ruffled his already-damp hair. "You're a weird one," he said.

"Let's find a place to camp," Istar said, adjusting her pack. The gully was long and twisting, parts of it underwater with runoff from the downpour. They picked their way down, half-blinded by rain, their boots slipping on the mud and their fingers chill from grasping at the freezing rock for balance. After an hour Istar was sure she was carrying an extra ten pounds of weight in the water that her cloak alone had soaked up. With the rain driving in her eyes, she could barely keep her gaze on the ground in front of her, yet from time to time she raised her head and looked around, seeking anything that might pass for shelter; but the whole side of the mountain seemed to be awash.

This was how she happened to see the figures come darting out from among the rocks above and leap on Kassien and Xiriel, who were in the lead. Her shout brought Xiriel's head up just in time to dodge the sword that would have parted it from his shoulders. In the next instant he had his axes out and was raining a rapid-fire series of blows on his opponent, who was caught off balance and slipped sideways in the mud. Istar glimpsed Kassien rolling down the gully, entangled with another attacker, before three more came leaping down on her with the blank faces and manic energy of the Enslaved. One fell at Istar's feet with Pallo's arrow in his throat; she gripped her sword in both hands and stepped over the body, shouting to Pallo behind her as she went. "The Sekk! Find the Sekk!"

She had no way of knowing how many more of them might be hiding in the rocks, but there were two swordsmen rushing up at her. Their faces were familiar; she was sure they were Seahawk Clan even before she had assessed their swordsmanship. All the savagery that she had expected to ignite inside her now subsided weakly. It was no use quoting back all of Pierse's injunctions about exterminating Slaves. They were her family. She could not kill them.

The flat of her blade caught the foremost across the face, but she had to lunge awkwardly to one side to avoid having her left leg sliced off, and she found herself trapped between the rocks and the tip of the second man's sword. She wove from one side to the other as he hacked at her head but caught only a flying braid; then, anticipating the stab that would be his next move when he realized her body was an easier target, she feinted, kicked him away, and slapped the sword out of his hand. It skittered across the stone; whirling, he went after it. Istar pounced on him, crushing the wind from his lungs and striking the side of his head with the hilt of her sword in hope of knocking him unconscious. But he writhed until he was on his back and she found herself grappling with him, unable to use her sword. He was far stronger.

"Kinsman," she shouted. "Listen to me! You are of the Seahawk Clan. I am your cousin. We know each other. Look! Look at my face, kinsman—"

"Istar! Istar, *don't*—"

If Kassien sounded frantic, she must be in trouble. The one she had slapped away had gotten up again, and Pallo apparently was not covering her. Kassien's boots flew past; there was a whistling sound in the air above her and she threw herself downhill, releasing her enemy and taking her chances rolling backward down the treacherous rocks. She eluded the strike from behind and came up with her sword ready, but she was too far away to act. Kassien was fighting for her, grappling with the swordsman bare-handed, and the man on the ground was crawling toward his own blade.

Where was Pallo?

She screamed his name as she scrabbled back up the hillside against a rush of water. Xiriel she could see out of the corner of her eye; he'd lost one of his axes and was still engaged with the Slave who had attacked him. There was no sign of the archer. When she got back on level with Kassien, the man she'd had on the ground was up and armed. His face was a rictus of fury.

She put her sword into the equation and was met with a hellish strength.

"Kinsman, try to fight it. You can wake up——"

She swung wildly, driving him back. Blood poured from his nose, and as the fight grew more intense she began to despair of saving his life. His sword cut across her abdomen and she leaped back with a hairsbreadth to spare. No. She couldn't measure her strokes any longer, or she'd be killed. The next time he came at her, she gripped her sword with both hands, whipped it back, and sliced his arm off at the elbow. It was a clean stroke, but the joint didn't quite sever. The arm dangled and the sword fell from lax fingers. Blood pumped out, hot in the freezing rain as it struck her face.

His face cleared, mindless anger giving way to astonishment. He slipped and sat down hard. She drew her sword back, poised to kill him.

"No. No. Don't kill me. I remember you now. You're the outbreed. Quintar's child."

Istar paused, chest heaving, rain streaming down her face. She ignored the emotional impact of being identified in such a manner, and instead ran a quick visual check of her eight directions. Xiriel had killed his opponent. Kassien's first Slave was either unconscious or dead on the hillside below. He disarmed the second and, as Istar watched, dealt him a mighty blow with the pommel of the sword he'd taken; the man crumpled. Pallo was nowhere to be seen, but the fifth Slave lay dead with his arrow in the throat.

Kassien turned and saw what had happened. "A tourniquet," he said. "Quick!"

Istar said, "You do it. And make sure Xiriel is all right. I have to find Pallo."

Before he could argue, she darted up the side of the gully toward the hiding place from which the Slaves had surprised them. Find the Sekk, she had ordered Pallo. But what if he had? Would he know what to do?

She stumbled among the rocks and splashed through puddles, her sword hand roving from side to side in a quest for opposition. Through the rush of water she could hear Pallo's voice talking to someone. She climbed between two boulders and saw them: Pallo on his feet, the bow all but forgotten in his slack hand, and the Sekk on the ground. Bleeding.

"Please don't," she heard Pallo say. "There's nothing I can do. Please."

The Sekk was golden-skinned, golden-eyed, and black-haired. It looked like a girl of about fourteen, her features yet half-formed—a mere collection of potentials. There was an arrow shaft protruding from its side. In its face was an animalian glint of fierce and uncrushable life. Its lips parted and it let out a cry. Istar knew immediately that the Sekk had Pallo. It must have forgotten about its other two Slaves, or lost control of them in the midst of their pain and its own, for all of its attention was now focused on the archer. It had not yet seen Istar, who ducked behind the rock again, breathing hard and wondering what to do.

The trick with the Sekk was neither to look in their faces, nor listen to their voices, which they could use to Enslave even without words. Pallo had made the mistake of doing both: the Sekk's cries of pain were laden with magic that played on sympathy. Istar could rush in and cut the life from the Sekk in one stroke, but Pallo might turn on her. Or he might be broken by the death of the Sekk, and then even if he pulled out of the Enslaved state as the Seahawk fighter had done, he would be forever vulnerable to all Sekk, his will crippled.

She was going to have to talk him through it. And hope.

She peered around the rock and saw Pallo jump at the sound of her voice.

"The Sekk is trying to kill you, Pallo."

"Istar? Don't come closer. I've shot her, but she's still alive. She's just a child, really."

"It's not a child, Pallo. It's a Sekk, and it's dangerous. Don't look at its face."

The Sekk emitted another cry. Istar could hear the hook in its voice that pulled Pallo in; the sound was almost sexual.

"Pallo, I need you to come back here now."

"You're going to kill her," Pallo said accusingly.

Istar ground her teeth. She was furious with him; but it would do no good to let him know this. "No, I'm not. Pallo, *you* have to kill it. You shot it. It has you trapped. *You* have to kill it."

Pallo laughed. "Are you insane? It would be like killing the sun. Being leader is going to your head. Bring Kassien over. He'll agree with me. She's *beautiful,* Istar. We can't let her die."

Now a series of escalating cries fluttered from the Sekk's mouth like a flight of birds. Istar stopped her ears.

"Leave us, Istar," Pallo said. "You don't understand."

Istar stepped out from cover. "Kill me, then."

Pallo turned to see her face; his own visage was bleary and indistinct. "What?"

"Kill me. Because if you don't kill the Sekk, I'll kill you. Unless you think you're a match for me. Here. Let's level the odds. Take my sword." She threw it at his feet, and he stared at it, uncomprehending. Slowly, he stooped and picked it up.

"Die or kill, Pallo. It's time you learned that. Come on." She got into a crouch, hands extended, body rounded to protect her midsection from the arc of the sword. Pallo looked stupefied. The Sekk was tugging at the arrow at its side, issuing a cry with every tug; and with every cry, Pallo jerked like a puppet on strings. Istar weaved from side to side, mesmerizing her opponent with her rhythm—then she feinted once and came at him. Her head rammed into his gut and she threw her shoulder against him. He staggered back, pushing at her and moving the sword around ineffectually. She stuck to him, continuing to drive forward as she tripped him. Once on the ground, they rolled over twice; he got on top, reared back, and struck at her head.

She blocked the force of the blow with a raised forearm, but the blade slid down her arm, laying the muscle open. She heard herself scream as she used the shock of pain to power her counterstrike—but Pallo was already out of range and she missed him. He was standing over her, his face no longer entranced, but horrified.

Istar clapped her hand over the bleeding cut and rolled out of sword range. She caught his eyes and willed him to stay free of the Sekk.

"Do it now, Pallo, or one of us is going to die."

Anguished, he turned, and half-blind with emotion drove the sword into the Sekk's body. It gave a last cry and slumped over, eyes wide. Pallo jerked the sword out, stared at the gore on it, and flung it away. The weapon landed in a shallow pool and slowly turned the water red. For a long moment neither of them moved to break the tableau.

"Istar? Pallo?" Kassien came leaping down from above. He saw Istar bleeding and immediately went to work. She was shaking. Her teeth chattered. After binding her arm, Kassien helped her to her feet, and she could see his mind working out what must have happened.

"Come on, Star," he said in her ear, supporting her. "Don't give out on me now. We've got two wounded Clansmen, and Pallo's a wreck. Pull yourself together."

With an effort, she managed to say, "I'm all right. It's just this rain. It's no good."

"There's a cave above," Kassien said, pointing. "They must have been using it for shelter and seen us passing."

She nodded wearily. "Get the others, then. I'll bring Pallo and meet you there."

Kassien went off. Istar gulped a few times and took a deep breath. Pallo had walked away and vomited. Now he just stood, arms slack at his sides, letting the rain pour over him. She went to him and put her arms around him, but his body was stiff and unresponsive, his face vacant.

"Come, Pallo," she said. "Come with me."

He suffered himself to be led. Istar allowed tears of pain to form in her eyes, knowing no one would see them in this rain. They climbed into the cave, which was relatively dry, and sat dumbly while Xiriel prepared heatstones to act in lieu of a fire. Her arm throbbed, but she couldn't complain: Anatar, the kinsman she'd crippled, lay curled on the floor, feverish. The other, called Pentar, had been pummeled badly by Kassien and seemed dazed.

It was Kassien who made everyone eat; Kassien who recruited Xiriel to hold Anatar down while he cut off the mangled arm and cauterized the wound with a heatstone. The others could do nothing but try to stop their ears to Anatar's screams. Kassien then sat guard by the mouth of the cave. He told the others to sleep; but although Istar was exhausted, for a long time she could not relax. She stared into the fire, feeling scarcely alive.

"Istar." Pallo spoke in a whisper; the others had fallen asleep. Even Kassien was dozing on guard. She looked toward Pallo, but his face was in shadow.

"Istar, will you teach me that charging thing you did? Like a bull, you know?"

Istar started to smile; then she sniffed affectedly. "I am not like a bull."

"Then a really vicious cow with horns."

She yawned. "The best you could aspire to would be a slightly temperamental goat."

There was a pause.

"I'll take that."

She closed her eyes at last.

"Tomorrow you practice your lunges, or else."

WOLF COUNTRY

"It took you long enough to get here," Mhani said snappishly. "Were you lost in the granary again?"

"That Ajiko will be the death of me," Hanji muttered by way of excuse. "He is such a stickler for organization. Every time something is lost or misplaced or displaced, he becomes incensed; but what does he expect? This is Jai Khalar, by the Animals!"

Mhani did not have the energy to discuss Ajiko.

"There is a strange being in the Liminal," she said. "I have Seen something of what happened to the Company in Jai Pendu. And it has disturbed me; but what disturbs me more is the sight of Ristale with a road cut by thousands of boots and hooves, yet none there to account for it." And she showed Hanji the image that appeared in the Water of Glass.

Hanji said, "What does Lerien say? Can he see this phantom army? Has he reached them yet?"

"I can't See into his Carry Eye. It's just like what happened in Wolf Country. Yet he is in Wasp Country, by my last observation."

"I doubt he is in danger, then. Even if Pharice attacks us, they could not have penetrated that land. It's across the mountains from Ristale. And if they had invaded Wolf Country, say, we'd have heard something from the people there by now. Anyway, there would be no reason to attack Wolf Country and then go back across the mountains and march down the other side! If they could have got across the mountains, they would have swept down on us across our own land."

"True," Mhani said, relieved. "For a moment I thought of the H'ah'vah tunnels that Devri saw, but you are right—Pharice could not have crossed over. Then what is the connection between the problems in Wolf Country and an army that somehow repels the Sight?"

"I don't know. The critical issue has to be communicating with Lerien. Could Pharice possess some Knowledge that interferes with the Eyes? For the Pharician army can't be truly invisible, if Tarquin saw it."

"How would they get such Knowledge?" Mhani said sharply. "Everything of Everien they have, they purchased from us."

"They purchased from Sendrigel," Hanji said. "He and Ajiko have their heads together all the time now."

Mhani, deep in thought, didn't answer.

"You're exhausted," said Hanji.

"I'm beyond sleeping now," she said. "I will return to the Liminal. Tell Devri to stand guard."

She didn't even see Hanji leave. She couldn't particularly feel her body, anyway. It wasn't hard to get back to the Liminal, to the thing that had spoken to her before—to the thing she had inhabited without understanding.

I knew oblivion for a long time. Someone must have called me; I know not who or why. I awakened in a strange land I recognized only from dreams, and now I knew things I had not known; but also I must have forgotten much, for I came up out of the hills alone and confused to find myself hunted.

They were men who hunted me, but they would not have done so had they known that I possessed a Glass. Humans are fragile, and the moment they brushed up against me they broke, one by one. They shattered on my Glass. They didn't learn from their mistakes, either. They continued to throw themselves at me. They pursued me clumsily, as if I were one of the H'ah'vah I later learned to call; they swung swords at me like enormous babies still learning to stand upright. They panted and stumbled up the hillsides, looking for me as if I were the manner of thing that lets itself be caught; I am not. I turned on the hunters and took my prey like a wave takes a struggling insect and devours it: with ease, but without intention. I was not yet fully aware: I did not know myself and I still don't.

The commander thought he was a wolf but he had come too far from his lupine origins, for his nose did not tell him I was waiting in the bracken and his ears did not register the disturbance of the scree when I shifted my weight slightly, overeager perhaps to touch and hold his soft mind. He was lean, with a long, thoughtful face and dun-colored hair, and his eyes never stopped moving—not until they alighted on mine. He had an ax in his left hand; now his right hand went for the other ax hanging from his belt. He gripped it but did not draw it.

There was a blood-soaked bandage on his left forearm; flies gathered on it. Behind him on the steep path hedged by miniature birches and fern I could hear his officers moving about, beating at the brush, looking for me. I could taste their fear on the air. Their aggression rose out of their fear and this blend fascinated me; their emotions were rich and intoxicating. The commander was in my eyes now.

You understand I hope that I wanted you, but in your absence I had to make do with the ones who offered themselves.

Taking him felt so right that I almost fainted on the moment of the Wolf commander's surrender. Now I had someone real. The Company were far away, scattered across the worlds, fighting with all the fire that had been put in them; but I had the Glass that was their essence wrought from the soul of their leader. It was my guidestar and my hope. It was my sword my food my love my dream. I used it to capture the Wolf commander and he looked at the blank space where my Sight should have been and freely gave me the Eye he was carrying; I crushed it in my fist and it died. I do not wish to be Seen. I do not wish to be Known. Instead I used his mind to look out of.

When I inhabited your commander I read his weaknesses, and I knew that the Glass could teach me how to move him and all his men, too. For it had the power to capture and bind, and I wished to hide among their numbers and move with their motion while I tried to discover what manner of thing I am this time.

"Bring me your people," I said through the Glass, "and I will attach them to myself."

He did not understand but he had been taught to obey anyone who assumes power over him. He obeyed me, and I took all his army in one swallow, and then I moved them about as if I had grown new limbs. It was easy, for they were accustomed to letting go of their free will and delivering themselves to a leader; and I had the Glass, which acted on them like an elixir of loyalty.

It is the Glass that is a thing of beauty. The Glass we made, you and I, out of the substance of the fight. When I held it, from far away I could smell the smoke and the blood; I could hear the horses screaming. Deep inside the Glass was the devotion of the body that every warrior knows, the offering of the fibers and fluids and electric motion, the flinging of the self onto the turbulence of chance. The ribs heaved and the fingers gripped steel with a conviction that is stronger than any love. The warrior had become the weapon and his heart swelled to bursting.

I called them and they came because they thought I was you.

You. That single syllable, pregnant with worlds and time.

I remember the last time we were together, how my fingers tangled in your hair; how the sun came singing through the long window. It was not a time of battle then. It was a time of meeting and recognition and the sharing of thoughts we could only tell each other. Some of these thoughts we had been saving for years and years, finding no one who could understand. Some of these thoughts we had spent ourselves in trying and failing to communicate, so that now we hesitated to offer them, expecting to be rejected, or misunderstood. We had believed ourselves alone under empty skies until at last we stumbled on each other, and remembered.

Quintar. Tarquin. How many other names I have called you by.

You will not know me this time. How will I make myself accept this? All that I am was made that way by you; yet you will think me your foe. It is not my fault to be what I am. Once I was something else and so were you, but you don't know it. If I could breathe the memory into you and raise you from drowning I would. As it is I can't even touch you.

The White Road is my only hope of salvation. You must take me to it, take me past its guardians—you must come with me. Home.

"Mhani?"

She didn't rebuke Devri this time, for she had begun to feel herself slipping out of control and she was glad to be recalled to the Eye Tower and her own body, weary as it was.

"What is it now?"

"The riders have come back from Wolf Country. It looks like treachery."

"What do you mean?" With an effort she focused her eyes on Devri's face. She was only listening as a formality. She could guess what he was going to say.

"It seems by all accounts that the various separate commanders have joined their armies together and gone up into the hills. Anyone who opposed them was killed."

"Is Pharice involved?"

"We don't know. That's why Ajiko wants to talk to you."

"Absolutely not. My utmost priority is to reach the king. Ajiko will have to wait. I am faced with many problems."

Devri had begun to sweat. "I was afraid you'd say that. Mhani, you've been up here a long time without relief. Please, won't you—"

She silenced him with a sharp gesture.

"If you want to be useful, help me See into Kivi's Carry Eye."

Devri said, "All right—but you must eat the food I've brought, and stand up. Move about. Do you have any idea what day it is? What time it is?"

"No. What time is it?"

Devri had lowered himself to the stone lip of the Water; now he gave a sheepish smile. "Actually, the clocks are running at so many different speeds it's hard to say for certain—but I can hear your stomach growling from here."

Mhani drank some mead and broke her bread into small pieces, chewing with an unfamiliar feeling. As Devri gazed into the Water and began to arrange the confusion of images, she closed her eyes for a moment and tried to remember how it had felt to *be* someone else—some*thing* else. She shivered.

"Here we go! I've got an image in Kivi's Carry Eye."

Mhani stood and walked stiffly to his side. "Show me."

Devri focused the image for her. It was the Company, riding on the White Road.

"Let me have control of that." She took the image away from Devri and began checking the other Eyes. Some were dark—destroyed, she now knew, by Night. Of the others, one by one they were all filling with the same vision.

"What does it mean?" Devri whispered. Mhani's reply was a murmur, which she wasn't really directing at him.

"If I say I seek the way to Jai Pendu for the purposes of my king and myself, is that true? Or am I really a pawn of Night? It is stronger than I am and all my Eyes are full of it. Night also seeks the White Road—if I find it, how can I prevent Night from using it?"

"Who is Night?" queried Devri.

"That's what I'd like to know," Mhani said. "Go back downstairs and stand guard until I send for you."

CHYKO'S IDEA OF FUN

Lerien had been counting on obtaining mountain horses in the Wolf hamlet of A-vel-Jasse, which was the highest settlement of any size in these parts; no one lived among the peaks that separated Everien from Pharice. But when they arrived, the place was deserted. There were no animals and virtually no goods left behind; nor were there signs of violence. Apparently the inhabitants had simply picked up and moved away.

"Tarquin, did these people tell you they intended to leave? It's scarcely a week since you were here."

"I didn't come this way," Tarquin answered. "I was on foot, and I cut down a watercourse two days' ride north of here."

Stavel had been walking through the empty houses. He said, "The Wolves who lived here are long gone. No one has been here for many weeks."

Lerien looked up at the mountains. "These horses will never make it up the mountain paths. We will not be able to climb to the monitor tower from here."

"We have to," Tarquin said. "If the Pharician army is moving on schedule, they are only twenty or thirty miles away across the mountains, marching down the border toward the sea gates. If we continue into Wolf Country before crossing the range, we will end up far behind them once we finally reach the other side."

"By all accounts our troops are still placed somewhere in Wolf Country, whatever the Eyes may say. Dario's is the second report we have had of Sekk amongst the army there—remember Epse and his tale of mutiny? The H'ah'vah are associated with the Sekk, and Mhani saw H'ah'vah tunnels in Wolf Country. Soldiers are finding eggs. . . . It is all very strange, and meanwhile Kivi cannot reach Mhani with the Carry Eye. I have a dilemma. Shall I climb the heights to get a view of Ristale and hope the Eye in the monitor tower can link me to Mhani, or shall I use that time to go directly to Wolf Country and round up the troops?"

"No one knows where the troops are," Jakse said quietly.

"Jai Khalar will be a Pharician outpost when you get back from Wolf Country," Tarquin said, shrugging. "You would have been better off had you stayed at Jai Khalar and prepared for a siege."

"I didn't ask for your opinion," Lerien said angrily. Tarquin suspected they were both remembering Lerien's failed attempt to join the Company.

"You were lucky that day Vorse beat you," Tarquin said. "You lived."

Lerien's face darkened. "Is that luck? I didn't ask for responsibility over Everien, and when I try to do anything I find my hands are tied by the Seers or the clerks. . . . Maybe it would have been better if I had died in a battle for something great."

Tarquin laughed. "Forget it. You should be grateful for what you have. I have never had a day's peace in eighteen years; I cannot keep a woman, or land. I have seen and done terrible things. If I do not find a reason to hurl myself at death, neither should you."

In a mocking tone Lerien said, "Even now you outdo me; nothing I have is as much as yours, is it? No one has ever suffered as you suffer. Or so you *say*."

Tarquin's sword came out at these last words. "Explain yourself! What do you accuse me of?"

Stavel and Ketar grabbed his arms from behind and he shook them off in a rage.

"Quintar always had a hair-trigger temper, didn't he?" Stavel remarked. "Some things never change."

"If Ysse found no fault with your conduct at Jai Pendu, then neither do I," Lerien said to Tarquin. "Miro will stay to guard the horses. We will climb to the monitor tower"—he pointed—"on foot, and I will consult with Mhani, irrespective of whether we see your Pharician army. Let us waste no more time guessing."

Tarquin put his sword away and directed a cold smile at Lerien. "Good," he said, and set off uphill at a pace fueled by anger.

By the time the others had caught up with him, climbing off-road through near-vertical fields toward the bare rock, Tarquin's fury had subsided to a vague annoyance that he had done everything he could to help Lerien and his people, but Lerien was a fool who never should have been made king. He was beginning to suspect all Lerien's armies had simply dissolved under poor leadership; he certainly felt like taking off on his own.

Ketar was the first to catch up with him, and he tried to commiserate with Tarquin over Lerien's indecisiveness, but Tarquin told him to shut up and eventually Ketar moved off ahead, quailed. The others didn't speak to each other. There was something about being on foot and confronted by a mountain that made everyone concentrate. Tarquin told himself he didn't have to compete with these green youths; gradually he fell behind the rest, until he found himself panting and sweating beside Stavel. Glancing uphill, he could see Taro's muscular legs moving like pistons, eating up the ground.

"If my grandson could see me now," Stavel gasped, "he'd laugh himself sick."

"Wait until the mountain fever hits them," Tarquin said knowingly. "Tomorrow half of them will be faint and won't be able to eat. You'll see."

Stavel cast him a grateful look.

"Ajiko broke his leg about two miles south of here," Tarquin remarked. "I haven't been back to these parts since then."

"I remember he had to stay behind when the Company took the White Road." Stavel glanced up at Lerien and Tarquin guessed he was also recalling how Vorse had defeated Lerien over Ajiko's place. "Ajiko told us how he fell down a chasm when fighting Freeze Wasps."

"That's not precisely how it happened," Tarquin said, laughing.

"Oh?"

"Ajiko broke his arm in a fall when we were training up here. It was a clumsy accident. While we were stopped, splinting Ajiko's injury, Riesel spotted a Freeze Wasp drifting on the wind. It probably wouldn't have attacked us, but Chyko was bored of waiting and he decided to go after their nest."

Tarquin hadn't thought about that incident in years. Now that he was in the same hills where it had occurred, it came back to him as if it happened yesterday: Chyko jauntily picking himself up, licking a finger and holding it to the wind before setting off among the rocks without so much as a by-your-leave. Tarquin remembered summoning the Wasp back, annoyed that one member of the Company was already injured and another behaving like a child.

"This is a training maneuver," he said sternly. "Chyko. Come back."

Chyko's backside wriggled suggestively as he climbed up the frozen watercourse.

"This is not a game, Chyko, you foul bastard," Quintar screamed. "You're a member of this Company. You can't just go off. . . ."

Chyko slipped into a crack in the rock and was lost from sight.

Lyetar was at his shoulder. "The Freeze Wasps are not pretty creatures. I saw one suck out a man's insides and leave only the clothes and hair behind. They have poisons that can melt your bones."

"Bastard!" said Quintar again.

"We should help him," Lyetar said. "He'll get himself killed."

"We are not helping him. Don't even think about it. Let him die! I'll dance on his grave, the bastard."

Yet the words were scarcely out of his mouth before Quintar was pelting up the incline after Chyko. The others fell in behind him almost silently, moving like fluid traveling paradoxically uphill. Scarcely a stone was disturbed as they climbed, and their dark cloaks looked like patches of exposed stone among the snow. Chyko had disappeared into a narrow aperture between two huge blocks of stone. Quintar did not like the look of it.

"He's dreaming," Lyetar murmured, "if he thinks he's going to shoot a Freeze Wasp. It's like putting an arrow through a snowflake."

"If the Wasps don't kill him," Quintar said, "I will. Cover yourselves up."

He squeezed into the crack, pulling himself along by judicious movements of fingertips and feet.

"Freeze Wasps love to hide in places like this," Lyetar remarked. "They wait in a half-frozen state until something with heat comes along and arouses them, and then they strike."

"Maybe Chyko will be all right, then," Quintar said. "His blood's too cold to wake them."

"Mine isn't," Lyetar panted, behind him. "I think I'm going to shit myself."

"Shut up. I'm not scared yet and I don't need you ruining my concentration."

The crack ended in a shaft whose walls were almost sheer. Above could be seen a scrap of sky.

"Chyko? Chyko?"

They could hear the wind above. Quintar turned to his cousin and said, "How best to fight them? How big are they?"

"About the size of a bat, I guess," Lyetar replied. "But they're . . . full of holes. They look like flying spiderwebs."

"Can you burn them?"

"Yes but—"

"Good. Give me some oil and send Ovi up here."

The Deer slid past Lyetar, his dark eyes fiery and keen. Ovi was the

only Deer in the entire Company. In general, Quintar found the Deer
Clan too intellectual, too soft, to produce the kind of fighters he needed.
Ovi, as if to make up for the lack in the rest of his family, was one of the
most savage warriors Quintar had ever seen. He could cut with the sword
as well as any Seahawk save Quintar himself and Lyetar, and he could
wreak havoc given a simple pole or pair of sticks of any size or weight.

"You want to fight a Freeze Wasp, Ovi?" Quintar asked, knowing
already how the Deer would react. "Put oil on your sticks. Lyetar, light a
torch. When you see the Wasps, set Ovi's sticks alight. But only at the
ends!"

Ovi said, "Just pour the oil on and I will spark it myself when I hit
Chyko over the head."

Quintar laughed. "Use a torch. Come, it's not a game."

Ovi climbed the shaft, Quintar and Lyetar on his heels. Ovi stuck his
head out the top and looked around. "Mother of Ysse," he hissed, ducking. "I think Chyko's done for."

Quintar pushed past him and looked for himself. "Give me the torch,"
he said grimly.

Chyko had finally met his match. Standing on an uneven ledge surrounded by vertical rock rising above him on three sides, he was motionless, unblinking, hand half-raised to ward off the enemy that must have
come flying out from among the rocks. There were no fewer than six
Freeze Wasps sticking to his back, his shoulders, and his head. They
looked like white mantises draped with such lace as was used on the
swaddling clothes of baby girls.

"You idiot," Quintar muttered. "You don't know when to stop." He
raised his voice. "Give me the torch, damn it. Will they suck out his
insides? Is he done for?"

"Their poisons melt you and then they feed off what's left. We could
try burning them, though. Maybe it's not too late." Lyetar sounded
doubtful. "I've seen people who survived. They're usually blind and deaf
and mad, and sometimes they can't walk."

"Give me the—" Turning, he seized the torch from Lyetar.

"We don't have many options," Ovi said. "The place where he's
standing is too narrow. There isn't enough room for all of us to stand,
never mind fight."

"Agreed," said Quintar. "Let's kill them anyway."

He flicked the torch at Ovi's stick; he heard it go *whoof* as it lit behind
him while he dragged himself out of the hole. Drawing his sword, he
advanced on Chyko.

"Captain!" Lyetar cried. "On your left!"

Quintar wheeled, ducked, whipping the torch past the place where his own head had just been. He glimpsed the Freeze Wasp as it slipped past him like a rag of smoke and spun again.

"There are three," Riesel yelled from the shaft. "Get under cover!"

Ovi was on the ledge; his sticks were slicing up the air, smoking and trailing fire. One Wasp was caught; it drifted gray and sizzling on the wind before it exploded to ash. Riesel cheered and thrust another lit torch out of the shaft, but just then several more Wasps materialized from cracks in the rocks. One of the ones on Chyko fell away from him, bloated and sluggish. It landed on the snow and sat there, now huge and bright red with Chyko's blood.

High on fear, Quintar ducked and dodged, never stopping, using the sword and the torch in a protective arc around himself. He was hard-pressed just to stay unmarked, and by the time he could get a moment to order a retreat, more Freeze Wasps had landed on Chyko. Ovi killed two others.

"Get back!" Quintar shouted. Lyetar obeyed instantly, hurling himself into the shaft, but Ovi wasn't listening. Quintar didn't have time to be angry at this dangerous disobedience; he was being pursued by four Freeze Wasps. He thrust the torch into a crevice ahead of him to burn out what seemed a whole nest; then he hid inside and put the torch in front of himself as a barrier.

"Ovi, it's not worth dying for," he called. "Get back *now*."

Ovi's back was toward Quintar as he advanced on Chyko, apparently intending some sort of brave but stupid rescue. He swatted away one of the preying Wasps with a stick and suddenly froze in place himself. There was no movement but that of the flames burning on the sticks in his hands.

Quintar began cursing, devastated. He didn't see a Wasp on Ovi, yet the Deer simply didn't move.

Chyko did.

Quintar gave a shout as Chyko advanced threateningly on Ovi, and as if the sound had broken a spell, Ovi suddenly screamed and fled from Chyko, diving for the shaft where the others waited. Chyko, looking a monstrosity still covered with Freeze Wasps, followed.

When he saw Chyko's behavior, all Quintar could think of was Sekk Slaving, and forgetting the danger of the Wasps he abandoned his hidey-hole and swung his sword at Chyko, who looked surprised and distressed.

"Cut it out!" Chyko said, slipping the blow. "Get under cover before the Wasps catch you."

Stunned but pleased, Quintar retreated to the cleft. In a matter-of-fact tone, Chyko said, "In a little while they'll figure out I don't taste good and then they'll leave us, but in the meantime we can collect lots of Freeze."

"What are you talking about?" Quintar asked sharply. "Why aren't you dead?"

"Don't sound so disappointed, Captain," Chyko laughed. "Don't forget, I'm a Wasp, too. I took a poison that interacts with their Freeze in my bloodstream. It Freezes back on them without affecting me. See?" He pointed to an already gorged Wasp lying on the ground. It didn't move. While Quintar watched, another bit Chyko and promptly fell out of the sky.

"Freeze is good poison," Chyko said. "It doesn't actually freeze you, of course; it just Freezes your perception of time so you can't move or think. You drop right out of time, and that's how they catch you. Then they inject their acids." He shook off the remainder of the Wasps, which drifted across the snow like paper. "Anyway, I think it's safe now. They're very intelligent, and the nest has decided that I'm not a very good choice of food. Stay there and I'll collect as much Freeze as I can."

"So there is a method to your madness," Quintar said.

"Not really. But it's a fun diversion from all that walking, don't you think?"

TO THE MONITOR TOWER

Tarquin paused for a moment, light-headed from talking and climbing together. Stavel, unused to the thin air, wheezed as he laughed. Tarquin noticed that his fair skin was beginning to redden.

"I still keep a vial of Chyko's Freeze," Tarquin said, fingering the thong around his neck. "I've never had the nerve to use it. As I get older, though, I think about it. Maybe it would be good to have a rest for a time. Just not be anywhere. Let a few years go by and not be there."

Stavel said, "The years run downhill, don't they? And we walk uphill." He mopped his brow.

Later they camped on a green shelf surrounded by snow, and even the sky was tilted. The mountains spliced each other's planes, changing angles capriciously so that the only way to find out the true vertical was to plant your feet and stand as straight as you could. Ristale could be glimpsed golden and serene through gaps in the rock; the ancestral home of the Deer Clan was a vast riverain flatland, bitterly cold in winter and lush in summer. It was a sparsely inhabited region of the Pharician Empire, visited only by the nomadic tribesmen who grazed their herds in the summer pastures and spent winters near the border towns of the Pharician homeland in the south. The people of Ristale were not bred of Pharician blood, and through the centuries of Imperialist policy, they had maintained an autonomous culture; but they submitted to the army that was based in a garrison on the edge of the forests to the west, overshadowed by the cliffs of the Everien Range. This garrison was the closest thing to a city in all Ristale, and it had been the focus of much of Lerien's conversation as they climbed.

"Any Pharician army in this region would have passed through that garrison by necessity. I suppose if they were planning a sneak attack on us, then they could gradually increase their numbers within the garrison without our noticing any large movements on the plain. But they might as easily have sailed to the edge of the sea plateau if they intended to rush through the gates of Everien. Coming down this side of the range wouldn't be a very smart policy."

"And they must know we have an Eye mounted at A-vel-Jasse," Taro said. "What would make them think they could sneak up on us?"

"Maybe they don't believe in the Eyes any more than I do," Ketar put in.

"That doesn't make sense. The whole thing is strange, don't you think, my lord?"

Lerien's head was down as he concentrated on climbing. "Sendrigel," he said cryptically. After that he fell silent, and in their camp that night he was an inconspicuous presence. He had ceased to ask Kivi about the Eye, but Kivi was seen peering into it from time to time and pacing, frustrated, back and forth across the ledge. At last he came and sat down where the others were finishing their evening meal.

"I'm too tired to concentrate," he said. "Every bit of my body is screaming at me."

"Eat something," Taro urged, but Kivi shook his head.

"I feel queasy."

Tarquin rummaged in his pack and came out with a packet of white powder. "Put some of this on your tongue and let it dissolve. The mountain people of the Wolf Clan use it when the mountain sickness troubles them. It comes from a plant that they claim has great magic, but this powder is difficult to make and requires much art."

"I thought the mountain people were like animals, having no speech or culture," Ketar said, surprised. Stavel growled low in his throat, and Ketar added, "Of course, I have only ever encountered them as Slaves. They fought savagely."

"They have a speech, of a kind, though they use it only at need, and not merely to hear themselves talk. I found this agreeable." Tarquin was aware of the eager attention now focused on him. He was tired of being a legend and a mystery to these men, so he added, "Eighteen years ago, when I left Jai Khalar, I meant never to return. I traveled in many lands. I sailed with the Dzellau and guarded the desert trains between Kolv and Pharice. I spent a year in an oasis far to the west of Pharice, before I grew bored with the sedentary life. I even went to the islands, looking for my distant relatives in the Seahawk people. Everywhere I went, the sky was big and the people were strangers. Nowhere did I find the Seahawk customs or language I had known all my life. They say the Snakes and the Seahawks and the Wasps came from far away before they settled in Ever-ien, but except for the wild folk in remote Wolf Country, I saw nothing that reminded me of the Clans."

"You must have grown lonely for home," Taro said.

Tarquin looked at the ground. "No."

"Even you must sometimes wish for a resting place," Ketar said softly. "Every warrior does."

Tarquin shook his head. "No. You're not seeking a resting place. You're seeking motion. You don't want to stop. You don't want it to be over."

"You *are* mad, then," Taro muttered.

"Am I? But how else could you do it? How else could you fight? You need this appetite. You have to want everything, you have to imagine how it tastes and know it even before you've tasted it, and when it's denied you, you have to go away and think how to get it. You have to sleep in readiness. You're a hunter. You want the big game, you want the thing that would routinely eat you but now you're going to have *it*. Kivi, the warrior spirit is an appetite, it's a way of life; I don't know how else to put it to you. But I think I have lost mine, or it is faded. My heart is not in this. My heart was in my Company, and without them I'm half a man."

There was a silence. Dismayed by the intensity of his own outburst, Tarquin stirred and gave a deliberate yawn. Lerien remained silent.

"I remember," Stavel said, "when there was joy in a clean battle. When there was pride in weapons."

"There still is," Ketar replied. "There will always be pride in destroy-ing Sekk."

"And what of our Clan brothers who are Enslaved, like those who destroyed that Wasp village?" Jakse challenged. "Is there pride in cutting them down?"

"You have seen what they do," Taro interjected. "The Enslaved are worse than criminals. To kill them is to save them from themselves."

"Maybe. But I can't take any pleasure in that kind of killing."

"Killing isn't about pleasure," Taro retorted.

"Sometimes it is," Lerien allowed, and everyone looked at him in surprise.

"Sometimes? I didn't know there were different kinds of killing."

"Kill enough," Tarquin said, "and you will become a connoisseur of all the varieties."

There was another silence. Kivi said, "Can't we talk of something more cheerful? I won't be able to sleep with all these tales of the Sekk."

"Hanji told me that in the old days, the Everiens made houses that the light could shine through, and the walls would change color depending on the color of the sky." Jakse pointed to the horizon, where the sun was fighting to stay aloft. "Right now, the houses would be rose-colored, and golden like the sky. And the walls would hold the light of the daytime and radiate at night, so that the Everiens could study the Knowledge at any time. They needed no lamps or fires, and maybe they didn't even sleep."

At the word "sleep" two or three of them yawned in succession.

"They made great statues of metal in the Fire Houses," Jakse went on, his voice dropping in pitch to a soothing baritone. "And they wove metal into their fabrics with some lost art, all for their pleasure. They opened the hills and brought forth jewels from places none now dare go. No one had to work like an ox in the fields all day. Some did nothing but make music, and turned their hands to no harder occupation."

"Like the court drummers of Pharice," Taro put in softly. Stavel's eyes were closed.

"Yes, like them. But the music of the Everiens was of a different type. They played instruments we have never mastered, although some of them turn up from time to time in Jai Khalar. You can hear the music there sometimes, if you're lucky. It is bewitching and strange."

Ketar began to snore lightly.

"And the women?"

"Ah," said Jakse. He smiled and the light flickered on his bald head. "The women often danced. Not for courtship, you understand—not with discipline. Just for the joy of it. Their backs weren't bent with toil, and their children almost always lived to grow up, so they were happy."

"Mmm."

Silence settled over them. Jakse drew breath to continue and then realized he was the only one awake. He sighed, stretched, and stood. His long shadow rippled across the sleeping forms like a melted blade as the sun finally went down.

IN THE MORNING they began the last leg of the climb, which would take them sideways and then straight up a shaft to the entrance of the monitor tower. Typical of Everien buildings, the tower appeared to be a natural outcropping in the stone, completely indistinguishable from the mountain itself from Ristale in the west; on this side, a series of regular windows punctuating the eastern wall made it visible to the travelers.

The king still said nothing, and following his example, the others slipped into a nervous silence. Even as they broke their fast, they didn't speak to each other except out of necessity. All were intent on reaching the monitor tower, and scarce air didn't allow for much speech anyway. By midmorning they were climbing more with their arms than with their legs, and Stavel was coughing as he struggled up a steep slab of tilted rock. Tarquin extended a supporting hand toward him and *found himself standing in a room looking at a window into another room.*

Through the window he could see a Sekk. It was male in appearance, and it had silver hair, papery skin, and eyes so blue they were almost violet. It was staring at him. He drew back from the window, and it drew back. He reached for his sword but had none, so he put his hands out defensively. The Sekk did the same. Tarquin's fingers brushed against the glass of the window.

It was not a window. It was a mirror. He screamed.

"He's coming around," Stavel said gruffly. "Step back. Give him air."

Tarquin opened his eyes to the concerned face of Taro, who was crouched on the rock beside him. The back of his head hurt. When he touched it, his fingers came away bloody. He got up shakily.

"It could be the mountain sickness," Taro said solicitously. "Do you feel dizzy?"

"I'm fine. I must have lost my footing, that's all."

Kivi was slithering down the stone toward them, face flushed, eyes bright with curiosity.

"That's right," Stavel said quickly. "I saw him fall. He caught a loose piece of shale and lost his balance."

Taro nodded, accepting the lie. "Could have happened to any of us."

But he hung back and walked beside Stavel and Tarquin for a spell. Stavel shot Tarquin a few sidelong glances that seemed intended to convey encouragement; yet he said nothing.

Kivi was not so shy. He waited until Stavel stopped to relieve himself, and then accosted Tarquin. "Tarquin, what are these fits of yours? Is it the old madness? Are you having Impressions? If you tell me, perhaps I can help you."

"I don't know," he sighed. "Kivi, you must not ask me questions."

Kivi's face was drawn with concern. "*You* would tell me not to trust you. You would ask to be treated as dangerous. You do not look well, Tarquin. Were you ever Enslaved?"

"No!" He collected himself. "I think it is because . . . it is because Jai Pendu draws near. Like when we saw those sailsnakes miles from where they belong. Like Jai Khalar being more illogical than usual. It is all related."

"Perhaps that's what is wrong with the Water of Glass," Kivi said. "It weighs on my mind, how I cannot See Mhani. I cannot See anything of use! This has never happened before. It leaves us too vulnerable."

"Better that you should learn to do without these things," Tarquin assured him. Stavel had caught up with them and now slowly went past, head down, pretending not to hear their private conversation.

"It is all very well to disdain the Water of Glass and sharpen your blade," retorted Kivi, "but you cannot pretend that the Knowledge does not exist, or that Jai Pendu isn't coming."

"Oh, I know it's coming! That doesn't mean I will surrender to its dreams."

"Dreams?"

Stavel was above them, laboring hard. Tarquin slowed, letting Stavel gain more distance and catching his own breath. He lowered his voice. "Sometimes it's as though I never left Jai Pendu. Sometimes it's as though there is a world behind the world, and if you rubbed hard enough you could see what's underneath. I don't want to see beneath this world, Kivi. This land, my sword, my bones and blood—would that they were true. Could not a glass of wine be only that, a flame only a flame. But to me they . . . they . . . oh, I have been mad for years and I can see it in your eyes, you shrink away."

"I do not!"

"Well, you should. Chyko would never have fallen for a word of my nonsense. Give me some water, will you?"

Kivi was only too willing to rest. He lowered himself to a shelf and rubbed his legs. He took out the Carry Eye, checked it again, and put it away. Tarquin drank his water and kept climbing, leaving the Seer behind. Above he could see Taro and Lerien pull themselves up a chimney in the rock and disappear from view. One by one the others followed. Tarquin glanced down and saw Kivi shoulder his pack and resume climbing. Stavel vanished in the chimney above. Kivi passed beneath an overhang. Tarquin was alone. He reached the bottom of the chimney and braced his back into position with his legs. He felt for handholds, balancing one part of his body against the other. Methodically he drew himself up the crack. Nothing stirred. He waited.

A shower of small stones tumbled down from above.

Ketar's voice, breaking pitch as he shouted down the chimney.

"Quintar! Quintar! Quintar!"

He stiffened.

"There are twenty thousand men on the plain. Quintar! It's just as you said! *Quintar.*"

He shut his eyes.

"My name is Tarquin," he said softly.

THE PHARICIAN ARMY

"Twenty thousand is a guess," Ketar admitted when Tarquin finally reached the top of the shaft. "It is still some miles away, but displaces a great cloud of dust."

"I know what it looks like," Tarquin said shortly, and heaved himself onto the roof of the monitor tower, which was made of moss-grown metal that made a hollow sound when they walked on it. The greenery had been cleared away from a double trapdoor, which Taro and Ketar heaved open to reveal a flight of stairs descending into the mountain. Strips of lightstone lined the walls, which were smooth and dark red.

They found a sunlit room looking out across the plain; a brisk wind blew in from the northwest. There was an Eye resting within a metal net suspended from the ceiling. Kivi approached it curiously. "It's active," he murmured, touching it.

The others fidgeted, their arms and equipment rattling. Ketar crossed to the window and gazed out on the view of the approaching army beneath, fascinated. Lerien said, "Wait for us on the stairs. Kivi and I will join you when we are finished."

Tarquin stood aside to let the others leave. Lerien ignored his presence, so he folded his arms across his chest and leaned against the wall while Kivi focused his attention on the Eye.

"This is the Eye that we would look through from Jai Khalar to See what is happening down below. The Water of Glass connects it to the Eye Tower there. Now, when Tarquin arrived and Mhani looked into the Eye, she would have been using one of the monitor towers further north, on the border of Wolf Country and Ristale. If those towers were to blame, then this tower should show us an accurate picture of that army down there."

"And does it?" asked Lerien, stepping closer to the suspended Eye.

"There's the plain below," Kivi said.

"Nothing. Not one fucking soldier." Lerien spun away, slamming into the wall with his shoulder as if tackling an enemy. "What about Mhani?"

Kivi said, "It's filthy."

"What's filthy?"

"The Eye. There are a hundred signals at least passing through it. Maybe more."

Lerien frowned. "I don't understand what you are on about."

"To get a clear vision, the Eye has to be kept clean, focused on the here and now—directed according to the will of the Seer. Like, imagine the Water of Glass became muddy and weed-grown. You wouldn't be able to see anything, would you?"

"But you just showed me a vision of the plain, and it was clear enough. Wrong, but clear."

"It's not a true vision. Someone is projecting it here. This Eye's being interfered with. I can't see out. Look! Here, look at my Carry Eye. It is the same way. It's like trying to look into a storm."

Lerien glanced at the sphere and backed away, blinking and rubbing his eyes. "Damned magic," he muttered. "There is always some excuse lately, isn't there, Kivi? You've got to get this Eye working. We can't afford to be out of communication with Mhani."

Tarquin left them fussing. He could tell by the look on Kivi's face that the Seer had no hope of reversing whatever was interfering with the function of the Eyes, and it was embarrassing to watch Lerien pace around the room in frustration over Knowledge he didn't begin to touch, much less grasp or use.

The others were waiting expectantly at the top of the stairs.

"They cannot use the Eye to any effect," he said, preempting their questions. "Lerien will have us go down and get a closer look at the army. He will need to determine whether they serve Hezene or are a rebel faction. If they are a rebel faction, I expect he hopes for aid from Hezene his friend." He took out his sword and began polishing it without looking at anyone.

They shuffled and murmured among themselves. Then Ketar said, "We would that you should lead us now."

"What?"

"Lerien was wrong," said Ketar. "He didn't believe this army was real. He can do nothing without consulting his Seer-glass, and now he will have us try to infiltrate an army that could crush us as easily as drawing a breath. Tarquin, did you return to take orders? You declared yourself Free, but you were Ysse's favorite. Everien is in your hands. Tell us what to do and we will be yours."

Still Tarquin said nothing. The others all looked at him expectantly.

"We don't care if you're half-mad," Stavel said bluntly. "It was so with many warriors of legend. Tarquin, do not fail us!"

Tarquin resisted the urge to laugh and sighed heavily instead. "I cannot."

Ketar looked shocked—offended, even. "What cowardice is this? How can you have changed so?"

"I am Free. I am my own master only. You must look elsewhere if you want a ruler."

"Rubbish!" said Ketar. "You led the twelve greatest warriors in Everien."

"I led them to their doom," Tarquin said. "Often I have asked myself, did I make them too savage; did I destroy their natural caution? For an animal will fight without thought and without reserve; but men are not animals, and my Company were fighting for the purpose set to them by Ysse and me, not for their own need to hunt and defend their territory. Did I make them into something too extreme? Did I push them too far?"

"But last night you said that was the warrior spirit—"

"And this morning you have told me I am mad. What are any of you thinking, asking me to depose Lerien?"

"If not you, then who?"

Tarquin shook his head, scowling at Ketar. "I'm through playing nursemaid to warriors. It is for you to determine your own actions; it is not for me to bring something out of you."

"But you are a natural leader. To refuse to use your gift . . ."

"Is what? Irresponsible? I became Free so that I need never face such a situation again. I am outside your Clan politics and your ethics. You must not see me as Quintar. He was destroyed long ago."

He knew he sounded commanding; it was ironic, but because he spoke in such a tone, they would have no choice but to accept his rationale. He could not help sounding like a leader.

"Then why do you travel with us?" asked Taro quietly. "Why did you come to warn us, and why do you help us now?"

"I have my reasons," Tarquin said, trying not to let his tone falter. "That is the point: they are *my* reasons. Do not look to me to save you! You will be disappointed."

He shrugged past them and walked away. Behind their backs, the king was ascending the stairs with Kivi; he had overheard these last remarks. Lerien drew his sword and said, "Shall we settle it with weapons? Ketar, you are mistaken if you think me effete. Come test me."

Ketar, seeing his plans dissolving, began backpedaling. He looked down, stammering apologetic refusals.

"I *would* kill you, Ketar, had I more men. You are nothing more than a wide-eyed boy. You would be better served to shut your mouth and do as you are told. Why Ajiko thinks you are officer material is beyond me. I wouldn't trust you with my horse after this."

Ketar fell on his knees. "Forgive me, my lord. Let me redeem myself."

"Redemption would be premature. I could care less what you do, Ketar. Follow instructions and not another word out of you. Kivi!"

The Seer had begun to edge toward Tarquin. He turned in response to Lerien's questions.

"Can we descend to the plain inside the tower? Where are the stairs? I don't wish to be seen by the Pharicians."

The others stirred and made helpful noises, acting a little guilty but relieved that Lerien had taken firm control. Kivi went to search the rest of the tower. Lerien repeated his intentions before the others.

"We will meet at the base of the next monitor tower, twenty miles south of here. Taro, you know where it is, and Kivi has Seen it with the Eye here, so we should all be able to find it. I want information," he concluded. "Ideally, we should try to capture an officer for questioning; but I will settle for knowing whether or not this group represents Hezene or some dissident faction hidden in his government. Pair off and be stealthy, whatever you do! This is no time for heroics."

No one looked as if he were even thinking of being heroic against such an enemy. Lerien nodded an invitation to Tarquin, and the two descended ahead of the others.

It was a long climb, and their aching legs rebelled at taking their weight on the way down. Tarquin was thinking how any fighting that might occur at the bottom would have to be concluded quickly, or he wouldn't be able to stand up. By the time they had descended, the army was marching past the monitor tower, parallel to the cliffs, at a distance of about a mile. The ground right under the cliffs might have appeared flat from above, but actually it undulated and sported many small streams draining from the mountains. The Pharician army marched on flatter land, but there was little cover, and Tarquin and Lerien could not afford to walk straight across the plain toward the army: they would be picked up by scouts in no time. Instead, they made their way parallel to the moving men, using ditches, high grass, and brush for cover; Kivi and

Ketar split off toward the north and the rear of the force; and Taro, Jakse, and Stavel made a dash to try to catch up with the vanguard, which was composed of the cavalry and a number of chariots.

"There will be outriders," Lerien assured Tarquin. "They have scouts constantly searching the ground ahead and fanning out to either side. So long as we can keep pace, we will encounter riders sooner or later, and then we can make our attack."

"We need to get closer as long as there's good cover," Tarquin said. "We might learn much without ever engaging them at arms, if only we could see!"

They crept through the long grass at an angle to the line of march, periodically glimpsing the formation of the soldiers. Tarquin's eyes were not so sharp as they had been in youth, but even from this distance he could see that the army was not as well trained as he'd first believed. Occasionally he would see a mounted Pharician officer with curving sword and body-sized shield passing between the files to enforce discipline, but the ranks were not particularly straight, and the pace was plodding. All that passed within his vision were decked out in standard Pharician army uniforms, carrying either spears or short swords with shields. If there were archers, they were not visible from this angle. Tarquin began to think that there might be hope. A couple of well-trained, mounted companies of one hundred or so could cut through an army like this, break it into pieces, and destroy its chain of command. An army of this size would be hampered by rough terrain; they could scarcely sweep through the mountain geography of Everien and wreck every single village—not if they were resisted as Tarquin knew they would have been resisted in his day.

The difference was that in Tarquin's day, every village had been well armed with men organized and trained by the Clan leaders who operated under Ysse. Today the villages were empty or half-empty. Ajiko had drained them to bolster his central army. Lerien would have to move fast to organize a successful resistance now. Tarquin wondered who was supplying matériel and foodstuffs to a force this large; it would be worth trying to cut the supply lines. Then he began to review what he knew about siege warfare. Yet he always found himself thinking as if the warriors of Ysse's days were at his disposal, and of course this was not true. He had no idea whether Ajiko's troops were as effective as the general claimed, and anyway he was many years out of practice at this kind of thing.

The Pharician cavalry was substantial, which meant that there were more than enough outriders to patrol the ranks and keep order on the troops. It also meant that Lerien's men would not find it easy to enter the columns undetected. At the rear of the formation, trailing more than a mile beyond the leaders, the supply trains wobbled slowly in the dust. That was probably the best point of entry, and Tarquin hoped Kivi and that fool Ketar would make the most of it. In the vanguard rode the elite Pharician horselords with their spears and standards; they were visible only as flashes of gold armor amid the dust of their chariots. It would be impossible to catch up with them on foot, and Lerien insisted on hanging back well out of bowshot, concealed in the vegetation. They jogged along this way for several miles; Tarquin's stomach was gnawing and his throat aching with thirst when at last the army began to break into sections and come slowly to a halt. They had reached a small river that flowed from a waterfall in the cliff and meandered across the plain in a deep cutting.

"Here's our chance," Lerien said. They picked their way closer to the army, which was now fanning wider across the riverbank; the columns had broken down while men and horses rested, gradually making their way across the river in small groups. A band of soldiers detached themselves from the main group and came along the river toward them on foot, leading mulecarts laden with water casks.

Tarquin was just thinking how they would get little information out of such underlings when Lerien leaped out from cover and attacked. He felled the first soldier with a single blow to the crown of the head and engaged the second, beating him back with sheer strength and already turning to meet the third. Tarquin was stunned by the ferocity of the king's swordplay and realized he had underestimated Lerien. For a man not born to the sword, he had certainly learned a few things while in Jai Khalar.

But by now the others had drawn their weapons and were entering the fray as the mules scattered, and Tarquin hastened to protect Lerien before the king was surrounded.

"Take one alive!" Lerien screamed as Tarquin fought two men at once. They were wearing uniforms, but they didn't carry the hooked Pharician swords. Tarquin's tongue caught in his throat as he looked at them and saw something he didn't expect. One was a stick-fighter, the other an ax-wielder.

He was so startled that he took several shots to the head and was almost choked by the stick-fighter, who leaped on his back and tried to pull his head back with one stick across the throat. What saved him was the explosive anger that came over him when he realized he wasn't fighting a Pharician. He flipped the stick-fighter over his shoulder and dispatched him with a gash to the head and a clean slice from throat to groin. Then, screaming in battle fury, he hurled himself at the one who used axes. He was met stroke for stroke, was driven back, recovered, and was driven back again. With his peripheral vision he detected Lerien, his own opponents defeated, standing by and watching.

"Alive, Tarquin! We need him alive."

Out of sheer insubordination, Tarquin abandoned all intentions of showing restraint. He saw his opening and drove his sword through the ribs; when his enemy fell, Tarquin went with him, for he'd held on to his sword, which was wedged between vertebrae. As the death twitching ceased, he rose and wrenched his sword free. The breath was hot in his throat and the blood in his temples sounded like a hurricane. He turned over the body with his foot and looked at the paint on the dead Slave's face. Wolf Clan. Rank in the king's army: captain.

Where is your army, Ajiko?

His own voice resounded mockingly through his memory. Nearby, the fallen Deer Clan Slave stirred and began to crawl blindly through the heather, trailing his own intestines. Tarquin lunged forward and savagely brought his blade down on the back of the wounded man's neck.

Across the landscape of dead bodies, Lerien was watching him. Their eyes locked.

"How many?" Tarquin said in a broken voice. "How many men are you missing?"

A WRETCHED PARADE

The pain in her arm woke Istar. She must have twitched in her sleep and jarred the wound, for it was the first thing she was aware of, an angry stab that subsided to deep throbbing. Her body was curled on one side. It rebelled at the idea of stirring, her fatigued muscles behaving as if frozen even though the cave was surprisingly warm. The heatstones had shrunk to little heaps of yellow and gray and their fragrance had faded, but they remained radiant.

She could hear the others breathing. Kassien was snoring.

She had not slept nearly long enough and didn't particularly want to be awake. Yet even before she quite realized where she was or what had happened, a thrilling sense of accomplishment rushed through her and negated the pain. They had seen real action. They had defeated a Sekk. No one was seriously injured—not of her own party, anyway. And they were almost over the mountains.

Satisfaction was succeeded almost immediately by a mixture of apprehension and guilt. Apprehension because the fight easily could have gone the other way, and she could have lost Pallo to the Sekk. Guilt because by now Mhani would be frantic. Well, maybe not frantic—the Seer had cultivated an air of serenity and reason for too long to ever appear frantic—but surely alarmed. Lying in the cave in the slowly graying morning, she could practically hear her mother's censure.

"You don't *think*," Mhani would remonstrate. "It's just a lark for you. Ah, you're more like your father with every passing year. The Wasp blood always tells, no matter what Clan brought you up."

She was fairly sure Mhani would be right, too: though she'd tried to develop the dignity and restraint that were supposed to characterize her adoptive Seahawk Clan, she couldn't now contain her elation. There were a million reasons why flouting Lerien's orders had been the right move, but inside herself she knew that she'd done it for the sheer daring.

Anatar jerked and cried out in his sleep. Istar unwound her body and got up, feeling old. She stretched and indulged in a few moans. Outside, the rain had stopped, but a thick mist had descended in the night. As she reached the mouth of the cave, she realized that she had slept longer than she meant to. Morning would be well advanced, but even the strong summer sun was not able to penetrate the fog. Barefoot, she picked her way along the rectangular shelf outside the cave, trying to remember the exact route Kassien had used to bring them here yesterday. The black stone had formed itself into long, tumbled blocks, wrenched from deep in the earth and then fractured at whiles to form castellated ridges and giants' staircases. Where two conflicting masses of stone met, there were sheer fissures, water-sculpted smooth as ice; and everywhere were unexpected pits and crevices, some of them partly overgrown with grass and heather, waiting to snap the ankles and break the balance of the unwary.

It was not the worst sort of terrain by any means, but in bad weather the surfaces were slippery, and more dangerous still, everything looked different depending on where you were standing. Stone formations that appeared distinctive from below sometimes didn't show up at all from above or from a different angle. The danger of a treacherous, deadly fall might not be so great, but Istar feared they could easily waste hours zigzagging across the same face because they'd lost their bearings or because a direct route could not be seen in the fog. With the two prisoners in such fragile condition, such delays could mean death.

For Anatar, she thought, gaining a ledge from which she could see the crevasse they'd been traveling down when the Slaves ambushed them, death might be inevitable anyway. She spotted the bodies of the other Slaves sprawled where they had fallen. Maybe a quick, unknowing demise would have been kinder than the slow, guilt-steeped decline that Anatar was surely now destined for.

Mist enveloped the mountainside so completely that it was easy to forget about the height. If the sky were clear, the tilting planes of peaks and distant valleys would be dizzying. But sound and light were trapped by the clouds, and Istar's heartbeat and breathing seemed loud in her ears, as if she were cornered in a tight space. She fought the impulse to look over her shoulder every five seconds.

She groped a way down to the place where Pallo had encountered the Sekk. She did not really expect to find evidence of its presence. Few Sekk bodies had ever been recovered, although a number of Clan soldiers, Istar herself among them, could boast of having slain a Sekk Master. She had engaged one a couple of years ago, in a village in Wasp Clan territory; but she had killed it by driving it into the pit of a Fire House. Afterward, there had been nothing left.

At first she saw no sign of a body. There was the pool where Pallo had flung her sword; there was the place where the Sekk had lain, crying to Pallo. No body. She dropped into the divide. Even her own blood must have been washed away, for she saw nothing to indicate there had been a fight. Then, turning slightly, she saw the Sekk. Oddly, the body seemed displaced a bit from where she remembered it being, but it lay in the same final position. Flies were at work, and a scavenger snake moved eerily beneath the soaking robes.

Normally Istar was not much affected by the sight of carnage, but to this corpse she found herself both attracted and repelled. She was drawn toward the body as if to something forbidden. It was safe to look, now that the Sekk had no power to Enslave. But her insides were twitchy and she felt as if she were about to go into a fight. She knelt beside the body.

It was beautifully proportioned, sleek as a racehorse. The skin and nails were in perfect condition. Relative to Istar, it was small, but otherwise the Sekk might have been Istar's age. She made herself look into the face, expecting something: some revelation, some insight. But there was nothing. Only a beautiful girl, eyes half-open, lips parted, dead.

The body stank. She stood up.

"Istar?"

Sounded like Xiriel. She bounded back the way she had come, shouting a reply. She was almost upon him before she saw him. He was standing on the ledge outside the cave, peering into the mist. Relief showed in his face when she appeared.

"Look what I found. Near the back of the cave." He held out a lump of disfigured glass, and Istar shied away.

"Should you touch that?" she said, alarmed. "What does it do?"

"That's just it. It doesn't seem to do anything. It doesn't resonate with the Carry Eye, it doesn't exhibit any of the telltale signs of an Artifact—not the obvious ones, anyway. I haven't had time to do all the tests. And it doesn't look like anything I've ever seen."

Istar said dubiously, "Even so. It's not natural, and it wasn't made by the Clans. No, don't offer it to me! I don't want to touch it."

Xiriel laughed. "For Mhani's daughter, you have a funny attitude toward the Knowledge. All right, then. I won't show the others. But I'd like to keep it, and see if I can figure out what might be done with it."

"Well . . . if you're sure it's all right . . ."

"It could be of use," Xiriel pressed. "Jai Pendu is not the only source of the Knowledge. Lesser Artifacts have been found in Everien."

"Very well. But I don't want to stay here, knowing that the Sekk have marked this place, with those bodies attracting buzzards outside." She raised her voice. "Are we all awake in there? Let's get moving."

Groans; vague shuffling. She went inside, hesitant until her eyes adjusted to the gloom. Kassien was occupied with Anatar while Pentar looked on. Pallo, not looking particularly awake, was attempting to dry his cloak over the remnants of the heatstones. One corner was singed and he batted at it sluggishly in midyawn; then he saw Istar watching him. He made an effort to compose himself but was overcome by another huge yawn, which he tried ineffectually to muffle against his shoulder.

Pentar didn't seem to know where to look when she approached him. She gave him a perfunctory nod and said, "How is Anatar?"

"Alive," said Anatar, "thanks to you."

But even these few words were clearly a struggle. Kassien was holding a bowl of medicinal tea to his lips, probably something to take away the pain, for the dressing would have to be changed. They had brought only a small amount of alcohol, and all of it would not be sufficient to sedate a big man like Anatar for long.

"He's come through the shock, and the bleeding is less, but there's fever," Kassien said. "There could be infection, or it could be his body reacting to the trauma."

"The wound looked clean last night," Istar said.

"Structurally, it's clean. Perfect amputation."

"Good cutting," Anatar muttered approvingly, and Pentar gripped his hand in a show of compassion.

"But . . . ?" Istar said, seeing the shadow in Kassien's expression.

"But that doesn't mean it won't become infected. I'll see more when I change the bandages."

"Don't wait, lad," Anatar said. "I can take it."

His face was so white it was almost blue.

"Food," Istar said. "He's weak from loss of blood. Pallo, cook us something."

She raised her voice but didn't turn; there was a scramble among Pallo and Xiriel, who by default had ended up doing most of the drudgery thus far.

"You, too, Pentar," she said, and began rummaging in their packs for the supplies she had brought specifically to remedy the effects of battle. Up to a moment ago, she had intended to push them all out of the cave at the first possible moment and break fast farther down the mountain.

Yet she found herself unable to refuse care to Anatar, and all of them, she realized, were dazed and unfit for travel. Leaving Kassien to do the medical work, she recruited Pentar to help with the meal. He chiseled more heatstone from the side wall of the cave, and she could see that many such recent cuts had been made, though there was little residue in the cave to indicate it had been used.

"You were kept in this cave, weren't you?" she said, helping Pentar haul the stones for Xiriel to activate. "You seemed to know where to cut."

Pentar stiffened. "I can't really remember." He was still having trouble looking her in the eye. It was disconcerting: her kinsman was an experienced soldier, at least ten years older than Kassien, who was Istar's senior by a few years. He ought to understand that Slaving happened; that although she might not trust him at her back, she would not hold him in shame.

"You can't remember anything?" Istar asked, looking at him searchingly. He was dark, with heavy features that made him appear lugubrious, and a growth of beard in one night that Kassien couldn't have managed in three weeks. "Often we learn more about the Sekk and their movements from recovered Slaves than from the Knowledge itself."

"I will . . . try," Pentar said. "It's hard to think about . . . you know. It. Like putting your hand into a fire. But my life is yours. I will try." He looked up then, eyes as black and submissive as a dog's for just a second; then he glanced away.

Damn it, Istar thought. *A sensitive one. Just what I need.*

"Pallo? We're starving to death and the day's half-gone. Move it."

While they were eating, Kassien said, "You aren't thinking of moving on today, I hope."

"That's exactly what I'm thinking." She reached for flatbread. "Fuel up. We've got ground to cover."

"Anatar can't be moved."

"I can walk," Anatar called. As if to prove it, he stood up and staggered forward. Xiriel made room for him in the circle, using his knife to push a heatstone in Anatar's direction. Kassien gave Istar a dark look.

Pallo didn't attempt to disguise the fact that he'd be happy to stay here until the weather improved. "How are we to orient ourselves in this mist? We'll never find our way to the sea."

He glanced at Xiriel for support, but Xiriel said nothing. Istar wondered what he had done with the piece of Glass he'd found.

Kassien pulled out a magnetic guidestone and fingered it thoughtfully. "I have some knowledge of this region," he said. "I can guide us, even in the fog. But it isn't easy going, and we all need the rest."

"In an ideal world, yes," Istar said. "But we're trapped here. We could hardly find a better way to attract another Sekk than to hang around where there are bodies of Slaves. Not to mention the body of the Master which I found this morning just outside."

Pallo swallowed uneasily. "I take it back," he said. "Let's leave."

They ate in silence for a minute, the tension palpable between Istar and Kassien.

"Not that my opinion matters," Anatar said, "but I'm a dead man already. I'll go ahead no matter what rather than bring danger down on you all. Last night Xiriel told me something of your mission. I—"

"You are prisoners." Istar cut him off harshly. "We will make the decisions."

Xiriel stared at her in distress. "There's no need—"

"Yes, there is," she heard herself say. "I can't trust you, Anatar. Either of you. You might still be under a Slaving spell. I am bound by duty to treat you as enemies until it has been proven to me that you are in perfect possession of your wits. I can't know that as long as we are in a lair used by the Sekk, within spitting distance of a Sekk Master."

She scooped the last of her breakfast from the bowl with her fingers and stood up. "Get ready to move out," she said, and began following her own orders.

No one said anything. She could practically hear them thinking, *Paranoid bitch*. She wasn't certain why she had taken this tack. It had been instinct. When Anatar had begun to speak, she'd realized that his air of self-sacrifice would compel the rest to stay, unless she played the villain and made them go. And they had to go. Maybe she *was* paranoid, but it would be too easy to relax, and ultimately too dangerous. Besides, it was plain that coddling Pentar would do him more harm than good. The others couldn't see that, and would resent her—but too bad.

Her arm ached and burned, and she belatedly realized that she had not had it tended. Well, she couldn't ask now. Not after what she'd just done. She gritted her teeth and clambered into the leather battle gear, heavy with yesterday's rain.

More rain, in fact, had begun to fall by the time they were ready to go. Kassien led off, keeping the pace deliberately slow. Xiriel followed, then Anatar and Pentar, and Pallo. Istar came last.

It should have been easier going, now that they were descending. But sore legs were uncoordinated in descent, and in the places where there was climbing to be done with hands, going down a rock face was always harder than pulling yourself up, because you couldn't always see where you were putting your feet. On one occasion, hanging by her fingers and kicking around randomly hoping for a toehold before the strength ran out of her arms, Istar wished she had relented and stayed in the cave. Her arm was not up to this kind of exertion. She could only guess what Anatar must be going through, scraping by one-handed.

Ropes were needed for Anatar, as it turned out. The rain got heavier. No one was happy, but there was no place sheltered enough to stop.

"I'm not sure where we are," Kassien confided in her during the afternoon. "I've done my best, but I can't see, and the guide stone is only good for determining general direction. We're going southeast, but beyond that . . ."

"It will have to be good enough," Istar said. "Just get us off the height and we'll be less vulnerable. It may well be clearer down below."

He nodded. Kassien was too good an officer to continue to make an issue of her decision this morning, and she knew he was doing his best even though he didn't agree with her. But they were all tired, and if even the absurdly fit Kassien was curt because he was conserving energy, matters really were getting bad. They stood chewing grimly on marching rations, water streaming unchecked down their faces, hair plastered flat.

"What a wretched parade!" Pallo cried suddenly, shaking his blond head and sending droplets flying. "I wonder what the Everiens did about rain. Was it a part of their Philosophy? If they were here, would their Knowledge keep our heads dry?"

The others chuckled dispiritedly.

"I don't know about rain," Xiriel said, "but it is rumored that in the far deserts of Pharice there are wizards who can make sandstorms."

"Sandstorms?" Pallo was unconvinced. "Is that the worst they have to contend with? Surely the visibility can't be worse than this, and at least in the desert it's flat."

"It may be flat, but it's hot enough to kill you in a day if you don't have enough water."

They all looked at each other: this was such an unimaginable proposition that they started laughing and could hardly stop. It was Pallo who led off this time.

"Come on," he urged. "The sooner we find shelter, the sooner I get my dinner."

It seemed the whole mountainside was awash, but even so, when they came to the river there was no mistaking it. The flood was audible long before they could see it, white with underparts stained brown and green in the half light like the belly of some huge beast. Generating its own fog, it burst from within the declivity it had carved for itself and flung offshoots to either side, claiming a whole region of the rock face. The main flow was more waterfall than river: this meant even more mist than before.

"This must be the Yrtaj," Kassien said. "Or one of the tributaries, anyway. If it is, we've come too far east."

"That means we're on my Clan's land, though," Istar said. "You fought here a few years ago, didn't you, Kass?"

Kassien said nothing, and Istar wondered if she'd judged his mood prematurely, earlier. He looked unhappy. The others stood dully, waiting for guidance; no one cared anymore about anything but rest. Istar could tell nothing about their surroundings, except that they were standing on a broad, grassy ledge. It was impossible to tell how high they yet were.

"We should follow it," Kassien said at last. "Even the Yrtaj is better than no landmark at all."

He adjusted his pack and moved forward. No one bothered to respond to the cryptic remark. Each of them was fully preoccupied with the simple act of placing feet and shifting balance, and their eyes were on the ground. Istar, from the rear, saw Anatar falter many times; Pentar was practically carrying him, and Kassien stopped often to wait for them to catch up.

Only a half mile or so downriver a valley opened up, wide enough to admit the flow of water and to spare. The ground began to level off, and trees appeared, furring the valley walls and cutting off all view of the sky. The river was too violent and its banks too steep for them to walk close to the water, so Kassien led them through the thickening forest on steeply plunging banks. They stumbled between vine-clad trees, ears full of the noise of water, often skidding sideways against the intemperate fall of the land. After a little while, Xiriel stopped Kassien with a shout.

"What's that?" He pointed, and the others saw a wall tracing a parallel course to theirs, higher up the side of the vale.

Kassien wiped the rain off his face and stared dumbly.

We've become a parade of idiots, Istar thought. If Kassien was losing his wits, it was time to stop and seek shelter.

"It looks like the verge of a road," Pallo said. "I'll go see."

Infused with new energy, he bounded up the hillside, eager, no doubt, for any sign of civilization. They saw him reach the wall, which was much bigger than it appeared, for it reached over Pallo's head. He turned, waved, and removing his pack, scaled it. At the top he turned and called back. "It is a road! Built by our betters, long ago, I'm sure."

Everyone brightened, and they moved to catch up with Pallo. Everyone, that is, except Kassien. Istar tried and failed to catch his eye. He had spent a fair amount of time in this part of Everien, and she wondered if he knew which road it was.

"Come on, Anatar," she encouraged, tugging at his good arm. "You can make it."

The road was paved with the same white porous stone from which Jai Khalar was built, even though the mountain itself was made of a black, dense composite of minerals. Both sides were walled, and the surface was strangely free from plant growth, though the trees arched overhead to form a long, twisting tunnel.

"This road's been well-maintained," Pallo said excitedly. "We must be in Seahawk Country already! Ah, I can almost smell my dinner roasting. . . ."

They set off with renewed cheer, Pallo now loquacious and full of verve. "I wonder how the Everiens moved all this white stone from across the range."

"Or why," put in Pentar. Kassien had dropped back to support Anatar, and Pentar now strode ahead. He, at least, seemed no worse for the beating he'd received yesterday. Istar caught up to Xiriel, who was talking to Pallo.

"I did not know any of their works had survived outside Everien. There are the Floating Lands, of course, but I thought that the miles between Everien and the Floating Lands were empty."

"That's what I was taught in Pharice," Pallo agreed. "I will have to set some people straight when I return there. What else haven't the old Scholars bothered to tell us, or forgotten themselves? I wonder where this road goes."

"Under the mountains," Kassien said tensely.

"Does it? Why didn't we take it instead of doing all that climbing?"

"There is a dead end before you come to Jai Khalar. And it would have been many miles spent in darkness."

"Really?" Pallo had begun to get excited, but Istar could see that Kassien was uncomfortable with the conversation. "What about the other way?"

"I have never walked on it. The Seahawk Clan avoids this road like a plague; they are superstitious about it. There is something unsettling about it, like all things built from the Knowledge. They say it goes toward the sea, but whether it arrives there I do not know."

Pallo's eyes bulged. He threw up his hands toward the sky. "It is joy!" he exulted, turning and walking backward to address the others. "Who needs cross-country slogging through marshes, up and down cliffs, when we could walk on a road? Hey, if only we had some horses . . ."

It was pure coincidence, Istar later convinced herself, that the manifestation should occur at the precise instant when Pallo uttered the word "horses."

From around a bend in the road behind Pallo appeared a band of riders. Judging by the variety of armaments and face paint, the group was comprised of a mixture of Clans, but all the saddle skirts were a uniform crimson, and the horses cantered in strict formation. Three Wasp archers with their painted bodies formed the first line, but ahead of them on a gray battle charger was a swordsman, his braided hair beneath the leader's helmet flying back with the wind of his passage.

As they approached, Istar strained to identify the riders, but the striped paint obscured their features and their standard was tightly furled. The leader's teeth were bared and the Seahawk paint brought a storm of triumph to his face. They were making as much noise as a landslide and within a few seconds they were almost upon Istar's party, who flattened themselves against the wall that bordered the road even as the host swept by. The horses' breathing and grunting was audible above the racket of hooves, and light flashed off weapons and armor. Istar could smell the hot animals, which bore aspects as fierce and ungentle as their riders despite their disciplined formation.

Pentar had the presence of mind to wave his arms in attempt to attract their attention, but none of the warriors so much as glanced at him. The blue-eyed Wolf fighters passed, the Bear warriors passed on their heavy horses, the half-naked Snakes with their poisons and charms netted about their torsos, and the Seahawk swordsmen—all passed oblivious to the presence of the small, sodden band of travelers by the roadside. It was a lucky thing that they were not trampled, in fact; or so Istar thought at the time. But after the strange force had gone by, riding hard up the valley toward the mountains to disappear around the next curve in the road, Pallo wiped the rain from his face and said:

"That's funny. Did you notice the sun was shining on them?"

THE SMELL OF NIGHT

"Prisoners." Lerien ignored Tarquin's challenge, gripped with an anger of his own that aged his face ten years. "You were to take prisoners. Now these men are dead and can tell us nothing."

Tarquin raised his gory blade and pointed it at the king. "Prisoners? What would you have them tell you? Why they betrayed you to Pharice? Or why they blindly followed their leaders to do the same? Ajiko could better answer that for you. He has spoiled them with obedience and order—did you see them march? It makes me sick." He drew breath to lay into Ajiko again and then caught himself. In a different tone he said, "How did they get here from Wolf Country?"

Lerien blinked. "H'ah'vah tunnels," he said grimly. "Now it makes sense. There are new H'ah'vah tunnels in Wolf Country."

"H'ah'vah are servants of the Sekk—or they used to be."

"Those men did not fight like Slaves!" Lerien protested. "They fought with spirit."

"Yet they showed no dismay to cross weapons with their own king. I cannot read these riddles, Lerien—have affairs in your country come to this?"

Lerien didn't have a chance to respond; the escaped mules had been found and a shout went up. Both men fled, Lerien leading the way back along the river and up a small stream, where the scent dogs might lose them. They threw themselves into the high grass and waited for sounds of pursuit. Horses galloped by fifty yards distant, and then returned going the other way. In a whisper Lerien said, "If they wish to attack Jai Khalar, why didn't they use the tunnels to go the other way, to bring the

Pharician army into Everien? They must have known they could come down from Wolf Country and take Everien one piece at a time. Why cross Ristale—especially when commanders like Jenji and Vortar know about the monitor towers in the western range? They would know we could See them."

"Perhaps someone has sabotaged your Eye system."

"Or perhaps," said Lerien, "they are not going to Jai Khalar after all."

"Explain."

"There is a secret political faction in Pharice called the Circle. They collect Everien Knowledge and Artifacts with a passion. Sendrigel has traded with them covertly; I allow it to go on because Hezene is too aggressive for his own good—I think he's riding for a fall."

"So you are lining yourself up with revolutionaries? A dangerous game, Lerien." Nevertheless, Tarquin was pleased at the thought that Lerien had *something* up his sleeve.

"The Circle is a mysterious group. I suspect their leaders are high in Hezene's government. I know that they are obsessed with the secrets of ancient Everien."

"There is too much wealth in Pharice," Tarquin agreed. "Too many rich men with nothing to do but make trouble. But it may be that Sendrigel has traded away your kingdom this time."

"What if they are trying to go to Jai Pendu?" Lerien mused as if he hadn't heard Tarquin.

"With three-quarters of the Clan army in their back pocket? Why? The White Road has only ever come to Everien—to Jai Khalar, specifically. They know they can't get to Jai Pendu by sea, and the Floating Lands cannot be taken by ten thousand any more easily than by ten."

"Every answer I can think of only brings more questions," Lerien said. "Come on. Let us round up the others before they get themselves captured or killed."

They crept back the way they had come, hugging even closer to the cliff this time. The army moved on, laboriously crossing the river and continuing southward. Lerien and Tarquin trudged to the base of the next monitor tower, where they found Ketar and Kivi already waiting for them. They had two horses.

Kivi said, "We went to the rear of the army and stole two of their spare horses. Ketar got us a couple of cloaks and we passed ourselves off as outriders. We worked our way up the columns. There is a Clan soldier for every five Pharicians. Our officers are mixed in with theirs. The Pharicians hold no special standard; nothing to show allegiance to anybody but Hezene."

"Well, we know where our army is now," Lerien said resignedly. "At least there is no doubt. Yet I don't understand any of it."

"Treachery," said Tarquin darkly, thinking of Ajiko and his damned maps.

Kivi said, "It was all very strange. As you know, Ajiko's soldiers are outfitted in dress not unlike that of the Pharicians, but we also saw Clan warriors on Everien mountain horses, and they wore no uniforms, but they were painted for high battle, just as they would have been of old."

"On horseback? How would they have gotten horses across the mountains from Wolf Country? What horse would enter a H'ah'vah tunnel?"

"Kivi is dreaming," Ketar snorted. "I saw no such men, and we were together all the time."

"You can only perceive them if you first See them through the Eye. You refused to do so."

"The Eye that has been proved false? Why should I look in it?"

"They were perfectly clear in the Eye," Kivi said to the others. "And then after a while, I was able to detect them without the Eye, like ghosts. They were terrifying."

"To you, maybe," Ketar said. "I saw many Pharicians and some Clan infantry, but they looked too tired to be terrifying."

Tarquin had gone cold. Lerien said, "Describe the riders you saw, Kivi."

"One of them was about your size, Tarquin, with a shaven head and blue bands painted across it, and he was wearing leather armor inlaid with Everien smooth-stone, and riding a white horse. The horse had spikes on its hooves. The other one was quite dark, hair all braided, and he wore practically nothing. His body was painted in red and gold, and he rode a small brown horse that had a long blanket covering it."

"What's the matter, Tarquin? Have you encountered these men before? Are they Clan or not?"

"I don't know," Tarquin said faintly. He felt dizzy. He walked a little apart from the others.

"Ketar, did you see the Pharician chariot squad? Did you see their leaders?"

"They have a strong chariot corps," Ketar said. "It wasn't merely ceremonial. We caught a glimpse of the leaders, but they were all packed together and surrounded by the cavalry. I couldn't tell you anything about them, other than that they fly a Pharician Imperial standard."

"The riders I saw," Kivi persisted. "There was something strange about them. They weren't exactly . . . solid."

"That's because they didn't exist," Ketar scoffed, and then snapped his mouth shut as Lerien glared at him.

"They flashed in and out of view," Kivi continued. "Then one of them came along, a Deer on horseback. He had blood all over his fighting sticks! They were actually *dripping,* and his clothes were torn. I stared at him; I thought maybe I'd recognize him, but I've never seen any of my kinfolk look so vicious. Then he was gone. He reappeared three columns away, and he spurred his horse and brandished his sticks even though there was no one for him to fight. The foot soldiers behaved as though he wasn't even there. Then he charged and I swear it, he passed *through* a chariot carrying a Pharician officer. I could see him flailing the air with his sticks. They were just a red blur, and the horse was striking out as well."

Tarquin said, "Was he wearing a yellow shirt?"

"You saw him, too?" Kivi spun to face him, wide-eyed.

"Tarquin, what is it?" Lerien caught his arm, for he'd reeled back on his heels.

Tarquin composed himself, stony and fatalistic. He loosened his sword.

"Then I saw the Sekk," said Kivi. His eyes slipped away from Tarquin, who lunged forward and grabbed Kivi by both shoulders. "What Sekk? What *Sekk*?"

Kivi's teeth chattered. "I couldn't look at it directly. It wore all black, and it rode in a chariot at the back of the chariot ranks."

"What Sekk—" began Ketar.

"Shut up, Ketar!" The Seer glared at the Seahawk. "I know it was a Sekk. All the army behaved strangely."

"Here come the rest," Lerien said, shading his eyes. By now it was late evening, and the shadows were sharp and warm on the summer grass. "If only we had more horses, we might easily keep pace with this army."

Taro had spent half his arrows in a fight with the Pharicians, Stavel glowered, and Jakse dragged himself along as one exhausted. Tarquin was too preoccupied with the sinking feeling in his own stomach to speak, but this did not stop him from listening to Stavel's report, delivered in a voice gray with despair.

"I saw our brothers like Slaves, and yet not like Slaves. What controls them? They have maintained their self-control but their faces are empty."

"What about this supposed Sekk of yours, Kivi?" asked the king. "Tell us."

"As I said, it was in a chariot," Kivi said in a low voice. "It turned toward me. It was attractive, like a Sekk. . . . But it—" He made a strangled sound and looked away. "It had no eyes."

Tarquin stopped breathing. He could not understand how the others could keep talking so calmly; it seemed to him that the very world was surely coming apart before his eyes.

"It could not have been a Sekk that Kivi saw," Ketar said. "The whole army would have self-destructed by now if infected by the Slaving spell."

"It's true," Jakse put in. "Sekk can sometimes rule over a handful of Slaves for a time, but never an entire army—not like this."

"Something else is going on," Lerien agreed and fell into a pensive silence.

"Let us debate it a little longer while they march toward Jai Pendu," said Stavel. "Kivi, are you taking notes?"

"Close your mouth, Stavel." Lerien's face showed white around the dark holes of his eyes and mouth; night was being gently run to ground by a prescience of sun.

"Stavel is right," Tarquin said. "Better to dive in headfirst, I think."

He strode away, Kivi hastening at his heels. They walked past the horses and climbed the side of a rock formation that jutted from the slope to look down on the army, which had passed them and camped to the south. Now quiescent in the shadow of the mountains, it was defined only by pinpricks of torchlight. The plain looked like a starry sky, but there were no stars above, only clouds that did not ever seem to move, despite the unceasing wind.

"Kivi," he said, "the rules are going to change now. I have no way of explaining this to you except to say that you must be prepared to do what you have never done, to see what you have never seen. You are young, and fast, but don't trust yourself. Not for a second."

Kivi looked uneasy. "Don't trust myself? What—"

"The Sekk have many tricks. When you have seen a few or a dozen, you begin to learn to recognize them; you begin to have immunity. But if you are taken in the first time, there never will be a second chance. You will be Enslaved."

Kivi looked affronted. "I was taught how to avoid the Slaving spells."

Tarquin guffawed and gestured to the army camped below them. "So were they. You hear me, Kivi?"

"I don't understand what you want me to do."

"In a fight against a man," Tarquin said, jumping down from the rock and tightening the girth on one of the grazing horses, "the problem is simple. He is only like yourself. His needs and means for killing are obvious. You are made of fear, of course, and if you have trained well and stayed alive in the past, then your technique and your skill will never avoid that fear, but rise out of it. Out of necessity, yes, Kivi?"

"They say it's like falling very fast," Kivi reflected. "There's no time to contemplate. You are reacting, and you'll grab on to anything that you can."

"And that," said Tarquin, "is where the Sekk can enter you. You cannot succumb to their sense of time. You cannot treat them as you would treat a bad dream and go about your business. Nor can you treat them like men. They are not men, and they will have you if you make that mistake. You must seek to understand them as something alien, unlike you."

"Seek to understand them? But Tarquin, isn't that how they take you? I mean, I thought—" He broke off, disconcerted.

"You thought what?"

"The Knowledge is like a wall. It is to repel the Sekk. What you are saying, it's like climbing over the wall. Going into their territory."

"The Knowledge excites them," said Tarquin, and began examining the contents of the saddlebags. "Have you not observed this? Does no one among you Seers trouble to make a study of the Sekk?"

"You cannot study them," Kivi said fervently. "They'll draw you in. They'll take you. Tarquin, if that's what you've been doing, you must stop." Exercised, he followed Tarquin around the far side of the horse, his voice trembling. "These fits you have. I respect you, so I have said nothing to the others. But I say it to you, and you must listen to me. I have worked with the Artifacts. I have read the texts in Jai Khalar and I have moved through the Knowledge in ways that I can't begin to describe to you. You have been adventuring hither and yon, but I have been in Jai Khalar, and I have seen as much of the Knowledge as anyone except Mhani. And I tell you that you are in peril. Do not study the Sekk. Do not seek them out. Do not attempt to penetrate their minds. It is more dangerous than even you can know."

Tarquin dug the blade of his hand into his thigh, separating muscle from tendon. "I have not asked for your company or your advice. Stay with Lerien if you are afraid of me."

"No. You can't get rid of me so easily."

"Do you understand my instructions?" Tarquin demanded. "Do you hear me?"

"Yes. I hear you. What do you want me to do?"

"Pay attention. Stay alive. It's not as easy as you think. The first time, you were allowed to escape." He lengthened the stirrups. "The Sekk wished for you to be a messenger."

"Messenger? How so?"

"This is not an ordinary Sekk. It can move the entire army with its mind, flex its muscles and swing men like you swing your sticks. It detected us sometime during our assay. If it wanted us dead, we would have been overwhelmed. We were not. Therefore, it wants something else."

"Are you saying this is a trap?"

"That's what I'm saying." He swung into the saddle.

"Where are you two going?" Lerien shouted. "Those horses are important!"

The rest started running toward them. Tarquin nudged his horse to a trot.

"If it's a trap, why are we walking into it?" Kivi demanded, holding the paint horse by the bridle and running alongside. He glanced back, saw Ketar closing on him, and leaped into the saddle.

"I am walking into it," Tarquin said, "because you tell me you have seen Clan warriors on Everien horses and a Sekk without eyes."

"I think you have a death wish," Kivi said with passion, gathering his reins clumsily.

"Thank you for your opinion. Now be silent, and follow me."

THEY RODE TO the edge of the Pharician camp and rested there. The sun came up in the south. The last ridge of Everien's western mountains sculpted the dawn like a frozen wave. In the dense light the ridge and each of the mountains behind it looked two-dimensional, as if each hill were a piece of torn paper lying on top of the one beyond it, faintly translucent. Everien, Tarquin thought, might be nothing more than this: some light-stained old record to be folded up and pocketed. By contrast, the meadow where they now stood was vividly alive with insects and birds. Nearby, the camp had sprung into action. The army was stirring. Using the long grass as cover, they walked their horses closer.

The soldiery of Pharice and the Clans did not look so different when seen in this formation, Tarquin thought with disgust. The Clansmen had retained their paint, but they wore uniforms not so different from the standard Pharician army issue, and their expressions were equally vacant. All had the looks of men who had been too long on the move. That their garb should be stained and scuffed was no surprise given the distance across the plains they'd lately crossed; but also their faces wore the kind of haggard expression that sets in after nothing in particular has happened for too many weeks running, and there is no reward to look forward to beyond a game of cards at the end of a long march. Yet Tarquin was not fooled by their apparent ennui. These men were Slaves—and when the Sekk willed them to fight, their eyes would burn with hate.

The real problem lay in their number. Tarquin had never had to cope with so many files of infantry, and he didn't know where to begin. He had not fully appreciated the size of the force until he had ridden past rank after rank of trudging soldiers and came to feel he would never see the end of them. Every so often an outrider would pass down the ranks with a routine air; one even nodded at Tarquin. He never once saw the same outrider return along the line, which gave him the sense that the columns of soldiers were infinite in length.

Their first objective had to be to get closer to the chariots at the vanguard; but this would mean passing close to the leaders, who would immediately see that they were not in uniform and attack them. Tarquin was debating the wisdom of this with himself when he saw Riesel riding among the infantry.

With the strange clarity of a familiar face glimpsed unexpectedly across a room crowded with strangers, the vision of his old comrade emerged from the dust and confusion of Pharician men and their arms, rendering them all meaningless. Tarquin's astonished eye bored all its attention into a detailed analysis of the rider he could scarcely believe he saw. Riesel had worn such a costume a thousand times before, mounted on Changeling his bay stallion, one ax thrust into his belt at the small of his back, the other hooked casually over his shoulder. Its haft had worn a shiny spot in the leather of his cloak where it always rested. Riesel wore the steel Wolf helmet painted with his family's symbols, and his tunic was made of leather tightly interwoven with deer bones.

Tarquin took all this in with even less faith than he invested in the waking dreams that had plagued him of late. He would not be taken in by the trick: seeing Riesel again was just another taunt on the part of his long madness, another insult born of a long night spent in Jai Pendu. He rode on in a strange calm, the horse blowing beneath him and jiggling the bit experimentally. The soldiers kept their heads down as he rode by them, and the nearest of the Pharician outriders was well out of earshot. Riesel on the bay wove through the columns of Pharicians mixed with Clan, head up, questing from side to side.

Kivi drew alongside him, fighting for the bit with his paint horse. "Tarquin, we're too close—we'll get caught!" he hissed.

Without taking his eyes off Riesel, Tarquin reached over and grabbed the bridle. "Sit back," he said. "Give her more rein and stop fretting."

Kivi said, "You saw him, didn't you? What is it? Who is it? See how he isn't really there?"

Changeling sidestepped, and instead of jostling two Pharician spearmen, he stepped through them as if they were made of air. Both of them shuddered and they looked at each other, then turned their gazes up toward Riesel, who was still oblivious to their presence.

"Get control of your damn horse," Tarquin snapped at Kivi. "We must overtake the leaders."

"I smell Sekk," said Kivi.

Tarquin said, "I smell Night."

SNUG AS A BAD DREAM

"Tarquin, I don't mind telling you you're frightening me," Kivi said. "You have the strangest look on your face."

"Shut up and pay attention to your horse," Tarquin said, just as Kivi slipped in the saddle when his mount swerved. The ground had become rougher, full of ditches, marshy patches, and thorn-brakes. They had to sweep well around the main body of soldiers and circle toward the vanguard out of bowshot, and their horses were hot and blowing when they overtook the lead chariots at last, a wall of flashing armor and shining pelts moving steadily forward. These were Pharician horse-warriors trained to the highest standards: their animals were fine and well kept, their armor was expensively and cunningly made, and they themselves wore the decorations of many battles. They were a composed, disciplined lot; they did not ride in circles and pull each other's braids as Clansmen might have done. Yet it could not be said for certain that they were Slaves, either. When one was summoned by an outrider and turned to cut back through the ranks, he moved with the grace of a man in full command of himself. Slaves were half-mad, often witless, creatures. Not so the leaders of this army.

They had hit a swampy area, which the Pharician chariots now began swinging wide to avoid; Tarquin decided to make the most of the cover and led Kivi trudging through mud and standing water and high reeds.

"What are we going to do?" Kivi asked, swatting bugs away and thrashing through the long grass. "What more do you need to see? If we go any closer they'll pick us out as strangers and kill us."

"Where do you think we will find this Sekk of yours?"

Kivi pointed out the group of chariots that he had seen the day before. He repeated, "What are you going to do, Tarquin? Do you think the Sekk is controlling this army, or is it just friends with the Pharicians?"

"I don't know," Tarquin said. He was scrutinizing the chariots, hoping for some glimpse of the Sekk. His body had started to harden with anticipation and anger like the point of an arrow hardening in fire, an anger that he would eventually release to a specific target. He could see the front line of chariots now, and his legs tightened against the saddle; his horse picked up its trot.

After a moment Kivi spoke again, and his voice cracked. "You do have a plan, right?"

There was another silence. Tarquin showed his teeth. He was starting to feel ready.

"Well, that's better," said Kivi in a relieved tone, seeing the smile but not the intent behind it. "You don't look worried, so I'm not going to be worried."

Tarquin loosened his sword in the scabbard. "There's nothing for me to worry about, for I'm about to be reunited with my Company—or whatever it is they have become. I'm not worried, my friend. But maybe you should be."

"Oh, brothers and sisters of the moon," Kivi moaned faintly. "What do you want me to do?"

"I think you'd better run away now."

"What? What about you?"

"Me? I'm *happy*, Kivi."

"Tarquin, look out!"

Arrows whizzed between them as they were identified as enemies. Tarquin's blade was out and he was charging; he heard Kivi's cries as the Deer was left trying to manage his horse. Mounted archers had cut in front of the line of chariots and were firing on him, but even on a substandard horse, he eluded them easily: this was old hat for him. He took in the archers on the periphery of his vision and dealt with them without really thinking about it: his eye was combing through the advancing chariots, seeking the one that held the Sekk. He guided his horse off to the right, looking for a way between the lines of chariots, and Kivi came galloping alongside him.

"That way," he screamed, pointing with one of his sticks. "See, among the Clan riders."

It was true. In the third line of chariots moved one that was surrounded by Ruarel, Lyetar, and Ovi. The chariot horses foamed, white-eyed behind spiked headpieces and iron shoes that churned up the dry ground as if it were surf. The driver was Pharician through and through:

lean, blue-black, shaven-headed, with visored eyes and witch-webs gild-
ing his bulging limbs with protection spells. His whip was out and he was
standing high in the harness as though he could barely wait to cut them
down where they stood. The one on the left was much smaller, clad in
black but preternaturally pale and almost ethereal by contrast. It was
unarmed and it had no eyes, but it turned toward them, head cocked to
one side as if it were mad or stupid.

Tarquin stared at it. He should not even glance at it, much less seek to
engage it over these yards of torn earth.

He was eighteen years beyond should.

The sky was blue, hooves drummed the plain, and voices shouted in
Pharician—*Prisoners,* they were saying to each other in a foreign echo of
Lerien's words to Tarquin yesterday, *take prisoners.* The wind carried the
smell of burning oil up the ranks from the siege towers, where black
smoke had begun to billow. Tarquin was aware of all of these things, but
he had zeroed in on the Sekk, hell-bent on discerning whether it was the
same creature he had seen long ago. Beside the Sekk, Lyetar threw his
head back and laughed. Bile rose in Tarquin's throat. An arrow was
coming toward him, and his sword came up automatically and sliced it in
twain. Then a Pharician rider passed between him and the Sekk, swinging a whip and singing.

He had forgotten about Kivi. The Pharician chased the Seer down
easily and lashed the fighting sticks out of his hands; then the whip went
around Kivi's neck and the Deer was pulled to the ground, where he
rolled, clutching his throat. His neck was surely broken, Tarquin thought,
and so must have thought the rider who had attacked him, for he tied the
end of the whip to his saddle horn and raised his arms to invite congratu-
lations. The other officers laughed and cheered. Kivi, still rolling, had
been drawn behind the hooves of the Pharician battlehorse. At first it
seemed there was no hope for him, but then he got his feet under him
and actually began to run behind the horse. Tarquin wheeled his horse
around and began to pursue.

It was a cruel sport, one that Tarquin had never seen the Pharicians use
on their prisoners; but as Kivi and the rider progressed down the convoy
toward the regular cavalry, it was obvious that the men were deriving
much amusement from Kivi's plight. Kivi's Clan was not called Deer for
nothing. The Seer could run, and when the Pharician reined his horse to
avoid trampling a stray infantryman, Kivi seized the opportunity to grab a
stirrup and vault to the animal's back. Tarquin almost reached him.

Then Chyko came crashing toward him.

The Wasp was riding high up on his horse's withers, bareback of
course, and he had a vial of some poison in one hand, a blowgun

clamped horizontally between his teeth, and a strung bow on his back. That light was in his eyes, and Tarquin got a whiff of his smell as Chyko's horse collided with his own and passed through like a wave of sound.

Tarquin suddenly felt nauseated. Chyko galloped across the front of the cavalry without heeding any of them, but the Pharicians and occasional Clan riders whom he passed suddenly became more alert. The Sekk in its chariot wove into view again, extending one finger toward Tarquin as if administering a curse; as one, the riders converged on him, and the light of Chyko's eyes had found its way into theirs as if it were a disease.

Tarquin hadn't realized how angry he was until he had cut down three of them with no effort. They were overaroused and sloppy, and they were Pharician: he had no qualms about killing them. But Kivi was on the ground beneath the rider and had lost his sticks. For a second it seemed the chaos would work in his favor, and Tarquin pressed to get closer to Kivi, thinking momentarily that next time he did something like this he ought to have a real fighter by his side, not a well-intentioned Seer who thought he could be useful. The sheer number of men and horses moving made it almost impossible to maneuver. The masses of soldiers had not even come to a halt: apparently to an army of this size, Tarquin and Kivi represented a minor distraction. This, too, annoyed Tarquin, but before he could penetrate to the place where Kivi was fighting, the first of the Enslaved riders caught up and hit him in the side with a spear, and he fell.

The point had not driven in, and as he tumbled in the air Tarquin grabbed the spear and pulled; the man came off with it and they rolled in the dirt while the horses shot off away from them, leaving an empty area of earth like an arena for the two to hack it out with their swords.

The Pharician was a captain, one of the foreguard, bearing a tracery of honor in the form of scars that altered the landscape of his face. Tarquin forgot about saving Kivi and focused on saving himself as the captain turned his weapon on him with total assurance, almost as if he recognized Tarquin. When they engaged, Tarquin almost didn't believe he could be a Slave. The Pharician had retained great skill and fought without a trace of the zombie quality that could affect badly made Slaves. Tarquin was hard-pressed at first and narrowly missed losing his sword before he woke up and began fighting with real concentration. In different circumstances, he might have taken more time to appreciate his opponent before killing him; but he knew he had only seconds before a mob surrounded him and slashed him to pieces. The rest of the elite were holding back for the moment out of respect for their captain, but Tarquin knew that even if he won this round, he'd have to deal with all of them.

The curved Pharician sword was not as long as a Seahawk weapon, but it could be deceptively quick in the right hands. The captain's blade was so swift as to be almost invisible; again and again Tarquin found himself sliding out of the way by a hairsbreadth and stabbing a hasty riposte, always moving to his opponent's off side in the hope of getting the sun behind him. Just when he was convinced this Pharician could in no way be a Slave, he spotted the Sekk Master standing in his chariot not a dozen yards away like a carrion crow. He quailed a little inside as he realized that only a highly accomplished Sekk could have cast a Slaving spell subtle enough to control the Pharician without blocking the man's talent and experience with weapons. There was his real opponent; but he resolutely kept his eyes on the Pharician captain, who now came at him with the sword clutched in both hands.

Going for the big one, Tarquin thought, and saw his opening. But he found little relish in cutting off the blow before it had been released, smashing his sword into his opponent's elbows just as they began to extend. Bone shattered and flesh rended. The Pharician fell to his knees, screaming, and Tarquin saw the light catch on the Glass in the Sekk's hand as it prepared its next move.

Now understanding seized Tarquin, snug as a bad dream.

The Sekk was tall and slender, with sleek black hair. It was clad all in black. It did not draw its weapon, but held the Glass before its face where its eyes should be. Grace was in its every movement as it stepped out of the chariot and came to meet Tarquin, unperturbed by the blood-blackened sword, the bared teeth, the overbright gaze. Tarquin could hear the cries of Kivi behind him, but paid no attention. He could make out the shape of the Glass possessed by the Master: three riders, fused together so that they surged as one out of the crystal base, their weapons drawn. The Glass was beautiful.

And he had seen it before.

Going into battle against a Sekk Master was like diving for oysters: you took a very very deep breath and hoped it would last you long enough. There was a trick of concentration, a way of shutting down parts of the mind that were vulnerable to the Slaving spells, which could mean the difference between life and death during those crucial seconds of an engagement. How long you could maintain this concentration was a factor of experience, training, and sheer will. But Tarquin was not dealing with an ordinary Sekk; he was dealing with his nemesis, his past, his loss, and the failure of his understanding—everything he had tried to forget. He was too incensed to be careful. That was how he made the grave error of looking into the Sekk's face with a naked mind, all his senses wide open.

He couldn't see her but he knew she was there. She smelled of lilacs and rain, and when her fingers touched his forehead he found he couldn't move and didn't want to. He made a sound low in his throat.

"I've missed you," she said. "Your face."

"Don't know how you can stand to look at me," he answered self-consciously. She moved against him and he didn't know where to put his hands. Everything about her was soft.

"It's not a handsome face," she agreed. "But it's yours. This one must have been painful."

Her fingertips traced a particularly virulent scar.

He pushed her away, tried to open his eyes.

"Who are you?" he said.

A sword ripped the air over his head and he found himself on his knees and the Sekk standing over him casting no shadow.

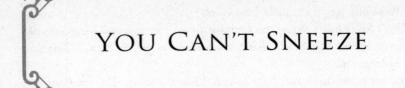

YOU CAN'T SNEEZE

Kassien spun to face the others and cried, "Get off the road. Now!"

Startled from their collective daze, the group obeyed him without question, scrambling over the rampart and down into the forest again. Anatar would have fallen had not Pentar caught the edge of his cloak and stopped him. At the bottom, the wounded man sank to the ground, shaking. Xiriel bent to offer help, but Anatar shrank away in fear when he came close.

"It is a haunted road," he whispered.

Pallo started to mutter something about a haunted road being preferable to an unhaunted mountainside, but Kassien spoke over him. "I knew we should not have set foot on it. The Seahawks are not an imaginative people, and if they say a thing is magical, they usually have evidence to support their claim."

Xiriel frowned and straightened. "Are you saying those riders were only visions? I felt the wind they made. The Knowledge is never so vivid."

Anatar gave a cry. "Don't speak of it!"

They turned their attention to him. He was clutching his shoulder where the arm had been and rocking from side to side.

"You're feverish," said Pentar, and removed his rucksack to search for medicine.

"The standard they carried," Anatar said, teeth chattering. "It was furled, but I could see part of it. There was a rose. I'm sure of it."

No one said anything for a minute.

"Quintar's Company . . ." Xiriel tried to catch Istar's eye, but she was staring off into space, trying to reenvision the riders and pick out which one among them had been her father. It had all happened so fast.

"Ghosts!" Pentar's voice became a whisper. "Those men are all dead!"

"Not all," amended Istar grimly. For it was not her father's face that had registered in her memory but the face of the leader. She tried and failed to equate the ferocious warrior with the gloomy man she'd seen on the tower roof at Jai Khalar. Again she went through each of the riders in her memory, looking for the one that must have been her father. But she'd had only a glimpse—not enough to say she'd identified Chyko. She set her jaw. "I'm going back up there."

"No, you're not," Kassien said firmly, grabbing her arm. "Show a little sense. Your own kinfolk who occupy this region avoid it like a curse."

"That was Quintar's Company. My father was among them. And it leads us to Jai Pendu. Why should we tramp through this forest when it could carry us straight to our destination?"

"No," Xiriel said. "It's not that simple. You might end up anywhere, at any point in time. The White Road is not an ordinary road."

"I don't care!" Istar cried, turning in Kassien's grip and leaning back toward the road. Kassien shook her. "Istar, stop it."

"Shut up, Kassien. You're just afraid of the Knowledge."

"*No,* Istar." Xiriel was insistent. "Think for a minute. If that was Quintar's Company that just rode by, we might have stepped into another time."

"Exactly!" Istar said. "Let's go back. Let's help them. Let's find out what happened to them. . . ."

No sooner were the words out of her mouth than she knew they were foolish.

"It's far too dangerous," Xiriel said. "Besides, they were going the other way! Our mission is to go to Jai Pendu. You cannot follow your father and fulfill your goal at the same time."

Angry and frustrated, Istar fell silent. She knew she was being childish, but the thought that Chyko's ghost had just ridden past her and there was nothing she could do about it—it ripped up what little self-composure she'd retained after the long march in the rain.

Still holding her arm, Kassien said, "We'll look for somewhere to camp. Anatar can't go on like this. Tomorrow we'll find our way down to the plateau."

"*Why* were they riding the other way?" Istar mused, ignoring his attempt to distract her. "They never rode back toward Jai Khalar, did they? Tarquin said they were all lost at Jai Pendu."

Xiriel adopted a patient tone. "That's what I'm trying to say to you, Istar. You must understand that the White Road isn't a road at all, it's a piece of the Liminal. It doesn't go in a straight line, and it doesn't make sense. We know from experience that when it appears in Jai Khalar you can take it to Jai Pendu, but we have no idea what might happen if we stepped on it in the middle. And Istar—*hey!* Istar, look at me!"

Glowering, she did.

"*The riders didn't see us,* Istar. Pentar was flagging them down, but they didn't even notice we were there. So we couldn't have spoken with them if we tried."

Istar turned away, her throat full of tears, struggling to master her emotions. When Kassien led them away, she didn't resist this time.

Silent and a bit unnerved, they picked their way along the valley for another mile, until the road was well out of sight and the sound of falls could be heard not far downstream. There was a dip in the slope where several large boulders had come to rest in some landslide long ago, now surrounded by a dense growth of hemlocks. It was the closest approximation of shelter they had seen since leaving the Sekk's cave, but even so it was a miserable place to camp.

Kassien set himself to looking after Anatar, and Xiriel crawled into the depths of the hemlock grove, where the ground was miraculously dry. He took out his axes and began chopping dead wood.

"Should you use your weapons to such purpose?" Istar queried, surprised.

"They were not meant as weapons in the beginning," Xiriel stated matter-of-factly.

"It's just that you Wolves are usually so proud of your iron. I've known Wolves to give their axes names and treat them as sacred."

Xiriel continued hacking at the branches neatly and efficiently.

"I've never given much credence to Clan superstitions. I'll sharpen these when I'm finished. They will be as good as ever for battle. I'm not afraid of offending the Wolf spirits."

"Don't you practice the Animal Magic?" said Istar, and then bit back her words. Clans never discussed their magic with each other. She had been startled into the question by Xiriel's cavalier attitude toward what she had expected him to revere.

He replied, "No, I don't believe in the Animal Magic. I am a man, not a Wolf; I practice pursuit of the Knowledge."

Istar hesitated. She realized that in all the time she'd known Xiriel, she had never spoken of personal matters with him; they only ever spoke of the Knowledge, and even that rather dryly. Because he was so reserved, she had come to take Xiriel as a font of information independent of people and society. Besides, Wolves were notoriously proud and aloof, secretive about their anecestral practices and protective of tradition. You didn't simply approach a Wolf and ask him, for example, about the intricacies of his Clan's death rituals, or refer to his sacred feasts—unless you had a death wish, that is. To hear him dismiss the traditions of his own Clan came as a shock, and Istar wondered what else she didn't know about Xiriel.

"You must not have been very happy growing up among Wolves," she ventured. "It's said that your Clan has more Animal Magic than any other in Everien."

"I have heard it said. But I have never experienced anything that convinced me the Animal Magic is anything more than men's wishes and fears. Whereas the Knowledge can be seen and touched; it is provable."

Because she had been adopted into the Seahawk Clan by Quintar, Istar had no Seahawk blood in her, and therefore no Animal Magic. Yet she believed it existed, and wished she did have some capacity for it.

"If I'd been born a full-blooded Wolf, I'd never have turned my back on the Wolf magic," she averred.

Xiriel tossed a last piece of wood onto the pile and slid the axes into his belt. "You can't turn your back on that which isn't there."

The wood Xiriel had cut provided them with too poor a fire for cooking, but the space he'd cleared let them crawl under the lowest branches of the dense trees, where the ground was slightly drier. There they huddled together in two groups. Istar found herself with Pallo and Xiriel, who took from his pocket the lump of Glass he'd found that morning and examined it furtively. She knew he was thinking of Jai Khalar, and the light on the towers, and his beloved documents and Artifacts. They leaned against each other for warmth.

"Have some nuts," Pallo said amiably, chewing. "We can pretend it's roast duck and herb butter."

Istar's cold fingers would barely close over the handful of shelled walnuts he offered. Water dripped from her hair onto the tip of her nose.

"What else do you know about the desert, Xiriel?" she asked with her mouth full. "I need something to think about while I'm drowning on watch."

BUT AS IT turned out, her watch was never called.

"Istar!" Kassien's voice brought her upright even before she was awake. Blearily she took in the fact that it was morning.

"What is it? What's wrong?"

His face was a scant six inches from hers, and she batted him away.

There was a nasty cramp in her middle back from being curled against Pallo's pack.

"I fell asleep on watch, and now Pentar's gone."

"Shit." Istar unrolled herself carefully. "How much time do you reckon's gone by?"

"Two hours, I guess. Maybe three."

"What about the other one?"

"Fevered."

Istar searched his face for signs of reproach that she'd insisted they press on, but found none. "I'll find Pentar," she sighed. "Start thinking about geography. We need to find a village or something and unload these two. They're slowing us down."

"I'm making a fire," Kassien said in a tone that brooked no argument. "Our equipment will rot if we don't get it dried out."

"Fine, whatever," she groaned, standing and stretching. Xiriel mumbled in his sleep and pulled his cloak over his eyes.

Istar left the camp and cast about for some sign of Pentar, brushing midges away from her head as she passed through a static cloud of them. It didn't take long to pick up his trail: he'd left slide marks in the mud, and after that she was able to trace him through the flattened vegetation. The thick bed of pine needles released water like a sponge as she picked her way down the steep decline, and the morning was loud with dripping leaves, bird calls, and the crash of water. The blended sound of many freshets and newborn brooks racing down the valley sides had eased her into sleep last night, and her ears were conditioned now to accept the constant noise. But as she descended through waist-high brakes of brilliant fern, the sound of water deepened and seemed to fill every cavity of her head, numbing her. She rounded a curve in the valley and the roar assaulted her straight on. Here the river descended into an ever-deepening chasm in a series of cascades that would have been impressive under any circumstances, but now, swollen with rain, overwhelmed the senses. The air itself was full of water, and bird calls became feeble overtones unable to compete with the falls, which appeared in flashes of white movement through the lush growth of forest. Trees had fallen across the chasm and made stark cruxes against the white background of water. The opposite side of the valley was all but invisible behind its wall of green; Istar, trained to think tactically, automatically indexed hiding places and ambush points as she considered the advantages and disadvantages of moving in such a landscape, where it was difficult both to see and to be seen. On the whole, she decided that she would rather be concealed here than exposed on the mountain, even if it was difficult to be sure they were alone. If they couldn't use the road, they could at least follow the watercourse all the way to the lowlands.

She spotted Pentar standing and looking over the falls with his hands in his pockets. He didn't hear her coming, and when his peripheral vision picked her up, he jumped in his skin. He seemed different today, she thought. Older. Beaten.

"Go back to camp," she said. "You should not be wandering this way."

"You don't trust me."

"No. I don't."

"I have remembered some of what happened," he said. "You know. When the Sekk caught us. You asked me about it."

She shifted uneasily. There was something odd and eager about his manner.

"Have you been standing here since the nighttime?" she asked.

"No." He waved a hand up the slope. "I went back to the road. At night it seems to glow. I wondered if it was really haunted."

"And?"

"I saw no more riders, or anything like that. But I remembered the Sekk who caught us. She was just a small girl. She sang to us."

Istar didn't like his faraway expression. "Go back to camp," she said again. "Shall I escort you?"

He gave her that pained look again. "I didn't mean it," he blurted. "I couldn't help it. I tried to resist, but Istar, you can't understand."

"Yes, I can. You have to be strong, Pentar. The Sekk know your weak points. I can't excuse you for falling victim to them. If you aren't careful, it could happen again."

He searched her face. "Strong. But you're female, Istar. Don't you understand that there are more things in the world than raw strength of will? No, don't glare at me. I understand you have lived as a man since your father . . . you know. Since he was lost. I have heard of you. But surely you want to let it go, sometimes. Surely you understand how it's possible to surrender?"

She looked at him pitilessly, unable to disguise the fact that she despised him. "If you surrender when the Sekk are around, you deserve to die. Your life is forfeit, Pentar. That's how it is. Your weakness is a danger to us all."

His eyes smoldered. "Kill me, then. Push me off the edge. I don't object. Honor won't let you, will it? But you want to. You want to. I can see it on your face. Aren't you meant to create life, not destroy it?"

"I'm meant," she told him with a tone of finality, "to seek out Jai

Pendu and bring back an Artifact for the war against the Sekk. You're
meant to go back to camp, like the prisoner you are. Anatar is sick. He
needs you. Kinsman."

She said the last word with a depth of hostility that surprised her. She
didn't know exactly why she was so wary around Pentar, but she kept her
eyes on him as he turned and resignedly started back toward camp. She
waited until he had disappeared in the foliage before beginning her descent to the river.

A quarter hour, she told herself. She needed that much time to herself,
to think, to be alone, to let down her guard. This need for solitude must
explain her attitude toward Pentar—that and her general level of physical
discomfort. Her arm still ached. She had slept in wet clothes and though
her body heat had dried the innermost of them, Kassien was right about
all the leather gear being soaked. She felt clammy and unkempt and cold,
and looked forward to partaking of Kassien's fire. She wanted to get
clean, and dry, and then to eat; after all of that, maybe, she'd be able to
think clearly about their next move.

She picked her way down to a quiet backwater near the foot of the
waterfall. Deer shot away through the forest as she approached, and insects touched the water and left silvery concentric circles on its black
surface. Stripping off her gear, she plunged in headlong. The cold was
shattering: she gasped, kicked, and felt her heartbeat triple. She stroked
across the pool, favoring her injured arm, submerged, and came up with
head pounding, shuddering as the air hit her bare skin. The air was hot
by comparison. She dragged herself onto a flat, sunlit rock, breathing
hard as she squeezed the water out of her hair. She combed her fingers
through her matted locks and refashioned the braids. She stretched out
and closed her eyes, thinking of nothing until her internal clock warned
her that a quarter hour was past. She sighed.

A snip of movement from the cliff above caught her eye and she leaped
to her feet. She could hear nothing over the water, but she could see
some kind of scuffle happening in the bushes near where she'd stood
with Pentar. She reached for her knife. Kassien appeared above. He had
Pentar in an armlock and was cuffing him lightly about the head and
shoulders. Alarmed, Istar got dressed and climbed back up to the top of
the falls.

"What's going on?"

By this time, Pentar was sitting on the ground, hands tied behind his
back, blindfolded. He turned his face away when he heard her voice.
Kassien was grinning lopsidedly. "I thought you said you went to look
for our little friend," he greeted her.

"I sent him back to camp."

"Oh? You were gone so long I came to see what happened to you, and who do you think I found having some fun at your expense? So to speak."

Istar cursed and blushed, and Kassien burst out laughing. He pointed at her and clutched his sides. "You should see your face!" he crowed.

"What was he doing? What did he see?" It was all Istar could do to stop herself kicking the miserable Pentar where he sat.

"He saw enough," Kassien said, still laughing. "He'll think of nothing else all day and most of tomorrow. But I knocked him down a couple of times for you."

"I would rather have done it myself," Istar growled.

"Ah, don't be such a prude. He and Anatar have had a bad time of it. You can't begrudge him a lucky glimpse or a bit of a—"

"That's enough," she snapped, and then laughed in spite of herself and shrugged. It was obvious that the more she made of the incident, the more Kassien would laugh.

Kassien managed to compose himself. He turned to Pentar and said sternly, "You haven't appreciated the freedom we've given you, Pentar. Now you *will* be treated as a prisoner."

Her kinsman said nothing, and Kassien pulled him to his feet and pushed him in the direction of camp. Kassien flashed her a warm look and a conspiratorial smile, which she didn't return. Instead, Istar sighed and trailed after them at a distance. She didn't know whether to be angry or flattered; and then she wondered why she should have to be either. It wasn't fair. If she'd only been born male, she would never have to deal with any of this.

By the time she got back, Pallo and Xiriel were giggling as they dried their equipment over the fire, and Kassien eluded her gaze. Istar joined them without acknowledging their mirth, and after a while they desisted. But Istar spent the day in a foul mood, even though the walking was the easiest they'd done since leaving Jai Khalar. She had every reason to be in high spirits: the forest made them feel safe, and Pallo shot a pigeon every few hours, until he had a bundle of them dangling down his back.

Xiriel fell into step with her.

"There's no such thing as an Honorary wood pigeon," Istar said peevishly.

The Seer gave her a blank look.

"I'm tired of being male when I'm *not* male," she explained.

"Oh." He frowned, considering. "You could change your status. Find a Seahawk man for a mate. Or take up a woman's trade."

"Are you crazy? There *are* no men—for mates or otherwise. I tried being a Seer. Believe me, I tried—Mhani begged me to become even the lowliest Scholar rather than take the sword. But I have no patience for it. Nor for anything else. I mean, can you see me as a weaver-woman or something?"

"I must admit you would make a rather mediocre woman, Istar. No offense."

"No offense? What do you mean, I'd make a mediocre woman?"

"You're bossy and you can't cook. And if I were your mate, I'd be afraid of you."

"Thanks! Any more compliments from you and I'll be blushing."

"Don't mention it." The Seer's mouth twitched with a suppressed smile. "What makes you think you want to be a woman all of a sudden, anyway?"

"I'm tired of having all the responsibility of being male and none of the fun. Pentar disrespects me, yet because I'm not a woman, I can't take offense."

"I see your point, but I don't know whether you'd like being female. Have you ever *had* a man?"

Of their own volition Istar's eyes went to Kassien ahead of them. She sighed wistfully.

"Yes. I dressed up as a woman and rode out into Deer Country last summer. I found this young shepherd and spent several hours with him. I wanted to make sure I'd got the hang of it."

Xiriel took a surprised step away, his eyes wide. "Just like that?"

"How else would I do it? In Jai Khalar you can't sneeze without everybody knowing about it."

"So how was it?"

Now she *was* blushing.

"It was all right as long as he didn't talk to me."

"That bad, eh? Why didn't you pick somebody you knew?"

"Because! I'm an Honorary. None of you even knows I'm female. Do you?"

Xiriel shrugged. "I never really thought about it. You're just Istar. Why are you worried about this, anyway? Shouldn't you be thinking about the Floating Lands instead?"

"I leave that to you," she answered, and leaned over to elbow him in the ribs. Out of the corner of her eye she saw that Pentar and Anatar had almost caught up with them; they looked a sorry sight, one badly injured, the other blindfolded, helping each other along. She didn't feel any pity for Pentar, whom she suspected of eavesdropping all this time. It was his fault that she was in this mood. After all the work she'd done to establish her authority among men, now Pentar had to come along and by his provincial ignorance disrupt her operation. Bad enough that the two had succumbed to the Sekk and now burdened the party with their injuries; but that they should also threaten Istar's leadership was intolerable to her. She began to wish she'd killed them both, kin or no.

Kassien's face when he alluded to what Pentar had seen—what was that look he'd given her? He had caught Pentar and roughed him up, yet he'd cast rather warm eyes on Istar himself. If he recognized that Pentar wanted her, did he not also acknowledge a kind of complicity? Had he, for a moment, seen her as female first and Istar the Honorary second?

Better not to think about that. It was easy to admire Kassien from the safe distance of being an Honorary and his comrade at arms to boot; it was another thing entirely to think of doing anything about it. Besides, there was too little to go on. Someone like Kassien would never have more than a passing interest in someone like her. She had lived among men long enough to know how easily they were aroused yet with what difficulty they were actually caught as mates. They could be incredibly indiscerning toward women, especially if they hadn't seen or touched one in some time—but if Kassien really desired her, he would be making a right fool of himself, and that hadn't happened.

She knew this, but it was pleasant to imagine that he was attracted to her. Actually, it was more than pleasant. She replayed that memory of his eyes on her again and again; it stayed with her like an actual touch, even after she'd grown bored of thinking about it and tried to wish it away.

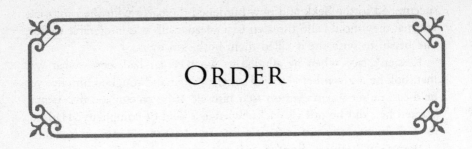

ORDER

$\mathcal{K}$assien said they had gained so much time by using the H'ah'vah tunnel that they could afford to rest more, and though Istar didn't like to admit it, she needed the reprieve as much as any of them except Anatar, who staggered along supported by Pentar, sometimes in a delirium. Eventually Kassien was obliged to remove Pentar's blindfold so that the hapless pair wouldn't go astray.

They rested at midday in a clearing beside the river, where Kassien tried to teach Xiriel how to catch fish with his hands. Xiriel bent his long body over a swirling backwater, hands poised to plunge, head bent as he focused on the dimly seen fish with total intensity. Kassien leaned against a rock and lay back, chewing on flatbread and chuckling. Pallo climbed around in the underbrush, examining the foliage minutely.

"That," he said excitedly, making a great show of pointing out something attached to a red leaf, "is surely a northern cousin of the rusted nail flying beetle we see in the coastal forests of Pharice. There are some dozen variations depending on the type of vegetation where they live, but I have never seen one with such dark eye stalks. I wonder if it is camouflage meant to disguise the feelers as sunburnt pieces of grass—that's what they look like, don't they, Istar?"

"Mmm." She wasn't listening. Having abandoned the river, Xiriel bent over and took a closer look. "It's a bug," he pronounced. "Whatever are you so excited about?"

"I think it's interesting, that's all," Pallo said defensively. "Look how he moves. Look at the coordination of the legs, and look at the way the carapace seems to float over the body. All the bits that are sensing and feeling are on the underside, beneath this shield. All the soft parts are on the inside—the bone, the structure, like our skeleton, is on the outside."

"So?" Kassien drawled.

"So you could study it for combat. It's got built-in armor. But mostly I'm just excited because it's unfamiliar to me. I thought I had seen and cataloged most of the plants and animals of Everien but I was wrong! I have stayed too close to Jai Khalar. There is much to study."

"Is that why you keep pulling leaves off the trees as you walk?"

"Yes, I'll press them and try to catalog them later."

"But . . . why?"

"It's how we study things in Pharice. We try to know as much as we can about the world, and write it all down, and learn from it. My teacher collected thousands and thousands of plants and insects to learn their characteristics. He had a room with hundreds of glass cases and everything he knew about each item was written beside it, and he could use these things to create new medicines or advise farmers how to control pests, or make poisons."

"My grandmother could do all that walking through the woods, tasting things and spitting," said Kassien. "Why make such a production of it?"

"That is how they do things in Pharice," Pallo said. "By keeping careful records. They believe there is an order in things, and they're always trying to find it."

"Here's an order," Kassien said. "Find us some watercress for supper. I miss eating greens. Only see you do not bring back poison mushrooms even if they look like a Pharician delicacy! Pick only what you know."

Pallo sniffed and went off.

"What are you looking at?" Kassien snapped at Anatar and Pentar. "You sit there all gloomy and disapproving but say nothing. Why don't you go help Pallo and earn your keep?"

"No," Istar said. "I want them where I can keep my eye on them."

Pentar hesitated; he had been about to follow Pallo. Now he glanced at Istar, at the ground.

"What is it with you, man?" Kassien said irritably. "This is not Ajiko's army. Say something! Raise your eyes."

Pentar obeyed, but there was no expression in his eyes.

"It's no good," Kassien said. "You can't behave this way. If you don't show yourself to be a man, what choice have we but to believe you still Enslaved?"

"The Sekk is dead," said Pentar. "Istar killed it. My life is now forfeit to her."

"I am not interested in your life," Istar remarked dryly, still annoyed about the waterfall incident. "Anyway, Pallo killed the Sekk."

"You live in a dream world!" said Kassien to Pentar. "Get your sword and let me remind you what it's all about."

"Kassien, calm down," Xiriel said. "It is no good fighting amongst ourselves."

"You embody everything about Ajiko's policies that I despise," Kassien told Pentar and Anatar. "Blind obedience, pigheadedness, self-sacrifice, and stupidity. I don't want you in my command anyway."

"My command," Istar corrected, bristling.

"Ajiko's army knows discipline and respect," Anatar said. "You four behave worse than a band of teenagers in a wine cellar. I have never seen such incompetence or lack of organization and purpose. I have no sword to give and I am ill and probably dying, but I'll crawl under the bushes and die like an animal before I submit to the likes of you."

He began to walk away, his upper body canted sideways as a consequence of the wound. Pentar started to follow and then halted, gazing at Istar.

"Why are you looking at me?" she asked shrilly. "You want to be a soldier. You want to give and take orders. You question my ability to wield a sword even after I sliced up your friend. I don't want your fucking loyalty." She spat. Then she walked away. After a moment, she began to smile. For the first time since the fight with the Sekk, she felt all right.

LATE THAT AFTERNOON the river emerged from its cutting and slowed as the land flattened out. They had reached the edge of the sea plain. Rain had brought a sudden riot of wildflowers and young grass to the sandy lowlands. As Istar's party came down from the hills they could see color steeping the plains almost to the fade-point of the long horizon, where the sea was imagined rather than seen. After the austerity of the bare mountains, all this beauty was intoxicating, and they walked captive to its dazzle. Maybe this was why they were only a mile uphill from the encampment before Pallo spotted the brightly painted wagons, partially hidden by a dense stand of pines lining a brook. Silk tents in vibrant colors were pitched in a rough circle nearby, and a number of animals grazed at the stake. The party ducked into cover.

"They are Bear Clan," Kassien said in surprise. "The king's own people."

Xiriel was peering over the grass. "Looks like a large family. Goats, chickens, everything. As if they've packed up their homes into those wagons."

Kassien and Istar exchanged glances. They were both thinking with relief of the prospect of getting rid of the two Seahawks. No one looked at Anatar; no one had to. Having cleared the air, Kassien and the Seahawks had made a grudging peace, but Anatar was at the limits of his endurance. Since the night before, the Seahawk man's face had been gray with pain, his eyes fevered. The stump of his arm was hot with infection. Pentar, for all that he was whole, behaved wretchedly now that he had been disciplined by Kassien.

Pallo said, "How can we be sure they're free?"

"We can't," Istar said, thinking that Pallo would not soon forget his encounter with the female Sekk. "Not from this distance. But the camp seems peaceful enough. No smoke, no loose animals. My guess is that they are safe."

Kassien said, "We've got to go and find out for ourselves. Who knows, Pallo? You may yet get your dinner."

At last, Istar thought, something good had happened. She and Kassien walked side by side toward the camp, breathing the smell of sun and flowers. When they approached the stand of pines, two large, longhaired dogs bounded from beneath the shade and stood, hackles raised, barking madly at them. A female voice called them to order, and out of the wood stepped a young woman. Her worried face lit up when she saw them. At Istar's side, Kassien suddenly straightened.

"Dhien!"

THERE ARE NO ROSES
IN EVERIEN

With neither thought nor effort, Tarquin's sword glided out in a long arc, forcing the Sekk to leap back or be slashed across the legs. In the interval between the start and finish of the stroke, Tarquin took in the fact that the scene had changed while he had been under the spell: there were fewer Pharician guards ranged behind and around their Master; Chyko was riding around like even more of a maniac than usual; and when Chyko passed through and among them, some of the Pharicians seemed to be picking up his attitude—but others were fleeing from him blindly. The careful order of the Pharician army had broken down.

There was black smoke all over the place, carried on the wind from the direction of the siege towers.

He could no longer see Kivi, but he was reassured by the audible rattle of Deer Clan sticks on Pharician armor. He took the measure of his Sekk enemy, sensing its rate of breathing, relative size and speed, and level of aggression. He felt also the eerie depth of the Sekk, a perception no less tangible than color or smell, yet impossible to describe. He knew only that the Sekk was a powerful magnet, a hole into which all forces conspired to draw him.

The sword reached the end of its curve. He lurched to his feet, parrying a counteroffensive automatically as he drifted sideways and aligned himself, avoiding letting his eyes be caught by the Glass. Then he saw that the Sekk was bleeding from its sword arm.

When had that happened?

When had the Sekk drawn its sword, for that matter?

Kivi was screaming from somewhere behind him, "Fight, Tarquin! You almost broke the spell."

Kivi had to be crazy. Tarquin entered the Sekk's range with a series of cuts that were repelled, then sprang back out. He had come alarmingly close to being Enslaved himself—what could he possibly have done to affect the Sekk spell? He pressed the Sekk again. It was slimmer than he, fast but not solid. One good slice across the abdomen was all that was needed. Yet he couldn't bring himself to close, and the Sekk knew it. He could feel its eyeless blank face pursuing him, and even if he couldn't see the Glass anymore, its presence in the closed fist was implied.

What had become of his violence now?

Kivi had come into view, locked in combat. His sticks whirled and snapped so fast they couldn't be seen. He had disarmed a Pharician swordsman and now closed, snapping the sticks across the unarmored hands, face, and neck with startling precision as he tripped his opponent neatly and continued to thrash him after he'd fallen.

Tarquin was heartened. He and the Sekk circled each other, exchanging test blows but never committing. Each held back, waiting for an opening. It was all backward: Kivi knocking down Pharicians like they were toy soldiers while Tarquin hesitated. He felt like he was in a whirlpool. Everything was becoming smaller and faster; he was being forced into himself. To break free, he had to kill the Sekk. He wanted to kill it, take away the Glass it wrongly held, destroy its hold on these men—for when he saw the Glass he had begun to understand what spell was at work here.

He couldn't do it.

There was fire all around now. Panic set in among the soldiers.

The Glass came out again: the miniature horses, the transparent men. Tarquin charged.

Her voice was in his ear.

"We sat in the cobalt shadows, and the moon was hunting in the leaves, and you were holding the rose in your hand."

"There are no roses in Everien," he told her. "I have never held one."

"You did that evening. We could smell it, like a chord on the silent air." Her lips grazed his spine. She did not touch him in any other place, but he could feel the heat of her all along his body.

"Everywhere the city was falling. You could sense the folds beginning, like striations on an egg before the chick's beak comes through. Something was breaking through from inside."

"I have never even seen a rose."

"Of course you have seen it. It is your sign—yours is the Way of the Rose. It is on your banner."

"Ysse gave me the banner, and the ownership of the signs. I do not know what they mean. I do not want to. Not anymore."

"And there was a rending sound," she went on as if he hadn't said anything. Her tongue probed an old scar about his kidneys. Her teeth closed on it, and she toyed with his flesh.

"I don't remember you," he said.

"Really it was folding, but we couldn't see the pattern from where we were. We were trapped inside it. But the whole city was folding in on itself, disordinating. We had no books to describe this, but you and I held hands and watched, for there was nothing else we could do. We knew we were soon to be parted."

"Where am I now?" he said.

"You are in the garden, where we always meet."

He let out a sigh of relief. *"I thought I was fighting. The Sekk Master, it held my Company in its hand, and all I could think was: How did the Sekk get my men? I thought they were dead. But it's worse than that, isn't it?"*

"They are no longer men. They are the Company of Glass."

"I saw the Glass in the hands of the Master. I don't understand. I remember seeing them die, but I knew it couldn't be as simple as death, if it happened in Jai Pendu. It's haunted me for years. Does that make sense?"

"There are years and then there are years," she said. *"There is sense and then there is everything else."*

She pulled away from him a little, and he wasn't sure whether she'd left him or not. He couldn't know whether he was in a large space or a small one: in that sense this was a place like twilight, endlessly mysterious. Then she spoke and he had to listen.

"You took your men to Jai Pendu. You stormed through the lost city and you climbed the Tower that is the Way of the Eye, and there you took the Glass called Water to bring back to Jai Khalar."

His men were moving all around him, their horses and their armor and their battle paint and their breathing and the easy way they floated in their saddles and everything else about them that was vital and true. The sensations took him over: the smell of saddle leather and the coolness of the gloaming that morning when thirteen riders had assembled before the entrance cave of Jai Khalar, and Hanji had showed the way to the White Road. Chyko had been whistling a jaunty Wasp Clan tune: it was infectious to the point of irritation. The steam came off the horses as they lifted their feet and placed them on the White Road, and Quintar's stomach had been in knots, his eyes heavy from lack of sleep. He had felt all sinew and nerve, but when he had exchanged glances with Chyko, the archer looked as if he were setting out for a day at the races.

"You rode the White Road fueled by hope; but you knew when you took the Water of Glass that you would pay a price."

At the end of the White Road they had come on a black triangle; when they stepped through it, they found themselves in a dark space with three doors. Only one of them would open: it bore the sign of the Eye. They entered it and began to ascend the Tower. Its very substance, its walls, floor, and ceiling were everflowing, made strong and changeful as water. They reached the huge open chamber at the Tower's heart. Everything here was water, as ice or snow or steam—but most of it was liquid that behaved as if bound together. Flashing across that liquid were images upon images. As they watched, a shining globe as tall as three men took form. It rolled from place to place on the polished floor; its surface wavered like liquid, but it hung together like a solid, perfectly round as a ball bearing.

Chyko approached the globe in a half crouch, one inquisitive finger extended. Between his teeth was a curved dagger, and the darts and poison vials rattled on the necklaces that draped his torso. He touched the globe, and its polished surface wavered as oil on a pond.

Quintar said, "Chyko, don't—"

Chyko gazed into the globe and as suddenly leaped back. "Something looked back at me!" he cried, and rebounded as if on a spring. He had another look. "I can see eyes. There's someone in there."

He thrust his hand into the Water and jolted as if stung. The tendons of his neck tightened and he screamed. Quintar rushed to his aid, but Chyko suddenly relaxed and withdrew his hand, laughing. He pranced and posed, gnashing his teeth at Quintar to show his amusement at his own wit. Quintar growled at him and looked into the Water. Inside floated a crystal with many facets, all bright but one. One of the facets of the crystal was entirely dark.

He started to reach toward it, but Chyko grabbed his arm. "No. There are eyes in there. See, one facet is dark."

Quintar did not see. "I've had enough of your games, bug boy. It's a Glass. It's what we came for."

Quintar reached into the globe and touched the crystal in its chill, watery home. The sensation of touching the thing was lost to his memory. It had been good—he was fairly sure of this. It had been good after the way of things that later turn out to be illusion or to possess an underside of unbearable pain. But he hadn't known of such things in those days.

In that instant, the world inverted itself, and where Quintar thought he was holding the Water of Glass in his hand, suddenly he found that *it* was holding him.

There had been a sound: not thunder, not rain, but something low and earthly and alarming. Maybe it was the buffeting of wind against the towers, for he had the feeling of the architecture of Jai Pendu swaying, growing unstable. Outside all the while the Moon dreamed its light onto the sea. It was time to go.

"That is the way of you and I," she said. "It is always time to go."
He sighed. Her hand slid over his hair as if she could stroke it all away, smooth his mind the way she might smooth a child's blanket before saying good night and leaving a kiss behind.

He couldn't get out.

He was in the Water and the Company were not. The Water filled his ears and lungs and bore him up. He was cocooned safely away from whatever was now stalking through the city. He remembered seeing Chyko slip his bow off his shoulder and notch an arrow.

"What's become of Quintar?" said Vorse.

"He's not in there." Lyetar prowled around the globe, looking straight at him but not seeing. "I don't like this place."

Chyko laughed his battle laugh. "It doesn't like you, either. Here comes something bad!"

Chyko was floating back off some invisible enemy. In his movement Quintar recognized the attitude of utmost respect that Chyko afforded to very few opponents, and he could see in the flare of his friend's nostrils that Chyko was alarmed. The chamber darkened. Quintar could no longer perceive its walls or ceiling, and the Water distorted the image of his men as they reacted to the attack. He couldn't see the Company's enemy no matter how he strained. Each of them was fighting, flailing at thin air, turning to track an invisible opponent—shuddering under mighty blows.

Through the medium of the Water, he could feel what was happening to each of them; and it was again as it had always been during the years he had trained them, blooded them, marched them across the hills, and pitted them against one another to make them all strong. He could sense what was going on in their minds; he could gauge their fatigue and their frustration and also their hidden reserves, the strength they didn't even know they had but he knew it.

"I couldn't reach them, but I could feel them. I tried to help them. . . ."
"You had become something else. You had connected."
"Connected to what? To who?"
Her fingertips stroked his brows.

He hurled himself upward. He couldn't get out.

"Quintar!" His name was called. "Hurry, and bring the Artifact. We can't hold out for long."

He shouted a reply, or tried to. He could hear the words in his own ears but they didn't penetrate the Water of Glass. "Don't wait for me. Get away while you can!"

Whatever they were fighting, whether men or beasts or something more alien, it was a powerful enemy. Their blood was spilled and it was not invisible; they were toppled from saddles; horses were skewered, the fallen trampled. The Company were moving like a force that finds itself hopelessly hemmed in, outnumbered. The brilliance of their weapons play was irrelevant. Their courage did them no good. They began to look desperate. They began to break down. He knew they were looking for him, seeking guidance.

He had lost all self-control. "Fight!" he screamed. "Don't give in to it! Fight fight fight!"

This they heard. He shouted instructions, directed them, conducted their weapons the way a choirmaster commands voices, all the while unable to see their enemy or to join them himself. Valiantly they strove to obey his instructions. They gave everything. They fought and fell; they lost limbs and mounts; they were disemboweled; they bled; they were dying. Some were decapitated, others crushed by the massive, unseen forces that opposed them.

All the while, he watched, screaming until blood flowed from his nose.

"Fight! Fight!"

But they faced an impossible adversary.

"You don't understand what happened after that, do you?"
"I . . . I wasn't alone in the Water."
"No. You will never be alone."
"Someone grabbed my hand. It was strong, but small, and the bones were so fine. I was startled. I inhaled water, and the thing was pulling me. I was terrified. This thing, it was no bigger than a child, but I couldn't see it clearly. It was so dark. I panicked and crashed through the side of the Glass. It was still clinging to my forearm, and it scrambled over my back. I can still feel its weight on me."

It had let go of him at last; he broke out of the globe of Water and shattered into the hall where he'd begun.

The place was empty. They were gone; there was no blood; and he had the Water of Glass as a crystal in his hand. That was when he knew he'd been tricked: for somehow his men had been taken, and he was free. Therefore there would be no escape for anybody.

He was free he was free he was free. That freedom, a curse.

Something large and white was waiting for him, moving with a flutter of what Quintar first took for feathers but then realized were filmy robes over a smaller human figure. The figure within was largely concealed, and its face was purest obsidian. The teeth were black and it had no eyes. The figure threw up its hands and darkness flew from its fingertips as liquid; but everything it touched turned to light as if soaked in the luminescent cave growths that the Snake Clan used for lamps.

It brought its hands together and darkness turned to light between them. The Company were still fighting. *He could see them through its fingers.*

In its hand was a Glass, and in the Glass were Chyko and Riesel and Ovi and all of the others.

It said, "Now it is your turn, Quintar, servant of Ysse. You have the Water of Glass and we have touched each other. There will be no going back. Come and join your fellowship."

The thing came at him like a serpent, a wind, assaulting from all angles like no opponent he'd ever known.

He tried to fight, but he couldn't hit it, and its light came after him like a spiderweb. Terror unruled him. In the thick, slow mire of dreams Quintar turned and began to flee; he could feel the white thing like a magnet behind him. When he glanced back he saw its color flash to black and then back to white again as with a terrible slowness he made his legs move him. Quintar was running through the mirror hall to the landing that led to the White Road, and the evil thing followed him, the white robes now pregnant with darkness.

He was down in the crushed grass and the Sekk was beneath him. There was thick, black smoke everywhere, and the sound of men and horses screaming. The ground shook. The Sekk had one hand on his throat and it bucked. He was hitting it again and again in the face, but it did not bleed.

He was not dazed at all by his abrupt return this time: his blood was full of outrage and he could think of nothing but destroying the slender body, slicing open the place where the eyes belonged. But the Sekk was cool and slippery as a fish and it slithered out from beneath him.

"You dare attack Everien with its own people? You dare use my men for your purpose? I'll grind you to dust, you—"

For the first time he saw her properly. She was silhouetted at the top of a flight of stairs. Her dress was unlike any of the traditional Clan garments, rather more like the type of heavy robe that Ysse had taken to wearing in later years, which gave little hint of the shape of the figure beneath. The staircase was strange: a metal framework with no stone or wood between the steps, so that tendrils of lit fog passed through from below. Behind her the sky was full of burning, whether from the falling sun or some other fire he could not tell. The light limned her red hair where it fell across her shoulders, and a shiver of uncertain recognition went through him. One hand rested protectively across her belly. The other held open a gate. Beyond were green and living things, incongruous against the desolate sky.

"We have no choice," she said. "It's awakening."

As she closed the door she turned slightly and he saw that she was pregnant. The door shut to silence and darkness.

His face was in the dirt. The Sekk had a forearm across his throat and was choking him, clinging to his back like a monkey. Inches from his face he saw the Glass lying loose on the ground. He worked a hand free and clasped it. The Sekk's black hair fell around him. He saw its pale hand grasp his own where it touched the Glass; but he felt nothing. He felt nothing at all.

STEW

Ajiko was the last person Devri wanted to see, and Sendrigel was the second-to-last. He had had nothing but grief from either of them for days, he was worried about Mhani, who never came out of the Tower, and he trusted no one else to follow her instructions, so he was always on watch in the office that Hanji had arranged for him at the foot of the Eye Tower. Fortunately, the seneschal's abilities had not failed him completely, for even in this solstice time of madcap behavior on the part of Jai Khalar, the little office had held its ground.

Devri was having a much-needed nap in the middle of the day when they all burst in on him: several guards, a Pharician prisoner, and the two busybodies who were running Jai Khalar in the absence of Lerien. The Pharician was unkempt and he smelled of leather and animals and sweat; he seemed to fill the room with an intense physical energy, making Devri feel dusty and two-dimensional by comparison. Sendrigel rushed up to Devri's desk, his potbelly drooping over his belt to disarray the paperwork—and burst out talking.

"You, clerk! Wake up! We have wasted enough time already just looking for the Eye Tower, and that crazy old man is worse than useless. He sent us the wrong way."

Surreptitiously Devri let the key to the stairs slide into the fountain as he cleared his throat and shuffled the papers on his desk with his free hand. "I am not a clerk. I am a Seer. What do you want?"

"We need to see Mhani. We know she's in the Eye Tower, and she's probably told you not to let anyone in, but this is an emergency so don't bother resisting." Sendrigel did the talking; Ajiko just stood there, gently slapping his fist into his opposite palm. The soldiers behind him stood rigid, eyes forward, unblinking. Obscurely, Devri wanted to laugh.

"I'm sorry, but she's locked herself in," he said. "I'd like to admit you but I can't."

Ajiko gave a slight jerk of his head and two of the guards—both childhood friends of Devri's, as a matter of fact, though they didn't show it now—stepped neatly around him, lifted the desk, moved it aside, and picked up Devri before he could react. Mice scattered from beneath the desk. The Pharician's lip curled.

"If my country *were* invading you," he remarked in a deep voice, "it would be much to your benefit. So this is the grandeur of Everien! Senile houseboys and mice!"

"Sendrigel, I have not asked this Pharician to speak yet," Ajiko said ominously. "Keep him quiet or I will have him gagged."

The Pharician composed himself to silence with the air of performing a favor. Sendrigel was fidgeting with anxiety. "Where's the key, little staglet?" he pressed. "Don't tell me you can't get in. You Seers have a way round everything!"

Devri squirmed as the soldiers' fingers bit into his skinny arms.

"Nirozi! Gen! Put me down! I haven't done anything wrong."

They tightened their grips.

"Your mother would be ashamed of this behavior, Nirozi," he chastised. One of the other soldiers reached out and slapped Devri across the mouth. His lip began to bleed.

Ajiko studied Devri coolly. "I am not here to fight with Mhani," he said. "We are in the midst of a diplomatic incident and the only way that I can communicate with King Lerien is through the Eyes. I know that Mhani would wish for Lerien to have all the information we have gathered. Lerien explicitly told Sendrigel to bring reports to her, and this is our report. If you obstruct us you are obstructing the king."

Devri wavered. "Who is this Pharician? What's he doing here?"

"He is a messenger from Hezene to Lerien. It is your duty to help us reach Lerien through the Eyes. You place us all in danger when you refuse."

"I told you, there's nothing I can—"

The other two soldiers were rifling the desk, and one of them came up with a ring of keys. Systematically he began trying them on the locked door.

"It's never the same door from one hour to the next anyway," Devri babbled. "So how could there be a key? I tell you, when Mhani is ready she will come out."

"She will get no food nor water till she does," Sendrigel said. "I will instruct my men to monitor the exit at all times, and Hanji will be warned to behave himself as well. She must come out eventually. Devri, will you not reason with her? Lerien needs this information. Has Mhani gone mad that she hides herself from us?"

Something must have shown in Devri's face, for Ajiko began to nod slowly.

"The Knowledge is dangerous," he said. "I would not be surprised if she were mad by now. I give you one day, Devri, to get us access to the Eyes, with or without Mhani's help. After that I will use any means available to me to break down the door. It may be necessary"—he smiled slightly—"for her own safety."

Devri drew himself up to his full height. "You cannot break down the door," he said. "You can do what you like with me, but you will not enter the Eye Tower by force."

Ajiko actually *believed* him: Devri could read it in his face. Emboldened, he went on. "Tell me your message and I will make an attempt to reach Mhani with it."

Ajiko rocked back on his heels and stuck his thumbs in his belt, sizing Devri up anew. *The swaggering bastard,* Devri thought, even as he quaked inside because he knew the general could render him unconscious with one blow from the back of his hand. Ajiko said, "Sendrigel, take your Pharician and wait outside. All of you go."

Sendrigel made a noise of frustration and complied. When he was gone, Ajiko cast his gaze on the floor and did not move for several seconds. Then in a flash he stepped forward, caught Devri by the throat, and hissed, "Pharice is not making war on us, you canting little wizard. Their garrison at Ristale was overrun with Clan soldiers."

Devri would have been speechless even if he had not had Ajiko's thick hand crushing his windpipe.

"What do you know about it, Devri?" Ajiko said suddenly, a canny light appearing in his eyes. He threw the Seer backward; Devri bounced off the desk and hit the floor gurgling and coughing. Ajiko stood over him.

"All of us are at the mercy of you Seers. If you tell us the troops are not there, we must believe you. If you show us a scene, we trust that it is a true vision, but we have no way of knowing. My men have been out of communication for weeks! For weeks I have listened to Mhani, and you, and Xiriel, and that old fart Hanji—whatever he has to do with it I've never been able to figure out—you all say, 'We're trying, General. We're working on it. We're doing our best.' Yet for all I know you are all part of the same plot. Don't give me that dumb-dog expression, Devri!"

"But I—"

"Did Mhani order my men to leave their positions and attack the Pharician garrison? Did Lerien? I have a sword in my hand, Devri. I think you should tell me where my men are and who told them to go there."

The general ran his thumb along the blade of his naked sword. Devri swallowed. His throat felt torn inside.

"There is no plot," he whispered. "I swear it. Mhani is trying to find the White Road. That's all I know."

"The White Road is a passage to death. You had better stop her, Devri. I must deal with this Pharician now, and in Lerien's absence I can do as I see fit. This room is going to be full of soldiers and you are going to be in the dungeon if I don't get some cooperation from you. You had better have something more satisfying to say to me by the time I get back."

He turned and opened the door quietly. "Nirozi. Gen. Stand guard outside this door until I return."

Devri listened to the receding footsteps of the men, still rubbing his throat. He got to his feet, tidied his clothes, finger-combed his hair. Then he plucked the key out of the fountain and opened the door to the Eye Tower.

He did not go to see Mhani this time, for he didn't expect her to be reasonable. He slid through her antechamber, under a carpet, and down a ladder. Here he expected to find Hanji's meditation chamber but instead came upon a larder positively swarming with mice. He backed out, climbed through a trapdoor into a gallery overgrown with vines, and began opening doors at random, hoping to find a way back to the part of the Citadel he knew. At last, in a small and dingy wooden corridor that sprouted unexpectedly from the rear of a disused bathhouse, he found the bright silver door he'd been looking for. Flustered and nervous, he entered.

The room was small and octagonal, tiled in yellow and gray. It smelled faintly of spices and water, the latter of which trickled from a carving shaped like an orchid high in one wall, snaked through a complex weaving of stone channels, and finally reached the slim basin that ran in a band around the floor. There was a quality of stillness in the rattle of reeds hanging in decorative bunches from the window ledges that made a constant hiss and slither in the air; in the play of light on the speckled floor; and in the attitude of the man who sat cross-legged on a woven mat, his hands open and lax.

Hanji's face was smoother in repose than in action, yet paradoxically he looked older. He even breathed slowly. Devri felt the air currents in the room eddy and shift with his arrival; then they settled and he was suddenly calmer. He cleared his throat.

"I knew someone would find my hiding place sooner or later," said the old man without stirring. "Didn't think it would be you. What do you want?"

Devri sank to the mat before Hanji. *"Help,"* he said.

Hanji continued to study his empty hands. "Stew," he said cryptically. "I am old."

"Stew? Can you no longer eat solid food?"

That old, familiar look: *Don't push it, Devri.*

"We have leftover venison from the most recent hunt. The head cook decided to do a stew, but the tithe collectors were late getting back from the villages with their load of produce because of a fire at A-vi-Khalar. Both of my assistants had been co-opted by Mhani for some project of hers, so I spent the morning personally organizing six girls to make an expedition down to the king's private gardens. I could not trust them to tell a turnip from a tomato, so I went with them. They spoke of nothing but their hair and the rumored sexual practices of the Pharicians. None of which, I might add, sounded remotely physically possible."

Devri stifled a laugh and Hanji frowned.

"When we got back with the food, there were numerous other problems piled on my desk, which I couldn't get to because of a line of confused clerks unable to work out the simplest schedules for the guard because none of their clocks agreed. Before I could get that sorted, the pastry cook burst in and said that the head chef and the entire contents of the kitchens had vanished, to be replaced by a segment of the records room that we lost last week. This left me with a mound of unwashed vegetables, three or four delinquent *assistant* assistant cooks who hadn't been in the kitchens at the time of the disappearance, and four Seers who somehow found out about the reappearance of the records and wanted instant admittance. In the middle of all this, a messenger comes summoning me to Ajiko. I told the messenger I would follow him shortly, told everyone else I was urgently needed by the general—and came here! I have been reduced to this by a stew. It is true: I am no longer merely not young. I'm not even *getting* old. I am old, I have been old for a long time, and I'm only getting older. Stew!"

"Is there to be no food this evening, then?" asked Devri in alarm.

"I shall let them roast me. Some little nourishment might be obtained by sucking my bones. What's your problem?"

"I know why Ajiko summoned you. Hezene has sent a messenger to inquire why we have attacked their garrison at Ristale—and to threaten us, presumably, with war. Mhani's still locked in the Eye Tower and Ajiko now accuses all the Seers of being in a plot against the army. He says we have been lying about the missing troops. He wants to use the Eye to talk to Lerien. But Mhani told me no one was to go up in the Eye Tower. And Ajiko will be back soon, and he'll find me gone. . . ."

"Ah," said Hanji. "Perhaps I should go have a word with Mhani."

He stood up creakily, swaying like a sapling in a wind. "I'm tired," he said. "And these mice are becoming a real nuisance." One of them scurried across the floor and disappeared into a small hole. "Come with me, boy."

THEY CREPT INTO the Eye Tower together and found Mhani slumped on the floor beside the Water of Glass. To Devri's educated eye, the surface of the Water was crowded with images, moving and still, piling on top of one another and changing places. It was a mess. But . . .

"I can See the White Road!" he cried. "Mhani, you've done it! I see it—but ah, it is too far away."

Hanji put a finger to his lips. "Where is it?" he inquired in a too-nonchalant tone, slipping around Mhani to get closer to the Water. He moved as if she were a sleeping lion. "Why does it not come to Jai Khalar?"

"Don't touch it!" Mhani said dully, beginning to rise from the puddle of robes on the floor. Devri spared her only one glance before returning his attention to the elusive vision of the White Road; but even in that second's glimpse he thought she looked weak and pale.

"It begins outside the boundaries of Clan territory, far away above Snake Country. I can try to trace it down. By your goldfish, Hanji, nothing's been properly monitored for weeks and there are messages piled up. . . . Mhani, why don't you let us take over the routine work, so you can concentrate on the Liminal?"

"No!" she cried. Springing to her feet, she seized Devri's wrist with a sudden strength. "You must leave. All of you must leave. What's been started must be finished."

"But Mhani," Hanji began in a placating voice. Still holding fast to Devri's wrist, she looked at him over her shoulder and Devri saw the tendons in her neck tighten.

"See me swim?" she hissed, and gestured to the image-murky Water. "It's what you wanted, old man. No good crying about it now."

She turned back to Devri. She gazed at him with melting dark eyes, and her mouth worked. "It is winter," she said. "It is winter in the valley of Everien, and I must return."

Her fingers on his wrist were chill, and they cut off circulation.

"You have interrupted me," she whispered. "I asked you not to do so."

Devri looked past her toward Hanji for support. The old man worked his way around to stand beside Devri, but he remained silent and steady as if he was treating with a wild animal. Devri had the feeling that Hanji didn't know quite what to do.

"You are a meddler, old uncle," Mhani commented. Slowly she began backing them toward the door. "Blame me not if your fingers are burned. Now both of you—get out. Get out of my Tower." With a sudden shove, she released Devri in the direction of the door. Her red robes spread behind her like a fan as she flew at them, spittle flying. *"Get out!"*

Devri felt himself propelled backward as if by a wind, and regained his balance only after he had stumbled down several steps, tripping over his own heels. He was quivering. Pulling his blue cloak around him with slightly more dignity as he descended, Hanji said to the Seer, "Now, don't be bothered by any of that performance, my boy. Just keep guarding the Tower, and don't concern yourself with the bad moods of the High Seer. She'll get over it."

BURNING

"They said he had lost his mind when he came back from Jai Pendu alone," Lerien remarked. "And to watch him go into one of his trances that he thinks no one notices, you would say he is still touched. But I tell you all: Quintar was a madman from the day I met him. Even when he was Ysse's pet he was mad. He was the greatest swordsman of his generation and all feared him, and he knew it. Sometimes I think it is *he* who makes the Eyes go wild and who made Jai Pendu perilous, for he was crazy enough to carve up the Moon and eat it, when I was young and under his tutelage."

Lerien's sheathed sword stood upright before him, and as he spoke he leaned on its hilt and peered into the dawn that slowly revealed the disposition of the enemy.

"What will Tarquin do?" asked Ketar in an ingratiating tone—for now that Tarquin was no longer on hand, he was trying to get back into Lerien's better graces. "What *can* he do?"

"He will attack the Sekk, I guess," Lerien said. "It is the most reckless of all options, and therefore he will probably choose it. If Chyko were here, maybe he could think of something wilder; but he is not."

Miro said, "Our bows have longer ranges than theirs. We might make something of that."

"Or we might find a way to poison their supplies," Jakse added. "I am not carrying enough tinctures to give so large an army a case of hiccups; but it is still some distance before they reach the end of the range and climb onto the sea plateau. We might contrive something."

"Their supply trains are surely the key," Lerien agreed. "They are poorly guarded in the rear, as Ketar and Kivi discovered yesterday. We must disable their pack animals, ruin their food stores, and burn everything we can. I am not entirely convinced they intend only to go to the Floating Lands. Why do they have siege towers, and oil, if not to assault Jai Khalar?"

"We might use those things against them," Stavel said. "It's not much, but it is our best hope."

The army had begun to break camp, so Lerien was compelled to finish his plans on the move or be left behind. He was extremely angry with Kivi for making off with the Carry Eye, even if it had done Lerien no good, but he said nothing of it. His small party had come close enough to a complete mutiny already; Lerien needed the support of these men, and if he was in the habit of getting it by diplomacy, then he supposed he had better stick with what he was good at and remain diplomatic—or they would desert him and then he would be a laughingstock.

"Think of it this way," Lerien told them. "The majority of our men have been captured by this force. As far as I'm concerned, the only army I have now are the five of you. Maybe you didn't expect to find yourselves in this position, but the real mark of what you are depends on your actions now. You will have to be as effective as a thousand men each. And you are capable of it. Remember, Quintar only had twelve in his Company."

Then he described his plan. It was a simple one: overtake the rear guard, slip in among the siege towers, set fire to everything they could, and slip out. Even if this only slowed down the advance of the army, it had to be better than doing nothing. Anyway, if slowed down enough, the Pharicians might not make it to the Floating Lands in time to catch Jai Pendu—for the floating city rode to land for only one day.

THE PLAN WAS outrageous, but its execution came surprisingly easy at first. Perhaps because of its massive size, and because it marched on its home territory, the Pharician army behaved as if it had nothing to fear from behind. The siege towers and catapults rumbled along among the oxcarts and mule wagons that bore supplies and matériel for many thousands; strings of spare horses and animals for slaughter were also kept at the rear, where they tended to be allowed to sprawl to either side of the ranks. The rear guard was on foot, and they marched amid such dust and noise generated by the war machinery that they must scarcely have monitored their perimeter, for six men on foot were able to slip in undetected, each at a different point.

After he had overturned an oxcart carrying barrels of oil, opened their spouts, cut down two startled guards, and set the whole affair alight, all of a sudden Lerien started to feel strangely free. He could scarcely concern himself with the politics of Everien when he found himself cut off with no Seer, no Eye, no army, and no horse in what was now enemy territory. His task was so impossible as to seem easy—he really had nothing to lose. And so he got into the spirit of things, releasing all his frustrations of everything gone wrong in the past weeks since the trouble in Wolf Country began. He slashed, and he burned, and if he could not burn all the documents and maps and records that filled his daily life, then damn it he would burn these towers and anything else he could set alight.

But the Pharicians were only complacent, not asleep. Once they realized what was happening, they acted to clamp down on the insurrection in their rear segment. He had told his men to act quickly and get out, and he intended to do the same. Lerien dodged through flames and among overturned supply carts, cutting down anyone who attacked him with the sword in his right hand, with the torch in his left setting fire to anything that looked flammable. He had almost reached the fringe of the supply train when he was lucky enough to spot an escaped horse trailing a long lead rope. He grabbed the rope and was trying to calm the animal enough to mount when a Bear Clan warrior he didn't recognize stumbled out of the smoke and fell at his feet. "My king!" he sobbed. "Forgive me—I think I have been lost to the Sekk!"

"Get up," Lerien commanded. "What's your name?"

"Ivren, my lord," answered the other, gulping.

"Ivren, where is your section?"

The Bear pointed to the rear of the infantry, where the columns had broken apart in the confusion. Lerien edged closer to the horse and caught it around the neck; the animal was well trained, if nervous, and it did not try to unseat him once he was mounted.

"Can I trust you?" he asked, looking down menacingly on the overwrought soldier.

"I think so, my lord. I have shaken it off; it was like a dream."

"Get up behind me."

Thus mounted, the two rode off to round up what men they could of the Clans. Everything was in chaos. Fires blistered and shook the air. Where the oil casks had been struck by flaming arrows, dense black smoke spiraled into the sky and gradually obscured the supply train and rear guard. Multiple blazes had caught nearby, spreading quickly in the sedge and dry midsummer grass of the border country. The main body of the army ground to a halt, with the ranks erupting into confusion. This gave Lerien hope: if Ivren had shaken off whatever spell bound the Clans, then others must have done so, too.

Still, they were surrounded by enemies, and the air was hot and hard to breathe. The remainder of the cavalry section detached itself to begin riding back down the columns. An elite mounted squad had already vanished in the smoke. A tight knot of spearbearers with shields had closed around one burning siege tower; the king could only infer that one of his men was inside that circle, but he did not have the luxury of rescuing any one person when he stood a chance of getting back whole regiments of his lost army. Everyone would have to fend for himself.

As Ivren guided him toward the rioting Clan troops, Lerien saw that some of the Clan soldiers wore their Animal colors instead of Ajiko's uniforms—a disturbing observation because it meant that even the newest and most inexperienced recruits were here, the ones for whom there had been no time to make regular uniforms. Everien must be drained of virtually all fighting-age men. At the moment, however, the lack of Clan uniforms worked to Lerien's advantage: it was easy to pick out his people among the Pharicians, now that they were at close range.

Ivren gave a shout and his comrades began to rally round the king.

"Get yourselves horses if you can, and fly!" Lerien said to them. "Quick, in case the Sekk tries to reassert its influence. I will wait for you at the base of the cliff—ride south along it until you find me. Draw any Clan soldiers you find with you, and forget any spells you have been subject to."

Ivren got down and gestured to his men to follow him. They struggled against the tide of Pharicians, who were having organizational problems of their own. Officers had begun riding among the infantry, screaming orders that were only partly obeyed in the upheaval. Then Lerien caught a glimpse of Taro, who had found himself a horse and was shooting flaming arrows at the supply wagons while he clung precariously to its bare back.

The operation was beginning to feel less foolhardy and more feasible; but now he had to bring his men to order. He signaled Taro to stay close by him and pointed to the approaching Pharician horsemen, who, Slaves or not, were not going to be friendly at a time like this. The archer responded by shooting one of them, first in the leg, and a second time in the back as he was bending to loosen the arrow from his calf. The second arrow caught a lucky gap in the striated Pharician armor and the rider slumped in the saddle. The horse checked his stride, sensing a problem. Out of nowhere came Ketar. He sprinted toward the animal from the off side. His sword surged ahead of him as if pulling him forward, cutting down two dead-eyed Wolf Clan Slaves and hamstringing a third; but Ketar scarcely broke stride. More horsemen were almost on top of him.

Arrows flew and dodging them he stumbled over the churned, uneven earth. The wounded rider was struggling with the reins, and the horse had wisely slowed to a walk. The smell of fire brought up the whites of the horse's eyes. Ketar took two long strides and vaulted over the shifting hindquarters. He ripped off the Pharician's helmet from behind and dragged the length of his sword along the rider's throat, then cast the dying man to the ground. The horse staggered sideways at the change in weight and then began to buck. Ketar was thrown up against the poll and had to scramble for reins and stirrups.

When he got the horse's head up and had established control, he looked over at Lerien for approval.

Lerien gestured that they should get out, and Ketar gave a roar of disappointed protest. The scene around them had fallen into a momentary lull. Slaves were lying injured or dead, and many more were running away from the formation, Pharician and Clan alike. Smoke blew sideways through charred grass. To his left Lerien could see a group of supply carts surrounded by Slaves, but the group seemed to be breaking up and some were running away from the conflagration. Others were attacking each other.

Yet he could not count on this chaos to last. The army was huge and it had been well-ordered. He couldn't hope to cripple it, only to sting it and then get out with as many men as he could. Lerien spotted a handful of Seahawks hacking their way out from among the Pharicians. There was a great noise of hooves as well as the clash and shout of hundreds of men as they reacted to what was, within the scope of the whole army, a smallish incident.

"Get out, Ketar," he ordered. "Take as many of ours as you can—but get out. If you get too ambitious, you'll be trapped."

Ketar obeyed with a snarl. Taro came within earshot again.

"Shoot the riders!" Lerien bellowed to him, seeing that all these were Pharician and therefore fair game. Then he spurred his horse against the tide of fleeing Slaves. Some of them fell in his path—the victims of each others' arrows, he thought at first, before realizing that they had simply lost their minds. Well, he could not expect to recover them all. Another rider overtook him and then turned in the saddle, still riding hard, and fired a crossbow back at him. The bolt went wide as Lerien's horse, growing winded, turned aside slightly; into this newly exposed line of vision came Stavel, his back turned as he trudged away from the fire. The Pharician bore down on the Wolf fighter, crossbow cocked. Lerien screamed a warning and Stavel turned, saw the danger, and threw both axes in succession. One bounced harmlessly off the corner of the boxy

Pharician saddle. The other smacked into the Pharician's helmet—as pretty as a song, Lerien thought, letting loose a spontaneous shout of appreciation—and unseated him. Lerien dug in his heels and rode down the fallen rider, jerking in the saddle as the horse's hooves struck armor and bone; meanwhile, Stavel began trying to catch the loose horse, which was badly spooked by flames that now roared toward them through tinder-dry grassland.

Lerien turned his horse's head into the fire and there was Kivi, staggering away through the surge of uncontrolled Slaves. The Seer grabbed hold of Lerien's boot for balance. He was breathing so hard he could barely speak, his cloak was gone, his sticks were charred, his face soot-blackened and his hair singed. There was blood on his boots and trousers, and his mouth was swollen and torn where someone had struck him a blow.

"Tarquin . . . gone . . ." he coughed, blinking smoke-reddened eyes. "Sekk Master—" Here he broke off, shaking his head and coughing.

"What happened?" Lerien's horse skittered sideways as a fleeing Slave made a wild gesture at it and then ran on, unseeing.

"They fought. . . . Sekk has a Glass. . . . Company are . . . there, but Tarquin . . . gone."

"What do you mean, 'gone'? Dead? In flight? *Where* has he gone?"

Kivi was shaking his head from side to side in wordless denial. "Something about . . . Glass. For a minute . . . spell . . . stopped. Men go free. Now . . . the Sekk . . . take over again."

Lerien dismounted and gave the startled Kivi a leg up. "Ride," he commanded. "Wait for no one. Get away. Use the Eye to watch the army if you can. Look for me. I will join you when I can. Until then, ride as fast as possible for the Floating Lands, and get out of range of their horsemen. Engage with no one. If you See Mhani, tell her what has happened and get guidance. I will meet you when I can."

He wasn't sure if the Seer was taking in his instructions, but Kivi nodded and rode off. Lerien ran into the smoke.

He passed his own subjects, and while he was glad not to have to fight them, for the Slaving spell, if that was what it was, seemed to be suspended or even broken, the sight of them in such a condition made his throat thick. They didn't seem to recognize each other, and where the Pharician cavalry rode, trying to restore order, many of the Clan soldiers allowed themselves to be trampled or cut down without resistance. When one of these riders made the mistake of trying to herd him like the others, Lerien was in the saddle choking him to death before the

Pharician knew what hit him. The king was furious, and though he believed that Tarquin was gone—probably through some new manipulation of the Knowledge about which it was best not to think too much—he had made up his mind that he would not turn back without mustering at least some of his people and leading them away from their Pharician oppressors.

Miro galloped up beside him, bow on his back and short sword already bloodied. He pointed into the fire and shouted, "Jakse!" The Snake had just picked up an ax from among the bodies and was turning to face one of the Pharician elite guard on foot. Lerien winced: Jakse was no Wolf, and the ax would be wasted on him. Miro checked his horse, got off two shots against the rider, and then had to put away the bow again after his horse leaped sideways around a gout of flame, reared, and started trotting away from the fire. Lerien swept down on the Pharician and drove his sword through his ribs; the dead weight spun him around and almost dragged him out of the saddle. As the Pharician's body hurtled past, all glimmering segmented armor, blood-red helmet, and flying black hair, two Deer fighters leaped back to avoid collision. They looked up at Lerien with understanding in their faces, and he was heartened.

Jakse looked dazed and weak.

"Get up," said Lerien, maneuvering his horse alongside the Snake. Then he raked the two Clansmen with his eyes. "You have been under the spell of a Sekk," he said. "If you want to stay free, get yourselves some horses from the Pharicians and ride after me. Bring as many of our people as you can rouse. Forget your shame and win back your lives."

They touched their foreheads automatically in the age-old custom and ran off to fight. Taro climbed up behind Lerien, and the warhorse again turned to avoid fire.

"Where's Tarquin?" Lerien asked, hoping for a better response this time. But Taro only clutched his arm and pointed to a sudden clearing in the smoke.

"The Master comes," he said hoarsely. "We'd better get out of here. Fast."

Lerien strained to see what kind of Sekk could rule so many men, but before the figure could resolve from the background of smoke, two Pharician riders swerved and came toward them, their horses bloodied and foaming.

"Clansmen!" cried Lerien, standing in his stirrups. "Flee the Sekk! Follow me or die!"

He whirled the horse and galloped away from the flames, seeking open space. Others of his party joined him, having acquired their own mounts somewhere along the way. But Lerien's horse, burdened with two, could not run fast. Some of the Clansmen remained free and began to exchange shouts of recognition with each other; draw their weapons; run.

"To me!" Lerien shouted as he rode. "If you don't trust each other, then follow me. But don't turn and look at the Sekk."

But even as he rode, some of the men were losing confidence, slipping back into Slavery as the mind of the Sekk and its mysterious Glass went to work on them. Lerien kept riding hard, making good ground against the remainder of the Pharicians, and wanting badly to believe that once they'd reached the higher ground, his escaping men might slip the range of the Sekk's control and fend for themselves.

Stavel, on foot, had gathered a group of mixed Clansmen and was marching them away, making them turn their backs on both the Sekk and their hostile compatriots, some of whom were consumed with the Sekk-induced madness that had slaughtered so many innocents in Everien. Lerien changed course to meet him and shouted terse instructions. "Get horses and follow us to the Floating Lands if you can. Otherwise—to the hills. Keep clear of the Sekk."

Stavel raised his fist as Lerien thundered by at the head of a growing band of Clan horsemen that formed a ragged wedge. The Pharicians seemed too preoccupied with rounding up and herding the errant Clansmen back into formation than with destroying the small band of riders, and soon Lerien found himself out of bowshot. He slowed his flagging horse and looked back.

The army had been lamed, but only because of the damage to the siege towers and the confusion caused by the fire. The ranks had begun to re-form themselves. Nearer to hand, the cavalry pursued deserters, but had not succeeded in capturing all. He found himself hoping that there were more men hiding in the grass and scrub and ditches and that they would find their way to him. It was desperately important to him that he should save as many as possible from the fate of Slavery, even if he wasn't sure how he was going to go on from here or what his next objective should be. He had been thinking on his feet when he'd instructed the others to get horses and meet him; now he wondered whether he might put together a solid enough force to brave the Floating Lands. They had come this far: surely it was worth trying for an Artifact?

His horse had caught a few breaths; now he pressed on. It was important that he gather his forces and make plans while the Pharician force was still regrouping. Any head start he could get now would pay dividends later, no matter what he decided to do. He needed to contact Mhani at once.

DAUGHTER OF A DAUGHTER-THIEF

The girl seized the collars of the dogs, which had been about to pounce. Before any of the others could react, Kassien had begun to run toward her, inspiring the animals to new heights of hysteria. Istar and the others trailed behind warily.

"Saxifrage!" the girl scolded. "Pebble! Behave yourselves. You know Kassien."

A laugh escaped Istar at such names being given to dogs the size of ponies. Pebble snarled at her. But when Kassien dropped to one knee and called the dogs, their behavior transformed instantly. They began to whine and wriggle, and once released by the girl they bounded forward and bowled Kassien over, all tongues and tails.

"Enough!" he gasped, trying to get out from under Saxifrage, who was sitting on his chest. "Enough. Please. I surrender."

Dhien stood over him, hands on hips, shaking her head in mock disbelief. "Do get up, Kassien."

Kassien wiped dog saliva off his face and rose. The dogs transferred their attention to the rest of the group. Their hostility was undiminished, with Pebble taking a particular dislike to Istar. He planted himself in front of her and growled elaborately.

"Don't back up," Istar said to Pallo, who appeared about to climb onto Pentar's back to avoid the snapping jaws of Saxifrage. "Don't show fear or you will only make it worse."

Pallo froze. He was breathing so fast Istar was sure he would make himself faint, and every time Saxifrage barked, he flinched. The dogs' mistress had occupied herself in brushing grass from Kassien's hair, an

operation he made no secret of enjoying. Dressed in wide-legged panta-
loons of Bear Clan spidersilk that rippled when she moved and a heavily
embroidered overshirt whose rich green hues offset her brown hair,
Dhien was extremely pretty. Kassien had eyes for nothing else—not even
his companions beset by slavering hounds.

"Don't mind Pebble," Dhien called after a minute, smiling apologeti-
cally at Istar. "We would give a better welcome to strangers if we were at
home and not afraid for our lives. I'm Dhien."

The dogs retreated at her whistle, looking ready to spring again given
half a chance. Kassien hastily introduced the others, and then before Istar
could speak, he said, "We're perishing for some hot food, and Anatar is
wounded."

"Wounded?" Her sympathetic eyes passed over them and focused on
Anatar. She grimaced. "Why didn't you say so at once? I will take you to
our fires. It isn't far. Come, Anatar." She took his uninjured arm and led
them through the trees. "Have you been fighting Sekk? Are they near
here? Should we move out?"

Kassien stopped her questions with a curt "No. It was far from here,
and it's over."

"How did you find us? We thought our camp well-concealed."

"Not with tents in those bright colors," Xiriel said. "And not to
anyone coming down from the mountains."

Dhien glanced over her shoulder at the Seer, seeming to take him in
for the first time.

"How long have you been here?" Istar asked before anyone could say
anything more that might allude to their quest.

"Only six days at this camp. We broke an axle not far from here on the
rough ground, so we are making repairs and resting the animals. It is still
a long way to the edge of the plateau, and there is no cover after this
point. The nights are so short that we cannot hope to travel by darkness.
Speed is our only ally."

"You cannot be going to the Floating Lands," Kassien exclaimed.

"No, no—we will go away west and then north toward Ristale."

"There will be trouble for you if you go that way," Istar said grimly.
"Lerien may well be at war with Pharice by now."

"We've made it this far. We won't be turned aside," Dhien responded,
and her lips tightened slightly. The dogs had gone ahead; now they
bounded back through the trees and fell into step with her as the little
group neared the far edge of the wood. Voices could be heard, and the
rhythmic clang of metal on metal. Saxifrage whined and bumped against
Kassien plaintively, but received no attention. Kassien was frowning.

"But it is ill-timed," Xiriel admonished. "Jai Pendu is on its way, and it is likely there will be battle all across these plains. You will not find anyone to trade with in Ristale, and you may have trouble making your way back."

"We're not going back." She lifted her chin, looking at Kassien as she spoke, but he didn't meet her eye. "They have taken all our men. Now we flee to save what's left of our line."

"You are leaving Everien." Kassien's tone was expressionless, but his jaw worked.

"We must."

She stopped. They had reached the wood's border, where a meadow gave way gradually to marsh, and then to water where the river widened and slowed. The tents were pitched in a crescent on the higher ground just under cover of the trees, but there were fire circles scattered across the meadow, and animals grazed at the stake all across the space between trees and river. In the cleared semicircle between the tents lay a wagon on its side, surrounded by various tools and a makeshift forge. A well-muscled woman of about thirty was laboriously hammering, the sweat streaming down her arms and her face smoke-blackened. Other women were engaged in various tasks from cooking to mending. An enclosure made of fishing net had been constructed among the pines, and within it a group of young children were playing. Old women sat among them talking in a halfhearted fashion, but they stopped as soon as the strangers appeared. One of them rose laboriously. She resembled her Clan animal as much as any human Istar had ever seen, her hazel eyes examining the strangers slowly and dispassionately from a wide face set on a wider body. There was power in her flat-footed, square stance, as if her bulk were saying, *You will not get past me so easily*. She looked directly at Istar, and the two took each other's measure.

"Great-Aunt Siaren, I'm stunned to find you here!" Kassien took three steps forward and went on one knee before her; the woman laid a hand on his head absently and addressed Dhien.

"You are sure they are safe, girl? Were they followed?"

"They're alone. I saw them coming. They have fought their way down from the mountains."

Siaren looked down on Kassien, whose head was still bowed. Her eyes shrunk to sparks within folds of leathery skin, and large, stained teeth showed in an oddly tender smile as she stroked his hair. "You look tired, little Kass. It has been a long time since you were home. You must see Hallen and tell him all about it. Dhien, see to their injuries, and bring them food, and I will tell Hallen they have arrived."

Istar felt weak in the presence of Siaren's calm. She had been so close to the edge of either panic or collapse ever since leaving Jai Khalar that the relief of being able to surrender decision-making to someone else was doubly sweet. She said nothing as each of her companions was led off in a different direction by Bear Clan women who seemed all too pleased at the sight of armed men. Then she shook herself slightly and realized she must not lose her sense of purpose. Siaren was watching her from a discreet distance, and when she caught Istar's eye she said, "You are Chyko's daughter."

Istar smiled. "You knew him?"

"Everyone knew him. He was a notorious gambler, dancer, and daughter-thief. He stole one of mine and sent her back three months later, pregnant and full of praise for him. He had convinced her he had a rare disease that prevented him from copulating with the women of his own Clan, and so was forced to spread his seed where he could. Hallen took six brothers and went after him with a pike."

Istar shifted uneasily. She was beginning to have doubts about Siaren's hospitality.

"What happened?"

"What do you think happened? They came back bruised and bleeding—Hallen's jaw was broken and he couldn't eat for weeks." She guffawed. "They said they'd been waylaid by a dozen bandits with clubs."

Istar suppressed a smirk and looked away.

The old woman said briskly, "The Clan chieftains are away hunting. But Hallen's too old for that now. He's working on the wagons, just around the bend in the stream. I've sent the children to fetch him, but he's never quick in answering a summons."

Then Siaren turned and shuffled off toward the wood again without another word, leaving Istar alone and puzzled. Her companions had disappeared into various tents. She made for the river and located Hallen by his feet protruding from beneath one of the wagons. Tools were scattered about nearby. Istar introduced herself and received no reply.

"Do you need help?"

"Hand me my awl if you would," said a deep voice.

A large, calloused hand appeared and she placed the tool in it. She could hear him breathing and grunting, and the wagon shivered slightly. The silence grew long. She sat down.

"You broke an axle?"

"Not on this one."

There was another long pause.

"The fitting for the harness has broken."

"Ah."

"We came over rough ground some days back."

"You must mean the borderlands, the steppes." She was eager to please the old man—he was a Clan Elder, after all—and her tone sounded young and breathless. He said nothing. She persisted. "How long will you stay?"

"Another day or two, maybe. There is good fishing here, and I won't push the beasts too much, too soon. We have a long way to go."

Encouraged by this veritable flood of words, Istar said, "How far do you make it from here to the Floating Lands? We are in some haste."

There was a thump and a muffled cry. Hallen emerged, white hair disarrayed, rubbing his forehead and looking consternated. "What do you want with the Floating Lands?"

"We go there on Lerien's business. I cannot say more." The lie escaped her easily.

Hallen covered his ears; he was a big man, and the gesture looked silly. "Ah, I will not hear such foolish reports of Lerien! I thought my grandson had some sense. If he sends you to the Floating Lands, he has lost his wits."

Istar settled herself on the ground beside the old man. "Have you ever been there?" she asked, and Hallen promptly dove for the underside of his caravan, presenting her with nothing more expressive than a large calf with a sandaled foot to talk to.

"They are bad places, those islands."

"Why? Tell me about them."

"No, no. You don't need to know more than that they are bad luck and to be avoided."

Istar said, "I place little stock in vague feelings. I am on an assignment, and I will not be intimidated by any inanimate object like an island, even if it appears and disappears; even if it sings and dances. I want facts. Hallen, you must tell me all you know of the Floating Lands."

The wagon shook as he wrestled with something. He coughed and threw a tool out. "Chyko was a right bastard. You are the daughter of a daughter-thief and I'm not sure what that makes you. I must think on this before we speak further."

His tone was decisive. She stood and looked down at his thick, hairy legs. She was thinking that all she wanted was to get to the Floating Lands on time, and it seemed every step of the way she had to struggle to prevent herself from being dominated by someone who thought he knew better than she did. Mhani, Lerien, Tarquin—and now this old man.

"I'm an outbreed and an Honorary," she said. "I've never had an ounce of privilege. I'll fight anyone I have to. Anyone."

He laughed. "You favor the left arm. Have it seen to, and get some

food in your stomach and some sleep under your ear before you challenge me. Even a fat old man like me has a few tricks you might not
know.''

Istar was amazed that he had noticed the way she carried her arm in
the few moments when he'd actually been looking at her, and she could
think of nothing to say. She was trying to think of a caustic rejoinder
when a boy of about fourteen appeared out of the trees, calling Hallen's
name. He paused and swallowed when he looked at Istar, clearly awed at
the sight of her weapons and armor. Hallen reemerged, flushed.

"Siaren says Istar's to be given a tent now," he said, glancing back and
forth between Istar and Hallen as if he didn't know whom to address.
Istar smiled at him, deeply pleased because she was only a few years older
than he was and could see that he knew it. She gestured to him to
precede her and turned her back on old Hallen. It had begun to drizzle,
and she was only too glad to crawl into the tent that had been set up near
the cooking fires. Pallo and Xiriel had already eaten and were bickering
halfheartedly over dry bedding; outside, children could still be heard
squealing in play as the shadows stretched longer. Istar was given fish and
wine, which made her eyelids droop and removed all need she might
have had to think. She didn't ask where Kassien was.

"It's silly to sleep in broad daylight," she muttered as she removed her
gear.

"If you take that attitude, you'll not rest till the equinox," Xiriel
countered, rolling himself in a blanket and presenting his back. "I for one
will sleep for a week, or would if Pallo here didn't snore like a Fire
House."

She didn't stay awake to listen to Pallo's retort.

IN THE MORNING, women came to bathe them and clean their
clothes. Honorary or not, Istar was taken to a separate tent for propriety's
sake; she didn't object as she was tiring of the constant company of the
others. She knelt in a basin while two girls her own age bathed her; they
acted as if they were afraid to look her in the eye, but their voices and
hands were extremely gentle, as though she, not they, were fragile. She
hadn't realized quite how rough she'd been living, and even the simple
pleasures of warmed water and soap made a great difference. One of the
girls timidly asked if she could rebraid Istar's hair and refresh her Clan
paint, to which she agreed gladly. While this was going on, the two girls
chatted about inconsequential things, slipping in and out of Bear dialect
and giggling softly. Istar began to relax and forget about her troubles.

Much clucking was made over the cut on Istar's arm; the girls behaved as if they were in pain themselves, just looking at it.

Just as she was beginning to feel really fine, Dhien came in to check on her. "You should not be using this arm at all," Dhien reproached her. "From now on you must keep it in a sling. Did you not know that when it is hot to the touch and discharging this way, something foul has got into it?"

"Of course I know that," Istar said, hissing as the woman cleaned the wound, which did truly look awful. "I have not had time to concern myself with it."

Dhien sighed. "I will have to speak to Kassien. He can be so stupid about such things."

"It is not his to say," Istar said, surprised.

"Oh?" The Bear woman drew back and the two studied each other. Initially, once Dhien had been out of sight, Istar had entertained the idea that she had only been imagining Dhien to be pretty—that she was, in fact, not much better than ordinary. Now, at close range, all such possibility vanished. The chestnut hair, worn long and loose as no Seahawk woman would ever do; the hazel eyes that changed color depending on the light; the flawless skin and perfect bones—these were undeniable evidence that Dhien was not to be competed with. Luckily, as an Honorary, Istar was not meant to compete—or so she told herself as Dhien went on to say, "Shouldn't the leader be responsible for those who follow him?"

"What makes you think Kassien is the leader?"

"He told me himself."

Istar felt her nostrils flaring. "What exactly did he say?"

Dhien glanced around secretively. The other girls had left. In a whisper she answered, "He said he was leading this secret expedition to Jai Pendu, commissioned by Lerien himself. But have no fear: the secret is safe with me. I will tell no one of your mission."

Istar was so furious she could not respond. She endured the rest of the consultation, teeth clenched as Dhien prescribed ointments for the wound and bandaged it. Then she went looking for Kassien.

"I only said it to impress her," Kassien said when she found him, not meeting her gaze. "Dhien has been holding out on me for years. I thought—well, you know how it is. You should have seen her when she heard we were going to Jai Pendu!"

"You had no right to say you were the leader. Now they are treating us accordingly."

"No they aren't. By the Knowledge, Istar, they are my own Clan. You can't expect them to ignore me. Anyway, we have always worked as a team. All of us."

Istar looked into his brown eyes and said, "I approached each of you with this plan. I did the research, I made the preparations, I set up the petition to the king, and *I* made the decision to go ahead even when we were refused. That makes me the leader."

"That was never formally decided," Kassien resisted. Their eyes fought for a minute; then he swore under his breath, kicked a stone, and said, "Damn you, Istar. What are you so uptight about? I can't believe you're making such a fuss about something so stupid. It wasn't a public challenge, it was something I said in bed. You want me to bow down before you and say, 'Yes, Istar, I'll do everything you say?'"

"No," she shouted. "But you might think twice what you say to civilians *in bed*." She almost choked on the last two words.

"You know, you don't have to act so high and mighty. You think you're Ysse come again, but you're still only a kid. I'll tell everyone you're the leader, all right? Is that what you want?"

Istar opened her mouth to fire another shot, then changed her mind. She had already lost any facsimile of dignity she'd possessed. "You've made your point. Let's just forget it."

He was glaring at her, still clearly game to argue. He gave his head a little shake when he realized she wasn't fighting anymore.

"Fine."

"Fine."

"Hallen wants to have a meeting. We were just waiting for you to be finished with your bath. Come." He stalked off toward the fire circle ahead of her.

HALLEN HAD BECOME positively loquacious overnight. They all sat on the ground, and he adopted the cross-legged pose of the storyteller. Pallo was still yawning behind one hand, but Xiriel had a look of cagey alertness about him. Istar thought, not for the first time, that he was wasted as a Seer. He had the build and the dark, scowling countenance of a natural warrior, yet seemed to possess no interest whatsoever in combat—or in anything other than the Knowledge. Istar studied his strong bones, his deft hands, and the concentration on his face and thought regretfully that such attributes were wasted on Xiriel. He could be a real warrior, one who could easily accomplish feats that someone like, say, Kassien, could manage only with hard effort—and Istar probably not at all. For she was not blind to her own limitations; in fact, the wound on her arm, though superficial, had reminded her of her deficiencies. She had had to work twice as hard as any man to achieve what skill she now possessed, and it rankled her that Xiriel should have so much unused ability. Yet he loved the Knowledge, and undoubtedly he could appreciate more than any of them the story Hallen was telling. The old man's deep voice was slow and deliberate.

"I can make the bees come. I can sleep my way through winter, and I can wait. This is the Bear way. It's in my bones and blood. But the jewels of the Fire Houses don't belong to us, and a lake of candles deep in the Earth is no place for our like. We don't know how to use these things."

"We can learn," Xiriel said. "We can solve the riddles of the Knowledge."

"Maybe. But why did the Everiens leave, my Seer? If their Knowledge was so strong, why did they leave it behind? Why did they flee Everien?"

"Lake of candles?" Pallo interrupted. The Bear leader cast a tiny censorious glance in the Pharician's direction, cleared his throat, and resumed the story.

"You believe," Hallen said, "that the land is true. The sun, the rain, the hills beneath your feet—these things you are sure you can trust. People are not reliable; they may betray you or be swayed by the Sekk. The land is something else.

"For almost seventy winters I have watched the snows come over Everien. You know how precious the light gets; when the clouds break and a piece of sky turns gold, all of the upcountry is reborn in a moment. What was flat steps forward. What was gray is colored. In the silence you can hear the sheep a mile or more below as if they were right beside you. The light will only last a few seconds before the clouds return, and you feel night following everywhere you go. In the upcountry you can see the shapes of the mountains change as the sun backs around them like a courtship dancer.

"It happened many years ago, even before the Fire of Glass. I had to get a message to Naethen, who had gone to serve Ysse in Snake Clan territory, far above the treeline. I was on my way back. White Screamers had caused avalanches all along the road by Fivesisters Lake and it was impassable. Despite the snow, I was obliged to make my own way above the line of the road and risk meeting the Screamers or walk into Sekk-Enslaved territory."

Xiriel nodded. "White Screamers would be the preferred evil, I think. They seldom actually attack people."

"No. They do not. But I was soon too preoccupied with the elements to even think about the Screamers or the Sekk. There was a storm and I was forced to take shelter in a cave. At first I thought it was a lion's den, and I was afraid to enter; but there were no markings in the snow, and I was too pressed to use much caution. I went in and rested. After a few minutes my eyes had grown accustomed to the darkness, and I probed farther back. I wanted to find the far walls, so that I could be sure to be safe from whatever might otherwise come crawling out. After a while I saw light, faintly. I kept going back.

"A warm breeze began to move and I realized I was emerging into a large underground cavern. I could smell and hear the water. There was a lake, totally still except for the sound of dripping water from the ceiling. A hundred or more vessels of light floated there, each only as bright as a candle; yet in that darkness, they dazzled."

Istar was scanning her memory for a cave entrance such as Hallen described, but she did not know the area by Fivesisters Lake very well, and if he had mistaken it for a lion's den, the entrance to the cavern could not have been very large.

"I went closer. It was warm in the cave; even the water was warm. There must be hot springs there, but at the time it seemed only to me that I had left the world of snow and exposure behind and I was now in a well-ordered place, where I might rest. I knew I had found some refuge of the ancient Everiens."

"Were they candles?" Xiriel asked. "Or were they Knowledge-lights?"

"They were not candles. One of them floated close to the shore, and I went down to the water to get a closer look. It was a simple globe of light, and it floated right into my hand. I looked into it, and someone looked out."

"What?" Xiriel spontaneously jumped to his feet. "Where is this place? Take me there!"

"Calm down, Xiriel," said Kassien, gesturing for the Seer to sit. "What's got into you?"

Xiriel subsided, looking embarrassed at his own outburst. Hallen appeared troubled. Silence fell. Kassien stood and pushed Xiriel back to his place around the circle. Hallen was deep in thought.

"No," he answered grimly at last. "I was afraid. I didn't like what I saw inside."

They waited for him to say what he had seen, but after Xiriel's question, Hallen seemed reticent again. Siaren leaned over and whispered in Istar's ear, "He is not used to being interrupted. Or challenged. He is an old man, you must understand."

Hallen said, "When I fled that place, I did not exit the cave where I had come in. I came out of the cave expecting snow and ice and wind, but it was not like that. There was ocean, and birds, and I was on one of the Floating Lands."

He fell silent again. The insight flashed through Istar's mind: *He is hibernating. He shuts down his mind when he cannot cope.*

"Hallen," she said. "Anything you could tell us, however insignificant it might seem to you, could mean a great deal to us. You may choose to leave Everien, but those of us who remain must cope with the Knowledge." She didn't want to say more; Hallen might react very badly indeed if he knew they were going to Jai Pendu.

The old man shook himself. He began to narrate again, not in answer to Istar's question, but as though reciting from oral tradition.

"There was a time when the world was different," Hallen said. "The Animal ways were strong, and of the many Clans that grew up out of Animal truths, all were rooted in the integrity of the land. Animal spirits moved among us, seen and unseen. The world was alive, and when we pressed our weight on it, it pressed back. When we looked at it, it saw us. When we called to it, it replied. This was before any of us became herders or farmers. Now the land and the animals are dumb and blind, but then all the world was alive, and we were just pieces of it. We died in droves. We remembered only what we needed to remember from one season to the next. We fought over women, but seldom over food, and never over land."

"How can you know of such times? Nothing has been written of them." Xiriel's tone was even. It was clear that he was not being taken in by romantic stories.

"I am old. I know."

"But how can you remember these days? You would be the same age as Ysse if she were alive, and when she was young the Clan ways were disintegrating. That was how she was able to unite us."

"That is not what I mean when I say I am old. Age is more than an accumulation of years and a slow wrecking of the body. You learn to see and understand more when you get older; life is more precious and so deserves your scrutiny and careful thought. It is not that I can see into the past, but rather that I can see inside the way things are. I can perceive the underlying nature of the world. I am not distracted by bright or elemental things."

"You mean the Knowledge." Xiriel's gaze locked with the old man's.

"It does not make you as fine and high as you think. There are virtues in the Knowledge; I could never deny this. But it belongs to the Everiens. We are only caretakers of their remains. And we have our own laws and ways, which you children would do well to remember. The day will come when you may need them more than you can now imagine."

Kassien said, "We do remember. We act *for* our Clans, on behalf of our ancestral ways. But we can't live in the past. The Sekk are a real threat. We need the Knowledge. These are hard times."

"It has never been easy for our Clan, Kassien," said Hallen. "We hoped by throwing in our lot with Ysse that we would finally have a chance at better lands, better weapons, better trade—a fragment of the Everien jewel. We have done everything right. We have adopted the sword, the common language, the Eye system. We have sent our men to Ajiko's army and we have succeeded in getting a Bear on the throne at Jai Khalar. But where does all this get us? The Wolves maybe no longer persecute us, and we have more goods than before, but our sons are all gone to war, leaving their children unprotected. Look at your Clan sisters, Kassien! Why is Sylden hammering at the forge? Why does Dhien have to carry a dagger? It is a disgrace; it is unnatural; and now in our homeland we must hunt Sekk when we should be hunting our meat."

Kassien said, "You will not like living in the Wild Lands. All of you are accustomed to comforts. You expect access to medicine, and lights for the long winter nights, and horses and goods from Pharice. There will be none of these things in the forests of the Wild Lands, only wild Wolves who will take the women for their own and make them servants, and relentless winter cold, and no herds at all."

"We are not afraid," said Dhien stoutly. "We will go back to the land sooner than see any more bloodshed for the sake of the Knowledge."

"Go to Jai Khalar," Istar urged. "You can shelter there while Lerien regroups the armies. Petition to have your warriors sent back to their own villages! Fight for the way of life you want; don't simply vanish into the forest."

Siaren shook her head. "Jai Khalar is already overburdened with land-less folk. They are spoonfed and coddled and the men are sent to fight while the women become a harem for the clerks and officials who govern there. It is not the Clan way. Clan men must protect their women and children first, their land second, and their country third. Any man who does otherwise has lost sight of what he's fighting for."

Kassien bristled. "You know nothing of strategy, Siaren. If you had your way every man would stand in the doorway of his own steading and brandish torches at the Sekk hoping to drive them away like bats. You cannot defeat the Sekk in a wrestling match. You must adapt."

Dhien said, "The years of serving Jai Khalar have changed you. The Kassien I knew believed in his family."

No one spoke. The reference to Bennen's death grayed the air.

Kassien stood up. His jaw worked. "I did all I could to save my brother. I could not stand guard over him every day. I did not understand him, but I tried. I tried to protect him. Ah—why do you attack me now? My own family!"

He spun on his heel and strode away. Istar leaped up and followed him. Pentar followed her. Istar glared at him and waved him back, but he kept following at a distance. She ignored him.

Kassien rampaged through the camp and out the other side, into open meadow where birds took flight, arrow-swift, before him. It was hot and windy; his hair, newly trimmed probably by Dhien, whipped back from his face as he reached up to his throat and tore the bearskin cloak open, flinging it to the ground as if it were an enemy.

He turned and saw her. "How could they say that about Bennen?" he cried angrily. "You know how it was, Istar. *You* know."

She met his eyes. "They're wrong," she said simply. "Bennen was . . . nothing could have saved him, not in those circumstances."

He wiped tears away. "The Knowledge is nothing more than a curse," he said, and she thought he sounded just like Tarquin. "I hate it. If it were a H'ah'vah, I would kill it."

"Bennen was happy in his way," Istar said, taking Kassien's hands. "His life was short, but it was not tortured. He really didn't care about Pierse. Half of him was always . . . somewhere else. Maybe it still is."

"Do you think so?" He searched her eyes.

"Don't be sad, Kassien."

He smiled a little, looked down, swung her hands from side to side. "You were a good friend to my brother," he said. "I know we fight, but—" He looked in her eyes again and she felt her face getting hot. Then she spotted Dhien walking toward them from behind Kassien, and she must have showed some reaction because he stiffened and turned as if anticipating an attack. As he recognized Dhien, Istar let go of his hands and stepped away. The brown-haired girl took her time reaching them, placing one foot before the other in a straight line so that her hips swayed from side to side. Istar drifted away.

"I'm sorry for what I said," Dhien said. "No one blames you for what happened to Bennen—that is the fault of Ajiko's policies and the crushing of Clan brotherhood. That is why you must return to us. You are a good warrior. We need you." She looked pointedly down at the cloak he had cast on the ground. She picked it up and put it on her own shoulders. Then she walked away without another word.

Istar kept her eyes turned toward the ground. For a long, wrenching moment, Kassien was locked in a silent struggle; then he suddenly sprang forward after Dhien.

"Wait!" he called. "Dhien, wait!"

Dhien turned. Kassien caught up with her. She threw herself into his arms. Istar pivoted and started to walk in the other direction, sickened. After a moment, Kassien called her name. She pretended not to hear: what was he going to say? *Thank you, Istar, for being such a good friend?* She didn't think she could stand that.

She had not planned on walking anywhere today, but after this little scene she found herself taking off across the open countryside, unwilling to be among people. Pentar was still following her at a discreet distance; she smiled maliciously, thinking that she would wear him out as well.

WHEN SHE GOT back to the camp it was full of activity. She found Pallo, who was carrying baskets of greens for Siaren. Catching sight of Istar, Siaren said, "I hope that the argument between Hallen and Kassien doesn't mean that the feast will be spoiled. I've been up half the night working."

There was something odd and hidden in her manner, Istar thought; but the big old woman made her feel secure, and Istar wanted to trust her, so she did not ask questions. She had the impression from the way everyone in the camp was acting that the tension had been broken and whatever had transpired earlier around the story circle had now been forgotten.

Pallo chimed in. "The Clan chieftains are back from the hunt, and Hallen has fixed the wagon, and they are going to give us a huge feast before we all go on our way."

"But there is still the matter of the injured to discuss," Siaren said. Pentar had been hanging around on the fringes of the discussion; now he spoke up.

"Anatar is weak now, but he will recover, and when he does, he may be of use to you. Ultimately he will wish to return to his own people, but at the moment, one cannot help but notice that you have few men to defend you."

"Yes," Siaren replied. "We will take Anatar with us, and be glad of his presence. But what about you, Pentar?"

"I will go with the others, if they will have me," Pentar said, and looked straight at Istar. She was annoyed that he had made it a public statement; she didn't wish to take him, but she also didn't want to have an open discussion about it in front of Kassien's family.

"We have not yet settled on our plans," Istar said to Siaren. "This is something we must decide amongst ourselves."

"But please can we do it after the feast?" Pallo begged. "I can smell something *wonderful*."

Siaren laughed. "Then take an ax and go cut some more wood for the fires."

Pallo stood and bowed to her. "I'll be happy to do anything I can to expedite matters concerning food."

They spent most of that day lounging in the sun by the riverbank, resting. The idea of a feast had reminded them all just how hard they had been going at it lately. The little taste of ordinary life that they'd enjoyed in the camp was proving seductive. When Pallo came back from chopping wood and joined the others, he was full of praise for the Bear Clan.

"I think I'll defect and become a Bear," he announced. "Do you think I'd look good in a fur cloak, like Kassien?"

"It is easy to think of reasons to go with them," Xiriel said, yawning. "We can't See Jai Khalar, so for all we know the White Road has opened and the king rides it to Jai Pendu."

"Or we can't see Jai Khalar because Pharice has invaded and destroyed the Eyes," said Kassien ominously.

"Even by the fastest reckoning the Pharicians could not have reached Jai Khalar yet," Pallo contradicted. There was a shadow in his eyes, and Istar pitied him, for it could not be easy to be an outsider among the Clans, and in a time of war surely his loyalties must be in conflict, no matter how much he purported to prefer Everien to Pharice.

"It is difficult," Kassien went on slowly, "to think of facing more monsters and probably worse when the bees are on the thistle like this. The world seems so peaceful, here in the sun. Look at all these insects and flowers; there's a universe in miniature here in the grass, and we sharpen our swords."

Istar cynically thought it more likely that Kassien was invested in the universe between Dhien's legs, but she kept quiet. Pallo also studied the thistle. "Their world is more violent than ours. The bees are not peaceful, and the butterflies are hunted, and the ants are positively rapine. I would rather be human."

"You say the strangest things sometimes, Pallo," Xiriel commented.

Pallo blushed, uncertain if this was a compliment or a complaint.

"The Bear Clan have been kind to us," Xiriel continued. "But I want to see Jai Pendu. So I vote we go on. After my nap." He closed his eyes.

Here in the sun, even Istar was having second thoughts. *I don't know if we can do it,* she wanted to say. *We may be fools rushing toward death when we could do some good here. And I am tired of traveling, and my arm hurts, and if I were not an Honorary would Kassien love me? Probably not.*

But she didn't dare speak her mind, so she simply said, "Of course we must go on."

There was a silence.

"You know what's strange about these moths?" Pallo mused. "They have these markings on them like eyes, so that birds will fear them and not eat them."

"How do you know that?" asked Xiriel.

"So they teach it in Pharice, and it makes sense, does it not? But what I want to know is, does the moth know about this? He can't, can he? Because it's like he's wearing a sign saying 'Back off! Don't eat me!' but it's not written in his language, it's written in the bird's language."

"Hmm," said Xiriel.

"So?" Kassien asked.

"So imagine you were walking around all your life with a message written on you, but it wasn't meant for you or your kind, it was only sensible to some other kind of creature. And you could go your whole life without knowing what it meant, or even that it was there."

"Pallo?"

"Yes, Istar?"

"Practice your lunges."

"No. I don't feel like it."

Istar closed her eyes. Tomorrow she would be a warrior. Tomorrow she would embrace death. Tomorrow she would be so fucking fearless they would all pull together beneath her brilliant leadership.

A moth landed on her face and she jumped, giving a little scream.

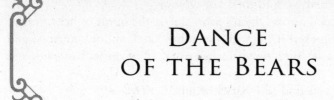

DANCE
OF THE BEARS

Istar had always associated feasting with winter and darkness, and it seemed strange now to find fires and music and food and drink all laid out under the sunlit sky. The reluctance of light to disappear altogether was a subliminal reminder that the midsummer arrival of Jai Pendu was now very close. To be among people engaged in revelry made her feel torn. The enthusiasm of the Bear Clan exiles was catching in its way, and it had been a long time since she and her friends had simply enjoyed themselves. The food was a simple matter of the meat that the chieftains had brought in from the hunt plus whatever fish and wild plants had been gathered while the family was stalled at this site, and the entertainment was improvised; but this makeshift approach actually made everyone participate more wholeheartedly than at any of the extravagant festivals Istar had ever attended at Jai Khalar, where the setting had a way of overshadowing the people.

It was the older generation of the Clan who seemed to let themselves go the most, Istar noticed. The children, of course, hurled themselves into the fun as she would have expected under any circumstances, but the young women seemed curiously subdued. Dhien, however, managed to attract a crowd at one point. Istar avoided the scene until the repeated *ooh*s and *ah*s broke down her reserve. She took her drink and went to peer through the circle of onlookers to see what was so exciting.

In her hand Dhien was holding a tiny replica of a bear. Istar had never seen anything so exquisite: it was a perfect specimen, exact in every detail, but only a few inches tall.

Then it moved.

They all jumped. Saxifrage, who seemed never to leave Dhien's side, gave a high-pitched yip and then sat, whining.

The bear padded across Dhien's palm and up the inside of her forearm. Delicately she plucked it up with her other hand, and it squirmed and clawed as it was set back down in her palm. It sat on its haunches and yawned.

"Where did you find it?" Xiriel breathed. *"How—"*

"It was made in the Fire Houses," Dhien said, looking sidelong at him out of her now-green eyes. "With the Knowledge."

"Who made it? How?"

"It was Resien, but he went off to war. We haven't heard from him in months. I don't know how he did it."

"A fusion of the Knowledge with the Animal ways," Xiriel said. "I've never heard of such a thing."

"It is never awake for long," Dhien said, smiling. "Maybe because it's a bear, it gets sleepy. . . ."

As she spoke, the bear settled into the hollow of her hand and closed its eyes. Dhien took Pallo's hand and gently transferred the creature to his open palm. He stared at it in delight. Fortunately, just then Siaren summoned everyone to eat and Istar was spared exercising her faculty for jealousy any further.

She sought out Hallen, sat beside him in the feast, and unobtrusively got him drunk. She wanted to pick his brain about what he had seen in the Floating Lands. She was wondering what the other Clan leaders might be planning without informing Jai Khalar. Hallen rambled a good deal at first, but as he got drunker, his mind seemed better lubricated, and he began to explain his thinking.

"You are much too young to understand. Ysse came into power only forty years ago. For a thousand years or more before that, it was the Clans. War was a way of life, but when I speak of war I mean the kind of war such as pits man against man, not army against army. Ysse herself was a product of those traditions, and for all that she induced us to put aside Clan quarrels to turn back the Sekk, she had a deep respect for Clan ways. She never attempted to build an army such as the Pharicians have, where the foot soldiers are faceless and expendable. Quintar's Company, Istar, was a miracle! He had the finest warriors of his generation, each alone a match for a dozen lesser men, and your father better than them all. Technically speaking, child, your father was outmatched by no man, not even Quintar his captain."

Istar felt her nostrils flare. "Why was *he* not leader, then?"

"He wasn't interested. Quintar's great talent was in molding men to his purposes without ever taking from them their essential dignity or

Had Kassien known? She looked over at him, but his eyes were absorbed in the sight of the approaching dancers.

It was too late now. She could not protest without giving offense; and anyway, if Kassien opposed her, her protests would probably do no good. She swallowed and sat back, watching the drama unfold with a sinking feeling.

The dancers began to appear. They had been painted with phosphorescent pigment that made them shimmer every which way they moved. They were wearing nothing else, and their hair fell wild around their faces as they complied with the music, which sounded harsh and dissonant to Istar's ears.

All of the musicians were female, but it was up to the audience—the men—to set the beat with their hands and feet. Despite her misgivings, Istar was enthralled at first. Unlike Seahawk ceremonies, the Bear dance did not tell a story. The shapes that each dancer made with her body were startling and dramatic: sometimes all tendons and strength, like a bow; sometimes soft as drifted sand. For some the music was an exterior presence, something unnatural to be coped with, and the effort of the dance was apparent. For others the music was a moving inside, a manifestation of some secret part of themselves. The latter was the case for Dhien. She was entirely unselfconscious, showing no embarrassment at the circle of men watching her. On the contrary, she attuned herself to her spectators' reactions, accepted them all, and responded through her dance. There was a magical quality in the way she made each of them feel she was dancing for him. Even Istar felt it, and she was no man.

But sooner or later these dances always got down to business, and in this case Dhien had already made up her mind whom she wanted. She was not alone in her preference, but she made the most stylish approach. She drifted along the circumference of the circle, letting herself be grazed by fingertips that came away shining; meeting eyes; touching foreheads; and then whirling away. When she got to Kassien, there was a crowd of other women. The drumbeats quickened and were punctuated by wild, birdlike cries.

By now it was not so amusing; in fact, the spectacle was almost enough to make Istar sick. A horde of eager females swarmed around her companions, oozing fertility. Pentar snagged two right away, and Pallo was dragged off into the bushes by an entire posse. Xiriel held himself aloof for a long time, but finally allowed a willowy young girl to sit on his lap and play with his hair. Although no one was particularly looking at her, Istar felt ashamed. She wanted to leave, yet she could not take her eyes off Kassien and Dhien.

Dhien's rivals had fallen away, either outmaneuvered or exhausted.

She was dancing now for Kassien alone, and his fingers glowed with her courtship paint where he had managed to touch her. His lips also sparkled. Her body now swayed from side to side, her pelvis in constant motion as her movements became frankly sexual. When she swept close enough to Kassien he would touch whatever part of her he could reach; then, teasingly, she retreated. Yet each time she approached, she stayed a little longer. The drums played on. She gyrated just out of his range, then inched toward him with little jumps. He ran his hands over her breasts, capturing one and covering it with his mouth. The music quickened and there were whoops and yips of encouragement. Dhien trembled and cried out, then tore herself from him and continued to dance, her hair now in total disarray. Kassien looked like a man possessed; as long as she was still dancing, the rules forbade him from leaving his place in the circle. Either she would have to draw him away from the fires, as Pallo had been drawn away, or he would have to make her forget the dance and stop. Otherwise, he was forbidden to move or restrain her. Dhien came in for another pass. She had pulled out all the stops now, and the drums beat furiously. The remaining men clapped and shouted.

She bent forward. His hands reached for her breasts, and her hair fell around him. The music paused; there was a shout; it resumed. He drew her closer. She continued to dance, but her movements were restricted now, for Kassien had leaned forward, resting his head against her belly and drawing his hands up her thighs. Her torso folded over him and her hands stretched down his back. There was a suspenseful pause—and then the beat went on. She turned her head to one side and her face was transfixed with desire. One of Kassien's hands curled around her haunch; the other reached its destination between her legs. Her hips began to move rhythmically against him. The drums stopped. Dhien did not. Her feet were still; only her pelvis moved.

She had ceased to dance. The audience roared. Kassien, triumphant, stood and picked her up. Now the music resumed, on a different beat, and the remainder of the single dancers returned to the fire circle, revived, to surround the couple. Istar did not wait to see whether Kassien intended to copulate with Dhien right then and there. She took the change in the scene as an opportunity to slip away, hoping to leave unnoticed. To her consternation, the two girls who had attended her earlier followed, making offers. Barely biting back her anger, she dismissed them, wondering if Dhien had put them up to it to insult her. Then she reminded herself that she had no right nor reason to be insulted. Custom was custom, she was an Honorary male, and there was nothing she could do about it.

• • •

THE NIGHT HAD all but run out, so she didn't sleep. When it was light enough, she went over their provisions and gear, making small repairs and taking stock of what they had. Saxifrage and Pebble cheerfully kept her company—excluded, it appeared, from Dhien's tent, which had been tied shut from within. When Kassien emerged to relieve himself, Istar waylaid him, before he could settle back in bed with his prize. "Don't get too comfortable," she said. "Time is short. We leave today."

He rubbed his eyes, face, hair. He was blushing and smiling. He scuffed a toe in the dirt. "Look, can you give me a bit of time with Dhien? We'll talk about this after breakfast."

"I think we should talk now. Don't look at me like that. This is an assignment, not a family reunion. Or a wedding."

He glanced at her sharply. "All right," he said seriously. "Let's talk." He led her off away from the tents. They saw Pallo and Xiriel coming up from the river. Istar didn't ask where Pentar was; she was glad to be rid of him.

"I can't go with you to Jai Pendu," Kassien said definitively. "I'm going to stay with my Clan. Protect them. I've thought hard about this and I know it's the right thing."

"Thought hard while you were pearl-diving between Dhien's legs?" Istar accused. She was being crude deliberately, hoping it would hide her jealousy.

He laughed. "Who could begrudge me, though? Istar, listen to me. These people are vulnerable. They need me."

"I need you, too. *We* need you."

He said nothing.

"Kassien, this isn't about what you want. It's about duty. You can't say that all bets are off now, because no one ordered you to take on this quest. You have committed to it and now your commitment is being tested. You enjoy wearing your rank, don't you? You enjoy the privileges it brings you. But there's a price to pay, and this is it."

"I have a duty to my Clan also."

"Is that truly why you are doing this? Or is there some other reason?" He looked away.

"I have no hold over you, Kassien. None of us has any hold over the others. I won't try to stop you. But consider what you are doing to us, who must go on." She gestured to Xiriel and Pallo, who had apparently overheard them and came blearily to join them, hastily donning clothes and rubbing eyes.

"That's just it," Kassien said heatedly. "*Don't* go on. Come with us. We'll start over, somewhere far away from the Knowledge and the Sekk. My Clan would gladly accept you all."

Istar could feel the relief forming in the minds of the others as they considered an alternative to the road to Jai Pendu, to the Floating Lands of which Hallen remembered so much horror, to the chaos and death that were surely to come. . . .

"I will go alone if I must," she said. "I am not afraid."

It was morning. Their shadows snaked along the ground, and the wind stirred the reeds. Birds could be heard but not seen. Impatient, Istar said, "You lot discuss it among yourselves, all right? I'm going regardless of what you decide; make no mistake about that."

She strode off toward the river, wanting to make a dramatic exit; then stopped. She could hear them talking. She started to go forward again, stopped again, and crept back along the path. They were having a heated discussion.

"She's Chyko's daughter," Kassien said. "And she's damned good. But we're all going to be killed."

"She got us this far," Pallo said.

"Pallo, you don't know what the hell you're talking about. I admit she has something about her—maybe it's the mystique of an Honorary—and it's true she's scrappy. She's a smart girl. That doesn't mean she's going to survive the Floating Lands. We have to be realistic."

"You can't say that to her," Pallo interrupted. "You'll only make her worse. She'll take it as a challenge."

"I don't want to be the one to tell her," Xiriel muttered.

"It has to come from you, Xiriel."

"She won't take it from me," Kassien agreed. "She's angry at me because I won't tell her what she wants to hear."

"That's not why she's angry," Xiriel contradicted, and then bit off his words.

"I'll go with Istar." It was Pentar's voice. *Shit,* Istar thought. *Just the one I don't want trailing at my heels attracting Sekk like raw meat for dogs.* "I will represent Anatar as well, for though he lies ill he would go with Istar if he could."

Xiriel said, "This is all getting too emotional. If I had my Carry Eye, I'd show you the paths I've found through the Floating Lands and we could—"

Istar turned and left. There was no point in eavesdropping. She went to the river to wait for them to make their decisions.

•   •   •

IT WAS LATE afternoon before Pallo came to find her, and he was in a hurry. "Kassien's coming," he said. "Xiriel talked sense into him. And Hallen is upset, so we have to leave right away. Come on!"

He grabbed her hand and ran toward the camp. Istar slid free and followed more slowly. She had begun to tremble. She was suddenly afraid.

They found Kassien and Xiriel beside the newly repaired wagons. They were sorting through their gear while a handful of girls and young boys looked on. Hallen and Siaren were nowhere to be seen; apparently the travelers were being officially shunned, but the few Bears who disobeyed their elders' orders now piled gifts and food on the travelers, most of which were useless. Xiriel patiently put the gifts aside and calmly organized what they needed for the next leg of the journey. Kassien avoided Istar's gaze. He looked as if the whole world were against him, and when they were packing and he tossed her a sharpening stone, he threw it at her head. It stung her palm when she caught it.

Dhien was even worse. When she came to outfit them with perishable supplies, her eyes were heavy from lack of sleep and reddened from crying. She was still beautiful.

Kassien took himself off to do some other errand, acting as if he found it too painful to even see Dhien. But his lover was slightly calmer. Dhien passed Istar some rolled spidersilk bandages and a bundle of medicines.

"You hate me," Istar said.

The Bear daughter stopped and looked at her searchingly. Thoughts passed across her face too fleetingly to be traced. "No," she said finally, her mouth snapping closed around the word so quickly it was as if she had not meant for it to escape. Then she sighed. "I don't hate you. But I think you are very foolish. You live in the same dream world as Kassien. And you're too young to have such responsibilities."

"I have no choice in my age."

Dhien shrugged and continued packing, but a barrier between them seemed to have slipped down. "He's been in love with me for years," she remarked. "I always liked him. But I was waiting to see how he would grow up. *Whether* he would grow up. Soldiers often don't. Especially officers."

Istar said nothing. She wasn't sure she wanted to hear this.

"I hadn't seen him in a couple of years. He's changed. And, to be honest with you, in our Clan there are five women for every man in my generation. I can't afford to be too selective." She laughed. "You think I sound calculating, don't you? That's what I mean when I say you are too young. You just haven't seen anything yet of life."

Istar ignored Dhien's condescension. It hurt to think that Kassien was infatuated with someone who saw him in such pragmatic terms. She was wondering what to say when Dhien suddenly leaned across the baggage and grasped her hands. Her expression was pleading. "Send him back to me."

Sympathy welled up in Istar from an unexpected source. She didn't say anything, but she met Dhien's gaze for a long moment. Then she went on with packing. Pentar had appeared at her elbow and she was suddenly furious with his constant shadowing. He had been getting on her nerves for some time, and now he was the perfect target for her pent-up frustration. She turned and seized him by the arm, dragging him away from the others.

"Pentar, you and I are going to have a conversation. Come with me."

She led him well away from the crowd. "Tell me what it was like to be Enslaved. Tell me what happened to you so I can be sure you're over it."

He shook his head violently. "Can't. Mustn't."

"Then leave me. I can't trust you if I don't know what you are or where you've been."

"I owe you my life, and the lives of those I would have killed if you hadn't killed the Sekk who Enslaved me."

"Pallo did that."

"Only with your help."

"This song doesn't sound any sweeter now than it did before. Let me reason with you. I have no use for you. I don't want you at my back. You say that you want to repay this debt, but you're a liability. Besides which, you were always one of Ajiko's boys, weren't you? He will not be happy with you if you come with me, assuming you survive. Which you probably won't."

She glanced at him to see if her words were having any effect. He smiled at her.

"Pentar, it's not funny! We're going to the Floating Lands—does that mean nothing to you?"

"Nothing but trouble," he said seriously. "We should go with the Bear Clan."

"You really are asking to be pissed on, Pentar," Istar said heatedly.

"Sorry."

"You annoy me like a sticky burr, and you're about as useful."

"You don't know that. Try me."

She snorted. "I beat you once and I could beat you again."

"I was Enslaved," he said. "How could I fight under the Sekk spell? My comrades would not have fallen to your party, either, had they been free. We were mad."

"Let's test it, then," Istar suggested, brightening. "Let's fight."

"Absolutely not," Pentar refused. "I won't fight you."

"Then I'll have to kill you," Istar concluded.

"I guess you will."

"Come—the others will support me." Still gripping his arm, she dragged him unresisting back the way they had come. When they reached the others, Xiriel and Kassien had all the packs ready to go. Kassien said he saw no point in their fighting among themselves.

"We'll use wooden swords," she said. "No blood. A training contest. If I win, Pentar stays here. If he wins, he's free to do as he pleases. Fair?"

"It sounds a bit vague," Xiriel commented.

"Fair, but silly," Pallo added. "I'll see if there are some wooden swords about somewhere."

"I don't want to fight," said Pentar. "Even wooden swords can be dangerous. I will not hurt Istar."

"Then Istar will have to hurt you," she snarled under her breath.

Kassien was watching her, and he smiled a little. "Are you having fun?" he mouthed.

Pallo came back with some sticks he'd found. The two squared off, Pentar protesting to the last. Istar sallied against him, knocking him back a couple of times, always going to his legs to try to unbalance him. Pentar fought left-handed and he seemed slow; she picked up on the periodicity of his movement and cut into it, stabbing for his midsection and slicing at his leg on the way out.

"Close with him, Istar," coached Kassien. "If he had armor on you'd never penetrate it like that."

Istar ignored him. If she closed with Pentar, he'd use his superior weight and strength against her. She had to dart in and out of his range, breaking him down a little at a time until he made a mistake.

"Those are butterfly kisses!" Kassien taunted from the sidelines. "Cut him, Star!"

Pentar showed no interest in the emotional byplay going on between Kassien and Istar. He behaved like a friendly opponent, showing no dismay even when Istar sliced him repeatedly and nearly disarmed him once. Then he knocked her down and backed off while she got up. As far as he was concerned, this wasn't a real fight.

All right, Istar thought. *I've had enough of you.* She charged, cutting angle after angle as she went, driving Pentar back so that the onlookers had to give way. All the while her eyes bored into him. She set out to destroy his gentleness, which she hated all the more because it was directed at her unasked-for. It was as if he had wiped out her very existence as a person, an Honorary. She opened up and let it out, and Pentar was forced to parry and retreat at a frantic speed. But she had spent herself, and he caught her a glancing blow on the shoulder; she ducked, went for his gut, and his blade came down on the back of her head with so much force that she was knocked flat, dizzied.

"That's it," Kassien called. "Match over. Pentar wins."

Pallo was bending over her trying to help and she knocked him aside effortlessly; he went flying. She climbed to her feet, weaving from side to side, and faced Pentar, of whom she was seeing two.

"All right, you bastard—fairly won. You're in. But stay clear of me."

"I'm sorry," he stammered. "Have I hurt you? I didn't want to hit you so hard but you pressed me."

Pallo interceded, steering Istar away before she could draw her real sword.

"He was lucky," he told her, tugging on her braids and slapping her back to distract her. "He was lucky, and in a real fight you'd have sliced his legs to ribbons before he ever got near you."

"He won," Istar said, astounded. "He's good. I overestimated myself."

"Hey, it was just a practice bout. Don't take it so seriously." Pallo squinted worriedly in the sun.

She took a deep breath. "Never mind," she said. "Maybe I needed something to wake me up."

Istar walked on ahead of the others, leaving Kassien to make his teary farewells out of her sight. As she walked, her stomach calmed. The others caught up with her one at a time. The light rested thick as honey on the sea plateau, and the grass was still in the evening heat. Their shadows walked tall and certain. Istar looked at hers and tried pretending she was big enough to fill it.

FINALLY A
CONFABULATION

$\mathcal{B}y$ $t\text{§}e$ $time$ Lerien had pulled together his motley collection of escaped Clan soldiers, they found themselves trailing the army on a parallel course, following the line of the last hills of the Everien Range. At their southern end the mountains ceased abruptly, giving way to flat grassland that stretched between the gates of Everien and the sea. All this land would have been a tidal plain, except that it had been lifted a thousand feet along the fault line of the Everien Range in a straight line: Everien, its bordering tide plain, and all its mountains towered over the neighboring Ristale from a height of a thousand feet. Thus the cliffs in which were hid the monitor towers; thus the virtual impenetrability of the high valley now deserted by its ancient owners.

The army was already approaching the geological anomaly that raised Everien up, and if Lerien attempted to overtake them, he would be trapped between the army and the side of the sea plateau and cut to shreds. Nor could he risk circling around the Pharicians from the other side. They had apparently regained control of their men, and they could easily send out a party to destroy Lerien's ragtag group without breaking stride if Lerien should make the mistake of getting too close. He had no choice but to hang back while the Pharician force began swarming up the ramps and steps that generations of traders had cut in the wall of rock supporting the plateau.

They were now only a few miles away from the sea, and decisions would have to be made imminently. He now realized that a good deal of the success gained by his mission of sabotage must have been caused by Tarquin's temporary wresting of power from the ruling Sekk. His new-found confidence was informed by caution, for Kivi had been the first of his original party to find him again, that night under shelter of the cliffs.

"It had an Artifact of some kind," Kivi repeated. "I wasn't close enough to see it closely, but it was not a mere Eye. To judge by Tarquin's reaction when he saw it, the thing was possibly a Glass."

"What Glass? The Glasses have only ever been found in Jai Pendu!"

"I know. But I can't imagine what else it might have been. They fought over it. Tarquin fought like a god. I have never seen such sword-play. He was tireless, and when he engaged with the Sekk everything around stopped. Even the Pharicians couldn't help watching. That was when I noticed the spell was weakening. The Sekk held the sword in one hand and the Glass in the other, and although it wasn't able to wound Tarquin, it eluded him in the most spectacular manner. No matter what he did, no matter how inspired his timing or his tricks, he could not hit it. But the men around began to wake up. Soon a shout went up that Tarquin the Free was amongst them, and the riders . . . the phantom riders, Lerien, they are his Company! They, too, came to a halt and watched."

While Kivi was talking, Lerien studied the swarms of Enslaved as they made their way up the side of the sea plateau. The steep parts were ruddy where nothing would grow, and the ramps used by traders' carts made zigzags up the thousand-foot-high incline. Stretched out thus into a long procession, the enemy force looked even bigger. Infantry climbed long flights of steps cut in the clay generations upon generations ago. There was something inexorable about their progress that held Lerien's attention.

Kivi was saying, "I went among the Clan soldiers and told them to run before they were Enslaved again, and the Pharicians did not take kindly to this, although they, too, seemed dazed. Then Tarquin faltered. It was as if he had lost his magic, and I shouted encouragement to him and I think he heard me, and he resumed the fight. After a moment he got his concentration back and again they battled. I didn't see all of it, for I was trying to wake up our warriors. When I looked again, they were on the ground, and Tarquin was holding the Glass and the Sekk Master was on his back. And the ghost riders, they put away their weapons and started coming through the crowd toward Tarquin and the Sekk."

He paused, licking his lips, his eyes darting away as if remembering some fear.

"And then what?" Lerien prompted.

"And then Tarquin disappeared."

"You mean he was displaced? Like a window in Jai Khalar?"

"I suppose. One moment he was there, the next moment the Sekk was standing up and looking through the Glass at the riders, and they drew their weapons again and rode off. Then the Pharician officers started whipping their men back to order, and I ran. I tried to take Clan soldiers with me but they would not listen to me. I guess I do not look very convincing."

"You look like a bleeding cinder," Lerien said. "Well, Tarquin has not defeated the Sekk. It is still a danger."

"My lord, there's something else. It's the Carry Eye—"

Lerien's eyes flashed bright, hoping to have finally a confabulation with Jai Khalar. "Have you Seen Mhani?"

"No, but—"

Lerien waved him silent. More riders were approaching from behind along the plain. Lerien dropped under cover of some scrub maples and drew his sword.

"Stavel!" he cried, and leaped out into the open, spreading his arms in welcome.

The Wolf looked weary, but he was unhurt, and Lerien was pleased with the complement of warriors that had managed to break free and ride off on Pharician horses. There were nearly forty men in good condition and a handful with wounds that would handicap them in battle. Of those he spoke to, some said there were more escapees on the way, and others spoke of Clansmen getting free on foot and hiding in the crevices of the hills. In the middle of the reunion, Ketar, Miro, and Taro came riding up with another group of Clan warriors and a bound Pharician prisoner.

Ketar gave Lerien a broad, proud grin. "This Pharician is a swordsman to be reckoned with, but he was no match for me on the ground. Jakse has taught me submission holds that work wonders with big brutes like this. Next time I see Jakse he's getting a big kiss from me." Ketar slapped the bound prisoner across the back and received a snarl in response.

Lerien said, "What's your name?"

"Sharek."

Lerien was bigger than most of his subjects, but the Pharician towered over him. When he was allowed to dismount, he stretched luxuriously as if to emphasize his physical superiority and indicate that, though captive, he was not afraid of any of them. The scarring on his body was symmetrical, the result of manhood rituals, unlike the random distribution of damage that told—for example—Tarquin's history. Sharek's musculature was angular and swollen, and with every small movement the chains on his arms and legs rattled. They looked more like a part of some costume than a real restraint. He sucked his teeth and spat. Very white teeth showed.

"You have been subject to a Sekk Master," Lerien said in Pharician, glancing sidelong at Kivi. "Do you understand what that means?"

"It was a privilege," Sharek said. "His is a mind of exceptional clarity. I would willingly have him rule over me. I've been separated from him, but I'll get back."

"Tell me about him."

"You are his enemy. I will tell you nothing."

"Are you a Slave now?"

"I don't know what that means. I belong to him."

"Yet you clearly have your wits."

"Great glory he has promised us," Sharek said, his eyes glossy with emotion. "He rides with Animal warriors out of history, and he will take us to faraway places, to see strange sights and be famed and go into legend. We could feel it as the moon grew. The round moon in the blue sky of evening meant that we were coming near the end of our journey."

Kivi had approached, still holding the Carry Eye. He glanced at Lerien anxiously. "He remains under sway of the Sekk," he muttered.

"Kill him," Lerien said. "Make it quick, and simple. And stay away from his body after he is dead."

He turned to the other Clansmen who had gotten free, scowling. "How many of you feel the same? How many of you still wish you were with this Sekk Master? Do not look away from me!"

He saw shame on many faces, and fear. He didn't see untruth. Ivren was the only one bold enough to speak.

"In dreams sometimes we do acts we would not do in life. Such was the feeling of walking behind the Sekk. We are awake now."

"See you stay that way," Lerien commanded sternly. He glanced at Kivi for reassurance.

"It's not a simple Slaving spell," Kivi said. "But I think these are free, or they would not be here."

"We're moving out," Lerien suddenly announced. "The sooner we get up onto the sea plateau, the happier I'm going to be. Take half an hour to see to your injuries and water your horses. Kivi—come."

He took Kivi apart from the others. The Seer said, "My lord, when I look in the Eye now, all I See are Quintar's Company with their weapons bared, riding and riding. It seems to me that this Sekk has invoked their ghosts, and uses them against us. It must have interfered with the Eyes, tricked us into seeing what was not there."

"The Sekk," Lerien said darkly. "One does not wish to understand them, eh, Kivi? They are like no other enemy. They don't hold land. They want no empire, or so it seemed until now, with this capture of

Ristale's army. They Enslave the strong if they can, use them to kill the weak, and spare the ones in the middle, like us. Or so it seems to me."

Kivi nodded empathetically. He held the Carry Eye in his cupped hands as if he wanted to say something about it, but Lerien was not in the mood to entertain new theories.

"All my life, Kivi, have I stood in their shadows. The great warriors, dead or vanished, they have left it to me to fill their places, and I cannot. Everything I do, I know it is not enough. I can never live up to the legends."

"Isn't that the nature of legends?" Kivi suggested. "They are larger than life, to inspire us."

"You don't remember Chyko, then. Or Lyetar. Or Ysse for that matter."

"When the great disappear, the ordinary can grow to fill their places. We have no choice but to perform. Maybe we, too, can become great, for whatever must be done, must be done by us."

"No," Lerien said. "Talent is talent. I will not delude myself that I have more of it than I do. Great warriors are born." He laughed. "You heard what Sharek said about the Sekk. Said he would do anything to stay with him. That he would die for him. That is a great leader. Yet you stand here and argue with me! I don't see you offering to throw your life at my feet."

"I argue with you because you allow me to."

"I'm not a dumb brute. Which is apparently what is called for in a war leader." Rain had begun to fall. Lerien paced toward his horse with no particular intention beyond getting out of the way of this irritating Seer. Kivi followed him.

Kivi said, "Our last leader was an Honorary. A female! I doubt anyone could call Ysse a dumb brute."

"She reaped the bounty of Jai Pendu. So, in his dark way, did Tarquin. So must I. I have no chance without the Knowledge." He looked toward the sea as he said it.

"Are we not returning to Jai Khalar, then? You promised Tarquin to mount a defense, to evacuate—"

"I'm the king," Lerien snapped. "I'm going to Jai Pendu."

Kivi fell silent.

"What is left to lose? Jai Khalar can resist a siege. The high villages have already been abandoned. Our army is lost, except for these few. I will not return to Jai Khalar only to sit and take advice. I'm not a Pharician emperor, as we have just seen. I'm a Clan leader and that's how I'll behave. If you doubt me, leave me: you are not of my Clan and I will

Free you if you wish. But I will not shame my Bear forefathers by skulking in some castle studying campaign maps."

"Your Bear forefathers didn't have to contend with the Sekk. Or the Knowledge."

Lerien turned and placed a heavy hand on the Seer's shoulder. He knew he was now resorting to the very approach he had just decried. "In Clan times, you would have had little status, Kivi. I could kick you up and down this camp and drink tea at the same time."

Kivi's eyes blazed. "You underestimate me."

"Do I?" The rain lay bright on Lerien's face and hair, and he whirled at the sound of hoofbeats. "I would like you to have the chance to prove it."

Jakse arrived, hell-for-leather out of the wind and rain, spooking the other horses and causing a commotion as he leaped from the saddle.

"Where have you been?" Ketar shouted, springing up from among his rescued kinsmen and running toward the Snake.

"There is a Pharician cavalry unit hard on my heels. They came across the plain from the southeast, near the coast. They looked as if they were making for the Floating Lands as well, but they have seen you lot and now they are on their way to sort you out."

Lerien took this in; then he turned to the young, blond Seahawk. "Ketar," Lerien said, "you know I don't trust you."

"No, my lord."

"But if you make a ruin of this order, you'll be dead I'm sure, so either way you are out of my hair."

"Yes, my lord. What do you want me to do, my lord?"

"Ride to meet this cavalry unit. Say that all of us are only a small party scouting for your king, Lerien—you can fill in all my titles and honors for yourself—and that if they trespass on the sea plateau that is grounds for war."

Ketar was practically jumping up and down. "Yes, my lord. A bold plan."

"See what they say, and then ride back to me. Under no circumstances do I wish Tash to know that this is the only army we have. You do understand that, Ketar?"

"Of course, Le—my lord!" Ketar was indignant. "It is only a ruse."

"Go on, then. Before they get too close. And Ketar!"

The Seahawk was fidgeting, eager to be off.

"Don't be too belligerent."

"I will be the soul of courtesy," Ketar said.

OF GHOSTS AND
GREEN EARTH

Tarquin was alone in a general darkness. He couldn't remember the details of the fight he'd been dragged out of, but he could feel its intensity guarding his back, for the fight was what he knew and understood, and this place where he was now, this state of mind—it was entirely alien. A sword and an enemy were all he'd ever wanted, but he had neither, and her smell was in his nostrils, the silk of her skin fingerprinting his memory. But she was gone, leaving her words behind.

We are in the garden, where we always meet.

He stirred. A warm stone surface was beneath him. He pressed his palms against it and slowly sat up, reassured by the grains of grit that stuck in his skin, for they gave him some feeling of reality. His body was relaxed, watery; like a seal out of water he was sleek and slow. Around him were fuzzy sounds. He focused his attention on the blur of noise and realized that he was hearing the rush of battle, but from some distance and as though underwater. The air here was still and heavy and green-smelling.

A little light began to come to him, and as he got to his feet his vision cleared. He was looking down a long, long hall draped in shadow, its double row of columns rising to support a roof made of nothing but midnight with its spilled stars. Running down the center of the hall was a rectangular pool set at the bottom of wide steps that ran around its edges. At the far end he could just make out the moon-etched outlines of a gate.

He began walking down the hall, weaving among the columns as a way of breaking the symmetry of this place by his movement; for its stillness frightened him and he would have been more at ease in chaos. When he passed behind the columns, expecting to find a wall, he saw instead that where the floor ended in darkness there was an edge, and beyond the edge of the floor there was . . .

"Don't look down!" The tone was imperious. He turned.

"Mhani?"

Her voice seemed to be right beside him, but he could not see her. Then he noticed the reflection on the surface of the pool. Mhani appeared to be coming toward him, red robes slithering across a stone floor in some other place. He had the impression that she was as surprised to see him as he was to see her.

"Quintar," she whispered, and there was fear in her voice. "How came you here?"

"I don't know. I was fighting Night, but then she took me away from all that."

"*She?*"

He swallowed and didn't answer. "Help me find the Company," he implored. "Help me find Chyko, if you will do nothing else."

"I want nothing more than to find Chyko. But I have more than one duty binding me," she said. "The place you are standing is a haven, but everything below us, everything over that edge—it is madness. You cannot go there. It is the Liminal, and the White Road is the only safe way through it."

"We will find the White Road together, then," he said. "I must return and undo what I have done. I must save them—all of them."

"Quintar—*what are you?*"

He didn't think this could be answered, so he crossed to the other set of columns and passed into the dimness beneath them.

"Don't look over the edge," Mhani said again.

"But they're there, aren't they? My men are out there somewhere, and they always have been, only now they're serving Night. Ah—you don't understand, why do I bother trying to speak of it?"

"I do understand," she said. "I know what happened. Night has been using my Eyes. You took its Sight when you took the Water of Glass, and now it moves freely among the Eyes of Everien."

"I told you the Eyes should not be trusted."

"But you did not tell me why! You should not have kept silent."

"I had to. My shame was too great. I let them be taken, and when it was my turn, I fled."

"You should have told us."

"You're all so fucking clever," said Tarquin. "With your words and your concepts and your images. You think because you can See out across

Everien that you understand, but you know *nothing*. You haven't been to Jai Pendu. You don't know what it is. You want to be told all about it for your Scholarly studies but the very idea makes me sick. Some things should never be spoken."

There was a pause. The image of Mhani had deep circles beneath its eyes—a haggard expression.

"Night is also looking for the White Road," she said soberly. "It wants to get back to Jai Pendu. It will take as many humans with it as possible, for it is full of a hunger for us. And Lerien must try to stop it, but I can't get to him. All my Eyes are full of Night. I cannot See without Seeing through Night. Even now. It sent you here, I am sure, Tarquin. Be wary."

"I still don't know where I am. Is this Everien?"

"This is the Liminal," she said. "You are no longer in Everien."

"And what about you?"

"I am in Jai Khalar, but I can See into the Liminal. I don't know how to explain—"

He cut her off. "I'm not interested. I just want to know what's become of my Company. Are they alive or dead? How is it that they walk, like ghosts on the green earth?"

"I don't know the answer," she said. "I do know that Night will march its army into the Floating Lands if it can."

"I told your daughter—the Floating Lands are impassable."

"If that's true, then how did Night get back to Everien after you left Jai Pendu? For I believe it went through the Floating Lands."

"I don't know." Tarquin was becoming increasingly agitated. He paced around the rectangular pool, followed by the cries and clash of steel that filtered up from the void. "What *is* it, Mhani? Is it a Sekk? How could a Sekk get into Jai Pendu?"

"There isn't time to speculate."

"I have to get out of here. I'll kill it this time. It won't elude me. I'll kill it and take its Glass. And I'll find my Company." He went to the edge and stood with his back to it. He could hear individual voices in the chaos now.

Mhani frowned. "You men are all alike. As if it were so easy."

"I didn't say it would be easy. I said I'd do it." He was only half listening to her. The other half was imagining Night, and building up a rage at having been sent away, prevented from killing it as he had longed to do.

"Tarquin, at the moment you're safe, but you're surrounded by what was once a collection of worlds, now torn apart and the scraps swept together in one pile. The White Road is only a thread, a way to quilt the worlds together to make some sense of them—but you can't put them back the way they were. Chyko, Lyetar, Ovi—all of them, they're mixed up in that mess. You say, 'Where are they?' but it's not a case of the locations of things being stable."

"Maybe. But if they're going to Jai Pendu, so will I. Simple, eh, Mhani?"

He turned and composed himself on the very brink, eyes closed, balancing the weight on the balls of his feet as if about to dive. He didn't want to see where he was going.

"As simple as death," she said. "What are you doing? Get away from that edge."

"There's nowhere else to go," he said, shrugging.

"Wait, Tarquin! Let me think. I may be able to help you. Maybe I can bring the White Road so you can follow it back into Everien."

"You can do that?"

"I can try."

Without turning to look at the reflection, he said, "You don't look well, Mhani."

She laughed then. "And you—do you suppose you look like a bridegroom? No, I will try. I warn you, though: Night has been coming to me through Impressions. If I open the White Road for you, it may take advantage of the opportunity to enter the Road itself."

"That's even better—it saves me having to hunt it down. I'm not finished with Night yet."

"Go to the end of the hall," she said softly. "I can See a gate with iron bars, and beyond it something green."

"It's a garden. I don't think—"

"Yes," she said with certainty. "That's the way. Open the gate."

He thought it odd that the gate was not rusty as he lifted the latch and it swung away from him.

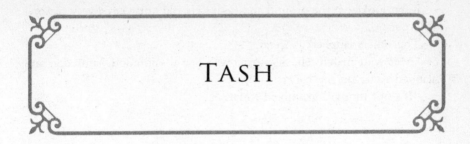

TASH

The bulk of the enemy troops had passed up the ramps and onto the sea plateau. By the little bit of dark that high summer allowed them, Lerien and his crew followed them at a safe distance, riding up the ramps until they emerged on the height. From here they watched Ketar approach the group of some two hundred horsemen. They waited for some time before he was seen to leave them, riding faster this time. Lerien paced and breathed loudly, impatient. When Ketar finally made his way up the level of the sea plateau, he was on foot, leading the horse. The animal was not lame, but it had been ridden down to exhaustion, and Ketar didn't look much better.

"Their leader is a man called Tash, a barbarian's son from the desert. He says he has been sent by Hezene to investigate the incident at Ristale. He has been riding along the coast, and he has seen the Pharician army climb the sea plateau. He blames us. Reports from the garrison at Ristale say it was taken by Clan warriors." Ketar could not keep the pride from his voice.

"I daresay it was taken by Quintar's Company," said Kivi in an undertone.

"Tash intends to take the sea plateau," Ketar said. "He says if we try to stop him, he will attack us."

"I don't wish to stop him if he intends on breaking up the army, but he doesn't know what he's dealing with in the Sekk Master or its Glass. Surely when he sees that Hezene's armies are not destroyed, only captive, he will want to work with us to free them."

Ketar looked at the ground and said, "He did not seem a very reasonable person."

The others laughed at Ketar.

"Met your match, eh, Sea-sparrow?" Stavel said good-naturedly, and slapped Ketar on the back.

"It's not funny," grumbled Ketar.

THEY WERE STILL discussing possible strategies when, an hour or two later, Tash's force came up the steep road in a cloud of dust and reflected light. They were well armed and fresh. Tash halted them not far from the edge of the height and, dismounting, began to walk toward them.

"Stay here," Lerien said to the others. "Except Kivi. Come on, Kivi—let's go parley."

Tash walked like he owned the Earth. He was not a big man, but he moved like a great cat, and his mahogany skin told the story of his conquests: it bore countless ritual scars and power trophies. Each place where his body had been cut or pierced represented a triumph over another man or men; the pain willingly endured by these glory scars was a testament to Tash's hardness. His eyes were cool with his accomplishments, but they contained an alertness, too, that made Lerien nervous. Tash said nothing, his whole attitude implying that he didn't expect to hear much of interest, and Lerien realized he had better speak before he lost his nerve.

Lerien opened his palms and tilted his head slightly to one side in a gesture of cooperation. His band stood a little distance away while the leaders negotiated, and he knew they looked ragged and impoverished in comparison with the sleek Pharician riders. The rain had slackened, and where the Pharician armor gleamed with moisture, Lerien's men were soaked and unkempt.

"This war is a mistake. I did not order an attack on the garrison at Ristale. The Sekk used my men against my will, and without my knowledge."

"A likely story."

"Would I be so foolish as to hurl my few soldiers against all the might of Pharice with no provocation? I have no quarrel with your country. My army has been stolen by the Sekk and now marches against my own country. Help me to recover it, and your troops also will be freed."

Tash's lip curled. "One does not lose an army. Either they are your men and they will die before serving another—or you are no leader."

Lerien, cut to the quick, said, "The Pharician garrison at Ristale was lost in just this manner."

"*They* are not my men." Yet Tash's expression darkened as he considered the implications. "Who controls them, and how?"

"A Sekk Master. I have not been able to get close to it."

"I'll kill him," Tash said simply. "As for you—go back to your disappearing castle, and disappear. If I see you again, I will liquefy you and your Animal boys. My emperor will treat with you later. If I were you I would prepare to join Pharice as a subject. You are unable to manage your own affairs."

Lerien thought about arguing and decided not to risk it. He was too severely outnumbered.

"Who has seen this Sekk usurper? Have you?" He cast piercing eyes on Kivi, who glanced at Lerien helplessly. "You are a Seer, are you not? With an Eye?"

"Kivi, show Tash the Company you have Seen in the Eye. And tell him of the Glass."

Kivi extended the Eye toward Tash, who gazed in at the vision of the twelve Clan warriors and raised his eyebrows. "*They* are something to see," he said.

Kivi cleared his throat and began, "The Sekk has a Glass—"

"Not now!" Tash snapped impatiently. "You will tell me many things, my friend; but not now. No, you will come with me as a token of your king's goodwill toward Pharice."

Lerien stepped between Kivi and Tash, who laughed. "You want to be cut to ribbons? Were it not for the long history of friendship between our people, I would have made myself a Bear cloak by now, Lerien. I'm offering you your life, one chance to go back to your citadel and stand by your people, in exchange for this Seer. The offer will stand for five seconds. Think fast."

He shifted his weight ever so slightly; just enough to make it obvious that the spear could gut Lerien with one stroke. Lerien stepped away from Kivi. Tash smiled. "It was the right choice for you, Lerien. Come, my little fawn. You will not be harmed."

Kivi didn't look at Lerien or any of the others. He cast his eyes down, and the Pharicians bound him.

THE FLOATING LANDS

In the morning it seemed that the entire episode with the Bear Clan had been a dream. The wagons had moved off in another direction, and they had walked a fair distance in the twilight; there was now no sign of the Bears. It was a fine day; the sun flew high and their way was flat and open. The sea plateau supported vegetation comprised of a mixture of marsh and dunes that sheltered thousands of birds, and after the recent rain there were many flowers. It was no hardship to walk freely over flat ground in the summer warmth, with their packs full of decent Bear Clan food and their injuries on the mend, their sore muscles rested. The Floating Lands had appeared, wraithlike, in the distance.

Xiriel became increasingly animated. "It remains a mystery," he mused, "what purpose the Floating Lands served, and why they were left behind. If nothing else, I hope to discover something of their true purposes."

"Surely it doesn't matter," Kassien said with a touch of irritation, "just so long as we can get across the bridges."

"Understanding the nature of their construction can only help us to find and cross the bridges," said Xiriel. "Anyway, it gives me something to think about."

"Why do you always need to think about something?" Pallo asked. "I don't need to think."

"So I've noticed!" Xiriel responded. "Pallo, I am trying to distract myself from my fear. Those islands are . . . alive. They don't wish to be crossed."

"We survived the H'ah'vah," said Kassien. "And the Assimilator. And a Sekk Master. We'll cut our way across."

"When we thought we were getting ten swords, that might have worked," Xiriel said. "Now we're going to have to become a little more inventive, I think."

Kassien scowled and trudged ahead. He was still sulking; but Istar was pleased to be free of the Bear Clan. It was simpler out here away from people. The wind from the sea felt soft and warm on her face, and as its blueness filled more and more of her frame of view, Istar had the feeling of waking from a long sleep. She had not come to the ocean for years, and now it seemed to emerge from memory as if it had been there before her all this time, present but unseen, and she found herself thinking, *Of course. Here I am again.*

The Floating Lands could be seen from a long way off. They were of varying heights—the tallest rose several hundred vertical feet from the ocean—and sizes—the smallest was only a matter of forty feet in diameter—but they were similar in that none of them looked like natural islands. Istar's party walked on a plateau that stretched many miles to the west at a height of several hundred feet above sea level, for the entire mass of Everien and its boundary mountains had been lifted above the continental plate like a loose tile, leaving a vertical drop all along its borders. To the northeast rose the cliffs of the Seahawk Clan where the Everien Range met the sea, but these were rough and craggy whereas the Floating Lands were sculpted from smooth stone in varying shades of gray. Their upper surfaces tended to be flat like the plateau from which they'd apparently been wrenched, and they bore some grass and moss, but their sides were entirely bare. The islands were blocklike and did not taper as they rose from the ocean, although one of them was twisted as though someone had grabbed it in the middle and wrung it like a mop.

"They have switched positions since the last time any of our people reported," Xiriel said.

Concerned, Istar asked, "Are they supposed to do that?"

"They are not grounded in the sea bed, so they will drift," Xiriel said. "But I didn't expect them to be in this particular order. I will have to think on it."

"How can we get across, then?" wondered Kassien. "I thought you said there were bridges."

"There *are* bridges, built by the Everiens," Xiriel said. "But they can be whimsical, and they don't seem to be extended at the moment. I suppose that's how the islands manage to drift. They're not always connected to each other."

"That one's broken," Pallo noted, pointing to a spur of rock that vaulted into the air to form an incomplete arc with crumbling edges. "And what about those ropes?"

"They are cables placed by the Pharicians the last time they tried to cross," Kassien told him. "They may come in handy for us."

"Where is Jai Pendu?" asked Pentar softly.

"Jai Pendu is the only one that moves completely untethered," Xiriel replied. "It sails in and out of the world, and it is absent."

"When will it come? And how will we know?"

"At the full moon, of course." Xiriel smiled. "That's in only a few days; but it won't become visible until it's almost upon us. And when it leaves, it will disappear very soon after detaching itself from the last of the Floating Lands."

Pallo said, "Wouldn't it make more sense to sail to Jai Pendu? You could wait until it arrived and then set your heading from here. You could probably row there."

Pentar laughed. "Pharician inlander! In a small boat, you'd be dashed to pieces. Look at those currents."

The tide was coming in, foaming and coughing at the bases of the Floating Lands. The water hurled itself hard against the stone, which was too sheer in most places to permit the landing of a boat even if the ocean had been calmer.

"Is it true, then, that Pharician galleons were sent to distant star settings?" Pallo asked.

"Several ships were displaced," Xiriel said. "Pentar is correct about the currents: I would not like to spend any time in that water myself."

"You shouldn't have to. Look, isn't that a bridge?" Kassien pointed to the nearest of the Floating Lands, connected to the edge of the plateau by what appeared to be a flexible rope bridge.

"The Pharicians must have made it," Xiriel said. "It is not an Everien-style bridge; those are governed by the Knowledge, and they endure."

"Let's go see," Istar said.

They quickened their pace, shuffling through windswept sand toward the cliff. The breeze picked up, singing among the sculpted stones.

"I feel dizzy," Pallo complained. "I didn't realize it would be so high. Kassien, if you can't sail among the Floating Lands, what are those boats doing out there?"

Kassien flung himself on the ground; the others followed suit as though choreographed to do so. Istar caught a glimpse of the boats Pallo spoke of, and she emitted a soft curse. Half-obscured by the line of the cliffs, there were two Pharician schooners moored just offshore almost directly below them and a contingent of Pharician soldiers guarding the first bridge.

Kassien swore. "Stay here," he commanded. "I'm going to get a closer look."

They waited while he crawled on his belly through the sea grass toward the edge of the cliff. He was gone for some time, and when he returned he didn't look cheerful.

"There are a number of smaller boats just beneath. That must be how the Pharicians got here. It looks like they've been able to navigate among the Floating Lands in light craft, but I doubt very much they have penetrated beyond this first island, as I can't see any figures standing on any of the other islands."

"How are we to know their disposition toward us? Are we at war with Pharice or not?" Xiriel said. "If only we had not lost the Carry Eye."

Dejected, they lay there undecided for a while. Then Istar said, "It doesn't really matter, because even if Pharice hasn't attacked Everien, we have no claim over this territory and they would probably turn us away if we walked up and asked them nicely to let us pass over the bridge."

"I wouldn't mind knowing how long those boats have been there," Xiriel muttered, embarrassed to have been proved wrong in what he'd said to Pallo. "How does Pharice plan to cross to Jai Pendu? They have far less information than we do, and I'm not even sure how *we're* going to get there."

"If only we'd had the White Road, we could have bypassed all this," Istar mourned.

Xiriel consulted one of the charts he had drawn in Jai Pendu, sharing it with Kassien, who concluded, "The boats are our best chance. We are only five. If we could manage to steal even a dinghy, we could look for another route."

"I can't guarantee we'll be able to get a boat close enough." Xiriel looked fretfully back and forth between the Floating Lands and the diagram before him.

"Kass is right," Istar said. "Let's try. It's either that or swim."

Pallo shivered. "I don't suppose anyone would like me to act as envoy and negotiate with the Pharicians?"

Istar started laughing and then suddenly grabbed Pallo by the shoulders. "That's perfect," she said. "You can create a diversion while we steal the boat. You speak Pharician. Go talk to them . . . if you're not afraid."

Pallo thrust out his chin. "Of course I'm not afraid. I'll tell them I'm a wandering botanist in search of Everien sea moss, and I lost my way while observing some rare snails, and—"

"Yeah, we get the idea. Come here, Pallo, and look at this." Kassien rapidly sketched a plan in the sand and told Pallo what to do.

WHEN THE GROUP left Pallo, Kassien was whistling. He led them along the cliff top until they were around a headland, concealed in the bay beside the place where the bridge hung from land to island. The boats were also out of sight from here, and they were able to make a smooth descent using ropes; by now all but Pentar had been tested in the Everien Range, and Pentar himself made a fair effort, being of Seahawk blood and inured from birth to the high places. They had to wait for the tide to recede, exposing the underparts of the nearest Floating Land with its shining dark skin of weed and glittering parasites. Their way into the next bay was also opened, and they slithered across the rocks of the headland, concealing themselves along a sheltered ledge below the bridge. There would not be total darkness so close to the solstice, but the sun was very low in the clouded sky, and the cliffs blotted out much of its westerly light anyway. They waited.

"How will we know when to make our move?" Pentar asked, his eyes bright with curiosity. Istar, too, wanted to know what Kassien had said to Pallo, but the two had fallen out of the habit of talking to each other directly. She no longer felt at ease with him.

"They're going to come right to us," Kassien said. "Provided Pallo doesn't make a mess of it."

For a long time nothing seemed to happen. Istar reckoned Pallo must have made contact with the guards by now, and he had had ample time to get down the cliff, for that matter, even without their help; for there was an ancient flight of stairs cut into the stone just to the side of the bridge. It led to a small landing, and as the tide rolled back in a number of Pharicians gathered there and built a fire. They could be seen milling around and eating.

"It would be easy to attack them now," Pentar said. "Pallo may have gotten himself captured."

"Wait," said Kassien. There was a pause and he turned to Pentar with a half smile. "Beating Istar has done you a world of good, Pentar. You've come right out of your shell, haven't you?"

Pentar demurred, but Istar took this an an oblique taunt directed at her and presented Kassien with a haughty profile. Just then a small boat slipped away from the landing. A dark figure rowed it toward their ledge, fighting the rough water. In the stern was a towheaded figure. Kassien began to chuckle.

"No need to kill anyone," he said. "We'll just find out whether this one can swim."

Pallo's exaggeratedly treble chatter reached them above the sound of the tide. Istar spoke Pharician only haltingly and with a thick accent, but she could understand most of what Pallo was saying.

"Just a little closer, please. This ledge is perfect. I'll show you some lovely luminescent slime mold if you'd like to step out of your boat. In my province we use it as a cure for overindulgence, although some say sloe-weed is better."

The tide had covered over their route from the next harbor, and now the boat passed by their ledge where earlier they had climbed on the weedy stones. Pallo reached out and caught hold of the rock, beginning to pull himself up toward the ledge. The Pharician stood, holding the boat against the cliff so that Pallo could exit. Kassien simply dropped on him, flattening him against the bottom of the boat. They wrestled a bit, and if Kassien was not particularly stylish about it, at least he had the element of surprise; he dispatched his opponent by tossing him into the water. The Pharician struggled just to keep his head above water, for he was wearing a good deal of metal and the waves were strong.

"Quick!" Kassien said. "And be quiet about it."

They dropped into the boat one by one, leaving the astonished guard to cling to the edge of the cliff and get his breath back before he could scream the alarm.

"I didn't have the heart to kill him," Kassien said. "They'll never see us properly in this light, anyway. Go on, Pentar: row!"

It was not quite as easy as that, for the tide was still on its way in and Pentar and Xiriel were pulling against it, but there was no reaction from the Pharicians either above or on the sea ledge, and they pulled alongside the first island.

"We have to get behind this island," Xiriel said, heaving the oar through taller swells. "Look at the map, Pallo."

Just as they were almost out of sight around the side of the first island, a cry went up from the guards at the bridge. A minute later the Pharicians had launched a couple of boats from the banks, which they rowed ponderously through the surf. Pentar and Xiriel redoubled their efforts. Istar untangled the climbing gear and Pallo struggled to read the chart Xiriel had given him to hold. He kept turning it around, and then it got wet, and then it caught on Pentar's oar. Finally Kassien grabbed the chart from Pallo and dumped an enormous coil of rope around his neck.

"Hold that," he said, and Pallo staggered under its weight, then ultimately sat down in the bilgewater.

Xiriel's chart showed an area where the cliff overhung the water around the seaward side of the first island. There were handholds within reach of the tall swells, and, farther up, an entrance in the wall. They maneuvered the boat into what felt like a rather tight space, and Kassien set about placing hooks in the stone and fitting ropes. Several times the waves bounced them off the walls, and the boat began to leak.

"Better hurry," said Pallo nervously.

"Go on, then," Kassien instructed, and gave Pallo a leg up to the first rope. "Climb up to that hole in the cliff and fix the rope. And be quick about it."

All long limbs and hair, Pallo jumped onto the end of the line Kassien had fixed to the stone as the first of the Pharician boats rolled around a bend in the cliffs and into the channel between the islands. The leader stood in the stern holding a torch, and six soldiers rowed. They were well armed, and as they drew closer their faces looked vicious in the yellow light.

Xiriel spun his axes and glanced up. "Oh, no," he groaned. Istar followed his gaze. The bridge between the first and second islands was broken. The first man dropped his oar and picked up a spear. Pallo reached the ledge. They ducked behind the gunwales for cover; Istar looked over her shoulder and saw Pallo frantically tying a knot, or trying to.

"Go on, Istar," Xiriel hissed. "Get up the cliff, quick."

"You go," she said. "I'll stay and fight."

Xiriel swung himself out of the boat, which bobbed and crashed against the stone. Arrows thudded into the hull. One bounced off Kassien's shield. Xiriel, in midair, flung first one ax, and then the other. One struck a Pharician on the arm and made him roar with pain; the other went into the sea.

"Istar, go!" Kassien stood up behind his shield and held the rope for her.

"After you," she said. Her sword was out and she was eager for battle. Kassien looked about to argue; then he simply grabbed the rope and started up. The Pharician boat reached theirs and the soldier with the damaged hand barreled aboard brandishing a curved sword. Istar sliced him neatly in the hand that wasn't hurt, and then shoved him overboard with her foot. But she didn't reckon on the imbalance this would cause in the boat, and to her dismay she went over herself. Meanwhile Kassien, hanging on the rope, was pulled away from the boat and had no choice now but to keep climbing.

Pentar was battling with two more Pharicians who were attempting to board, and a third was throwing spear after spear at Pallo and Xiriel, above. Pallo threw rocks back. One of them bounced off Pentar's helmet. Pallo covered his mouth in dismay.

Istar dragged herself back into the boat, feeling humiliated and foolish, just as one of the Pharicians got past Pentar, losing his sword in the process. Undaunted, he dove at her legs and knocked her down in the bottom of the boat. She could not get her sword free and quickly found herself entangled in the Pharician's arms while his body weight pinned her. Istar was protected in part by her armor, but this did not stop the Pharician from attempting to lock one arm and strangle her at the same time, perhaps not as neatly as a Snake would have done it, but effective under the circumstances. She could hear Pentar screaming as he cut at any Pharician who came near the boat, and the rest of her companions shouted encouragement and advice, but she could not maneuver in the tight space. The Pharician seemed to be feeling no pain: she bit, gouged eyes, and loosened teeth, but he relentlessly crushed her into the bilges. She could barely breathe and the Pharician was too well armored to feel any of the short-range body blows she directed with her legs.

She was a fingersbreadth from panic when the man was abruptly pulled off her and dumped into the water by Pentar, who then wheeled and engaged the remaining enemy with his sword, giving Istar time to get onto the cliff. Her muscles were not responding well: even three minutes of hard wrestling had been enough to sap her strength, and she had to carry herself and her wet armor and her pack up a retrograde cliff, where the rope had been fixed by someone much taller than she, with longer reach. She managed it, but only barely, with Pentar crowding behind her. Kassien managed to draw up one of the ropes but had to cut the other, as one of the officers had caught hold of it and was preparing to mount the cliff. Istar watched with satisfaction as its coils landed on his head.

They ducked inside, winded but triumphant.

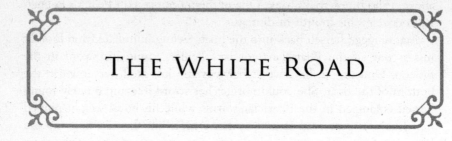

THE WHITE ROAD

Tarquin never saw the garden because a dark figure was coming at him with a long sword. He leaped backward, fell, and rolled, getting his sword out on the way. The air was freezing and aswirl with windblown ice pellets; snow blanketed the uneven ground, broken in places by metal structures like skeletons arching across the clouded sky. At his back was a roar of heat, and as he turned over he glimpsed a river of white fire spilling across the snow, which was evaporating into thick steam where it touched the lava.

The swordsman pursued him.

He no sooner got on his feet then he had slipped again, for he was standing on a slab of melting ice. The ground shook in a slow rhythm. His chest had seized up in the extreme cold and he could scarcely breathe; but the lithe figure that scuttled after him seemed to have no such troubles. His opponent's skin was bare and lightly coated with sweat.

Chyko was coping with the cold in just the same way he coped with every adversary.

Tarquin threw his sword on the ground and opened his arms in delight. Chyko kept coming, a familiar intensity hardening his ash-reddened eyes. Just as Tarquin realized it was too late now to defend himself if Chyko did not recognize him, the Wasp skidded to a halt, lowering his sword by degrees. Then he reached out, grabbed the edge of Tarquin's cloak, and dragged him to the ground, rolling him over several times in the snow, cursing all the while.

"Enough!" Tarquin yelled, sitting up. "You *are* a crazy bastard."

Then he realized his cloak had caught on fire in the lava, which was even now oozing toward them. Chyko checked to be certain he had put out the flames, then jerked Tarquin to his feet and wordlessly led him uphill and along the top of a rough gully. There were rusted remains of buildings of some kind, but Tarquin was overcome by the noise and wind and the rushes of hot and cold; he could not take in all the details of his environment, and anyway, the visibility was terrible.

There was a rush of water down the gully. Where the snow and ice met extreme heat, steam shot up into the air and obscured the sky. From beyond the broken teeth of destroyed buildings Tarquin could hear a terrible screaming—a hybrid sound that possessed the harshness of metal scraping metal and the expressiveness of a wild animal. There was a constant thumping that grew slowly nearer, but its source was invisible behind the fog.

They squatted in the lee of a snowbank, as high as they could away from the liquid fire, shifting their feet as their boot soles overheated. Chyko's dark skin was dusted with white ash; even his eyelashes were whitened.

"I wish you were really here," he said. "If you were really here, I think I would kiss you."

"I am really here. Do not kiss me!"

Chyko laughed and grabbed his head, pulling Tarquin's forehead to his own. "My friend, I don't care if you are real or phantom. It is good to see you."

True to his word, he pressed his lips against Tarquin's brow.

"Do you remember the thing that caught you?" Tarquin asked. "Can you speak with it?"

"It?"

"Night, the creature that holds you here."

"I don't remember."

"Do you remember Jai Pendu?"

Chyko reached into a pouch around his neck and took out a small pipe. He stretched out one long arm and held it against the hot ooze to light it. "Inside the Water, I could see Eyes. Many, many Eyes. If you go through the Eyes, it's a place where . . ." He hesitated, licking his lips. "You can't touch anything there; you can't feel anything. It is all at a distance. I would rather die." He puffed meditatively, then offered the pipe to Tarquin.

"I thought you were dead. What have you been doing all these years? Where have you been?"

Chyko's eyes were a vacant black. "Here. *Fighting.*"

As Tarquin passed back the pipe, the metallic screaming grew suddenly louder, and the earth shook. Overhead a section of ice dislodged itself and they leaped up in the interval it took to come crashing down. They were running alongside the fire river through eddying twists of smoke and steam, Chyko firing arrows behind him without breaking stride.

"Quintar!"

Suddenly he couldn't see Chyko. The mist closed in on all sides. The snowy ground was cracking and heaving.

"Quintar, stay with me!"

He turned toward Chyko's voice and there was an explosion, louder than the most violent workings of the Fire Houses. He fell. The ground shook for several seconds. As the disturbance subsided, Tarquin could hear nothing at first, though his heartbeat swelled in his ears and throat. He began to crawl. The snow yielded to white stone, but he could see only a few feet in front of him, for the fog was thicker than ever, and laden with the smell of ash.

There was something black on the ground ahead of him. He crawled closer and saw that it was a dark-robed body. His heart began to race again. He sprang to his feet and drew his sword. The robes didn't stir.

"Night," he said, still deaf to his own voice. The air was no longer cold, and the stone beneath his feet was smooth and seamless. The fog cleared a little, and he could see the familiar curves of the White Road passing beyond the black robes in one direction, and on into unknown mist in the other.

He gripped the sword in both hands and brought it down upon the prostrate figure. When the sword reached its destination, Night was no longer there. Tarquin's sword skipped off the White Road, sending shocks back up along his arms and rattling his teeth. Nearby, Night was now standing, leaning slightly in his direction.

Tarquin was afraid.

I'll kill Night, he'd told Mhani. And she had laughed at him.

He charged at Night again, and again it slipped away from him quick as a flame in wind. Angrily, he began running away from it along the White Road, wondering what it would do. At first it didn't seem to be following. He ran flat out, expressing his frustration in long strides and cutting the mist with his sword to make himself feel he was doing something. He still could not hear properly after the explosion, but he felt hoofbeats shuddering along the stone.

He spared a glance behind him. Night was following, stumbling and groping like a beggar, dragging itself along the Road. As fast as Tarquin had been running, it seemed to have kept pace though it barely moved its feet. The Glass it carried must be very heavy, for it was clasped in both hands and it seemed to throw the slight figure off balance, as if Night were wrestling with the contents of its own hands.

The hoofbeats went faster. They were made by only one horse, but caused the road to tremble. Tarquin halted. If he went forward, he would lead Night forward. If he stood his ground, Night would catch up with him. He hesitated, and the black robes crept toward him.

The hoofbeats accelerated, and the White Road shook.

Tarquin thought, *No horse runs that fast. This horse is so fleet it meets itself coming; it stands in two or three places at once, not laughing because horses don't—but if they did this one surely would.*

He didn't know what to do. Closer and closer came Night, till Tarquin could see the threads on its robes, and hear its thin breaths, and feel the air stir where it moved. In a moment it would touch him. The hoofbeats became a roar.

Night's shadow fell on the white surface just before Tarquin, shining like a pool of oil. Night stopped. Something within its shadow began to move. A shape rose out of the blackness, swelling the stone as if it were skin. The White Road stretched and gleamed as within its fabric some living creature thrashed, struggling to break through. Even as the form of the animal became apparent, there was a trumpeting scream. The head came up and ripped the white membrane apart.

It was a horse of light and shadow, and its scream was a stallion scream, unmistakable in its ferocity. When it reared, all glinting teeth and flying mane, its forehooves struck Tarquin down and slammed the door on his senses.

IF THE SEA
HAD A PURPOSE

t was something resembling nighttime when Tash had Kivi
brought to his tent in bonds. The Pharician sprawled on the ground on
his spread cloak, propped half-clothed on one elbow, dark and gleaming
like a panther. He was cleaning under his nails with a dagger and smoking some fragrant herb in an intricately carved pipe; his eyes were wide
and shining. He dismissed the guards with a jerk of his head and pointed
to the ground. Kivi sat. A flask was passed to him.

Kivi brought the flask nervously to his lips. He had neither eaten nor
drunk during all the long, hot hours of the afternoon, and he was now
parched. He took a sip; the Pharician liquor burned all the way down.
He coughed.

Tash laughed. "You drink like a child."

Challenged, Kivi took another swallow. He could see no reason to
remain sober under the circumstances: who knew what Tash intended for
him? He hoped the stories he'd heard of Pharician soldiers and their
fondness for slender young men did not apply to Tash.

"Are all men in your country children, or is your king some excep-
tion?"

"Lerien is not a child," Kivi said. "I make him older than you."

"All the more disgrace for him, then, that he is no man yet. Drink up,
boy!"

Tash took a long drag on the pipe. Smoke made the blue-gray light in
the tent seem almost solid, as if sand were suspended in the air. It was
very pleasant, Kivi thought, and began to wish he were Tash. If he were a
powerful warrior he, too, would be obeyed when he spoke; he would

have the best liquor and the first meat, and he would ride the fastest horse. Kivi was finding Seerhood tiresome outside of Jai Khalar; in the physical culture of road and field he found himself ever in a subordinate role, treated with a scorn that was thinly disguised at best.

Yet Tash treated him with some privilege, and he felt gratified by that. Kivi took another swallow, and some of the ache of his recent exertions dissolved from the muscles of his back.

"And what of you? You are a Seer. I would like to know what this means. See something for me."

"I cannot," Kivi said, brandishing the flask. "We are not permitted to use the Eyes when the mind is clouded."

"Ah, nonsense," Tash said. "Spare me your pathetic excuses."

Kivi shook his head; the tent spun and he laughed, slipping sideways onto his elbow. It was the strongest drink he'd ever had. "Seriously, I cannot," he said. "Anyway, there is something wrong with the Water of Glass. I have not been able to reach the Mother Eye in Jai Khalar. I can only see the Company, and I have already showed you that. Perhaps by tomorrow we will be out of range of the interference of the Sekk, and then I can hope to use the Eye effectively again."

Tash blinked. "I will not be confused by your esoteric terms," he said. "Can you See visions in it or not? If you cannot, surely it is no use."

"I'm not permitted to look in it with an undisciplined mind."

"Give me this thing," Tash said, holding out his hand. Kivi clutched the Carry Eye protectively. "It's not a toy," he slurred.

"Will you look into it or will I?" Tash asked, snorting. "I am sure I can manage to break it, and then how would you feel, rabbit-boy?"

"All right, all right. I'll look." He felt guilty as he focused on the Eye; but not very much so since he could be excused doing what he must when his life was at stake. "It's not working. I can't See a damn thing."

Tash sat up. He moved like a snake, holding out an arm. "Give," he said.

Feeling weak, Kivi gave it to him.

Tash ran the globe around in his hands as if pleased by its very touch. He looked inside it and made a sound low in his throat. "Ah, there they are!" he said. "Many riders; how wonderful they are. It's so easy, a baby could do it."

"I wouldn't advise—" Kivi began, but Tash put a finger to his lips. Suddenly he gave a shudder and his eyes crossed.

"Oh, no . . ." Kivi moaned, and covered his face. "Tash, don't—"

When the Pharician spoke, his accent was gone. His voice was very soft, just on the verge of audibility. Kivi found himself leaning closer in spite of himself, aware that he had broken a cardinal rule in allowing a neophyte to come under the Impressions, but too fascinated to attempt to break Tash's trance.

"Those who think they know should be summarily chopped up and fed to the pigs," the warlord whispered. "They are useless. The only ones I want are the ones who know and respect the tide. If the sea had a purpose it wouldn't tell you, would it? Purposes are hidden but actions are expressed. Action is what interests me. Can you move? Can you feint? Can you dive? Do you have something inside you or shall I cast you aside? If you have something in you that you recognize but don't understand, that you have tried and failed to control, that asserts itself in the moonlight and under cover of various other darknesses, then maybe I will take you and together we will go into the pathless places and find things, but if you are sweet and content do not come to me for it is only the hard and difficult way that interests me, and if you wish to feel good you should drink wine and sleep and produce many offspring none of whom will respect you."

He fell silent. Twitched. Kivi started to move toward him, and in a sighing tone he said, "My head is loose on my shoulders. Will you come for me yet, my strange and errant lover? Or do you wish me upright like a statue, like eternity damned to stone—no I would not dream it of you. You worship the changes and the coming darkness and you laugh always. How I seek you over fields and under clouds who think they are animals but they are only vapor, they will not commit themselves, they laugh in the sky but—"

His voice cut off with a strangling sound. His expression came alert and he pushed the Eye back into Kivi's hands. "I don't want it," he said. "You take it. You do it."

Kivi didn't look into the Eye. He knew it was polluted at least, and damaged at worst, for even a Carry Eye required skill in the use. Yet he dared not disobey Tash. So he looked down on it without focusing his eyes, for once trying *not* to See.

"It's not working properly," he said. "I don't know if I can get a clear image."

"Nonsense," Tash barked. "I used it, and I'm not even a Seer. Do you know what you're doing or shall I have you executed?"

"No! Wait, I'm starting to get something."

Kivi had been about to make something up, to lie about what he Saw simply for the sake of keeping Tash at bay; but when he spoke these words, an image did appear in the Eye. Through the haze of alcohol he tried to make it clearer. When suddenly the picture came into focus, he leaped back and dropped the Eye as if it were fire.

"What is it? What do you See?" Tash was excited, raising himself and lunging across the tent on all fours, eyes bright.

"Mice!" Kivi shrieked. "Ugh . . . thousands of mice!"

MOUSE

Finding the White Road for Tarquin had used up the last of Mhani's strength. As Hanji might have put it, she could no longer swim; she could only drift with the current of the Liminal.

It was winter in the valley of Everien, and the river was a frozen black strip on which lit boats with black sails skated. Snow lay over all the land, its moonlit sheen haunted by gray-violet shadows where the wind had banked and curved its surface. The sky was indigo and once in a while the silent wings of some aerial thing passed across the stars. A-vi-Khalar looked like a cluster of luminous mushrooms, the lights of each building oozing from the windowless, rounded walls. Overseeing it all like guardians, the Fire Houses climbed the sky.

Where are all the people? Mhani wondered, and then noticed two figures standing in one of the boats as it glided to a halt on the edge of town. She found herself there, observing from the banks as they tied the boat and slithered across the ice to the dock. One was larger and faster; it turned to help the smaller one. Both were heavily wrapped against the cold, their faces invisible. She saw no weapons.

As she followed them down the street she gazed in wonder at the town. The frescoes and arches were no different than the ones to be found in A-vi-Khalar even now, but there were flowers in bloom everywhere, despite the frost, and they cast colored light about, tinting the ice. The smaller of the two reached out and snapped off a cluster of them in passing. Sparks flew. Mhani willed herself to look more closely at the plants, but her sight was not really under her control. She had no awareness of her body and no volition: she was a captive spectator.

The two figures moved rapidly, almost furtively, past door after door, all of them shut against the night. She recognized some of the symbols etched on the doors from the murals and maps in Jai Khalar, but there was no time to memorize their placements or analyze them, for the walkers had nearly reached the base of the Fire Houses. The conical black towers looked like the rending teeth of some giant predator, and they blotted out the moon.

The larger figure held a gate open for the smaller, and they both plunged down a steep ramp into the underground, where a warren of passageways and rooms awaited them. The underground town had been the ancients' way of coping with the severity of the Everien winters, but in Mhani's time most of these tunnels were collapsed or blocked. She would have liked to have Seen more of the town, but as it was she had no more than a glimpse of a bright-lit avenue crowded with moving bodies, accompanied by a burst of weird music that she recognized as Everien in origin, for its like sometimes played uninvited in Jai Khalar. Then the two figures plunged down a flight of stairs. Mhani thrashed inwardly in frustration at not being able to see more.

What does any of this have to do with the White Road? she wondered. *Is it now hidden beneath the Fire Houses?*

Although it was warm underground, the pair did not uncover their heads. They had reached the base of the middle of the three Fire Houses, the largest of which in Mhani's time held the Fire of Glass, and they climbed up a flight of metal stairs that was no longer there. They emerged at the bottom of the forge pit. Several small, ordinary fires were burning, but no one was at work. The interior of the Fire House was spectacular: on the inside it resembled a living structure woven from red and gold fiber and impregnated with both light and color. From bottom to top the interior gradually became brighter, until at the apex of the cone there seemed to be no ceiling at all, only a muted, red sun that was the Fire. The place reminded Mhani of a womb, and at the same time it reminded her of the embers of some conflagration that now lay at rest. There was no other source of light, so the nature of the equipment and furnishings that rested in and around the forge pit were obscure. There were metal structures in the forge pit which seemed to hold unfinished work of some sort: whether weapons or other tools, she could not tell. She was not at liberty to study anything in detail, for the two Everiens had stopped at one of the fires, and one of them was adjusting the brackets on a device made of metal and glass. Mhani found herself wishing urgently for the assistance of Xiriel, who had a way of understanding machines.

"I brought a young one," said the smaller of the two. "Perhaps it will be easier to capture when its mind is soft and unformed."

The voice was feminine, and the gloved hand that reached into a pouch beneath the outer robes was delicate. It clasped a brown mouse—tiny, struggling.

"Hello, little sister," said the tall one in a soft baritone. "Don't be frightened."

"Of course it's frightened," said the female. "You'd be frightened if some giant seized you in your nest and brought you here, to end up under magnification."

The man had contained the mouse within the restraints of the apparatus; Mhani could not even see his eyes, for they had both put on tinted masks. The woman now began shedding her wraps under the heat of the fires.

"You won't be harmed," said the man to the mouse. "There will be no need for blood or pain. You will not feel anything, and afterward you will go free. We only wish to take an impression."

"Once there was much pain," said the woman. "I'm glad we don't have that dilemma. How could they have hurt such a tiny creature to gain Knowledge?"

"They killed not one, but millions, in thousands of ways," said the man.

"We are gentle now," she said as if to reassure herself.

"Yes," he answered absently, busy with some fine adjustments on the equipment. The mouse held very still, paralyzed maybe. Nothing was happening that Mhani could see.

"Do we have anything?" asked the woman after a while.

He shook his head. They were silent, tense.

"Anything yet?" She sounded nervous.

He breathed out through his nose. "No."

The mouse began to move.

"Got it?"

"*No.*"

"What's wrong?" she whispered. "Why is it moving?"

"I don't know."

The mouse was writhing in earnest now, its fluttering respiration and shivering nostrils impossibly tiny and fast. A deep tone like a bass string throbbing began to build, way up in the cone of the Fire House. The sound traveled down the ropy strands of red glass like blood surging through arteries, and the structure visibly shook.

"Ah," said the woman. "It must be working now."

Mhani wondered what sort of a face she had, and whether her eyes now on the frantically struggling mouse were kind. *The stupid mouse,* Mhani thought. It would not understand that it was trapped. It thrashed in the grip of the restraints, which only held it tighter the more it moved. Exhausted, it sat still, panting. Then it started fighting again. It flipped and twisted in the grip of the apparatus, flashing a minute white belly. The phalanges of its digits might have been made of the finest grains of rice, not bone. The mouse would not give in.

"Why do they resist?" said the woman in frustration. "Can't they relax? We are no threat! We only want your patterns, little mouse. We only want to understand you."

"In the old days they would have cut up this mouse piece by piece and then tried to put it back together."

The woman cringed. "That's horrible! How could they?"

"You cannot reason with an animal," the man said. "Wait for it to be tired and then its pattern will appear. All we need is one impression from you, little friend, and then you can go free."

The Fire House was vibrating from top to bottom. The Fire in the roof dimmed and brightened in pace with the mouse's pulse. The floor, which was all black and smooth as the river outside, began to steam. The arterial cords in the walls had become pliant and they glowed and dimmed, stretched and relaxed in an inconstant rhythm.

"Anything? Anything?"

"*No,* Carmyn!"

The mouse stopped moving. It was limp.

Probably dead, Mhani thought, and didn't feel especially sorry. Mice were a damned nuisance. They would overrun Jai Khalar if given half the chance. She spent half her time seeking cats in hope of keeping pace with them, but most cats disliked Jai Khalar and would not stay there unless caged.

"Is it dead?" Carmyn whispered. "You haven't killed it?"

"Here it comes," he answered. "Here comes the impression."

Mhani didn't know what he was looking at that she wasn't: he seemed only to be watching the mouse, but with the visor over his face it was hard to be sure what he was Seeing.

"Aha," breathed Carmyn. "There it is. It's . . . beautiful. . . ."

She opened the brackets and gently lifted the mouse.

"It's alive. I think. But it may have struggled too hard."

"It's gone into shock," he told her. "They don't usually live long once they've passed that stage."

Mhani could hear the tears in Carmyn's voice as the man put down the mouse on the table. "But . . . but . . . you said we wouldn't harm it."

"We didn't! We can't help it if the thing resisted. Look, Carmyn—"

He had started toward her with a conciliatory gesture, but the Fire House flared with red light and the sound grew louder.

And louder.

And louder.

And *louder*.

The two humans clutched each other in panic. The mouse on the table stirred. It crouched, nose twitching. It seemed to Mhani that the mouse had a tiny sideways canny smile on its face.

The Fire House shook like some gigantic musical instrument.

I should never have come here, thought Mhani. But she thought it too late; much too late.

A POACHED EGG

jiko planted both fists on Devri's desk.

"She could be in trouble," he said. "She's been up there a long time, hasn't she? For all you know she could be dead."

"She's not d—" As soon as the words were out of his mouth, Devri knew he'd been tricked into admitting he'd spoken to Mhani since Ajiko's last visit.

"Give us the key."

Devri swallowed and shook his head. Ajiko's hand shot out to grab him by the throat again, but Devri leaped back, warier than before.

"I'll fly you from the battlements, Devri. I'll make you wish you were a poached egg. The key. Now!"

Devri quivered behind the desk. He would not betray Mhani.

"Sir!"

Tiemen reached into the fountain and withdrew something shiny. "Here's a key, sir. . . ."

MHANI'S EYES WERE crossed and she was saying words no one knew. Saliva glistened on her lips and chin, whenever anyone moved she flinched, and she kept covering and uncovering her face with her hands.

"You are a disgrace," Ajiko said to Devri. "How could you let this happen? How many days has our country been without a monitor system? Look at the Water! Even I can tell this place is a mess."

"I'll start getting things in order immediately," Devri said. Thinking it was the sort of thing the general would like to hear, he added, "I could not disobey Mhani's instructions."

"You should have!" Ajiko exclaimed. "Couldn't you see she was insane? Ah, never mind, Devri. Just get her out of here."

Devri went along with Hanji and a couple of guards, to make sure that Mhani would live. When they carried her down to her bedchamber a mouse ran across the passage, and Mhani began wailing and then singing a song of lamentation. Hanji had Ajiko's soldiers place her on the bed; then he dismissed them and left the room himself. Worried, Devri trailed after him.

"Shall I fetch the healers?" Devri asked. "Has anyone seen Soren?"

"I will take care of Mhani," Hanji said in a kindly tone. "You have done enough."

"But where should I go? What should I do?"

"Lose yourself," Hanji said. "If Ajiko has no Seers, he will not be able to use the Eye Tower."

"But if he doesn't use the Eye Tower, how will we control our armies? How will we contact the king?"

Hanji gave him a sadly tolerant look, as if he were an idiot or small child. "Go on, Devri! Do not let Ajiko find you. There are many hiding places in Jai Khalar."

"But I want to stay with Mhani."

"I will take care of her. You've done well. Now look after yourself."

"Hanji—"

The section of floor Devri was standing on shot upward, and he found himself in the aviary with his ears ringing. No one seemed to be attending to the birds. They were screaming and hostile. He wondered when they'd last been fed and decided to let them out. They didn't appreciate his help any more than Mhani or Hanji had done: they flew at his face and he had to throw his arms up over his head and run for cover, bleeding from multiple scratches and feeling wholeheartedly rejected. He returned to his room, curled up, and went to sleep.

AJIKO WOULD HAVE been jealous if he'd known the Seer was sleeping. He was tired and perplexed and now even the defeat of Mhani brought him no satisfaction. As he paced the Eye Tower waiting for the Seers to come and clean up the Water, he wondered whether it wouldn't really be better to consult with Hanji, but the old man had vanished and there was little chance of catching him as long as he was busy removing ferrets and bumblebees and those damned mice.

The general had not been sleeping. Refugees swarmed through Jai

Khalar. It was bad enough for the veteran inhabitants that the Citadel misbehaved more often than it functioned properly, but for the strangers who had never set foot in such a place before, Jai Khalar caused untold grief. Ajiko had made some effort to collect the fighting-age men who came straggling in and to keep them ready for action after he debriefed them. They were not a large contingent, the majority of the homeless being women, children, and the old.

Civilians bored Ajiko, especially when they had a way of being always underfoot. It was not easy to maintain discipline in such a social environment, and as furious as he was with Mhani for locking herself up in the Eye Tower and refusing to come down, there were times when he would have liked to do the same. The reports had come back from Wolf Country at last, borne on foot and on horseback by witnesses. The events they described, if they were true, would represent the greatest military revolt in Clan history. Mhani, curse her, might well have been right when she suggested his own troops had turned on him. Last night he had gathered together all his maps and plans and burned them on the training ground. He had instructed Sendrigel to offer whatever was necessary to keep the outraged Hezene in check; but it was impossible to get anything done quickly without the Eyes. So, as much as he might like to rest, he had to be here, in a position to send and receive the messages that had been delayed by Mhani's breakdown.

The young Seer Soren looked half-asleep as he stumbled into the Chamber of the Eye. "Hanji has sent me, General Ajiko. Will you pardon me while I put the Water in order?"

Ajiko waved him through. "It's about time," he said. "Show me my troops."

For all the accounts of Clan officers taking their soldiers out of position and killing anyone who objected, no one had been able to tell him where all the rebel troops had *gone.* Until he knew where they were, and what they held as objectives, he could not act. And he was frustrated after weeks of inaction.

Soren avoided looking at him directly. The Seer went to work right away, yawning slightly as he began to scan the messages recorded in the Water. "Something's amiss," he told Ajiko, who bristled at the ridiculous understatement. "Look in the Water."

The Water was all white, and an image within the whiteness showed a battle in progress.

"Where is that? Who's fighting?"

The Seer was too nonplussed to answer, but Ajiko could see for himself: it was Quintar's Company, looking more or less as they had eighteen years ago.

"What does it mean?"

"I don't know. Mhani. I . . . let me see if I can fix it."

Ajiko turned his back on the pool. "The whole business disgusts me," he said. "Bring me some useful information or we will close the Tower completely. How much damage Mhani has done already, I shudder to think."

"But, sir . . . We mustn't close the Tower. Hanji said—"

"Hanji is the seneschal. Let him worry about the bed linens. Show me my armies—or else."

PALLO'S GRANDMOTHER'S BEARD

$\mathcal{I}$t was dark and cool in the narrow passage in the stone.

"Thank you," Istar said awkwardly to Pentar, but there was no time for talk. Xiriel was soon leading them into a rough cave and thence up a long shaft laddered with metal rungs.

"They'll get up that cliff without ropes," Pallo said. "It's not such a hard climb."

"I know," Xiriel called over his shoulder. "Move as fast as you can."

The inside of the island was a maze of tunnels and chambers. Xiriel was making decisions about which way to go every five seconds. There was no time for anyone to argue or even pause to consider the way.

"They'll never find us now," Pallo said. "Unless we're going in circles . . ."

They eventually climbed all the way to the top of the island, emerging from beneath a broken slab into a ragged dawn dulled by cloud. They could hide behind the damaged stone walls that laced the top of the island and make their way around without alerting the dozen or so Pharician guards who prowled the ruins. Istar was beginning to enjoy herself again; the Pharicians hadn't been too clever, so far.

"If we can just lose these ones following us, we may be all right," Istar said.

But Pallo was pointing over the mainland, across the sea plateau, which was now slightly below them. Some miles distant to the northwest was a dark smudge on the landscape that had not been there before.

"What on earth's that?"

"I don't know," Istar said. "Let's just find the next bridge and go. The Pharicians are bound to notice us sooner or later."

But there was no next bridge. As they learned when they performed a covert search of the top of the island, the Pharicians had been trying to make a bridge to the nearest of the adjacent islands. One of their boats had impaled itself on a rocky outcropping below, a testament to their failure. Several of them had gathered on a disc of white stone above the ruined boat, where the original Everien bridge was meant to extend.

"They don't understand how to do it," Xiriel said.

"Do you?"

"Maybe."

"Well, after what we did yesterday, we can't very well send Pallo in to offer our assistance, can we?" said Istar caustically.

"There's more than one way," Xiriel told her. "For one thing, that island to the left is fairly close. We can probably get there. We'll go back underground and find a different bridge."

"Not underground again," Pallo moaned as Kassien went off amid the rubble to look for a way back into the island.

"If we stay here they'll find us sooner or later," Pentar said.

"We could take them, and then Xiriel would be free to extend this bridge." Istar was feeling spunky again after her near escape at the boat; but the others looked at her skeptically.

"I hope you're kidding," said Xiriel. "The ten swords we were meant to have isn't much, but without them what chance have we got? Pallo couldn't fight off a puppy, I'm a Seer, and you're a woman."

"Not by law."

Pallo's voice cracked. "Istar, will you remove your head, give it a good soak, and put it back on properly? You can't hope to defeat so many. Nobody admires you more than I do, but if you don't calm down you're going to get us all killed. You're not your father any more than I'm Tarquin the Free."

Istar knew he was right, but at the sound of Tarquin's name her blood lit on fire.

"I should have challenged him while I had the chance."

Xiriel gave a bark of laughter. "He would have taken your sword, cut off your braid, and spanked you with it before you could say 'girl-child.' "

Istar glared at the Seer, speechless with rage.

"Don't tease her," said Pallo.

"I'm not teasing her. We can see some of the past in the Eyes. I have seen Tarquin before he was Tarquin. I don't know how much he has changed, but.in those days the least of his men was worth a dozen of Kassien. And Chyko was worth twenty."

"You've Seen my father?"

He averted his eyes.

Before she could press him, Kassien came around the corner.

"There's another shaft going down. I think it goes to a different section of the underground than where we came up."

He led them stealthily among half-ruined walls and dark pits to a hole in the stone like a mossgrown wound. They could see the beginnings of a steeply pitched flight of stairs leading down into darkness.

"We can't risk a light yet," said Kassien, and plunged into the tunnel. Xiriel went after him readily enough, but Pallo ducked behind Istar and then kept a hand on her shoulder as they left all light behind. There was a metallic, unnatural smell that reminded Istar of the Fire Houses, and always the amplified sound of the sea, distorted like a breath blown too close to the ear. Suddenly Kassien turned and grabbed Istar's hand, pulling her past Xiriel and down the stairs until they reached a wide landing and a gust of warm wind hit them, indicating the presence of a larger space. She bumped into Kassien in the dark and he steadied her, still keeping in contact with her with his hands. It distracted her.

As they had been crossing the sea plateau, Istar had worked on convincing herself not only that Kassien would never desire her, not really, but also that he was not worth the trouble anyway and would fail to match up to her expectations in the long run. But now finding herself in his immediate physical proximity, her attitude began to soften. Even if he didn't really want her, that didn't mean it was all over. Maybe, someday, there would be a sudden, unexpected encounter between them, a feast of passion after which she could coolly go her own way; or maybe something would happen to make him see her in a new light; or maybe he didn't know what he wanted, only *thought* he did but would be proved wrong in the end, or would mature, or change, or . . . something.

She had no business thinking about any of this, of course. In the back of her mind something in her marveled that she could be so preoccupied with the question of Kassien's affections at a time like this, when all her resources ought to be focused on the task at hand. And then she decided that that was the difference between herself and the others: they could put aside their emotions when they needed to, and she, it seemed, could not. Or maybe she was just stupid.

And then it occurred to her that if she was thinking about Kassien and what was between his legs, she was spared thinking about what fate she was leading the other four toward, and whether she was ready for it.

"Feel along this wall," Kassien was saying, placing her hands on the surface and moving them for her. She felt incisions like writing in the smooth wall, which was warmer than the surrounding stone. Then her hand passed across something soft, like cool flesh. She inhaled with a hiss. "Xiriel, come and touch this."

Xiriel hummed from the bottom of his throat as he passed his hands across the surface. "It's a door, and it's covered with Everien symbol-writing. I might be able to do something with—wait, what's this?"

A gentle light flared, and Xiriel's silhouette could be seen in the flow of his Knowledge-light. He plucked a broken dagger from a seam in the wall and handed it to Istar. "Someone has tried to come this way," he said.

"It's Pharician," Istar said.

"They've jammed the door," Xiriel muttered, and then gasped as the sound of steel-shod boots rang in the stairwell above them. The Knowledge-light went out.

"Get back against the walls," Istar hissed. "Wait for my signal to strike."

Torches sliced the darkness as the Pharicians barreled down the stairs, talking among themselves. "These Everien tricks are mind-breaking," one of them said to the other. "I wish I could understand how to open the door."

Her back was flush against the wall, but Istar knew the torches would sweep over all of them and catch the shine of their armor. She let them descend, two steps, three steps, four . . . she willed herself not to panic. The Pharicians would not be expecting to find anyone in this tunnel. She must wait. They came down eight steps and Istar leaped out, drawing her sword and shouting, *"Now!"*

As her sword went between the ribs of the first Pharician, it occurred to Istar that if Lerien had not declared war on Pharice yet, she had done so now. Pentar and Kassien flanked her on either side, chasing the surprised Pharicians back up the stairs.

"Don't let them escape," Istar cried, and turning to the one Pentar was fighting, knocked him down and cut his throat. She did this easily: fighting the Slaves in the mountains had put a fine edge of ruthlessness on her, and she was out to prove herself against Pentar, anyway.

Kassien was not so brutal. He disarmed his man but did not deliver the killing stroke. Instead he stood over his vanquished opponent for a long moment.

"Tie him up," Istar spat. "And gag him. He's too dangerous if he brings the rest down on us."

Kassien did so, and Pentar went to the top of the stairs to be sure no more were coming.

"Hurry, Xiriel," Istar said, stepping over the bloody bodies and into the pool of illumination where Xiriel had returned to his examination of the door. Pallo was giving her a frightened look, but she ignored him. She was jumping inside her skin as Xiriel calmly pored over the incisions in the wall.

His hand lit up and he pressed it into the wall.

"Pallo, press on that Eye symbol," Xiriel said.

Water could be heard rushing somewhere beyond as a section of the wall yielded beneath Pallo's hand. They were in a rough passage through which a stream flowed into thin blue light. Steam rose from its waters.

"Pentar! Kassien!" Istar called, stepping into the cavern. "Hurry and get through here. Xiriel, can you shut it behind us?"

"I can try," Xiriel said. The others came through the passage and Xiriel stayed behind; a minute later he could be heard loping behind them, laughing at having foiled the Pharician pursuers. The stream turned twice, and then light began to grow. They emerged into a breeze and under the shadow of the next island. The stream disgorged in a white spray that shot out over the sea, falling sideways in the wind. The ledge where they stood was tiny and exposed. Pallo pressed himself against the stone, white-fingered. Below, the waves swirled hypnotically against the base of the cliff. Gulls made idle patterns. "How are we going to get there from here?" he asked faintly.

The shadow of the second island fell on their faces; its sides were almost sheer, apparently without blemish except for tiny white beards painted where gulls had somehow managed to perch, staining the rock. A pair of seahawks was sitting on the cliff opposite, observing them. Istar took this as a good sign. Directly across from them, the semiarch of a half-extended Everien bridge hooked out into the air like a claw. It was much too far to reach from here.

"Something's down here," Xiriel said. He bent and wiped fungus and dirt from the tiles of the tunnel entrance and ledge. They were ornately inscribed with symbols the others couldn't read. "Ah! The other island comes when called, but how to call it . . ."

Openmouthed, Istar stared at Xiriel. "Comes when called?" she said. "What's got into you?"

"Shh, Istar. Go away. You smell of intestines."

Kassien and Pentar had busied themselves with ropes and grappling hooks, but it was evident to Istar that they were too far away for such simple methods. She studied the cliff face, wondering how scalable it was and whether they might swim across, climb to the unfinished bridge, and enter the underground door there. This didn't seem very feasible, either, but it occupied her mind while Xiriel was doing whatever it was he was doing.

Then she wondered if she could be suffering from vertigo, because it seemed to her that the next island was slowly *turning*. Xiriel was chuckling gleefully. On the next island, several pieces of loose stone tumbled into the water from beneath the tongue of the viaduct.

"By my grandmother's beard!" Pallo exclaimed. "The bridge is moving!"

Xiriel was looking exceptionally pleased with himself as the other island extended its arm toward them with a heavy grinding noise. The span was not supported in any way but appeared completely stable. It slid against the stone at their feet and stopped. There was a deep humming and they felt vibrations pass through their boots; then nothing.

"One bridge, as requested," Xiriel said. "Let's get across fast, before it changes its mind."

They ran. Halfway across, they came into view of the original Everien bridge, which the Pharicians were still attempting to extend to reach a different neighboring island. At the same time they came into the line of the wind, which tackled them and drove them to their knees. Pallo clung, unmoving, flat on his belly on the stone. Istar turned and saw him.

"Crawl if you have to, Pallo!"

Arrows flew among them, driven harder on the wind. They struck the stone around Pallo, who could not even bring himself to look.

The rest of the group had almost reached the far side of the bridge.

"*Pallo!*" Istar screamed. Xiriel had reached the entrance to the tunnel in the new island, and he waved them on.

"It's not going to last long!" he yelled over the wind. "The time for the bridge is short and there's nothing I can do about it."

"What's he talking about?" Kassien said to Pentar.

"*Pallo!*" Istar was frantic. Pentar ignored Kassien's question and ran back out across the bridge.

"Leave him," Xiriel called to Pentar. "The bridge won't stay!"

"*Pallo, damn it!*" they chorused. The bridge began to retract, moving beneath them. They scrambled onto the solid ledge on the other side, where Xiriel waited. More Pharician arrows flew, but although Pallo was unmoving, none struck him. Pentar reached him and began dragging him back. The island was slowly turning back to its original position, forcing Pentar to pull the resisting Pallo into the wind. The bridge flexed and bent in the wind, which sported eddies that could be seen in the irregular flight of the endless Pharician arrows.

Pentar trudged toward them, his face flushed, his dark eyes half-shut against the gale, one arm clamped around Pallo's neck as the Pharician stumbled after him uselessly. Istar stretched out her arms. The bridge was carrying Pentar forward anyway, but as it came toward its final withdrawn position, it tilted and the two figures nearly fell. Istar leaned out and caught Pentar's swirling cloak, then his hand, and he thrust Pallo bodily at her.

"Here he is," Pentar gasped as he fell into the tunnel. "For whatever he's worth, he's all yours, Istar."

Pallo was trembling. "I'm sorry," he said. "I'm sorry, I really really tried, I did, but I—"

"Shut up," Istar said, placing her hand over his mouth to illustrate. The others had already started down the tunnel.

Pallo had begun to recover. "Always underground," he complained.

"Always moaning," Kassien answered. "Someone get a light going."

"Yes," Xiriel agreed. "We are going to be underground for a long time. Get used to it, Pallo."

After this, there would be no end to the sound of the tide, night or day, near or far. Everywhere they went in that space that was larger than itself, they could hear the sound of the ocean as if it were about to burst in on them through the rock. Even after they had descended many levels below the point they knew to be the waterline, the rush of the surf filled the empty spaces between footfalls, words, thoughts.

Kassien in the lead had reached a dead end. He placed his hands on the wall, which was smooth and possessed sources of light the size of grains of sand buried deep within it. He shuddered.

"What is it?" Xiriel asked sharply.

"Look." Kassien uttered the word without removing his gaze or his finger from the wall. They looked. The lights seemed to get larger without getting any brighter, and they began to move around, gradually elongating until they resembled slugs, and then, stretching more, worms. Istar was not disgusted; on the contrary, the slowly wriggling lightworms were soothing. She could feel her anxious brows soften. After a few seconds it seemed that each of the lightworms had a personality, and she found herself singling out one in particular and following everything it did. She could no longer take her eyes away. It grew larger and larger until it filled the entire panel before them. Then it turned its mouth toward her and the wall wavered like a jelly. The lightworm's mouth stretched wide and engulfed her. It began to swallow.

Pentar caught her other arm and pulled her back. She couldn't see anything but the worms of light, but she could hear the others asking her concerned questions and making a fuss in general.

"I'm fine," she said, shaking off their hands. "Don't look at the worms, whatever you do."

"This octagonal tile in the floor, I think I remember it from one of the maps," said Xiriel.

Istar felt vertiginous. She turned in a circle, off balance as if drunken, almost falling. She heard Xiriel exclaim, "Aha, it *does* move!" and the next thing she knew her stomach had been left behind and she was falling—they were all falling, to judge by the screams.

QUICKSILVER

The floor was still beneath her, so the stone itself must be plunging downward.

It slowed and then stopped.

She still couldn't see, but the faint glow of the lightworms had been replaced by pure darkness. An ice-cold draft rushed over them. Xiriel coughed, and his Knowledge-light came on faintly. They were on an octagonal tile that had fallen down a shaft and landed on a pool of intensely reflective silver liquid filling a roughly circular chamber measuring some hundred feet or more in diameter. The disc rotated slowly as it floated. The walls of the chamber were not stone: they threw back weak reflections where Xiriel's light touched them. He was holding the light over his head and peering up the shaft. His teeth chattered in the cold.

"I think we've fallen past the ledge that leads to the level we need. We're going to have to get back up."

They craned their heads and looked up the shaft, where the rim of the ledge Xiriel spoke of showed silver in the darkness. Kassien took out his grappling hook and rope and made a toss. The hook struck the ledge perfectly on the first try, but there was nowhere for it to catch on the polished surface and it slipped off as though greased, landing in the silver liquid with a low-pitched *thunk*. Globules of silver flew into the air; one settled on the tile where they stood and lay in a little lump instead of draining off as water would.

Pallo nudged it with his toe, laughing. "It's quicksilver," he said delightedly. "I've never seen so much of it! Isn't it fun?" He bent and began playing with the stuff, which behaved like no liquid Istar had ever seen.

"Quicksilver?" Xiriel exclaimed. "It expands when you heat it, doesn't it? I wonder if this level is meant to be higher, so we'd reach that ledge from here. Maybe it's too cold here."

"It *is* freezing," Pentar said, hugging himself. "Could we build a fire?"

"It would have to be a huge fire. And it would have to come from below." Xiriel dropped to his knees to examine the tile they were standing on. He dipped one of his axes in the liquid and hooked the blade beneath the tile. The whole thing tipped slightly, surprisingly light and buoyant.

"We're definitely floating," he said. He turned his attention to Kassien. "I wonder whether we could paddle our way to one of the walls, and get a hook into the wall and climb. . . ."

Kassien gazed dubiously at the ceiling, and then down into the silver pool. "I don't think anybody wants to risk falling in *that*," he said dubiously. But Pentar had already lowered himself on his belly, placed his sword into the fluid, and begun using it as a paddle. It was not a very good method, but the tile did move, and when the others joined him they were able to navigate slowly and laboriously across the chamber. As they drew near the wall, the light reflected back from it grew brighter and more complex. Pallo lit a torch, and as its flame caught, the others gasped. The chamber was made of crystal laced with fine filaments like the veins of a leaf. The crystal was utterly clear, but cut in such a way that light sent to it came back multiplied, diamond-sharp. Slowly their raft drew up to the wall until they could see at intervals tubes of clear glass protruding from the crystal. Kassien reached out and caught hold of one of these, attempting to use it to hold their position; but its end broke off in his hand and there was a hissing sound as an invisible, foul-smelling gas poured out.

Before anyone could react, Pallo's torch had lit the gas with an explosive whoof. His hair caught on fire and Kassien leaped on him in an instant, smothering the flames with his cloak. All at once they were overwhelmed with the impressions of burning hair, burning bear fur, sudden heat, and blue light. A blue gout of flame shot out from the wall; within, the veins that had looked as if they were filled with water now were shown to be filled with the flammable gas as they flared to life. The entire chamber filled with light and heat. It was as if they were inside a hollow crystal egg that had suddenly caught the sun.

Pallo staggered to his feet, sooty-faced but not seriously hurt, as the raft began to rise.

"Hurry!" Xiriel said. "We have to get back to the center or we'll be crushed against the ceiling."

They were moving upward rapidly. Abandoning all caution, they thrust their hands into the now-hot liquid and paddled madly. The quicksilver rose higher and higher, and the air became searingly hot. Soon they were crouched beneath the roof of the chamber, pulling themselves along the crystal by their fingertips in an effort to reach the hole in the center. The heat became unbearable.

Xiriel was the first to stand up and step onto the ledge, which was octagonal with eight tunnels leading in different directions. The others piled after him, gulping down the cooler air that blew in from the eight tunnels. Pallo smiled and stretched. "It's a good thing I lit that torch," he said. "We probably never would have guessed we could—"

The quicksilver had risen to the level of the ledge. It lifted the tile and began to ooze out from beneath it.

"Shit, which way?" Kassien blurted.

Xiriel hesitated. "I've lost my sense of direction," he said. "They all look the same. . . ."

Quicksilver crept up their boots. All the tunnels were dark and straight. There was nothing to discriminate among them.

Istar whirled and picked one at random. She shot down it, shouting for the others to follow. Splashing through the silver liquid she just kept thinking, *Please let it not be another dead end.* She came to a flight of steps and bounded up them as if wing-shod. Light filtered in from around a bend; she took the corner and halted, grabbing the wall for balance as yellow summer light smacked across her face and the tunnel opened onto thin air. The sea soughed far below. A piece of blue swayed in her vision as the others shuffled and wheezed to a halt at her back, spitting with exertion. The next island reared high above them like a wolf's fang. There was no bridge other than a thick strand of weed-covered cable that hung slack between a ring in the stone at the end of the tunnel and some fixture on the opposite side.

Pentar was breathing down her neck. She shoved him back with a twist of her hip. Pallo was uttering what she assumed were oaths in Pharician.

"Uh . . . Kassien?" she said in a high voice. She turned and caught his eye, and he moved Pallo and Pentar aside to reach her. Gently he took her shoulders and pulled her back from the edge. "No need to stand *there,*" he said, and dropped to his knees, examining the cable.

"I picked the wrong tunnel," she babbled. "But there was no time, and I was afraid—"

"Shut up, Star," said Xiriel.

"Can we go back?" she asked weakly.

"Not unless the fire stops on its own. The quicksilver's reached the bottom of the steps."

"Never mind," said Kassien. "This is good enough. It's not rope, it's something much stronger, and it's thick enough to grip well with your legs."

"Did the Pharicians put it there? Could they have got out this far?"

"I don't think so. I doubt anyone's been out this far," Xiriel answered.

"We're crossing *that*?" Pallo squawked.

"I am," said Kassien. "Perhaps in Pharice you all just flap your wings and *wish*. . . ."

"It can be done," Pentar agreed. "Just don't look down."

Kassien secured all the fittings on his pack and gear and then climbed down the rope. It was draped loosely between the two islands, and dropped against the cliff for a little way before curving out across the ocean in a long parabola that eventually rose to the opposite side. Kassien spun on the rope so that he lay with his back to the water and his head toward the next island, legs wrapping the rope and hands gripping it above his body so that he could pull himself along.

"It's too overgrown to attach to a safety loop," Pentar observed. "The thing wouldn't slide and it would only slow us down."

"I wouldn't mind," Pallo said in a small voice.

"If you fall, just swim for it," Xiriel advised him philosophically.

"But you'd never get up the cliff opposite," argued Pallo.

"We'd drop you a rope. Or you'd make a nice fish food. Come on. I'm going, and you're coming next." Istar swung herself out onto the cable. Kassien was already well over the open water. She had gone down about twenty feet and had shifted position to copy Kassien when she tilted her head back to check his progress.

He wasn't there.

"Kass?" She peered back at the others, but they were obscured from below by the ledge.

"Xiriel! Where's Kassien?"

Her voice projected only weakly over the sound of the ocean. She couldn't see Kassien in the water, but it was rough with whitecaps and might easily hide a swimmer. She shut her eyes and kept going, wrestling with clumps of hanging seaweed that made the rope thick and slippery. She saw Pallo climb down after her as she'd ordered. She shouted to him, but he didn't respond—probably too terrified. She looked ahead again. The rope disappeared ten feet beyond her clasped hands.

"Xiriel?" Still no response. She could see the terminal section of the rope where it reached the next island, but a whole length of it was gone. It hadn't been cut, for it didn't hang slack. It was invisible.

Istar edged right up to the place where the rope disappeared. The edges were not frayed. Nothing beyond looked different than it should, but for the absence of the rope.

"Kass?"

She looked down the length of her own legs. Pallo was creeping along the cable like a little old lady.

Closing her eyes, she slid her hand up the rope. She felt it go off the end. There was nothing solid beyond, but the air was hot and dry on her hand, and cool on the rest of her. Something was dragging at her hand without touching her, a tugging like a magnet's. Or like gravity. . . .

She gripped the rope hard with her legs and her right hand, and stretched her head and shoulders off the end and into the heat and drag of the other place. She was hanging at the bottom end of a line suspended above a pit of volcanic fire. Below her, dark and hot and red at once, lava seethed and spurted. Her sense of gravity was completely confused, for although most of her body was lying horizontal under a rope over the sea, her head felt as if it were dangling over the pit. She wondered whether she could go back, or if she would fall off the end of the rope and into lava if she tried. She looked up and saw that the rope stretched toward some kind of girder. She began to climb, buffeted by heat. Sweat poured from her skin and into her clothes. The rope was hot to the touch and it seared her hands, burning her legs even through her leather trousers; but there was no way she could think of letting go.

When she reached the girder it was all she could do to pull herself onto it. The fact that the metal was burning hot was further incentive to keep moving, or she probably would have collapsed there. She staggered along the girder so fast she couldn't possibly lose her balance, screaming Kassien's name. The girder was slippery; she skated the last several yards and fell to her knees on the brink.

"Istar?" She could hear Pallo calling her name from somewhere above. A tiny splotch of blue light was visible like a fleck of paint on the general darkness. She didn't know how to get to it. She stood up again, muscles trembling. Her feet didn't want to stay under her. *I'm going to fall in a minute,* she thought—and someone grabbed her foot and dragged her sideways.

It was Kassien.

She was lying on a ledge above the sea, half her body draped over the edge. The rope stretched out over the water above her. Kassien's hand pinned her foot to the rock, and she saw that somehow she had reached the other side, but she was well below the end of the rope where it met the cliff. The others were all standing on that ledge above her; Kassien had a rope around his waist and a precarious hold on the cliff.

"This is a funny place to take a nap," he said. "You almost fell in. How did you get here? We thought you fell in the water. Nobody could see you."

Istar said, "Thirsty," and licked cracked lips.

"Your face is black," Kassien said. "Your hands are burned. What have you been up to? I thought Pallo was the pyromaniac among us."

The lightness of his tone, meant to reassure her, instead made her feel like an invalid being coaxed to drink soup. She wondered how close she had come to falling.

"Come on," he said, and drew her up. "Put this rope around you."

They had to pull her up; she was too weak to climb at all. Kassien free-climbed after her.

"Show-off," she croaked, swigging from Pentar's water bottle. "Where are we?"

"Dunno, but I'm starving," Pallo said suggestively. They had almost reached the summit of the island, which was rugged and sported ivy and moss among the ruins. It was a logical place to rest before attempting the next bridge. They trooped up a vine-covered staircase that had once been white, curving among reclaimed parts of buildings. Pentar turned to look back and gave a startled cry. He pointed to two of the islands that floated to the south. They hadn't come near either one, but they could see that a legitimate Everien bridge had been extended between them and the horde of soldiers was passing across it like an army of red and black ants.

"How are they doing that?" railed Xiriel, pushing Pentar out of the way to get to the highest position on the island. "How do they know the way?"

"And why so many?" Kassien mused. "What do they think they're going to have to fight at Jai Pendu, to bring such a large force? How did they get across?"

Pallo strained his eyes, bouncing up and down with excitement. "Kassien . . . by Ysse, look carefully. See, there on the mainland? There must be thousands of them. There are horses. There are—"

"Yes, we can see for ourselves," Kassien snapped.

"—siege towers!"

"That could be the army Tarquin warned of," Istar murmured. She had recovered her voice, but not her energy. "But why here?"

Xiriel called down, "Come! Hurry! There's an intact bridge to the next island!"

This was all anybody needed to hear; even Istar was able to move forward when offered the incentive of a proper bridge. The next island was taller than the rest, so they could not see what was on top of it. The bridge was a perfect white curve, graceful and strutless. It ended at the mouth of a dark tunnel in the side of the island. They crossed it hurriedly, and when they reached the other side, Xiriel looked everywhere in the tunnel entrance and around the foundation of the bridge, hoping to find some way to block the bridge behind them.

"There's nothing I can do," he said.

"Never mind." Kassien pointed to the island they had just escaped. "There are figures coming up out of the ruins—I think they're catching up. Let's get going while we still have a lead."

XIRIEL LED THEM under the island. There was very little light, and a powerful wind was blowing from somewhere in the depths; eventually they reached the end of the tunnel, where the wind originated somewhere far below. A panel slammed down behind them. Kassien turned and flung himself against it, but it did not yield. Ahead of them was a chasm of indeterminate depth, out of which roared a deafening wind. At the end of the tunnel loomed a highly decorated wall covered with, among other things, glowing tiles marked by mysterious symbols. Xiriel addressed himself to it; Istar's esteem of him went up another notch as she observed his total concentration on the task at hand.

The other three huddled out of the wind, watching Xiriel. His tall form was bathed in flickering lights of orange and green—weird, unnatural colors such as they had never seen. The wind blew his thin garments so hard against him that they seemed painted on his taut lineaments. His face was completely still but for the flickering eyes. Sweat beaded on his upper lip.

"Where is all this wind coming from?" Kassien said in her ear. She cast a concerned glance at him, knowing that he was even less at ease with the Knowledge than she. He looked as though he would bolt if there were anywhere to bolt to.

Before Istar could answer, the pitch of the wind changed. As one they covered their ears—all except Xiriel, who stood alone in the light, swaying slightly as the air currents pressed him. The wind sang higher. A bass drone slid below the original pitch. The dissonance made Istar's teeth tingle; then the sound resolved to a chord. A fourth tone came on waveringly, and then a fifth.

The light went out, leaving them in pitch darkness.

Kassien stiffened at her side. Pentar gripped her arm and spoke into her ear, but she couldn't hear anything but the wind, which was now throbbing through the chasm in distinct waves. When the sound hit them it was hard and soft at once, like water under great pressure. Istar experienced the unnerving sensation that the ground had dropped away be-

neath her and that they were all floating in the sound. She didn't know if
her eyes were closed or open.

That's it, she thought hopelessly. *That's the end of us.* For she didn't
dare move.

Then a pencil-thin line of silver drew itself across the darkness, reas-
serting the presence of matter in a world that had seemed empty; the line
of light broadened to outline the entire wall before which Xiriel stood. It
was a crack, for the wall slowly began to fall away backward, admitting a
clear blue illumination that rendered Xiriel like an ice sculpture in starlight. And indeed he remained still enough to have frozen.

Beyond him, in a space the size of ten Fire Houses, something bright
and terrible was moving.

The thing before them was not a beast, but nor was it a mechanical
system. It was something less abstract and dismissible than a vision though
indisputably a strain and a terror to the already fevered imagination. Istar
found herself gaping at a monster with a thousand aspects: some human,
some made of fire; some nothing but mouths that spoke unheard languages. There were wheels made of teeth that dripped blood; there were
dark, sulking things that rode on the shoulders of merciless gearboxes and
gazed soulfully at the travelers before turning tail and disappearing in the
hidden cracks between the monster apparatus and itself; there were claws
and fins and animal sinew hard up against metal and wire humming with
light; and there were hundreds of wings that beat in apparent futility,
until one looked at their undersides and saw whole cities writ there in
miniature, or large irregular windows leading to star-strewn nights. And
then an architecture began to show itself through the horror of displaced
body parts and repellent smells, and a disjointed geometry became apparent. This was not a visible structure: its joints and supports could not be
seen like the abandoned buildings of the Everiens above. It was not a
thing for the wind to blow through, or one on which the shadows might
change through the constancy of days and seasons. It was a structure of
implied connections, mistaken meanings, cancers of design in which
slightly damaged details replicated out of control and through their dumb
purposelessness acted deep in the mind to make the skin crawl with
revulsion. Mechanisms were firing off without reason. Pieces of the
whole changed places and jumped locations without warning, creating a
sickening sense of movement. It was, Istar thought, like looking at a
bucket of worms in which some of the worms, on closer inspection,
turned out to be people you knew, or songs that had been turned to
helpless flesh with no other option than to squirm blindly, bereft of
context, or the summer days you most fondly remembered now become
nothing more than pieces of tissue whose meaning and memory would

have done better to leave them. And just as you were about to turn away or shut your eyes, you saw within the noisome mess a sort of pattern—and the pattern in this case was discernible first to Xiriel, and then slowly, horribly, to the others.

"Look at it carefully," he said. "It's a staircase."

"No it isn't," Kassien said. "It's a nightmare. Close the gates. We'll find a different way."

Istar was inclined to agree with him, but Xiriel said earnestly, "This is the only way. You mustn't be squeamish."

Kassien looked angry, but he shrank back. "You're mad. It's alive and it's hostile and I'd rather fight the whole Pharician army bare-handed than go one inch closer."

As if his words had come to life, two things happened in rapid succession: first, the behemoth of the gates shot a section of itself toward them, something resembling a green and diseased system of genitals that spat a luminous arc of liquid. This struck a section of the landing nearby, eating through it with a sinister hiss of yellowy smoke and revealing a white swirl of water beneath. Second, the chorus of wind ceased all at once, save for a soft and plaintive wail of air beating a wavering melody through some overlooked crack. In the ensuing silence the tramp of many boots could be heard.

"Here they come," Xiriel murmured. He sounded in a trance and Istar wanted to strike him.

Pentar leaned out into the tunnel they'd just left. "There must be a better place to fight them than this."

"I don't like it, Xiriel," Istar said. "But if you can lead us to the top, we'll go. Let them follow if they can."

Kassien didn't look at her, or the others, or the gate-creature. "This is suicide," he said in a low voice.

Xiriel grabbed Istar's hand. "Get hold of one another!" He sprang away just as Istar managed to get a piece of Pentar's cloak. Pallo was clutching her, and Kassien was somewhere behind them. Istar concentrated on breathing, just to stop herself gagging.

"They're following us!" Pallo shouted. Xiriel turned around and Istar saw the whites of his eyes. She closed hers and let herself be drawn forward.

TERMS OF SURRENDER

"Sir? Sir! Wake up! I think I found Kivi!"

Ajiko spun and looked at the place on the Water where Soren pointed. His eyes slowly focused. It was a bright morning on the sea plain, and Kivi was surrounded by a blur of armored bodies. Ajiko's spirits shot up. Lerien must have found the army.

"Kivi! Report!"

The Seer licked his lips and said, "General Ajiko, sir, I am a prisoner. I have been asked to contact you to offer terms of surrender."

"What!" Ajiko turned to Soren accusingly.

"It's a Pharician army, sir," whispered Soren.

"Where's the king?"

"I'm instructed to say that the Pharician commander Tash has declared this entire valley forfeit to Pharice following Pharician losses in the incident at Ristale. King Lerien and his men were last seen on their way to the Floating Lands. We are en route to you and will overrun your land in a matter of days. Tash gives you a choice. Surrender and allow Jai Khalar to be entered, and you will retain your position as steward in the occupied territory."

"And if we refuse?"

"Then you will be besieged and Tash will take the valley out from under you."

"Tash presumes much if he believes the Clans will not defend their land."

Kivi said, "Tash knows you have no army. It has been seen under the dominion of a Sekk Master, marching toward the Floating Lands."

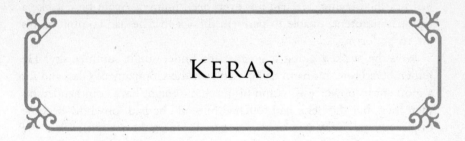

KERAS

$\mathcal{F}$or a long time, Tarquin couldn't work out what was going on. He was not in the melée at Ristale anymore, though his sword was naked and black with hard-set gore. Night was gone, the woman he knew yet didn't know was gone, Chyko was gone, and the demon horse was nowhere to be seen—yet his cloak was half-burned as proof it had all truly happened. He was walking along a narrow track in uncut green hay: his eyes came to focus on a small spider hurrying across his path, one of many that moved among the trampled blades of grass.

This was not Pharice. The grass was different, and he was among mountains, not beside them. It looked more like Snake Country. He was walking northeast up a teardrop-shaped valley set in white peaks. There were two hawks overhead.

He had been walking for a long time. He deduced this by the blisters on his feet when he stopped to rest and the lack of rations in his pack. And the length of his fingernails, which had not been trimmed for days.

Even simple inferences like this took time for him to reason out. His mind was utterly battered and spent. Tears of frustration filled his throat. He was lost. He could trust nothing—what he had said to Kivi applied doubly to Tarquin: he especially could not trust himself.

He had had another chance to kill the thing that stole his men. The white fragile being that he'd thought he left behind in Jai Pendu was the same creature that now controlled the mixed army of Clan and Pharician warriors. It made them Slaves of a kind, and it would be taking them back to Jai Pendu. There was nothing he, Tarquin the Free, could do about it, for he had not destroyed the Sekk in combat and moreover he had not died trying. He had not even been injured! Again he felt like a coward: impotent, unable to perform the act that he had committed his life to perfecting.

Now he walked along a green path under sunlit summer sky. He remembered how his hand had closed over the Company of Glass and for a moment its power was within his reach; he might have commanded his men then, but the Sekk had touched him and he had somehow become displaced here. Why was he always spared? He could not spit back at the sun that shone on him; he could not help being relieved to be alive and not sucked into the Glass that the Sekk held, as he knew it must have intended. Yet nothing made sense. His throat tightened when he recalled the unexpected meeting with Chyko after all these years. Could Chyko really be alive, unchanged? Or was it all just a cruel trick?

Chyko had thrived on the irrational; he would have delighted at finding himself in such straits as the ones that had Tarquin trapped right now. But Chyko had never subscribed to the notion of sense—much less practiced it. Take Mhani, for example: Chyko had fallen in love with the one woman in Jai Khalar—maybe even in the whole world—who was not taken in by his charms. He had wasted far more time and effort in trying to win her over than she deserved, Tarquin thought. They had nothing in common: she was an intellectual, and he could neither read nor do arithmetic. Her looks were average bordering on plain; he was a stunning piece of manhood, even if his features were exaggerated and bore the marks of many battles. He was a rampant extrovert; she was quiet, even secretive. He had an outrageous sense of humor, and she was serious out of all proportion to her age. Yet in the end she had capitulated and had given him three children in as many years, first Istar and then the twins. And he had paraded her around, pregnant, as if she were a goddess of the jungles of Anaya and he her chosen servant.

Mhani. He wanted to curse her for setting her daughter on a path of madness; but in thinking about it, he realized that if Istar had even a fingernail of her father in her, Mhani would never have been able to stop her from doing anything. He had told Istar there was no way across the Floating Lands. How badly he had wanted to believe them too damaged to permit crossing—and how wrong he had been. How else could the Sekk have gotten from Jai Pendu to Everien?

He startled a deer and her two offspring, and returned to the present. The track topped a slight rise. Where the ground dipped at his feet, a river traversed the valley, passing through a small stand of young trees. Then the grass continued, uninterrupted except for a sizable piece of woodland about two miles away, near the head of the valley. In the distance he saw horses grazing. There was no bridge and he saw no fences, so the horses might be wild; but he thought not when he noticed a thin curl of white smoke rising from the far side of the woodland.

He forded the river and rested for a few minutes on its farther bank, where he drank and cleaned his sword and stretched wearily. Gossamers glided over the disturbed water and came to rest like golden filigree on the giant ferns that lined the shady part of the banks. When the gossamers sunned themselves a certain way, the sun shot rainbows through their wings. Tarquin was charmed. The slow river, the heat, and the silence recalled him to the summers of his youth spent by the rivers of the Seahawk Clan that led to the ocean, and the long hours with his friends playing war games as they browned in the sun, making slingshots and racing in the water and telling stories.

Am I now to live only in memory? he wondered, and immediately became annoyed at the sentiment. His mind felt soft, but his body had become like the stuff of the mountains where he'd been spending his time, and he moved off feeling stiff, tough, and hungry. The path left the trees and he began to jog across the rolling, open field. As he drew closer to the larger patch of woods, the grass became shorter, grazed down by the dozen or so horses that roamed it. Still he saw no buildings or fences. The path widened into a general area of mud and then veered off into the trees. He followed it and had just come into the deeper shade of oaks and chestnuts when loud hoofbeats sounded ahead of him. The horse was moving fast; it barreled around a bend in the track and was upon him before he could do more than turn and try to stand aside. The rider was holding a wicked-looking Pharician spear, which pointed at his belly.

The horse had no saddle, and the rider was dressed in leather softened of long wear. She was a wiry, small woman several years younger than Tarquin, with unkempt dark hair that had been tied back but most of it escaped anyway. She had brought the horse to a halt using only her legs, and now moved with the animal as if welded to its back. She looked him over with an expression on her thin face that was amused but not happy, if this were possible. The horse danced in place, but she contrived to hold the spear steady. Tarquin took a step back.

"You are trespassing," she said in a Pharician accent. "This is my place, and you have not been invited."

"I'm lost. I mean no harm. Can you tell me where I am?" Her accent confused him: the landscape looked like some remote part of Snake Country, but her voice belonged to Jundun or maybe even farther south.

"Where are you trying to go?" She answered his question with another, suspiciously.

"Jai Khalar." He didn't sound very sure of it; how could he plan where he wanted to go when he didn't know where he was to begin with?

She laughed. "You aren't lost. You're mad. Well." She pointed with the spear through the trees, where a small footpath cut through the underbrush. "There is a quicker way back to the river if you follow that path. It's a nice day for a swim, so you won't have wasted your time completely. Now, if you cross the river and go back down the end of the valley the way you've come, and cross the mountains avoiding the Assimilators and the roaming Slave bands and the lions, after several days you will come to Fivesisters Lake, and thence it is only a few hundred miles to Jai Khalar."

"What? On foot?" he said in despair.

She gave a derisive toss of her head, but beneath her cavalier manner he detected a hint of fear when she said, "Who sent you here? How did you find us?"

"No one sent me," he responded hastily. "I told you, I'm lost."

"You've been lost for a long time, then—unless you have wings that can fly you across from Fivesisters Lake, which is the nearest settlement."

He sagged, thinking of the distance to Jai Khalar.

"What Clan are you?" she asked. "You wear no signs, but you speak like one of Ysse's army."

"I was Seahawk Clan. But that was a long time ago. It doesn't matter anymore. Let us just say that I find myself here, and my life means little to me if I am as far from Jai Khalar, and Jai Pendu, as you say. For by the time I get back there, it will be too late for me to redeem my errors."

"Look," she said flatly, and turned the horse. The mare began to walk again, and Tarquin strode by her side along the path that led through the wood. "We both know you are here to bargain for my horses, so spare me the long and colorful stories of your adventures."

"I'm not—"

"It's a time of war," she said. "I cannot take them back over the mountains to my homeland, and I will not trade them away to strangers who will only use them in battle. I will not trade them to their deaths."

"I'm not a horse trader," he managed to get out. "I'm lost. Still, one of your animals would be of great use to me, if only to carry me far away from Everien."

She looked down her nose at him. "You have not looked once at the horse I ride," she said. "That alone prevents me from giving you anything to ride."

"I'm no expert on horses," he conceded, now giving a cursory glance over the chestnut mare and concluding she was a fine animal, although she had an unusual face and exceptionally sharp hooves. "Tell me how it is that a Pharician such as yourself ends up high in the Everien Range, breeding horses."

"It is a long story. But I am not the only Pharician trainer you will find in your country. Among your Clans there are none who know the magic of the horse. Horses are not among the Clan animals, and your people have no gift with them."

"And your people do? Since when do Pharicians have Clan animals? You are all too busy being civilized and building your empire to appreciate the Animal ways."

"How little you understand! The Animal Magic is older than all of us, and it is not unique to Everien. We may not have the Knowledge in Pharice, but we, too, have the Animal Clans—or did at one time. Their ways are all but buried now in the common culture, but traces can be found still, especially among the horse tribes of the desert."

"Your people." He realized that her origins should have been obvious from the first moment he laid eyes on her. She was a desert nomad, now far from home and apparently alone.

They had emerged on the other side of the wood, where there were several roughly constructed buildings and a pond fed by the river. Beyond the trampled earth of the yard, goats and chickens roamed nearby; the horses were scattered farther, some of them chasing each other or rolling in the high grass.

She gestured to the field scornfully. It easily filled three hundred acres.

"It is like teaching them to dance on a dinner plate. In my country, the plains stretch for miles on miles. I would have these horses running day in and day out to condition their muscles. They would run without food or water, on pure spirit, and they would fight like whirlwinds. So I would teach them. But we are closeted here. I was not able to take them across the mountains to Pharice while the danger from Sekk is so high. I would not risk the journey. So we must cope with this confinement."

"They seem fit enough to me," Tarquin said, squinting to see the young animals scattered around the field.

"They are passable. But they have not awakened their true country which lies within them. The fires of the desert lie in ashes. They will run if driven, fight if challenged; but it is not their passion. They are asleep. All except Ice, their sire. He knows what it means to run and never stop. He can eat the wind and polish the sky with his mane."

"You can't mean the same Ice of legend. Not the Pharician demon-horse, the one who ran races in the Deer Country thirty years ago?"

"That's him."

"But . . . how old would he be now?"

"Age does not run the same for Ice as it does for us," she said. "What are you called?"

"Tarquin," he answered shortly. She gave no indication that the name was familiar, and he was relieved.

"I am Keras."

"Which one is Ice?" Tarquin was trying to remember clearly the gray he had seen at the races, so many years ago. If he were still alive, Ice would be as old as Tarquin by now; he was surprised to hear Keras talk of the horse in the present tense.

"Never mind," she said cagily. "I must ask you to go now. I have much to do, and whatever you may have heard, my horses are not for sale."

"Not so fast." He stepped in front of the chestnut mare, who rolled her eyes at him; he realized she was thinking about having a go at him. "I just got here. There are no other people for miles. Perhaps I could help you, lend you my back for labor. And surely we might exchange news. You might like to know that Everien is at war with Pharice."

Her eyes sparked, but she quickly concealed her reaction. "War? I have no interest in it. I have had enough of fighting even in my own country. I've seen too many of my horses abused and killed in war, and for what? They don't need men. We need them, but they don't need us. You can see this. Ice and his bloodline live quite happily away from people."

"Yet you said you taught these animals to fight." He was still watching her mount warily.

"To protect the herd. That's all."

"Protecting the herd is what I do," Tarquin said. "The Sekk are the wolves in the hills. They steal people from the villages and send them back, Enslaved, to slaughter their own kind."

"*We* don't need your protection."

"How hard you are, Keras."

"And you as well," she retorted. "You think that everything in the world belongs to you in your time of need, just because you are a warrior."

"If I'm to lay down my life for the land, for your life, for their lives, then yes—I do think I have a right to ask for a horse."

"I told you. I haven't asked for your protection. I doubt you could offer it, anyway. I will keep my own, and trust to my wits to survive."

"And what about your homeland? What about Pharice? Did you know it is on the brink of being overrun by Sekk?"

Her expression sharpened. "You lie."

He drew breath to release his rapidly fraying temper and then changed his mind about arguing. He let his shoulders sag. He had no appetite for an argument with this woman. He had already done battle with a Sekk today, and this piece of Pharician girl-talent who thought she was so fierce was really just an ignorant bit of fluff who would be blown to death by the winds of the Knowledge that were sweeping the world this mid-summer. Yet she obstructed him.

"I do not lie, Keras." He sighed. "Put the spear away and come down off the horse, and I will give you news of what is happening elsewhere than in your high valley."

She eyed him for a moment. Then she said, "Go over to the house and wait for me. We will sit down and talk, if that's what you really want—like the *civilized* people of Pharice."

She accompanied this remark with a shrewish little smile, and then twitched her legs against the horse and was off. Tarquin followed more slowly. It was tempting to just make off with one of the animals in the field, but with his luck they would probably all attack him. The mare was a strange one: he had never seen such a predaceous-looking equine and wouldn't have believed it possible for the species.

The steading was primitive and simple. He fell asleep in the shade of its wall; when he woke up, the sun had moved into his eyes and Keras had watered the mare and was brushing mud off her legs. The horse swiveled her head to look at Tarquin and he read a certain intelligence there that he had never before associated with horses. He didn't think this one liked him much, though. She turned away dismissively, and Keras said, "Tell me why you think Pharice is in danger."

So he told her. He described the army in detail; told her what he knew of the recent intrigues in Hezene's court; added in some informa-tion of his own that had come his way in his travels to convince her that he knew what he was talking about. While he talked, he followed Keras about as she collected eggs, threw down hay for the goats, cleaned her saddle. She began grooming her horse in earnest. Downplaying the role of Night and the Company, he added, "Pharice is likely to try to cross the Floating Lands, just as that fool Istar is doing. I used to think it was impossible to get across those islands, but now I'm not so sure. Certainly I fear what Istar may do if she is unlucky enough to find herself in Jai Pendu with the Sekk bringing an army of twenty thousand there."

"Twenty thousand Pharicians?"

"Not all of them, but more than half are your countrymen. They are under the sway of a Sekk and the Glass it wields."

"Who's Istar?" Her question startled him; he had forgotten she was there.

"Her father's daughter, I'm afraid." He sighed. "Yes, that is my real fear."

There was a long silence, ended when Keras abruptly chucked the brush into a tack box and slapped the horse's rump. The mare shot off into the grass. She moved beautifully, Tarquin thought, and wished that his problem could be solved so easily, by the use of a fast horse. He was simply too far away.

"It is a hard thing to suffer, this failure. If only I could have gotten to Jai Khalar, I would begin to rally the people to leave Everien entirely. I would not allow Ajiko to hold the people to the land. Better that they should flee and live as you do."

Keras began to stroll away from the buildings and into the open grassland. The shadows had grown long and blurry with gathering cloud. "You are a strange manner of thing," she remarked calmly, plucking a stem of grass and placing it between her lips. "Listening to you now, there is even less reason for me to risk one of my horses on you. I suspect you are quite out of your mind."

Tarquin didn't say anything to this. His words sounded vague and ill-conceived in his own ears, so how could he blame Keras for not cooperating? He wouldn't give himself a horse, either, if he were her.

"Tell me about Ice at least. He is still alive, you say?"

She softened then, as he'd guessed she would. She walked a little way into the field and called the horse. Two heads came up, observed her, and returned to their grazing. Tarquin smiled. So the mysterious Ice didn't even know his name. Maybe Keras was all talk after all.

Then Ice came over a rise and Tarquin's spine snapped erect. He was lost for breath or thought.

It was hard to believe this was the same animal he had seen as a child. He remembered that horse being fast, and he remembered the unusual color; but the sight before him now was astonishing. The horse fixed his gaze on Keras and moved easily toward her. Everything about him was motion and light, like a storm tide in sunset when the water goes white with its own force, and whiter still where the light shines through it.

"He moves like a song," Tarquin breathed.

"He moves like the wind demons in my country," said Keras, "when the sky draws the sands up into the blue and drags the earth itself behind it. The *majalah,* we call them. The white winds. Ice is no name for him."

Ice did not seem to approach; he merely *arrived,* his flanks dry, unwinded. His eyes were blue. The horse sidled up to Keras, sidestepped her, lowered his head, danced away again. Her head did not even reach the animal's withers, so she looked like a child; but Tarquin had no eyes for her. He was studying the stallion's conformation. Ice was leaner than a warhorse, with slender legs and a narrower chest—beautiful to see, but not built to carry an armored man over any distance. A hothouse flower,

Tarquin feared, dismayed by so much beauty. The animal looked as if he'd been dipped in ink: black where his hooves touched the ground, which darkness faded until above the hocks it became a silver gray, and finally alabaster on the body. Mane and tail were also white, flown like flags from the arches of the horse's body. Ice picked up his fetlocks prettily in an excess of enthusiasm, pawing the ground and snorting as he played with Keras. She was laughing.

"Want to see him run?" she said.

"I think I just have," Tarquin answered, letting amazement heat his tone.

"No you haven't. Watch this." She vaulted onto Ice's back and they shot away before he could blink. The horse took the perimeter of the field, leaving a trail of flying earth. Tarquin could just descry Keras stretched out along his neck and bit his lip with fear for her; the horse could barely be seen at all. His legs were a blur. All too soon they arrived again from the other direction, Ice trotting easily, barely breathing harder and sweating not at all—and Keras winded, red-faced, exultant.

"How do you ride such a thing?" he queried in amazement.

She gave him the first genuine smile she had yet shown. "A horse is a mechanical creature. He operates on his gaits, and when you can feel his rhythm, you can direct it."

She wrapped her arms around Ice's neck in an excess of affection.

"You should have seen Nemelir, my teacher. He was a ghost. He could get so deep inside the horse, the horse would think it *was* Nemelir."

"But how do you make them fight?"

"Ah. As I said, that is the Animal Magic. No one writes of such things. How is it that Seers of your Clan can fly, Tarquin?"

"I have no Clan," he corrected defensively.

"Let's not split hairs. How can they fly?"

"They can't *fly*, actually," Tarquin said, exasperated. "They can read the birds. That's all."

"Well. Our horses can read us. But as I say, those secrets are carefully guarded, and I don't claim to have mastered them. Whereas Nemelir—"

"Yes, yes, Nemelir. But he's not here, and I have need of such a horse as this." He was excited. With luck, he might make it to Jai Khalar before all was ruined.

"Ice is no one's to give. He belongs to the herd. He is too precious to risk. And I doubt you could ride him."

"Try me."

She dismissed the suggestion with a wave and a laugh. "It is out of the question. Look at yourself, Tarquin the Free. You are all but dead on your feet." By the time he'd realized she had deduced his identity without being told, she had dismounted and the horse was gone; and he realized she was right—he was too tired to be good for anything. He trailed after her as she returned to the steading.

KERAS HAD CONVERTED a section of the barn to a home. There was a stove, a table littered with pots of liniment and broken saddle leathers and unwashed dishes, and in the corner, a straw pallet covered by a horse blanket that looked more or less clean.

"I am a very lazy cook. I have only flatbread which is days old," she said, scrubbing vegetables in a bucket. She added gruffly, "You can have some to take with you when you go; I'll make more for myself."

"I would thank you. But you know I want a horse. Does my situation move you not at all?"

"I didn't say that." She glanced at him over her shoulder, brushing the unruly mass of hair away from her face. She had decent, clean lines, he thought: like her horses, a little savage, but interesting. It was a pity about her temperament; he supposed she had been too long alone, unaware that he was coming across much the same to her. "My horses are like children to me. You are dreaming if you expect me to give one to you. And to have the balls to ask for Ice!" She chuckled. "It's like asking to be given the Moon down from the sky. It just isn't going to happen."

He sighed and ripped off a section of bread. "Maybe you're right," he said. "I'm tired. I've had enough of losing, whether by inches or by miles. Maybe I should just give up. It is peaceful out here, isn't it? But it must be terrible in winter."

"We don't stay here in winter," she said in a clipped voice. He didn't ask where they went instead; he didn't feel like being rebuffed for his curiosity.

"Do you have anything to drink?" he said instead, and the plaintive tone in his voice must have elicited some sympathy from her, for she laughed and passed him a bottle.

"It's better than nothing, is it not?" she said.

They ate and drank randomly for hours as it finally got dark. After a few drinks, Keras began laughing for no reason, lying back against the Pharician-style pillows she had inexpertly made for her bed. They talked about nothing in particular. It had been weeks since he had thought about anything but the Pharician army, and Night and Jai Pendu and his Company; now, as if they were wounds to be guarded, he was not willing to touch any of these things in his mind. It was too late. There was nothing he could do. But Keras didn't care about Jai Pendu or about any of it. She really didn't care. And perhaps it was time he understood that life would go on, away from Everien—away from the past.

It was a barley liquor they drank, and it had a kick like a H'ah'vah's bad mood. Tarquin was lounging on the floor, looking at the line of her outstretched leg, the faint gleam along her shin leading to the high arch of her lax foot. It was a shapely foot but the soles were black and tough with deeply ingrained dirt and hard wear.

"Civilization is not for me," she told him. "Your armies are so silly, the way you ride around saving things from each other. It's all a game, isn't it?"

It wasn't, not to him, but he was well drunk and agreed heartily.

"I don't play those kinds of games. Horses are my *life*, Tarquin," she continued. "I was born in the desert southwest of Jundun, among the Horse Clans there. My feet scarcely touched the ground when I was a child. Always we were on the move. I slept and ate on the back of a horse. I thought I was one of them. I drank lying on my belly and sucking the water up without a sound. I tied my hair in a switch on my belt and used it to chase flies. My given name was Keras, but my father called me Aneeki, which means Two Lights, because my eyes were always open."

She fell silent, fixing those eyes on the subdued fire. Tarquin rose, walked outside, and smelled the darkness. He found a clean bucket and filled it at the well. The surface of the water stretched the Moon almost to breaking, reshaped it like a wobbling egg. When he went inside again with the water the room was close and he could smell her. He emptied the bucket into the iron pot and stoked up the fire. Keras stretched.

"I was so happy then," she said after a while. She began to unwind her hair. "I didn't know anything and I didn't have anything. It was better in those days. I can still feel the sand and I can see the way it lifted when the wind came. I thought the sand was alive. It danced in the air. Out there in the desert, the world starts to fray apart. It isn't the same world as this one, and there are spirits there which are indifferent to people. They don't live by human laws, and they can break your mind. But that was my world, do you understand?"

He put his finger in the water. It was still cool. Keras yawned and leaned back, sinking against the wall.

"I hated it when we sold our horses. We sometimes ate them because we had to, or because the horse was sick or injured and couldn't carry on with us. But always the Pharician traders came from Jundun looking for warhorses, or hunting animals for their courtiers, and my family dealt with them even though it meant our horses would be slaves after that. My ancestors had been driven off their land by the Pharicians, who were

intent on bringing everyone under their rule. My people used to raid the
lands the Pharicians stole from us and then run free under the sky, but by
my father's time the army at Jundun had grown so strong we were forced
to give up the horses that once had fought for us, so they could fight for
the emperor and expand his territory. It burned my heart. And when the
Pharicians came on the trade caravans to see our stock, they looked at us
like we were something to be spat upon. How would they treat our
horses, if they had nothing but contempt for us?"

He poured the warm water back into the bucket and set it at the foot
of the bed. He knelt and picked up her right foot.

"A Pharician nobleman purchased me when I was twelve," she stated.
Startled, he looked up at her. Her eyes were closed but the flare of her
nostrils betrayed her emotion. "He liked me far too well, and he offered
more money than my family had ever seen. He took me back to Jundun
with him. There I learned many things."

Her voice shook slightly on this last sentence. Her foot was still between his hands. He scooped up water and began to bathe it.

"I cut a deal with him, you see. If my family taught me one thing it
was how to bargain. So at first I kicked up a huge fuss with Beres, my
captor. I let him know what I was made of, what a little savage I could
be. The fights we used to have! He was not a bad man in his own way;
slavery was customary in his land and within its bounds he had no wish
to mistreat me. That was his weakness. I fought and fought until he was
out of his mind with what to do with me. I was the one in control and he
knew it. Then I pulled the switch on him. I offered him pleasures without being asked. I discovered what his body wanted and gave it to him
better than he'd ever had it. And then I said, 'Beres, I wish to have a
tutor.' By this time he could not refuse me!" She snickered. "I learned
mathematics. Botany. Art. Languages. I learned to write in several
tongues, but when I came here I realized there are as many dialects in
Everien as there are in the desert."

Her feet were calloused and hard. He had to scrub with the pad of his
thumb to loosen the dirt that was embedded in her heel. After the skin of
the right foot was clean he continued to massage the muscles and stroke
the joints to loosen them. She had stopped talking. There was no sound
but the trickle of water back into the bucket and the slight pronounce-
ments in her breathing that he elicited when he touched a sweet spot. He
trailed his fingertips lightly along her sole and the dark hair on her leg
stood up shivering.

He put the foot down and took up the other one.

"Sometimes I wonder what I would have become if I had stayed in
Jundun. It didn't take long for me to forget my childhood. I'll tell you

one thing, Tarquin. I hope my father took the money and brought our horses to the other side of the desert, away from Pharice. I hope he returned to the old way of life and stopped trading away our lifeblood. I hope he didn't use it to become just like one of them, only more foolish for he had no education in Pharician ways. What you are doing right now—"

And he froze, looked up again at her face, and now she was gazing back at him with something like amusement.

"—they used to bathe each other this way in Pharice. I was Beres's favorite so I used to have two younger girls to attend me. I got accustomed to it. I was always very clean, in Jundun." She gave a soft wheeze of laughter. "It was all right, really. It was all right until I got pregnant."

Tarquin kept scrubbing. He didn't know what else to do.

"Then everything fell apart. I ran away. It was as if I'd gone mad. I became like an animal again. I was out of my mind and at the same time I was exactly certain what I had to do. Have you ever been so sure of something it became the only thing you could see? And you didn't care if the rest of the world was against you? Because they couldn't even perceive what it was you needed—but you just *knew*?"

"No," said Tarquin.

"So I tried to make my way back to the desert. Mind, I didn't know what I was going to do when I got there. My family would not be able to take me back without bringing Beres down on them like a storm; it would have meant they'd gone back on the deal. And I had become very soft, living in Pharice. I had forgotten about hunger and cold, and the horse I had taken was little hardier than I. And we were attacked by wild horses and my mount was driven off with the saddlebags."

"I have never heard of wild horses attacking anybody."

Keras seemed suddenly to come awake. She shifted her weight and in the movement of her body he sensed how easy it would be to simply glide his hand up her bare leg and, rising after it, cover her body with his own. She seemed to be waiting for it to happen.

He dried her foot on the edge of his tunic and placed it on the ground. He stood up and went to the door. He had stayed too long.

"That's how I met Nemelir, and that's where I had my son. I had to cut a deal with the wild horses. I had to cut a deal with Ice," she said. "It was the craziest deal I ever did. And that's why you'll never have him."

They locked gazes in the darkness. He wasn't sure what she was challenging him with, or what she meant; but they were both drunk and he wasn't really thinking. Her eyes held him fast. It was even more absurd than the average staring contest, Tarquin thought; they could barely see one another. Yet neither would be the one to look away first. He fixed

his eyes on her face, determined that she would not win. He swayed with
exhaustion, his eyes swimming with tears.

Her leg twitched and a snore escaped her. He blinked and smiled; then
he picked up the blanket and tossed it over her as he was leaving, so that
she would know she had lost. She stirred, grabbed the blanket, and rolled
over violently, clutching it.

"You'll never have him, you bastard," she murmured as he shut the
door behind him.

THE BLACK ISLAND

No one but Xiriel could really see the staircase for what it was, but as they passed through the monstrosity they could feel their legs working on an ascent. Kassien began to retch. Istar clenched her teeth as she nearly gagged in tandem with him: the staircase was as full of smells and sensations as it was sights, and these were so disgusting that she shut her eyes against them.

"Just keep going," Xiriel said confidently from the lead. "They're only Impressions. They can't really harm you."

Istar thought she heard Pallo whimper a bit, but he didn't speak. At last they emerged onto the top of the island under a moody, dark sky. Blue showed patchily between the clouds at intervals out over the sea, which was azure where the sunlight hit it and steel gray everywhere else.

Istar looked around carefully at the smooth black stone. A little jolt of surprised curiosity went through her as she took in her surroundings. It was getting hard to tell what was hallucinated and what wasn't. She reached out and tugged feebly at the Seer's cloak. "Xiriel," she said. "Feel my forehead. I think I'm sick. When we came across the last bridge, the easy one, the island we were heading for was white. Wasn't it?"

Xiriel stared at her, touched the rock, squinted.

"Was it?"

"Yes, it was," Pallo said. "I remember."

Xiriel scratched his head. "I'm confused. I don't know where we are. This island wasn't on the maps I studied. Look, the nearest one to us is the twisted one—it wasn't like that when we crossed that last bridge, was it?"

He was right. They were in a completely different part of the archipelago, not far from the island that looked like a wrung cloth; but none of them remembered seeing a black island among the white ones while they were on the shore.

"But that's good, isn't it?" Pallo said, licking his rope burns meditatively. "Because it would mean we've skipped a couple of islands in the process."

"Only if we are still going the right way," Pentar muttered. He still stood at the entrance to the tunnel, looking back down the stairs. "How long before they follow?"

The island proved to be made entirely of some kind of soft black stone, and it had a weird aspect even though it was relatively bare. They walked all over it looking for a new bridge, or a way back down into the ruins, but everything they found seemed to be a dead end. The only bridge led back toward the nearest landward island, where the other end could be seen protruding from the clifftop. The severed segment rose up and out over the sea, ending high above the waves. Xiriel climbed out on it, leaned over the end, examined it from every angle, yet although it was not damaged, it didn't seem to extend in any way, either. The wind kicked up, and his robes were blowing wildly as he came back down the bridge. His Knowledge-light shone weakly through the gloom.

"Why is it so dark here?" asked Pallo. "Everything is desolate. Jai Khalar at least has light, even in the deepest vaults."

Xiriel said, "Some of the old Scholars used to think that the Floating Lands were an ancient battleground, and that they are too scarred to be repaired."

"But who were the Everiens fighting? The Sekk?"

"Possibly."

Kassien said, "I'll never believe that. The Sekk never could have competed with the Everiens. They don't have ways to bend metal and shatter rock."

"Not now they don't."

There was a silence.

"Others believe there are monsters here, and the Floating Lands belong to them."

"What kind of monsters build stairs?"

Pallo said, "None of this explains why the Floating Lands float."

"They could be giant ships."

"With no sails? No oars?"

"Maybe it was an earthquake or something," said Istar. "The islands look ragged, like pieces of broken glass somebody's going to set back together, but they've left spaces in between."

"Broken glass. That's an interesting choice of words."

"I wasn't thinking of the Glasses," Istar said hastily.

"I know. But Jai Pendu draws closer, and we're stuck."

"They are following." Pentar's voice sounded oracular and strange. He was pointing to the broken bridge on the landward island. Figures had begun to gather there.

Kassien was cursing. "They keep finding different ways—ways we don't know!"

Xiriel stalked off. "*Do* something," he said to himself.

The sun had been playing tag with storm clouds for hours, and now it was hidden beneath the horizon, throwing a coda of remembered light into the clouds, which had gone deep blue as they moved inexorably toward land. Nearly dead calm, the sea plashed quietly against the base of the island far below. At this hour, the peculiar drama of the landscape made itself felt even more eerily: they looked across a blasted, pitted surface whose edges seemed to make jagged slices into the sea. Pieces of unknown machinery were half-buried in the black stone, as though arrested in the process of being birthed by the ground. As the five combed the island for an exit, they encountered deep shafts whose sides seemed hewn from murky glass, too slippery to scale. An unhealthy green glow came from these pits, tiring the eyes without really illuminating anything. As night came on, the shafts could be seen from a distance by the green beams they fired into the storm-bringing sky.

There were other holes that were entirely lightless, and Pallo nearly stepped in one, mistaking it for the shadow of a warped pillar—for many such architectural aberrations decorated the bleak scene.

"I think there are creatures here," Xiriel said, half to himself. He was looking in the piece of Glass he had found in the Sekk's cave. "They are not described in the texts. But this place is not empty."

Kassien had gone very quiet.

"Am I the only one who sees that?" he said, pointing.

Istar looked. "What are you pointing at?"

"The smoke. And it's full of light. It looks like firedust, only—"

The others glanced at each other. None of them could see it. Still absorbed with the rough piece of Glass, Xiriel said, "Things are not where they appear to be."

Kassien gave a ragged scream and leaped backward, staring down at his own legs in horror. "Where are my legs?" he cried. "What's my head doing on the ground?"

"Xiriel," said Istar. "Find the damned bridge, will you?"

"I think," Xiriel said slowly, "that the entire island is alive. It moves things so that . . ." He passed his own hand in front of his face. "They aren't where they are."

"Oh, nice," muttered Pallo.

Kassien had frozen in place. "Everything's upside down. The sky's falling. . . ."

Istar reached toward him.

"No!" Xiriel exclaimed. "Don't try to help him. Istar, look at this."

He passed her the warped piece of Glass she had refused to look at, back in the cave. Now she peered into it hungrily. She could See what was happening. The architecture of the island was shifting from place to place, shuffling like tiles that make up a puzzle. It bent where the wind struck it. It wavered like a reflection on water. The same thing must be happening to Kassien. Now he was all but paralyzed, completely taken in by his perceived rearrangement of his own body. Istar strode over to him and gave him a shake.

"Kassien, there's nothing wrong with you. Don't believe in your senses. You're absolutely fine."

He didn't even seem to hear her. He was looking around frantically, but she couldn't imagine what his eyes could be focusing on. He began walking off toward the edge of the island, and when she grabbed his arm she got a shock that made the hair on her arms stand up. He shook her off. Beyond him, she could see soldiers spreading out across the adjacent island to turn its surface black. They stood right at the edge of the cliffs, and Istar wondered whether they would jump if ordered. At the far side of the broken bridge, the crowd cleared a little and one figure stood apart. It was a little smaller than the others, and unarmed. Istar had the peculiar feeling it was looking at her.

"I found something!" Xiriel shouted. He was moving aside pieces of rubble to reveal a round hole like a well. The gleam of liquid showed several feet below.

"We can't go in there," Pallo said. "We'll drown."

Xiriel was tugging at her cloak.

"Come on," he said. "This is our only chance."

"Xiriel, for once I agree with Pallo. What good will it do going down there?"

"Things are not what they appear," he repeated. "If you look at it through this piece of Glass, it's quite different."

"Maybe, but a Sekk made that. I wouldn't trust it. Probably it will get us killed."

Kassien began running in mad circles, swatting something around his head. "I can't see!" he screamed, but he must have been able to see, because he was somehow avoiding the obstacles and pits that were around him.

"Pentar, you might have to knock him out for his own protection," Istar said, and then stuck out her arm to prevent Pentar taking the remark literally, for he was already on his way to obey her.

"All right, I'll go," she said. "It can't be any worse than any of the other nasty tunnels I've been down today."

To her surprise, when she got inside the well, it wasn't filled with water at all, but with light. And there was a ladder set in the side of the shaft. Pleased, she climbed down it. She called back to Xiriel but could no longer see any of the others; this sort of thing was ceasing to bother her very much and she climbed on down blithely until she reached a flat area with turnings going in several directions. None of the openings was high enough to permit her to stand up; they were all crawlways.

She picked one at random and started down it. It was made of warm gray stone and it twisted and turned smoothly, not unlike the H'ah'vah tunnel. Then it opened into what seemed a perfectly ordinary room that might well have been part of Jai Khalar. There were tapestries on the walls and a locked door at the far end. Knowledge-lights glowed from ornate sconces in the walls.

Istar turned and went back the way she came to call the others. No one answered. She climbed back up the ladder and poked her head out into a rainstorm. Thunder sounded through the walls of the well. Rain pelted down, and the sea below could be heard like a whole flock of dragons. She climbed out all the way, still calling. Nobody.

It was dark.

"Xiriel? Pallo?"

Nothing.

"Damn you fools, did you follow me and pick different tunnels? What is this, a picnic? Why do you idiots have to go getting ideas of your own?"

She paused, wiped rain off her face that was soon replaced by even more of the infernal downpour.

"Pentar?"

She would have been glad to see even him, but there was no one there.

Then she picked out black shapes moving among the wreckage. She opened her mouth to call out again, but something silenced her. These were not her friends. There were too many of them, and they moved silently, and they scared the shit out of her. She ducked back inside the well and slid down the ladder without using the rungs at all.

A pool of rainwater should have collected at the bottom by now, but it hadn't. Her hair and clothes were soaked, but the floor was bone-dry except for the puddle she made.

"Pallo? Kassien?"

She hissed the question, afraid of being overheard from above. Although it was warm and dry here, her teeth were chattering with anxiety.

"Pallo, you'd better not be dead," she warned.

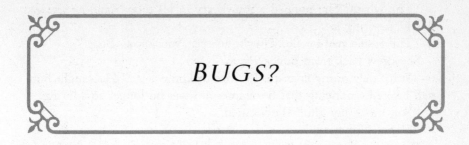

BUGS?

Pallo was not dead. On the contrary: couchant on a silken divan, he was having his feet massaged and being fed exotic fruits by a woman with eight breasts and a tail. He was pleased with himself, but only because he assumed he was dreaming.

"I am fond of you," she said.

"Really?" he asked with his mouth full. "That's nice. I wonder what this is all about."

"As do all of us," she said gravely, and dropped something red and delicious onto his tongue. "I think you should consider looking at these."

She moved away from him and he sat up. She came and knelt at his feet with an enormous book.

"You don't have to sit at my feet," he protested, embarrassed.

"Don't talk," she said. "Just look."

He obeyed—who wouldn't?

It was a book of maps: maps of many places far and near, but especially maps of islands, and a city that traveled forever, made all of glass.

"Ah," said Pallo in a pleased tone. "This is lovely of you."

"I know many things," she purred, stroking his forehead. "I have traveled in many places."

He flipped through the pages, his brow wrinkling as he suddenly had a thought.

"Say—you wouldn't happen to know anything about the rusted nail beetle of Ristale, would you?"

"The what?" She popped a strawberry in his mouth and he chewed slowly, savoring it.

"The rusted nail beetle. They're insects. You know. Bugs."

She drew back from him. *"Bugs?"*

"Yeah, they're my favorite. I'd love to know . . ." He caught himself, belatedly noticing that her expression was no longer so adoring.

"You mock my gift!" she accused.

"N-no! Not at all!"

When she drew herself up to her full height, she was quite large, he realized. Quite long, and her tail had a sting on the end of it, which was now quivering as she flexed the muscles of her back.

"I'm sorry, I meant no offense, really!"

She brought her nails together and they sparked; a tiny dancing light appeared between the tips of her forefinger and thumb.

"Come here, my sweet," she beckoned. "If you like bugs, then you must come into my little world."

"That's not necessary," he demurred, backing away. He didn't stand a chance.

FOR HER PRINCE
TO COME

Ajiko spent the morning explaining to the Council of Elders why he was taking the hard line with Tash; fielding questions about the Eyes; and vainly asking everybody for some kind of insight as to where all the mice and other miscellaneous animals were coming from.

"Jai Khalar is besieged within and without," he jested. "Does anyone have any ideas about the cause?"

Yanise murmured something from the sidelines about the Animal Magic, but none of the others had anything to say. Half of them were dozing, too old to stay awake all morning without refreshments; the other half fidgeted, waiting for their chance to pester him about getting rid of the Pharician invaders. He had no plans to do so for the moment, so he adjourned the meeting abruptly and slipped out with the air of someone who has just remembered he has other, more urgent, business. He hoped to elude the old men of the Council this way; but he could not elude Sendrigel, who was lurking in the hall waiting for the meeting to end. Sendrigel came running after him. "Tash's men are camped in the field below. Only two hundred, but they ride desert warhorses and carry the red halberds of Hezene's highest order."

"Horses cannot harm us in a castle," Ajiko said, unperturbed. "Let them graze all they want. Let them grow fat on our grass. We can wait."

"This is only the beginning," Sendrigel said darkly. "How can you be so nonchalant? If we negotiate now, we can hope to retain some control. But I am sure Tash's threat is not idle. Hezene will have sent more troops behind these; this is only the foreguard."

"Let them come. I think this Tash is bluffing." The general started walking away from the crowd of officials and clerks and hangers-on. His guards flanked him on either side; they stuck to him everywhere he went.

"*What?*" Sendrigel trailed after them, bouncing onto his toes to look at Ajiko over the heads of the guards.

"I'm not convinced he's one of Hezene's boys. He could be one of the Circle, looking to capitalize on our misfortune and using Hezene's name, and our isolation, to frighten us."

"I have no information pointing to such a conclusion," Sendrigel stated, huffing as they climbed stairs. "Why do you appoint me to monitor affairs in Pharice if you aren't going to listen to what I have to say?"

"*I* didn't appoint you," Ajiko answered. "But I'm operating on a hunch. I just don't believe this Tash is telling the truth. He's overeager."

"A hunch? What's come over you, man? You're not yourself, having these fanciful ideas. What's put this wishful thinking into your head?"

Ajiko shrugged and kept walking. He turned into a courtyard but just as quickly spun round and left it: the fountain with its ornamental sail-snakes had clogged and was overflowing everywhere. He began looking for an alternate route to the battlements.

"You don't think the king is going to somehow save us, do you?"

Ajiko said nothing.

"Ajiko, you behave like a girl who keeps herself virgin waiting for her prince to come back from war. Lerien's not coming back! And if he does, the Council won't have him for king anymore. It's time we had a change."

"I will never give Everien to Pharice."

"Then you are stupid. They can help us." Sendrigel swerved to avoid a posse of purposeful-looking mice and followed Ajiko into a work hall filled with looms and girls hard at work weaving. He nodded apologies to them and touched his head; one or two looked vaguely amused as the armored men crossed the room slowly, avoiding the looms.

"Help knocks on the back door," Ajiko replied. "It doesn't come crashing through the roof with fire in its jaws. You like the Pharicians too well, Sendrigel. For all I know, you have been plotting with them all along."

"Now hold on a second—"

"Lock him up," said Ajiko crisply. His guards leaped to do his bidding. The looms fell silent. Girls stared, openmouthed.

"General, have you gone mad? You act like a despot! The Council—"

"Oh, stuff the Council—they're halfway there already. As for you, maybe a dark cell will foster your creativity and you will think of a more profitable means by which to get us out of this jam with Hezene." There were a few gasps at his hard tone. From the corner came a feminine snicker of appreciation.

"But—"

"If not, at least I don't have to worry about tracking down a traitor."

"I'm not a traitor!" Sendrigel cried as they dragged him off before the astonished eyes of the weavers.

"Then you'd better start thinking," Ajiko called after him. The girl in the corner laughed again; he glanced in her direction and saw that she was plump, and young, and red-haired. He adjusted his cloak self-consciously and swept on through the room without the guards. There were a few titters. Under his dark skin, he blushed.

A Bearskin Cloak

There was no point in staying in the intersection. Istar hurried down a different passage from the one she'd taken before; this one, too, was gray and plain. It let out into a room identical to the one she had left. She rattled the handle of the locked door. Cursing and dripping, she returned to the bottom of the well and took the third passage, with the same result.

"Is this on your map, Xiriel?" She addressed the air at large in a sarcastic tone. Then she took out her sword and hacked at the door until she could get a hand through. Ignoring the splinters, she unlocked the door from inside and jerked it open.

The room she entered was richly appointed with velvet brocade and deep carpets. Knowledge-lights cast a subdued glow over an ornately carved bed draped with red silk, a tall wardrobe whose dark wood gleamed with polish, and a dressing table and chair with beautiful inlays of leaves and flowers in blond wood. A fire had been set but not lit; on the mantelpiece was a single unused candle and a matchbox. There were no other doors, but there was a curtained window holding a single, thick pane of glass that looked out over a twilit sea. Rain beat against it. The floorboards of the room creaked beneath the carpet when Istar walked on it.

She felt completely out of place. She searched the dressing table, but all the bottles and jars seemed only to contain perfumes and other unguents unfamiliar to her. She sniffed and abandoned them. She lit the candle.

Something dark writhed inside it, as if an insect had been trapped there and was burning. She stared. It was Pallo in miniature, as tiny and precise as Dhien's bear. She called his name and he spun in circles, burning.

"The hole's not big enough," he screamed back, and his voice was as tiny as his form. "You have to enlarge it."

"How? Where are you?"

She jerked her face back from the candle, baffled, and the flame flared brighter in the draft of her movement.

"That's it!" he cried. "More! Bigger!"

She fanned it again and as the flame flared larger, so did Pallo.

"It's still too small," he sobbed, beating at the flames around himself. By all rights he should be dead by now, Istar thought. It couldn't be a real flame.

"Bigger!" screamed Pallo in agonized tones. As far as he was concerned, the fire was real.

She bent and lit the fire on the hearth. Pallo appeared in the flames curled up and clutching something protectively to his abdomen. He was larger than before, and huddled in a ball.

"Now I get it," Istar said, and held the candle to the fringes of the bedsheet. The flame didn't catch right away. She went to the dressing table and doused the bedclothes with perfume and oil. This time the fire caught instantly, roaring high over the magnificent bed. Pallo rolled out of the fire, himself alight, clutching a large album to his breast. Istar dragged him from the room and out into the gray passage, beating at him with her cloak. It wasn't really necessary; the flames disappeared as soon as they left the room, and Pallo was unscathed except for the real singeing his hair had taken earlier.

"I got some maps!" he announced, and held up the book.

"How—?"

"But they're all burned," he added miserably.

"Where are the others? How did you get inside a candle?"

"I think I made her angry," Pallo answered dreamily. "She turned out to be so unkind! But Istar, the places I saw when she was burning them all! She shrank me *into* the map. It was the strangest thing—"

"Yes, I'm sure it was. Where are the others?"

"Oh—the others. After you went down, the leader of the army made a bridge extend, and they started crossing over. So we climbed down and Kassien and Pentar went down one tunnel, Xiriel took another, and I took a third. Here, I'll show you."

When she looked at Pallo's book of maps, Istar had to agree that they weren't of much use; still, without Xiriel around, they were better than nothing. She was able to locate their position now, and according to the

map, although the four doors at the ends of the four gray passages looked
the same, they weren't. One led to a maze of tunnels ending in a large
cavern with a picture of a snake for its label. Another led to a small
chamber that Istar guessed must have been the bedchamber where she'd
found Pallo. The other led to a wide tunnel and thence into a series of
rooms that had writing on them; this section of the map was burned, and
neither of them could read the writing, although Istar recognized some
of the characters as similar to the ones on the bridges Xiriel had manipu-
lated.

When they got back to the intersection at the bottom of the well, a
wet trail led off in the direction of the door that led to the writing.

"I think Kassien and Pentar went this way," whispered Pallo.

"Did anyone follow you down?"

"No. They must think this is an ordinary well."

"Good. Let's go get Kassien."

They found the wooden door broken open and swinging from one
hinge, and using Knowledge-lights they stole from the walls, they followed Pallo's map into a large central room. They emerged into a chamber with a high ceiling, lit from a bright beam coming down a shaft near
its center. In each of the walls were either doors or open passageways
leading into darkness through which the wind whistled to eddy unpre-
dictably around the metal and ceramic rigging that littered the area.
There were cylinders of various sizes, and ropes made of metal, and
frames and poles all jumbled together. Istar had seen the like of such junk
in the Fire Houses, but she had never understood what it was all for and
at the moment, all she could think was that there were a lot of hiding
places for enemies in the shadows. Toward the far end of the hall, a large
metallic structure had been overturned against one wall, blocking a door.

As they entered the room, Kassien and Pentar stepped out from the
shadows where they'd been hiding. Pallo pointed to the blocked door.
"That's the way we're supposed to go," he said, showing Kassien his
charred map. "It looks like this shaft might lead back to the surface, but
it's a bit hard to be sure. . . ."

Kassien swatted the book away. "Useless documents," he said. "We'd
be better off following one of those open tunnels. Where's Xiriel?"

"I don't know," Istar said, and then the light from the shaft above
began to move, just as if the shaft itself were moving. It picked up speed,
dodged from side to side, and spun around them, giving them the impression that they were inside a globe being spun and the light-filled shaft
was therefore sending its beam into different parts of the cavern. This was
impossible, of course—they had no sensation of moving—but it would
be equally impossible for the shaft to be moving. Yet the light flew

overhead, and the skeletal forms around them cast shadows every which way. Everything danced and changed, and there was a hissing noise that, like the light, seemed to locate itself in different places at whim.

Pallo said, "Does anyone else hear boots?"

Istar looked at Kassien and the light flashed off his teeth and eyes. Then shadows hid him. She was apprehensive. Their eyes had no time to fix on their surroundings, in which there were a hundred blind spots and hiding places. They could be easily surrounded.

"Let's climb the shaft," Pentar said suddenly. "Quick. Come on."

He hurled a line into the light, pulled it back; threw it again; pulled it back and threw it again, but each time the light moved and the hook came clattering back to him. At last it caught and held. Pentar stepped back. "Go on, Pallo—you say you know the way."

"There's someone here," Kassien said, whirling and drawing his sword. Pallo leaped on the rope and began to shinny up; but the shaft and the light and now the rope continued to rove around the cavern at high speed. Pallo was taken along for the ride, whipping through the air as if being dragged by a powerful beast. Yet he clung to the rope and made his way closer to the light. The others crouched with their arms out for balance, disoriented by the impossible motion. Kassien had begun to stalk among the metallic structures, perfectly balanced even as the others were nearly nauseated with sensory confusion.

"Come on," Pallo called back, sounding not much bothered even though the rope was snapping behind him wildly. "It can hold us all. Don't waste t—"

"There you are at last," Kassien said. He was facing away from them, into the shadows near one of the shut doors. "I know she is your daughter. I would not let harm come to her."

"Who are you talking to?" Istar demanded.

"I knew you would return."

Pentar's arm shot out and grabbed Istar just as she was starting forward. Was her father still here, somewhere . . . ?

"You can save us all," Kassien said.

"Your father's dead," Pentar said in her ear. "Let me deal with this. Go with Pallo."

"Who's he talking to, then? *Kassien!*" This last was a whisper, for a hollow space of fear had opened in her gut.

"Go with Pallo. I'll see." Pentar, his face full of fear and simultaneous anger at that fear, went after Kassien. He walked through the mad carnival of moving darkness and light as if balanced on the bowsprit of a ship in high seas.

"Come *on!*" Pallo insisted. She couldn't see him anymore, but the rope was still flying out of the light, which was itself still jerking all over the place.

"This place is crazy," she whispered, just as the hissing localized itself in the spot where Kassien was—or where he seemed to be. Istar only got a glimpse of him every few seconds, and she couldn't be sure whether he was staying in the same place and she was moving or whether it was the other way around. Everything was blackness exploding with sudden light and collapsing to blackness again. She could hear booted feet growing rapidly louder, their rhythm thundering in the passage beyond Kassien. Pentar heard it, too. He turned and looked at her and the light flashed across his face as he mouthed the word *"Go."*

The light stopped, fixed itself on the door from which they'd come. Kassien walked over to the door with Pentar behind him. The footsteps crescendoed and suddenly stopped. Echoes died away. There was a sound of someone knocking on the door; a quotidian sound that was civilized and chilling in this otherworldly context.

"Let us in," said a soft voice from beyond the door.

"No," Istar mouthed, unable to make a sound. At the same time, Pentar moved to stay Kassien's hand, which was moving toward the door. Kassien turned and slapped Pentar back with the flat of his sword. Before Pentar could recover, Kassien had shot back the bolt of the door.

"Istar! Kassien! Come on!" Pallo was calling for them, not merely shouting, but screaming from out of the light, which had stalled again.

The door opened and a horde of Pharician soldiers rushed in, overcoming Pentar and Kassien in a heartbeat. Istar got her sword out, trying to position herself behind some scaffolding for protection; but Pallo's voice reached her from the light-filled shaft.

"Don't fight. There are too many. I can see them all from up here. Come *on.*"

Istar grabbed the rope. She looked back for Kassien and glimpsed his fur cloak among the dark Pharician uniforms; then the rope was tugged from above and she was pulled off the ground. Everything went still. She was climbing, shutting her eyes against the light. There was no more movement, no more noise.

Pallo was dragging her onto a ledge of some kind. He ripped the length of rope up after her, and they looked down on the cavern they'd just left. From this vantage, the entire complex of chambers they had just come from was transparent, and whenever the light tore past, the train of soldiers could not only be seen swirling around the chamber, but filling every sinuosity of the island around and beneath; for the light now revealed the island to be as riddled with holes as wormwood. Where the light rippled over it, the island seemed made of glass.

At first Kassien and Pentar could not be seen, for the chamber below was full of Pharicians, but within minutes they dispersed to the edges of the room. The light stilled, shining straight down the shaft, where directly below them lay the dismembered remains of a man. There was a bearskin cloak, wrung and twisted, tangled about the legs; the rest of the body had been hacked up and was pure red. Other fallen bodies lay nearby, most of them Pharician. There was no sign of Pentar.

From out of the metal nets and wires stepped a dark-cloaked, slender figure holding some sort of Glass. Istar strained to see the object more clearly as the figure moved directly beneath her and Pallo. They looked down on the top of his head as he approached the bearskin cloak and stood over it.

Istar spat.

The figure raised his head and Istar saw that it was a Sekk—but it had no eyes. It raised the Glass before its face.

"Get out of the light!" Pallo hissed. "Hurry!"

He pulled her away from the edge and the light went out. Below, they could hear the footsteps of the Sekk Master stalking back and forth under the shaft.

Istar went limp. There wasn't enough strength in her body to permit her to sob. She lay with tears trickling sideways across her face, her fingers twitching sometimes with unreleased battle electricity. Pallo nudged her. "Istar. Get up. We can't stay here."

It had gone strangely quiet. It was warm here, and the air smelled different. She wondered if Pallo really knew where they were.

"Star."

No. Not Kassien. Not after everything.

"*Star*. Get up." Someone was tugging her arm.

It was the unreality that she couldn't take. If she held his head in her lap and his eyes went sightless and his throat rattled, then it would be all right. Well, it wouldn't be all right, but she'd be able to accept it better than this. She lurched to her feet, wishing she were drunk but she was only tired.

"Right," she said. "What now?"

THE MOON AND ICE

Keras was slightly friendlier the next day. He wasn't sure how much she remembered about last night, but she fed him breakfast and suggested he help her clear out one of the sheds, so she would have a dry place to put the hay when she took it in.

It was strange, but he didn't feel alone around Keras. She was bristly as hell and took offense about a thousand times during the course of the day, but none of it was serious. He watched her work two of the younger horses and thought them formidable; but Ice was nowhere to be seen all day. Tarquin wondered if she had sent him away out of fear that he would try to steal the stallion. He would have been tempted, if he really had somewhere to go. But his noble ideas about riding to the rescue of Jai Khalar had been replaced by a more pragmatic selfishness. He was sick of futile quests.

In the twilight after supper they walked over to the river.

"Is today the longest day of the year?" Keras asked. "Or tomorrow?"

Everything reminded him of Jai Pendu.

"I don't know," he said. They were near the place where Tarquin had forded the day before, only now the light from the west was horizontal on the water, making it a mirror. In the distance a white horse moved in the grass, just on the periphery of Tarquin's vision. Before his eyes could follow the movement, the scene of the river and the plains and the mountains beyond had become something quite different.

Where the trees had been there was now a polished sky flown with tarnished cloud. The river spread to become an ocean. He could still smell the horses and the smoke from Keras's fire, but he could see a moon-bright path on the water, stretching and receding over a great distance of dark ocean and then, just on the point of disappearing, reaching three towers whose outline he would never forget.

Keras touched his shoulder. "You can't go there," she said.

Startled, he turned. "Can *you* see it?"

"Yes, but if you walked on that path you would not be able to come back. It's never the same road twice."

"The White Road," Tarquin said. He shuddered. "Sometimes I . . . see things. I thought for a moment it was following me. But you see it, too. Why is it here?"

Keras laughed condescendingly. "You thought it was following *you*? No, no; you may have stumbled on it before, but it belongs to Ice."

His mouth fell open. Ice was ambling through the field beyond the river, apparently without purpose. Was this the horse that had erupted from the fabric of the Road? Keras said, "Come, let's go in," and when he looked again, the vision of the White Road was gone.

"Keras," he said. "You must tell me what is going on here. How can Ice call the White Road?"

She turned to face him squarely. "No, I think it is you who ought to tell me what is going on here, Tarquin the Free. I am not afraid of you, or your reputation, or your madness, or your Knowledge."

"Let's go inside," he said. "I may as well tell you. I don't know why I've never told anyone before."

And he did. He told her everything, omitting nothing—spilling out every detail of an event that was burned into his mind with more clarity than events that had happened only days ago. He told her of Chyko and his Company; of Ysse and their unusual relationship; of the horror of Jai Pendu. She put food in front of him while he was talking, but he didn't eat it. She ate hers slowly, as if mesmerized, her eyes never leaving his face. After a few minutes she put down her knife, the meal forgotten.

Finally he told her of Night, and the way the horse had risen out of its shadow on the White Road. "I think that horse saved me from Night," he said. "It's hard to be sure, but it's almost as if I was led here—don't you see that, Keras? I *need* the White Road."

He stopped talking and suddenly began eating voraciously. Why had he told her all this? There was no way she was giving him the horse. He had kept silent for so long, and to people who had so much more right and reason to know—like Ysse, and Istar, and even Lerien—why now did he speak to her?

Keras filled his cup and pushed it toward him. Her eyes were slow and dark, lashes half-lowered.

"I don't know how Ice does it," she reflected. "Jai Pendu sounds a terrible place. I would not want to go there."

"If I go back, Night will probably take me. It has nearly done so already, more than once. I will become like them, like my Company. I will be used to lead that army into Jai Pendu and out of the world."

"It sounds as though it will be your doom."

"It is my doom."

She leaned across the table and took his hands. Her fingers were small and strong. "You must not go. Stay here for a time if you like."

He shook his head automatically.

"Why not?" she said. "Start again. You are not as old as you make yourself out to be."

He shook his head again. He found he couldn't look at her. "There are reasons why I have remained alone. I dedicated my life to training men for war, when I was not waging it myself. It would have meant a compromise to take a mate, for we do not now live under the ancient Clan laws which lead every man to protect his own family. My family had become everyone. If I had a home, children, then I would ever concern myself with them. And all my attention had to be given to my men, my task—the affairs of Ysse's country. I could not live divided."

"By your own admission it is a long time since you were in command of men," Keras remarked.

"Not long enough to forget," he said. "Nor will it ever be. For eighteen years I have lived as one dead—for I should have been taken with all the others. I should not be alive. And what can a dead man offer to a woman? What can a dead man offer to his sons? I even ignored Chyko's brat, Istar. I would not taint her with my failure."

"Your life means nothing to you, then?"

"Nothing."

"You are a fool," she said. "Pass the salt."

He did. Her brow was wrinkled with annoyance. She shook salt violently across her food and chewed noisily, all the while fidgeting in her seat like an impatient child. He watched her jaws work, their action sharpening the line of her fierce cheekbones and tightening the tendons on her neck.

"Are you that good, then? That Ysse would have you train her soldiers? Did they not come from their Clans well skilled already? It is said in my country that in those days every man in Everien knew how to fight because of the monsters that came down out of the mountains."

"They knew how to fight with their traditional Clan weapons. And some of them knew other weapons, secret techniques taught only in their families. They did not know how to fight as a group, and that was what was needed to stand against the Sekk. It was a kind of warfare entirely new to our people. I was the one who had to make it work. And for that I was given an elite cadre of warriors, to shape to Ysse's purpose. But I lost them."

"Perhaps it was meant to be. Perhaps we each have a destiny, and this was yours. Not all things are within your power, Tarquin the Free."

"That I know well. But tonight . . . tonight Jai Pendu will be on its way, and your horse can open the way to get there."

"So you can ride it to doom in Jai Pendu? Better you should walk."

"You are impossible, Keras."

"Thank you."

She was so calm; and he was tired, tired with the exertion of years. Tired in the wake of so many secrets that, in the end, he couldn't keep.

"You bring much drama," she said with a yawn, and parting the curtain, looked outside. "It is almost the full moon. The dogs will howl tonight; but don't be troubled. I've tied them up."

She stood up and turned, then pulled the shirt over her head. She turned sloe eyes on him over her shoulder and he swallowed hard.

"I'll be back in a minute," he said gruffly, and left her snickering to herself.

The dogs, he thought, stumbling to the privy through the clouded moonlight outside, sounded more ferocious than Keras herself. He peered into the forest, knowing he must get moving and wondering if he could find his way back to the ford in the dark. Wondering whether he could get a horse across it before the dogs caught him. Wondering if Keras had ever killed anyone. And concluding, ultimately, that he was too tired to do anything bold tonight. He wanted to sleep.

When he went inside, she was under the blanket, eyes half-closed. Her clothes were folded neatly on a chair. She stretched a bare arm toward him.

He put out the last candle and got into the bed with her.

"What's this?" she asked, touching the vial of Freeze that he wore on a thong around his neck. For a moment he hesitated; this might be a way to get access to the horse without Keras's knowing it. He had kept it all these years without using it. Maybe this was the time.

"Nothing," he said, resisting the idea for some reason. "Don't touch it."

Her bed was rough. Stuffing poked through the cloth in places, which was itself little better than burlap; but because the whole operation smelled of her musk, and because he had been sleeping on the ground for many nights, it was paradise. Similarly—and maybe it was just deprivation but he didn't care—Keras proved sweeter than he would have guessed on first impression. She was smallish but took his full weight readily; he could feel her soft breaths accelerating against his chest. Her skin was grimy. She drove up to meet him and he moved into her, trying to go slowly and savor the experience, but she forced him to accelerate, drawing him in and goading him on until he was beyond himself, spiraling into brightness.

Afterward he felt like a felled tree. She was sucking his fingers. He opened his eyes in the starlight and saw the liquid gleam of hers looking back at him. She was still keen. Very.

Sleep. He wanted it. And yet. In the whispers and idle touching that ensued, he had begun to see how he might get the Moon down after all. He began to tease her with his tongue and fingers.

"I know what you're doing and it won't work," she said suddenly, and then drew a ragged breath in spite of herself; he had parted her legs decisively and hooked her knees over his shoulders.

"Go to sleep, then," he suggested.

"I'm not tired."

She certainly was not. Tarquin muffled a yawn of his own and got on with his persuasion. He made a pillow of her thigh and used his tongue in a desultory, noncommittal fashion. He was half-asleep, but she was on a knife edge. Her breathing grew fast and desperate, but every time she began to climax, he stopped. She began to sweat and tremble, and then to plead.

"Maybe I should stop," he whispered. "Because I can't give you what you want without some kind of fair exchange."

"Don't stop!" she begged.

He stopped.

"It's only a horse," he reminded her, stretching one arm down her legs and the other up her torso. He drew his fingers along the sole of her foot.

She thrashed, seized his other hand and brought it to her mouth. She took the flesh below his thumb between her teeth and tugged.

He winced. "Be nice, Keras."

"Please."

"Say it. Say, *Ice, Tarquin* . . ." He slid his tongue inside her and she made inarticulate sounds. ". . . two words."

Finally she said, "You can have Chaser. The chestnut I was riding."

He sighed, and the muscles of her legs tightened spasmodically. A tendon pressed sharply against his cheekbone. "Close, but I need Ice," he chided.

"She's a great horse," Keras cried. "The best I have."

"Except for one." He picked a hair from between his teeth.

"It's for your own good." She squirmed against him. "Believe me."

"All right," he murmured. "I'll take it." He came up for air. She had thrown off the blanket and her arms were flung over her head, covering her face. She was panting, and in the pellucid light her flesh swayed like lilies on waves. He thought about taking her again but knew if he did, he would probably sleep all night and most of the next day. So he fulfilled his end of the bargain, and when he was finished with her, she was still as twilight.

While she was asleep he stole Ice.

IT PROVED TO be one of the more ill advised of a lifetime's bad decisions. Ice seemed determined to kill him—if not by actual violence, then by fear and especially shock—for the horse was reassuringly placid at first. Tarquin was sex-dazed and smug, or he would have been more suspicious of the calm way the stallion meandered across the field, swishing his tail, and chewed some oats Tarquin offered. The animal lowered his head obligingly for the bridle, even though Keras had used no rope or tack of any kind. Tarquin figured he needed all the help he could get, so he cinched up the saddle twice to be sure it wouldn't slip, checked the stirrup leathers, and fastened a martingale just to be safe. All the while the horse sighed and blinked, patently bored. Tarquin threw on the loaded saddlebags and mounted.

Ice was taller than anything he'd ridden, and the muscles of his shoulders gleamed where the scant light struck them. Tarquin felt him playing with the bit, felt the stallion's breathing move his calves. The sky was argentine with breaking clouds and the trees stirred. A vaporous light had begun to filter slowly from the east. Tarquin touched Ice with his heels.

He felt the upsurge, like a pendulum rising to swing: a perfectly coordinated musculature was balancing itself for action. He glimpsed the wind lifting the pale mane, and as he was lifted he clamped his legs hard against the horse in the split second's premonition that something big was about to happen. Then the sky whirled, the wind went out of him, and it was all down, down, down as the horse took off. Ice ran so fast he seemed to leave his body behind, accelerating all the time like a fall from a high place. Speed pulled back the flesh of Tarquin's face, stung his eyes, and nearly made him faint. The impact of hooves on the forest path shook his teeth. Branches streaked by. The body beneath him gathered and released, stretched itself forward as if trying to run straight into next year. If Tarquin were a boat, then Ice would be twenty-foot swells in a gale, with lightning in the rigging. If Tarquin were a salmon going to spawn, Ice would be a hundred-foot waterfall pounding him down every time he tried to leap. If Tarquin were a candle, then Ice would be the messenger wind of winter darkness that blows open the shutters and blackens the house. He had never been mounted on such fury incarnate. The martingale snapped. He hung on to the reins but Ice had the bit in his teeth and was snarling like no horse Tarquin had ever known.

For one single instant Tarquin understood something, and then immediately forgot it. Something abstract. Something difficult. Something like: Ice *is* the White Road.

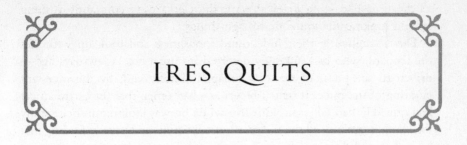

IRES QUITS

$\mathcal{H}$anji $\mathcal{W}$as no$\mathcal{W}$here to be found: even his meditation chamber had disappeared, and Devri's head got all turned around in the process of looking for it. To think what might happen to Jai Khalar if the seneschal somehow failed in his duties gave Devri gooseflesh. Jai Khalar was as unpredictable as a pregnant woman nowadays—one whom only Hanji, it seemed, knew how to soothe.

Devri had followed instructions and stayed away from Ajiko and his soldiers; none of this was a hardship. But he had family in the Deer Clan villages not far up the valley, and with Tash's army sitting on the doorstep, he was nervous about their welfare. If only he could get to the Eyes, he might send a message to the Seers at the Fire Houses, who would advise his relatives to go to the high pastures in the hills at once; or else to open up the Lower City and hide underground until the Pharician danger had passed.

He was also hoping to make some sort of arrangement for Mhani, who was quite unable to fend for herself. Yet he daren't go near the Eye Tower for fear of having a run-in with one of Ajiko's underlings. The Citadel was a hive of activity: the Council were hysterical, the refugees clamored to know why they could not find their chamber pots, or, for that matter, the walls themselves; the soldiers were forced to do their drills and maneuvers in the open stairwells and galleries, as access to the training grounds had been blocked off a few days before as a result of the flood that had been in turn caused by mice chewing through some crucial ropes in the clock tower; and with Hanji appearing and disappearing all the time like some magical wart, the clerks were constantly rushing around looking for someone to sign things.

Devri laughed at their hidebound foolishness and took up with Ires the leopard, who had sulkingly deserted his usual post a few days ago—driven to the point of nervous collapse, Ceralse said, by the incessant taunting of the mice. It struck Devri as a bad omen that the guardian cat had quit. He had fallen in with Ires while he was looking unsuccessfully for Hanji, searching all the old man's usual haunts and usually finding that he had missed the seneschal by a matter of minutes or even seconds; once or twice he even thought he glimpsed a corner of the telltale blue cloak, but always too late to catch Hanji.

"Fine," he said to Ires at last, reaching down to touch the leopard's head where he trotted alongside, munching mice. "It seems Hanji doesn't want to see me. Damn you, Hanji!" And he shook his fist at the nearest flowerpot.

The next thing he knew, he had fallen down a flight of stairs into the aviary again, where the falcons were flying about madly as if he'd left them there only a moment before and not days ago. They launched themselves at his eyes.

"Leave me alone!" he shouted, and running in wild circles he ended up inside the cage that had once been their home. There was a gaping hole in the floor and white light poured out of it. Over the edges began to spill a flood of squeaking brown mice. The falcons swooped on them; Devri closed his eyes against the carnage and began to run away, but then the wall to his left collapsed and white wind hit him, and he heard hoofbeats. He fell down. All of Jai Khalar seemed to shudder, and he had the sudden fear that the entire castle might collapse.

A woman's screams were blown on the wind from the light. Devri plunged forward into the noise, only to find the whiteness guarded by some fierce animal. He didn't see the whole beast, but he glimpsed flaring equine nostrils and the black stripe of fur running down the gray belly as its prodigious hooves just missed cutting him; then he was rolling along a carpet of white fur like a child among dandelions tumbling downhill much too fast, until just at the moment he was sure he'd be sick, the surface beneath him heaved and tossed him roughly aside. The light faded and he was inside a disused linen cupboard. The white sheets were yellowed at the edges and populated by white mice. Mhani was there. He thought at first that she had been bound and gagged, but then he saw that she was caught in a net of white fibers. When he took a closer look he realized that the white fibers were Jai Khalar's roads and bridges and passageways and staircases, and they had locked themselves around her like a spiderweb.

"Help me," she said. "I'm trapped in the Liminal and I can't get out."

"But how can you be here? You're in your rooms. They carried you off and you were raving."

"Please help me. Get me out of Jai Khalar. I can show you how to get out, but I can't do it alone."

"No, no, I must be dreaming. I'm only wishing you were sane; none of this can be real, there is no such place as this and what was that horse, how did I get here, where am I?" He sneezed suddenly, and standing, began to move aside crates that blocked the only exit.

"This is the Liminal, and you came on the White Road. It has gone wild, it has reverted to the animals; it is no longer ruled by the Knowledge. I can't get out, Devri. The Knowledge has been broken and I can't get out. I was seeking the White Road and I found its source, I found the mouse, and what they did to it but I can't understand it, what they tried to do that broke the world, the Animal Magic . . ."

"Mhani, Mhani, I'm only dreaming, I know. . . ." He cradled her face tenderly between his hands, feeling helpless.

"Help me, Devri. Save me. Take me away. Take my body to our people, to the Deer Clan, to the Fire Houses where it all began. Help me!"

"I can't," he said feebly. "Perhaps I should get Hanji."

"No! No, Devri. You must not trust Hanji."

"B-b-but, Mhani. First you say not to trust Ajiko or Sendrigel, and now you say don't trust Hanji. Forgive me, but isn't it all a tad . . . paranoid?"

"Listen to me, Devri. Hanji appears to be a man but he has become an outgrowth of the Citadel itself; I would not be surprised to peel back his robes and find that part of him was made of white stone."

"Don't be silly; he's just a fussy old coot."

"He's fooled you as well, has he? Devri, please." And the High Seer, playing the last of her feminine mood-cards (Devri thought cynically) burst into tears.

"All right, then! Can you walk? I guess not. I'll have to come back for you."

He heaved the last crate out of the way of the door and opened it enough to slip through. On the other side were the ovens of the main kitchens, where he nearly collided with an apprentice baker carrying loaves on a board. He twisted to see back the way he had come, but of course the door was not there. The apprentice muffled a curse, then gave a shriek as Ires came shooting into the kitchen, gazing accusingly at Devri as though the latter had deliberately deserted the cat.

"Come on," he said. "We'd better go check on Mhani."

• • •

TWO FEMALE APPRENTICES were attending the High Seer, who would not stay in bed but paced back and forth before her window, talking to herself. Her black hair was tangled and dull, and she was naked; the apprentices rushed to cover her when Devri entered, but she cast off the blanket and went to sit in the corner.

"She's having a bad day," the small blond apprentice called Lestel told Devri. "We asked if we could move her to a chamber that doesn't over-look the Pharician camp, for it upsets her so; but the healer said she must stay in her familiar quarters if she is to have any hope of getting better."

Mhani sprang up, wrapped the blanket tightly around herself, and began pacing again. Ires tilted his head back and forth, following her with his eyes.

"Is this the only exercise she gets?" Devri asked. "Pacing up and down a ten-foot length of floor with you two watching her?"

"We tried to take her for a walk in the evening," Lestel said defen-sively. "But she kept trying to go to the Eye Tower, and we didn't want to get in trouble."

Devri sighed. "Get some clothes on her, at least. You two must make an effort to be more forceful."

"She is the High Seer," Lestel protested. "We cannot disrespect her."

"She needs help more than she needs respect," responded Devri. "Get her dressed."

"We must get out of here, Devri," Mhani said. She hadn't looked at him, but her voice was entirely calm.

"What did you say?" He moved toward her, but she shrank away and put her hands over her face. Ires sat down and began licking his back.

"Don't touch her!" Lestel warned. "She'll cry."

The girls brought out Mhani's red robes.

"Not those," Devri said. "Something she would wear when she's relaxing."

He stood in the doorway of the closet and watched them select more simple garments, while behind him Mhani continued to pace.

"She's put on too much weight to wear that. Hand me the green."

"Ooh, is that gold embroidery? How lovely."

From behind him Mhani's voice whispered, "It is absolutely crucial that you get us both out of here. Tonight, Devri. Please. I'm begging you."

This time he didn't turn, hoping she would keep talking; but the apprentices bustled out of the closet loaded with enough clothes to stage a play. Mhani stood like a doll while they dressed her, and Devri averted his eyes—not so much from her nakedness as because he didn't like seeing her reduced to this passive state.

"That's enough," he interrupted after Mhani was at least decently covered, preempting their efforts to dress her hair. He picked up her shoes. "Thank you for your assistance. I will take the High Seer for a stroll. She needs fresh air."

She drooled and tripped on his arm, and he was beginning to feel silly as he led her along a gallery open to the sunset, the sort of place where young couples went to sit on the windowsills and make exaggerated vows while stroking each other with tongues and fingers. Devri had been accosted here a few times himself, profiting by the absence of the majority of the male population. Tonight Mhani by his side sang off-key, and he hastened her along, jarred by the incongruity of her madness in such a romantic setting. Ires walked at her other side as if sensing that she needed some kind of support, the tip of his tail moving in that pensive way of his.

After a little while Devri realized that Mhani was not well enough to be out and about, and whatever she might have said that sounded lucid, she wasn't about to elaborate. In this condition she couldn't very well leave Jai Khalar even if he could think of a way to get her out with a siege going on outside. He decided to turn and take her back to her room.

Ires stopped in his tracks and sat down. A shaft of light fell on the leopard's face; he blinked. Devri looked up and the ceiling of the room had opened, exposing a square of yellow evening sky. A rope ladder tumbled down as though thrown by an unseen hand.

"Yes," Mhani said. "That's where we have to go."

IT WAS THE full moon that night, cooling the white cliffs of Jai Khalar, which lay silent and invisible in the mountain folds while its sister city exploded into reality beyond the Floating Lands. In the field beside the entrance stream, Tash's army slept, their fires dimmed. Within the Citadel, the mice threaded their way from shadow to shadow, and the liberated falcons roosted in the eaves, full of the day's catch. High in the confusion of rooms, a silent, cloaked figure glided along a picture gallery to a small, gray door with a silver keyhole. There was a musical sound as the key turned in the lock and the door opened, revealing a closet. The door at the other end had been left open weeks ago by Tarquin and the cat. Surefooted, the cloaked figure passed through, following the same route as the escaping cat, until finally a hidden door opened on the fields where the king's horses no longer grazed in this time of siege.

Tash's army was camped right under the shadow of the cliffs, and when the door opened, a sentry on patrol halted in his tracks and then came forward, perceiving the dark aperture when it suddenly appeared in the alabaster stone.

The sentry's sword preceded him, but the cloaked figure melted back into the darkness. Wary of the confined space, the sentry gave an alarm shout, and ten men immediately leaped from their rest to run across the field toward him. Torches were lit.

"Shh!" said a soft voice from the door. The words that followed were Pharician. *"Do not raise the alarm. Enter quietly, and the Citadel shall be yours."*

"Where did that door come from?" said the sentry, lowering his blade slightly. "And who are you?"

The slight figure stepped forward into the moonlight. He pushed his blue hood back to reveal silver hair and old, cunning eyes.

"A friend," he said.

Tarquin could not fear the White Road, for as it cast itself playfully down at Ice's feet it revealed its true nature. All roads bear within them some promise of a surprise or delight that could be just around the next bend, but the White Road was the very essence of such possibilities: it was the wellspring of newness and the unexpected from which all roads must draw in order to entice their travelers onward. The sights flew by too fast for words. Like butterflies released from the grass in a storm of wings, visions of unknown lands and creatures and peoples whipped past the horse and rider. There were flocks of great birds that sailed on the sea with their human tenders passing among them in tiny boats, playing irresistible songs on their flutes—to what purpose Tarquin would never know. There were houses like paper lanterns that drifted through the sky, supported only by the heat of their own flames, and the shadows of the winged inhabitants made dramas on the see-through walls; there were creatures of vast bulk that lay beneath the sea, guarding caves whose treasures were only glimpsed as a flash of light in the deep; there was the roar of a squadron of bright monsters like legless beetles, which skated on red and gold ice through starless nights while the clouds lurked upstairs like thieves; there were visions of earth torn open to reveal palaces resembling exotic flowers; and high places where the wind has a form and strange voices cry. There were pitched battles fought by young boys with glowing whips. There were lamplit nights with the rain like jewels on the windowpane and the traveler settled by the fire, giving news for wine.

Ice broke them all as if running through a field of new snow, and as every image yielded to the next, the road's destination was seen first in a shadowy way, and then more clearly as the worlds peeled away from the floating city and the Moon rolled up and balanced itself on the edge of the ocean, and the evening came open.

HERE COMES YOUR CHANCE TO GET POWER

"But I don't believe in the Animal Magic," Xiriel heard himself protest. "And anyway, I'm a Wolf, not a Snake."

By the time the words had come out of his mouth, Xiriel had already forgotten what he was protesting about. He didn't really know what was going on. He knew where he was: he had chosen the passageway that led to this cave because he'd hoped to find Istar here—he'd sent the others on ahead in what he was fairly certain was the right direction. But when he got into this cavern and met the man and ate the flower, he promptly forgot about everything he had been doing.

What had come over him? He'd never ever behaved like *this* before. He probably shouldn't have eaten that flower. It had tasted so good, though.

And he was enjoying himself . . . kind of.

At the moment he was standing over a pit of snakes. The strange man was there, already submerged in snake flesh, lying with their weight draped all over him. They were all colors and sizes, and the banded ones could be seen wrapping themselves around his limbs, forming a circuit of endless motion. The man seemed afloat in a living sea; he did not move except for an occasional shudder of pleasure, but all around him the reptiles were twining and untwining, massaging his body.

The man was called Se. Xiriel remembered that much, at least. Before he climbed into the snake pit, the man had given the Seer a flower to eat. It had been an exotic, blood-red flower on a woody stalk. Maybe that had brought on this irresponsible and confusing state of mind. Maybe not.

"They're warm," said the man in a languid voice, as if he had not heard Xiriel speak. "They've been basking in the sun all day. Now that we are here, they seek out our heat instinctively. They are . . ." He paused, and his eyes rolled back momentarily. Se sighed, and when he spoke again his voice was pitched lower. "They are fond of warm orifices."

"I don't know. . . ."

"Ah, coward. You can't begin to imagine what you're missing. They are extremely supple. When the smaller ones wrap you and flex, it feels better than any woman's cunt, I assure you. See these yellow ones? They are trained. Lie down and they will come to you."

Xiriel was feeling the effects of the flower, this much was certain. He didn't step into the snake pit so much as he seemed to deliquesce into the reptilian flesh. A myriad of fine and delicate sensations enveloped his skin, and a fabulous smell rose up from among the snakes; he couldn't identify it, but it aroused him beyond words.

"It is the Animal Magic," Se told him. "It is sacred to my Clan. We never share it with outsiders. But you won't be an outsider for long."

His gold-green eyes dragged at Xiriel like a tide, irresistible. Xiriel clasped his outstretched hand and let himself be pulled through the heavy, sleek mass. Se's skin was pale and shining beneath its armor of snakes; as they moved they revealed and then covered sections of muscle and skeleton, delineating the body piecemeal. Two golden snakes had enveloped his phallus with their curves, endowing his genitals with a size out of all proportion to the rest of his body. He held out a slender golden creature of the same type to Xiriel.

"Here," he said. "Take one. They know what to do."

But Xiriel could barely move. One of the largest constrictors had wound itself around his torso and had restricted the movement of his shoulders; his legs had long ago been taken out from under him, and he felt now like he was swimming in a sea of pressure and smell. The constrictor's body vibrated slightly as though thrumming to some deep bass music beyond the threshold of hearing.

"Of course, they can be scary," his tutor murmured as a banded red viper slithered across his lips. "That is part of the thrill."

Xiriel didn't know whether or not to struggle. The constrictor was pulsing tighter around his body; it had not interfered with his breathing yet, but it had a tight grip on one leg, and his range of movement was limited. The other snakes moved randomly against him. Several had worked their way inside his clothes; he wondered what had happened to the yellow one until he felt its greeting, which was more intimate than anything he'd ever experienced. He began to gasp with excitement.

"You are quite strong," Se observed. "The constrictors don't even go near me. They know I am no match for them. This one senses your strength and she's challenging you."

"Well," Xiriel gulped, trying to laugh, "At least it's a she."

The other man's eyes narrowed. He stood up and the snakes suddenly fell away from him.

"This is how we learn to fight," he said. "It is how we learn to love, also. They are almost the same thing, and both involve initiation rites."

He came closer to Xiriel and began to stroke the great constrictor.

Meanwhile the golden snake worked up and down the length of Xiriel's penis, contracting rhythmically. It felt like a woman having an orgasm, only stronger; Xiriel's hips began to fire out of control, but every time he came to the brink, the snake squeezed him hard and his erection subsided slightly.

"It's good, yes?" Se's whisper tickled his ear. Xiriel tried to answer but only an inarticulate noise came from his mouth.

"Don't come," Se said. "It gets better."

The yellow snake went back to work. Again the stimulation increased, and again he began to gallop toward climax.

"No," the other man advised. "Don't."

Somehow the injunction only made Xiriel more frantic. Every time the word "don't" was spoken, he nearly lost it; and every time the snake gripped him and pulled him back against his will. Then it would begin again.

This time as he was beginning to reach a peak, something slithered lightly along the inside of his thigh, between his legs and across his scrotum. It penetrated him briefly, then retreated. He heard himself bellowing with pleasure, and he was entered again, and yet again. The intensity of sensation shocked him to the point of blindness.

"Don't come," whispered the other. But there was nothing he could do this time. It was too late, and now the constrictor was around his neck, preventing blood and air from flowing—"Don't come!"—and he exploded. His body transcended itself, soared exponentially higher and higher as if the release would never end, the ecstatic flood unstoppable. He lost consciousness.

He wasn't sure when or where he came back, but his body was still out of his range of command, tingling and sparking. From somewhere distant he heard his companion chuckle.

"You had better move fast. You have been weakened, and now they will kill you and eat you."

This didn't make sense and he felt inclined to ignore the words, but they tickled at his mind even as pleasure continued to flow sluggishly through him. His mind was much happier when it wasn't thinking—why had he never noticed this before, or if he had, why had he forgotten about it? He felt sure that it would be best if he stayed this way forever. The constrictor was still wrapped around his throat; yet it had also managed to contort itself so as to stare at him with both eyes at such close range that he had to cross his eyes to focus on it. Its tongue began to slide in and out more rapidly between its jaws, tasting him. Again he tried to take in what had been said, but his body was still captive to ecstasy and he only wanted to laugh. He was breathing hard, soaked in sweat, light as dust in sunlight. The snake tightened fractionally.

Kill. That was the word Se had used. *They will kill you and eat you.*

It had to be a joke.

The snake's mouth yawned open.

"Here," Se remarked, "comes your chance to get power."

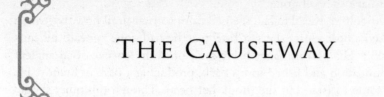

THE CAUSEWAY

"*We are still* in the black island," Pallo whispered. Below they could hear the soldiers passing through, but the light had gone out and they could no longer see through the rock where the light shone. "But it's got these displacement connections inside it that can take you to other islands in the chain, depending on which way you go. Remember how we seemed to skip when we got across the rope before?"

"Sort of . . ."

"Like how Jai Khalar displaces parts of itself?"

"Yes, yes, I get it."

"Well, if I can get us up to the surface using the correct way, we'll be able to skip to the last island. There's a causeway there that leads to Jai Pendu."

"How do you know these things? The maps in your book are all burned."

"They're burned because she put me inside the book before she set fire to it. I've been to all these places while they were going up in flames."

"Never mind!" Istar said, holding up a hand. "I don't want to know. Can you get us there without getting lost?"

"I *think* so."

She gestured for him to lead the way. Through the darkness they climbed and turned and trudged, until at last they emerged onto the smooth grass of one of the most seaward of the Floating Lands. The storm had cleared and the sun was low on the horizon.

"Where's the army?" Istar asked, looking around and seeing the other islands all empty. She couldn't see the black island from this position. "Where have they all gone?"

Pallo didn't answer. He had seemed calm to Istar until now, but when she looked a little closer she saw how pale he had gone beneath his sun-gilded skin. His posture sagged. He sank onto the corner of an ancient stone foundation and fished in his pack, producing a flask of brandy. He offered some to Istar, but she shook her head. Though this quiet should be a welcome respite, she didn't trust it. She lowered herself by Pallo's side and they both gazed out to sea.

Their vision had become a triptych in blue: sky, ocean, and massed clouds divided the world into three equal parts. Whitecaps appeared and vanished; shorebirds clustered on the water where schools of fish swam beneath; and then without warning the scene shattered and fell away and Jai Pendu was there.

The sister of Jai Khalar resembled it the way ice resembles stone. Where Jai Khalar was largely invisible, Jai Pendu's every surface reflected or radiated light. Its towers and arches released a superfluity of illumination that admitted no shadow. The floating city hurtled toward them, massive and yet delicate, its angles contrived with a spiderweb precision. If the Moon were to be rendered according to the logic of a mad wizard, it might resemble Jai Pendu, for in the floating city some secret geometry of light was expressed with a virtuosity that stole breath and thought. Starspun, spiralline, anchorless, Jai Pendu looked more like a blown seed-pod or a tangle of mating insects than a city. The sky showed through gaps in its delicate, weightless structure. Its underparts were mirrored. They cast the sea's light back on itself.

There were three towers, groundless and ethereal; they seemed to overlap one another, and the central one rose above a mass of filaments like firelit hair, at whose center was a red jewel the size of a house.

At length, Istar and Pallo wrenched their gazes away, turned, and looked back toward home. With each step across the Floating Lands, with each bridge or hidden way, they had felt another thread sever itself from the rope of reason that bound them to Everien. Now it seemed that they were held by one trembling strand to the world they knew, and overnight the dew had collected on this thread and they could see reflected in the wavering droplet a miniature vision of Jai Pendu, like a promise.

"We're never going home," Pallo said. "Are we?"

He offered Istar the flask again. This time she took it. Pallo took a long swig himself, leaned back to look at her, and with a forefinger deliberately wiped the streak of fresh blood off her cheek. He added, "You know, I'm starving."

They perched on the edge of the world and Pallo broke apart flat-bread, which they shared. As her jaw worked on the stiff crust, she thought nothing had ever tasted so good. She became conscious of vague aches and pains in her legs and back from all the climbing, and the rope burns on her wrists began to throb. Jai Pendu was mushrooming into being as it moved inexorably toward them, its vast detail and endless light making a kind of visual symphony in the background of their meal. She stifled a yawn.

"You've had too much," he remarked.

"Too much of what?" She groped for more bread greedily.

"Everything," Pallo answered, and wrapped a long arm around her. "Sleep if you want. I'll watch the tide."

They both fell asleep for a while; Istar awakened thinking about Kas-sien, and tears clogged her throat. She swallowed hard. Brushing herself off, she pulled free and stood, rousing Pallo. She was still hungry; Pallo gazed blearily up at her, startled, and offered more bread as if he were afraid she'd strike him. She took the bread and tore it with her teeth while Pallo wandered to the edge of the cliff and looked out on Jai Pendu.

"Where is that damned Xiriel?" she muttered.

"I don't know, but look! The causeway is starting to surface."

Istar joined him and watched as the city came closer. As the tide drew out, the underside of Jai Pendu was revealed, and the causeway that connected it to the Floating Lands now appeared as a strip of white, several feet underwater.

There was only one problem. The causeway connected Jai Pendu to the island adjacent to the one they were now on.

"How are we going to get down there, Pallo? We're on the wrong damn island."

"I know, I know."

"I wish Xiriel were here," Istar moaned tactlessly.

"Xiriel would apply logic," said Pallo. "Think. The army we saw is led by a Sekk Master. It's probably using that Glass to control them somehow—it got Kas—" He broke off and looked away. "I just think that's what it's doing. I mean, did you see the way it turned toward you? It would have had you in another second. So all this time they've been following us, and we've cut off the way behind us, and yet they keep finding other ways. Just now, we climbed the shaft but they might have passed through that door that was blocked, the door that I originally wanted to take."

"I don't want to go back to that place," Istar said, thinking of the body cut in pieces. Her throat closed.

"We have to. We're on the wrong island, and I don't know how to extend the bridges even if there are any."

She clambered to her feet, yawning. She was feeling slightly better for the brief sleep, but not much. She capitulated. "At least give me some more bread."

They weren't able to retrace their steps exactly because Pallo's memory was not too reliable, and he was beginning to be anxious, which caused him to make mistakes. Eventually they found themselves back on the top of the black island, emerging from the side of a half-ruined column.

"It's just like Jai Khalar," Pallo muttered, before Istar dragged him to the ground with her. The army was camped on the surface of the island.

"They're waiting," Istar said. "I'll bet they can't all fit inside the tunnels. Pallo, look! There are Clan soldiers there—see, a whole rank of Wasp archers."

"Maybe our countries are not at war after all," Pallo said hopefully.

Istar wasn't listening to him. "We have to get back down that well. How are we going to get past them all without getting slaughtered?"

She studied the movements of the soldiers for some time, noticing that the Pharicians and the Clan soldiers did not mix and that the Clan leaders were holding authority over their own men although the Pharicians outnumbered them. Those who were on this island seemed to be resting or conferring. Among the Clansmen, discipline was not especially tight. The army was using a bridge that had been extended from the nearest landward island, and it was crowded with moving soldiers, most of whom were slowly filing into an equally well-guarded pit in the ground—one that Xiriel had explored and found useless. By contrast, the well that Istar had used for access was being virtually ignored. It was guarded only by two low-ranking Pharician officers. One of them was actually holding a bucket on a rope.

She spat on her hands and rubbed what was left of her Clan paint off her face.

"Let's go."

"*What?*"

She walked out of cover and toward the well, taking out her water bottle and neatly dumping its contents behind a wall. Pallo followed suit. Istar asked for water in broken Pharician and the bucket was passed to her. The two soldiers didn't seem very interested, even when Istar dropped the bucket in and then herself afterward. She dangled, groping for the ladder with her feet, and slithered down as quietly as she could. She could hear Pallo chatting in Pharician to the guards.

"Hurry *up,* Pallo," she whispered, looking around at the gray tunnels and trying to remember which one was which. She could hear the movements of the army echoing from the center tunnel and had started to move off in that direction when she heard a soft noise from the one tunnel she had not yet been down. She drew her sword. It was a kind of hissing, like steam.

Or snakes.

She took out the lightstone she'd retrieved earlier and held it ahead of her at the mouth of the unknown tunnel. She could just descry something lying on the ground. It looked like a human body. She took a step forward and the light glinted off a snake as it shot away from the body. Just as she was about to turn away, the body moved again as two more snakes slid off it and disappeared into the shadows in the gray tunnel. She shuddered.

"Istar?"

She leaped back as the figure started to sit up. It wasn't—?

"Xiriel?"

"What a terrible nightmare," he said.

"Where are your clothes? And your *hair?*"

Xiriel looked down at his own body in dismay. He was wearing a close-fitting suit of snakeskin that left his arms bare, and his axes were gone, replaced by a tightly coiled strangle wire and a steel net that hung about his torso. Yellow Snake Clan paint marked his features. His head had been shaved; he ran his palms all over it in dismay, then buried his face in his hands. "Oh, no," he moaned. "I never asked for this."

"What happened?"

"I had to fight the Snake. I think . . . Istar, I think it ate me."

"Of course it didn't," she said. "Can't you remember what really happened?"

Xiriel looked down at his own body again. "No—no, I don't want this! Let me go back to sleep, maybe when I wake up it won't be true."

He started to roll over.

Istar grabbed his arm. "Don't be an idiot. We lost Kassien and Pentar, and we have to get over the causeway to Jai Pendu but the entire army is ahead of us now, and there's a Sekk Master with a Glass, leading the Pharicians. Xiriel! Stop looking so stricken. Think! This is what we brought you for. *Think* what we should do."

It took some time for Xiriel to unfold and get to his feet. He looked a bit like a rag that has been wrung out a few times. He was not standing to his full height. "I feel sick," he said. "How could a Sekk Master get hold of a Glass?"

"What about that thing you found in the cave?" Istar prompted. "The one I was afraid of. You can See things in it, can't you?"

Xiriel felt about his person anxiously, giving a sigh of relief when he came up with the lump of raw glass. "It seems to be a half-finished Carry Eye—or something of that nature. It's a poor substitute for the real thing, but it has been useful in exposing some of the illusions here."

There was a loud thud behind Istar, and she whirled to see Pallo in a heap at the bottom of the well. From above came shouts and cries.

"Come on, Xiriel," Istar urged. "We're almost there, but we don't have much time. Just blend with the crowd until we get across the cause-way."

She raced past Pallo, leaving him to pick himself up and cope with the apparition that was Xiriel. She took the tunnel that led to the room where Kassien had been cut down, forcing herself to put her sword away. Men were entering through the door that Kassien had opened for them, moving slowly through the room to the exit that had been blocked by machinery. It was now open. Istar waited until a group of Clan soldiers were coming through and slid into their ranks. They didn't seem to notice her: their eyes were turned inward.

Then there was an outcry from behind; Pallo's guards must have caught up with him. Istar broke from her position and barreled through the ranks of soldiers, shoving aside startled officers, Pharicians, Wolves, Seahawks, Wasps. She simply put her head down and scurried forward, and before anyone could grab hold of her she had slipped between their legs and kept going, using the bodies of the soldiers to pull herself along. The shouts and hysteria from behind increased, so she ripped out her sword as the passage began to open to daylight.

Suddenly she was out in the wind. As Pallo had suggested, they had used the black island to jump to the final island. Now, carried along by the momentum of the host, she was running across a greensward high over the sea. The causeway was gradually emerging from beneath the tide. Spray flew at her face, turned to handfuls of jewels by the light of Jai Pendu. A Pharician lieutenant grabbed her from behind as she charged forward onto the causeway, and from there on out it was one big fight.

A series of impressions raced across her like reflections on water. There was brine and wind and her arm felt seared where the wound had re-opened, and she could sense the innate composure of her own skeleton as she met the onslaught. The situation couldn't have been worse: she was completely surrounded by well-armed opponents—yet somehow she felt sure of what she was doing. Her muscles were responding when she asked them, and her eyes picked up the arrows directed at her and taught her to dodge without breaking focus on the nearer opponents who came at her with spear and sword. There was visceral fear and hostility in plenty, but in some remote part of her there was also a detached satisfaction at being able to ride the currents of the battle. And if the fight had been only a fight, Istar would have felt herself able to rise to its demands.

But it was not only a fight. For Jai Pendu cast its light over the scene, and even when her back was to it and she could not see it directly, she could feel a disturbance in the air. Every so often she jumped or twitched for no reason, as if someone had touched her with a needle.

She had not reckoned on the sheer mass of them. No matter how many she struck, there were always more to replace them, pushing through any gap they could find with the force of thousands behind them, spilling across the bridge to Jai Pendu. They climbed over one another, knocking each other into the sea and sweeping up Pallo, who was borne out into the water. Istar kept pressing forward along the causeway, wading up to her thighs. She found it hard to use her legs with the tide sucking at her balance, and swung wildly. There were too many; far too many. She lost sight of Pallo; Istar whirled with her sword outstretched, cutting herself a circle of free space in which to work, and two poorly equipped Pharicians fell into the deeper water. A heat, a fury on the edge of madness, swept through her loins and belly and chest, and she could hear herself gasping and crying out as she made each frenzied stroke, stabbing and darting and turning and swinging the sword like an extension of herself, her feet moving of their own accord and taking her into a crouch, then kicking her free of a descending stroke at the last second. She sliced someone's fighting sticks in twain without missing a beat and dropped to one knee to avoid a spear, only to catch an arrow in the upper arm. She jerked it out while parrying a sword cut; the pain spurred her to drive her blade through the pelvic girdle of some untrained Slave, whose blood poured over her as he fell.

The causeway dipped in the middle and she lost her footing, swimming a few clumsy strokes before she found it again. The soldiers were foundering in the water, surging forward like panicked animals trying to cross a flooding river. Istar began pulling herself up the roadway on the other side with the waves smacking her right and left. The causeway was slippery beneath her boots. The current nearly pushed her over the side altogether, into deep water. Gasping from deep in her lungs, she threw herself and her armor and weapons forward, and suddenly a fortuitous break in the waves freed the way before her, and the road led up milky and calm into Jai Pendu. Behind her, the gray of midsummer night swallowed color.

The men around her had altered their disposition. They ceased to take notice of her or of each other. They moved like a great herd; they could not be bothered to fight, for they were fixated completely on their glittering destination. Istar let herself be borne along by the crowd, straining for some glimpse of the Company—but she was too far back in the ranks, among the common soldiers. She raised her gaze to Jai Pendu where it loomed above her.

The scale of things had changed. What from the Floating Lands had appeared to be filigree and mesh as delicate as a butterfly's wings now turned out to be solid columns and awnings of a light-bearing substance as hard and fixed as stone. As she reached the top of the incline and came among the arches that led through the outer walls, she had the feeling of being inside a living thing. There was not a straight line anywhere, nothing was symmetrical—yet every part contributed to the whole, which was beautiful and a little frightening.

The arches passed into a huge space containing a mountain of irregular white spheres culminating in what must be the base of one of the towers, but its top could not be seen, for there was an opalescent ceiling forming a vault around the tower's treelike base. The army was crawling up the surface of the white mound, moving very slowly, for the curves were steep and smooth, difficult to grip.

She was beyond tired, and her arm hurt so much she could barely move her fingers, so she slipped a little to one side and hid herself among the folds of the mound. The soldiers were so focused on reaching their destination that no one seemed to notice her departure. She rested for a little while and then began to wander along the base of the mound, curious as to what this place was and who had made it. The mountain seemed to be one thing yet many, like a pile of eggs all fused together— and it was perhaps this fanciful association that caused her to give the base a good kick with her booted right foot.

It didn't break; but it was hollow.

Intrigued, she kept walking around and looking. Eventually she came to a place where the mound had cracked open, revealing a honeycomb of chambers whose walls were translucent. They appeared tissue-thin—until she came up close to one of them and realized it was as thick as her hand was long. Within the membrane she could see more honeycomb designs, as if the structure were repeated on a tiny scale inside the wall itself. Something had broken a path through the inside of the mound, as if a rush of water had come down from the top, splitting into a number of streams along the way and shattering the dividing walls of the chambers as it went. She found she could climb up quite easily by following this passage. Above and around her she could feel and hear, and sometimes vaguely see, the progress of the army as it slowly oozed up the sides of the mound.

Heartened, she climbed faster, and at the top she cut her way out into a semispherical bowl. She had managed to get here ahead of the Sekk and its vanguard, and for a moment she was alone at the bottom of Jai Pendu. What she had taken for the bases of the three towers was in fact an empty space. The towers climbed through the roof of the vault, but they were not rooted in anything: they floated over Istar's head, their bottoms mirrored just as the underside of Jai Pendu was mirrored where it rode the sea.

She had no idea how to get up there. The bowl was completely empty and featureless, except for a black triangle set in the floor at the center. When she stood inside the black triangle she could see the faint outline of three doors around her, each one set on a side of the triangle—but they were like phantoms and she couldn't touch them.

She heard hoofbeats.

Stepping out of the triangle, she wished Xiriel were with her; maybe there was a code for these doors, also. She climbed up the inside of the bowl and peered over the edge, down the white mountain. The chariots and siege engines had been long ago abandoned and the Pharicians climbed hand and foot; but there were twelve in Clan armaments who rode horses even over this impossible terrain. The standard they carried had been lost, but Istar recognized them at once. They moved among the mass of men, and infantrymen and officers alike looked to them for guidance. At the head of the army walked the Sekk Master. She knew that it was the same one she had seen inside the black island, for it had no eyes; but now its robes were white, not black. It carried a Glass, which it held before itself like a torch.

Istar couldn't move. She could only watch it coming toward her, closer and closer until within the Glass she could glimpse a bit of movement, like tiny people. A group of Pharician soldiers broke out of the front of the army and charged toward her, but she couldn't look anywhere other than at the Sekk. She tried to strike, but instead of raising her sword, her arm relaxed at her side and the hilt bumped the outside of her thigh.

She gazed into the Glass. The soldiers surrounded her but did not attack. Instead, they pushed her back toward the black triangle and in among the ghostly doorways that she couldn't touch. Still she was transfixed by the Glass, for she had begun to make out the figures inside it. For a moment she thought she saw—

"Chyko?"

Her rapture lasted only an instant; then something bit viciously into her back, bruising her flesh even through the heavy leather. She was dragged off balance and lost sight of the Glass as darkness swiftly snatched her up.

THREE DOORS

The White Road passed into the mirrored underside of Jai Pendu and ended in darkness. The sea was twilit behind Ice and Tarquin, and Jai Pendu was as luminous as ever, but the place where the Road ended was smothered by a rag of impenetrable darkness; this place must still be held under the influence Night had put out when it spoke its name and killed the light eighteen years ago—if time truly ran that way in Jai Pendu. Here, in what he remembered as an in-between place among the three towers, Tarquin could not see boundaries, and though he felt something under his feet, he could not see the ground, either. Dimly lit by the Moon were three doors against a black sky, set around him in a large triangle; but there were no walls. There was no ceiling, and the constellations that lived overhead were ones he had seen only once before. Each door had a symbol carved in its lintel: the Eye to one side, the Sun to the other, and the Rose straight ahead of him. The doors stood in isolation, like stage props: he could walk completely around them without passing through.

The horse Ice prowled the darkness, nostrils red, pawing at the ground that was not there. Insubstantial forms moved without: the horde was somewhere adjacent, unable to penetrate to this final stage, but waiting. Like Night. Waiting for him to make a mistake.

Outside in the darkness there was a commotion. Ice's head shot up and the horse lashed his tail like a cat. Tarquin drew his sword. Beyond the place of the three doors the soldiers surged as though trying to enter, and among them was a white form: the Sekk with its eyeless, shadowy face. The air rippled. They were going to break through.

Ice stretched out his neck, the blood vessels swelling in his wide nostrils, and opening his mouth to reveal dreadful teeth, he bit into the darkness.

There was a cry, and an armored figure tumbled against the horse, braids flying, sword extended. Tarquin took a step in to engage, but Ice blocked him. The figure kept rolling and landed right side up. Dark eyes fixed on him. It was Istar.

"My father!" she exclaimed. "Where is he? Where did he go?"

Tarquin fell back. He was at a loss for words.

"My father's in that mob out there! I saw him through the Glass. He looks like a ghost. Tell me what you have done."

"There is no time to tell tales."

Sword still out, she pursued him.

"You will answer to me, Tarquin the Free. Or I will start opening these doors and discover the answers for myself."

He felt the blood drain from his face. "Do not, Istar!"

"Then tell me. Why are they here? What is the Glass the Sekk holds, and how does it control the army? What has become of my father?"

Ice continued to guard the darkness. The army without was stalled. Tarquin haltingly began to speak. It was easier the second time—what had been a story stammered out piecemeal in a whisper to Keras became more coherent the second time around. As Istar listened she paced, and he could sense the pressure building within her.

"We must save them," she said in the end. "We must get this Artifact away from Night and liberate the Company from their prison."

"Not we—*I*. This has nothing to do with you, Istar. Keep out of my way."

"No, you keep out of *my* way!" she exploded. "You're just a broken old man—and this is your fault. I came through the Floating Lands. You said it was impossible."

"Yes," he said bitterly. "You led Night through the Floating Lands. That is the good you have done. And now Lerien rides behind you, does he not? All of us gripped like food in the jaws of Jai Pendu, food that doesn't yet know it's dead."

"Don't be such a doomsayer, Tarquin. The Sekk found its own way through the Floating Lands—we were lost more often than not. Besides, that's how it must have gotten back from Jai Pendu in the first place, don't you think?"

"It has changed. It wears white in Jai Pendu, and its face is black."

"Well, do not blame me for the Floating Lands. I closed the way behind me several times, and the Sekk found another. They would have come whether or not I had got here."

"Istar, I mean no insult to you. But this is no time for posturing. You can't just reach out and take the Glass away from Night. This Sekk, it has aspects you cannot see. I saw it crawl from the Water and I saw it take the strongest warriors in Everien like a cat takes mice. The Company of Glass is dangerous; you are not equipped to deal with it—or with Night."

"My father is one of the Company. I'm sure I'm equipped to deal with him."

He said nothing for a long moment. How could he make her understand something he barely had begun to grasp himself? "There are places among the worlds so twisted and forgotten that an honest human emotion is worth more than gold. Even if that emotion is hate."

"My father was many things, but he was not a man of hate."

"You never saw him fight."

She had been listening carefully. Now she looked pointedly at his hand on her wrist. There were tears shaking in her eyes, but her voice didn't break when she said, "All this vague talk of other worlds doesn't help us in this one. I'm not going to just stand here with you and wait for the tides to turn over. I'll get another Artifact for Everien."

"That would be a stupid mistake."

"More stupid than what you have done?"

He said nothing. He felt old. He tried to think of a way to explain, but she was wriggling in his grip.

"Let go of me!"

Suddenly he released her. "Find out for yourself," he said angrily. She took a few strides, rubbing her forearm where he had grabbed her. She went to the door with the Eye symbol, but it would not open for her. She went to the Rose door, and that wouldn't open, either. Her face set in hard lines that reminded Tarquin spookily of her father, Istar strode to the last door and gave it a jerk. It opened.

"Ah," she said, smiling her father's battle-smile. "The Sun. I will go this way."

Tarquin glimpsed a flight of steps going up into grayness before the door shut behind her. Now, in spite of himself, he was curious. He went after her, but the door was locked. He went to the Eye door and this one opened, but the way was blocked by water falling so hard he couldn't even stick his hand into it. He shut the door.

The only choice was the Rose. Tarquin loosened his sword in Ysse's scabbard and opened the door.

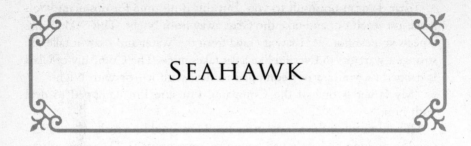

SEAHAWK

Istar counted eighty steps before her wind began to go and she slowed. Hunger gnawed. Her head hurt. In the brief pause she'd made to argue with Tarquin, her muscles had cooled and stiffened, and bruises were swelling and aching. When she looked down she could see a white city, so complex as to confuse her eyes; but she couldn't see the Floating Lands, or Everien, or even the other two Towers. The stairs went on, dazzling in their alabaster symmetry, curving slowly out of sight behind violet and gray spires that rose like grass. She lowered her head and kept climbing. She couldn't feel any wind, even though she was higher and more exposed than she had ever been on the Floating Lands. She could hear nothing but the creak and scuff of her steps, the explosions of her breathing, and the wild rattle of her heart as she struggled to keep up the pace. Gradually she was forced to slow down. The stillness had become oppressive. There was nothing up here but architecture—no birds, no clouds, nothing that moved at all.

How not to be defeated when there is no opponent?

Her mind began to get lost. What was at the top of the stairs? What if they went on forever? What if she fell—no one would ever know what had become of her.

What if something even worse than the monsters of the Floating Lands was waiting for her at the top?

The Sekk-controlled army no longer seemed such a threat.

She couldn't see the Floating Lands, or the mainland, even though she was now at a great height. There was only white stone, glass, and the blue sea and sky all around. As if she were in a bottle.

She felt small and panicky. She kept going for a long time. She realized that night had fallen because the sky above deepened its hue; there was still plenty of light coming from the city itself.

The steps ended suddenly and she found herself on the top of a sheer pillar of smooth stone. She turned to take in the view; the stairs could be seen spiraling away below, but the buildings she had passed on the way up were no longer there. The city had rearranged itself when she wasn't looking. Now there were no obstacles to her view. She was in a lonely place above everything and the wind had begun to blow sunlight ferociously into her eyes. There was nowhere left to go.

She had expected something very different—something more like Jai Khalar: a long and convoluted journey, maybe, through a giant puzzle, or a series of tests, ending in a hall or room where the Artifacts were kept. A room not unlike the Eye Tower, perhaps. All she would have to do (she'd thought) was rise to the occasion. What she hadn't appreciated, and what began to dawn on her, was the fact that her entire rationale had presupposed that the builders of Jai Pendu had planned it as a test of human pilgrims; as if her quest had been laid out by some higher authority, predestined.

The queasy feeling in her gut was the realization that she had been mistaken about this.

There is no reason to this place, Istar thought. *It's a problem without a solution. How can I defeat an enemy I don't understand?*

The sky was greening with dawn. Earlier she'd been struck by the absence of birds; now when a shadow passed across her, she startled like a rabbit. The wingspan was unmistakable, and the distinctive tail spread identified the seahawk immediately. Her Clan's namesake was among the largest of the birds of prey to be found anywhere from Pharice all the way up through the Wild Lands. Seahawks were known for their aggression, and they had been seen picking off baby seals on occasion, although their usual diet was ocean fish. There were stories of a single seahawk going on a killing spree in the gull colonies, not eating any of its kills, but simply taking out dozens of birds as if for the joy of it. The seahawks lived under clifftops and on ledges all along the coast, always seen alone once they'd reached adulthood. They were not well understood, and no one hunted them.

The sight of this one, now, created an odd psychological friction, reminding her of the world she had left behind, of which there was nothing now to be seen. Yet her heart could not help but lift: the bird was a majestic sight, cruising effortlessly on the thermals. She could see its head pivoting from side to side, but the only other movement in its body came from the subtle vaning of its wingtips.

For an instant as it began to dive she had the wonderful fantasy that the Animal Magic of legend really was true: that her Clan totem had come to snatch her up and fly away with her, back to a world in which there were no Sekk, no Knowledge, only the hunting tribes and the rough justice of the Wild Lands. But as the bird careered out of the sky it occurred to her that she was far too heavy to be carried and anyway, this bird was full of vicious intent. She threw herself flat on her face just as the hawk pulled out of its dive. Its extended talons raked up her back and she felt the downdraft of its wings as it began to climb again. She sat up, astonished. A pale, downy feather flew past her in the wind. The bird had looped away and was slowly ascending in the distance. The wind died.

"What in the name of Ysse was that all about?" Istar yelled after it, and the sound of her own voice made her feel better. She spun on her knees and looked down again.

"What are they doing? Where are they going?"

She could see knots and curls of darkness where the army worked its way up the white mountain. The spirallene nature of the city meant that they moved in many different directions. Now they passed into the black triangle and vanished. She had taken the wrong door. The army was in there with Tarquin right now, or maybe it had even gone past him. She glanced up for no reason and the hawk was back, circling easily over her head.

She drew her sword and shook it pugnaciously.

"Come on, you fucking chicken!" she screamed at it, hopping up and down in frustration. "You've turned against me, too, have you? Come and taste this!"

Imperturbable, the bird circled. The city below spoke its silence.

"Calm down, Istar," she whispered suddenly, lowering her sword and blinking to clear wind-tears from her eyes. "You can't kill the seahawk. The bird is sacred."

She looked at the sky again. The sun had cleared the sea and it shot its rays at her. Never before had she associated dawn with violence, but this one seemed torn protesting from the seam of ocean and sky.

The hawk hurtled out of the sky, screaming.

Istar put her sword up.

She stabbed her Clan's animal, and its momentum took her off-balance. She went to her knees in the rain of feathers and blood. The bird on the end of her sword dragged her arm over the side; its wings made a final thrashing at her head. The sky where the bird had been turned red in the shape of its spread wings and she was dragged into the red hole by the weight of her sword.

•   •   /   •

THERE WAS NO sense of landing, no collision of any kind. She was inside a segment of an enormous red crystal, trapped as if frozen in ice. She could only move her eyes. To her left she could see a twisting pathway that rose to the crystal and seemed to pierce it in several places, for the crystal was irregular and spiky in shape. The path below was black with a moving line of soldiers, but empty above her. To her right, in the red light within the crystal, she had an impression of the bristle of many weapons, and movement that did not seem human. The dead seahawk was still attached to her sword; she was disgusted and wanted to fling it off, but she couldn't move.

The man before her was not Seahawk, but he carried a huge sword on his back. His lithe body resembled the bow he was drawing slowly, thoughtfully. He posed and aimed at her. Crimson reflections shone on his dark scalp and jagged profile, and despite combat erupting all around him, he appeared to be smiling.

She flinched, but the arrow went past her. He drew his sword and dashed straight at her. He was dressed in black Wasp Clan leggings. A scant leather harness bound his torso, holding various darts and poison ampules, and a blowgun hung around his neck. His face was painted for war and his feet were bare, but he held the sword with a familiarity at odds with his Clan: he held the sword like a Seahawk. His eyes were wide and black and there was blood on his heaving chest. Steam was coming off his body like smoke from a coal. She shrank away in fear, but he didn't seem to notice her. He hurled himself at the wall of the crystal, and she realized that his target was somewhere outside.

Istar couldn't take her eyes off him. He was like a spirit.

"Let us out!" he screamed savagely, and she realized he was not merely angry—he was desperate. From behind his back there was a roaring, and out of the red smoke and chaos, a shadowy form was looming. It was larger than man or beast, its shape indistinct enough to remain a mystery; yet its threat was felt, even on the edge of visibility. "Let me out! Enough of this fighting! Quintar, where have you gone?"

He paused, almost sobbing, gasping for breath, and glanced over his shoulder. He pressed closer to the surface of the crystal, straining to see out. And then, in the movement and shape of his face, she knew him without any doubt.

"Chyko!"

She flexed her muscles, unable to escape. "Chyko, can you hear me? It's Istar!"

But he was gripped in some rage that she didn't understand. She was scared. He was screaming out through the red barrier. "Quintar, you bastard, *come*! Don't leave us! Where are you?"

The shadowy presence behind him was advancing. Istar watched the action of his body as he cut and slashed at the inside surface of the crystal, raining blow after blow. Every muscle flowed perfectly in the action: tendons tightened and breathing exploded. She was witnessing the relentless application of a human being at the very limits of great ability, and the sight transfixed her. Yet it was no good. The shadow-thing was coming closer, and the sphere remained unchanged. War cries had changed to screams of terror; yet Chyko fought. Istar stiffened against the crystal, nails biting at its surface without gripping.

Suddenly Chyko stood still. The sound of his breathing broke through the background noise of fighting. The sword hung in his lax arm. His eyes were vacant, except where pierced by two uncannily bright points.

"Father," she whispered.

Then the wall behind her shattered and she tumbled out, narrowly missing being caught by the backstroke of Tarquin's sword. A moment later she landed at his feet.

"Get out of the way, boy!" Chyko cried hoarsely, and then booted feet were trampling her as snow flew out among the shards of red crystal. She curled up instinctively, wrapping her arms around her head to protect herself, and rolled out of the way.

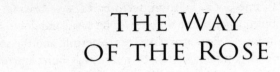

THE WAY
OF THE ROSE

The middle door was one of those peculiar multidimensional creations of the Knowledge that Tarquin most loathed: it opened three ways. When he tugged on it, the door yielded on one side to the army that had been seeking a way in and on the other side to a spiral pathway that soared up into the light of Jai Pendu, winding around and through the red crystal that floated high in the netting of the center tower. The crystal had a complicated, inverted geometry that caused it to intersect with the pathway in many points, so that a maze of red light was thrown in varying degrees of intensity over everything.

When the door opened, Tarquin inserted himself into the Way of the Rose only a moment's breadth ahead of the first of the Pharician warriors who rushed ahead of Night. He slapped the Pharician down with his sword and ran up the pathway until it was blocked by the crystal, which sliced the ramp with a thin red sheet like the petal of a flower. He could see the other side of the path as it led on upward, but when he looked at the crystal he could also see something within it.

It was a world full of fire, and things of terror the like of which even the darkest reaches of Everien's mountains could not have housed. A man was there, fighting a serpent with two flaming axes. Tarquin turned and Night was just behind him with its Glass.

"No," Tarquin said. He did not draw his sword. He stood, arms folded across his chest, blocking the way to the red-lit crystal facet. The Sekk stopped. "You cannot take them."

There were a thousand men pushing into the passage behind Night.

The Company ranged ghostly in the front rank, still horsed. Their grim eyes bore into him as they came on.

Tarquin's sword came out as he spun, teeth bared, eyes blazing. Gripping the sword in both hands, he swung it over his head and down against the crystal wall. The crystal flew apart like ice shattering, and the sound it made was a deep and complex snatch of music that burst up into the tower like a flight of birds. The world beyond was full of fire and terror and the sound of serpents. Out of the smoke leaped Riesel. His cloak was burning and his face was black. He shoved Tarquin aside with the haft of one ax and charged into the crowd of soldiers behind the Sekk. They parted instinctively, one Pharician falling to his knees with a supplicating cry. The ghost warriors had begun to step forward through the ranks, slithering like morning light through mist. Riesel stepped into himself and turned to Tarquin, recognition in his eyes.

Tarquin wanted to throw his arms around Riesel, so great was his pleasure at seeing him again past all hope; but Riesel's face was hard with fell purpose. He took in Tarquin, acknowledged him for a moment; then he turned and began to kill.

"Night, release them," Tarquin commanded. As Riesel went to work, there was a sound of steel on steel; the thud of bodies; a squealing slaughterhouse scream; and the Sekk drifted over the crystal shards and ash, up the steeply tilting path as though sleepwalking. Even as he was driven backward up the ramp, Tarquin began to laugh.

"Have it your way," he said, and rushed at the next facet of the crystal. It sang as he hacked it with his sword, his feet leaving the ground with the force of his blow. He spun out of the way a second before Mojise's whip preceded him into the chamber—and Mojise, too, found himself among the ghosts and came to life. Laughing, Tarquin rampaged up the spiral, eighteen years of pent-up rage releasing themselves along the length of his sword and into the huge, light-soaked crystal. The barriers to the worlds broke. Lyetar and Vorse and Irisel came pounding out of the same facet, and Lyetar's sword was already blood-blackened. Chyko arrived like a cyclone out of a white world and leaped into himself almost absentmindedly; scarcely bothered by any of the events about him, he scrambled along the underside of the spiral and blew darts into the host. Tarquin almost tripped over Istar as she was carried out with Chyko, but he didn't stop for her. He didn't spare more than a glance for each as he freed them, running up the spiral in an excess of physical expression; he began to sing as he cut. He could smell battle, like an old dog in the morning standing and stretching and realizing the miracle in one more day of rabbits and sun and running head down on the trail. Something in Tarquin awakened and stretched and was glad to pit itself against any enemy. He burned for the fight, and his men rallied around him. Each of them was different in some way than the last time he'd seen them: Chyko had a scar on his face, and Lyetar's hair had burned off; and Vorse had silver teeth that made him look more menacing than ever. There was no time for words or sentiment.

At last he had them back. Tarquin set his teeth and led the Company into the swarm of Enslaved soldiers, and everything fell away.

There is no noise in battle. How this could be was a mystery to Tarquin but it was one of the few truths in life that he had ever discovered. There is no noise. There is only a series of events, each one perfect as a ripe fruit where it sways from the summer tree; and you can't predict the order or nature of these things but you recognize them when you see them and you act. You see the blade coming at you and you aren't there. Your blade—pure as intention, vile as thought—goes singing out to violate your enemy. You kill and that is all.

Inside this simple tune are myriad variations, but if you learn one you recognize all of the others and there's no noise. There's only truth. What transpires is not open to debate or interpretation. Blows are sent, blocked, countered; attacks are delivered and gravity drives one opponent backward, the other onward. It is not fire. It is not mind. It is some devil outbreed bastard of life and death that casts itself on the boards like a die in a game, and chance roams the battlefield like a vulture. It will prey on the unwary. You have to assert yourself always, your eyes wide and inclusive, your breathing like it's your last breath. You are a sinuous line of power and you never give up.

But twenty thousand pushed against thirteen, and the harder the Company fought, the more the mob pressed, still linked to their spirits by the Glass. For Night held the Glass. In the passages and staircases of Jai Pendu, the men of the Clans and of Pharice pressed toward their doom; and Night holding the Company walked through the middle of it all, silent, unscathed, untouched. Resolute.

Tarquin set himself in the path of Night. "You cannot have the men of Everien," he said. "Their spirits belong only to them."

Yet even as he spoke, he feared that his words were untrue: the Enslaved soldiers had no spirit that he could see. They clamored for some gratification he could not comprehend; they crowded behind Night like sheep competing for space at the trough. Only the Company were alive, and the single uniting thought that lit the air among them was *Kill*.

"Your game is over," Tarquin said to Night. "I for one have had enough of being your thing. Go back where you came from, you skulking piece of nothingness."

"I skulk behind the stars," said Night. "I live in the centers of your eyes. Hide there and I will surely find you."

"Come fight honestly, then," said Tarquin, spinning his sword in a glittering eight. Like a horse in the spring when the grass is wet and the light is thick as ambrosia, he wanted to run. He wanted to feel his tendons stretch, his body respond the way the clocks of Jai Khalar could never aspire to respond: with truth and passion. "Come fight me, and it will turn out differently this time."

But Night didn't like to fight with swords.

"It is nothing for me to take you," it said. "The spark which you feel and call life is as light as a word to me, a word that it's on the tip of my tongue to say just for the pleasure of the sound of it, and that would be the end of you, of course."

Tarquin was not daunted. He went forward, and Night spread its arms to welcome him.

He could see her now from afar, but she did not see him. She was sitting in a garden, at an alabaster stone table surrounded by dark foliage threaded with white vines. He was standing among the hawthorns at the gate, shoulders sagging, sword hanging with its tip almost in the dirt, covered in mud, blood, bruises—bone-tired. He was so empty he couldn't speak. All through the battle, all through the legion pains, irritations, discomforts, and frustrations of the journey, he had dreamed of such a stopping place as this. Just to be still and hear the birds and the faint harmonies of falling water, and to smell the flowers that lay like drifted snow on shadowy leaves—it was enough. To look at her was also enough; not more than enough, not too much—but exactly enough. He could have stood that way forever. He could see the breaths move the hollow of her throat. Her red hair was braided simply, but even thus contained it captured the sunlight and did something wondrous to it. It draped her shoulders and snaked down her back, which was left bare and pale by the moss-green tunic she wore. She had been intent on some object on the table, and for those moments while he stood taking in the set of her body, the expression of balance and unforced concentration in her slender arms, her poised back, her legs crossed at the ankle beneath the bench, he thought her perfect. He thought everything perfect.

And then she perceived him. Without turning, she tilted her head slightly, and even this subtle reaction transformed the scene. The set of her eyes changed, and her lips parted slightly, and everything else remained still. Then in one smooth movement she turned and, slipping whatever it was she had been handling into a pocket with a furtive movement, she brought her eyes to bear on him, large and steady.

When she spoke, he found he was trying to memorize her voice, knowing she would soon be gone—and that he'd find himself being trampled or skewered, or in the middle of some other predicament. There was a tingling at the back of his head at the sound of her voice.

"I know you don't know who I am. It's all right. Come and sit here, and let me look at you."

"I can't," he said, but his legs were taking him toward her. They sat at the table and she held his hands in hers, making him feel large and uncouth. Then she whispered to him of things she said he must try to remember, but afterward he couldn't remember, no matter how he tried to recall the bewitching tones of her speech.

He did remember how she stood and in the gray gloaming she went among the dark-leaved plants and returned with a red flower, and she gave it to him.

"There," she said. "Now you can't tell me you have never seen a rose."

VORSE'S WHIP

Lerien king of Everien had lost his castle, his army, and his Seer. But he still had a sword and fifty-odd men who were just crazy enough to chase a mob of Pharicians across the bridges of the Floating Lands and toward the exotic sight of the city that appeared only once every nine years, for a day.

They had been riding hard, and it had taken every bit of animal affinity the Clan warriors possessed to persuade their horses to cross some of the bridges that the Sekk had left extended. Time had become their enemy, and it was evening when they reached the last island. They found it deserted. The Sekk and its army had already passed over into Jai Pendu.

"It's too late," Stavel said. "They are already gone—and look, the sun is on its way down."

There was a deep cutting in the top of the island where the causeway of Jai Pendu had landed. The causeway lay in a parabola, its center close to the waves, each of its ends reaching high into the Floating Lands and Jai Pendu, respectively. Lerien stood at the head of the cutting and looked down the white stone causeway at the magical city. A pale thread could be seen arching over the sea and entering the base of the city. The White Road was still there.

"Come," he said. "We cannot turn back now."

THEY WERE HALFWAY across the causeway when the army began to come back toward them, no longer marching deliberately, but running pell-mell.

"Retreat!" Lerien cried. "Use your bows. Hold the end of the bridge!"

But this proved impossible: the army was no longer composed of half-tranced automatons, but terrified men of Clan and Pharice alike, ranked and unranked. They plowed through Lerien's men, who desperately tried to muster their countrymen and make some order out of the madness.

Fighting was not Lerien's job here. He had to gather his men and try to get them away from the Pharicians—for now that the spell was broken, the Clans and the Pharicians had all begun to attack each other with a wild energy. He collected a unit of Clan foot soldiers who had managed to come through the entire experience intact; with their wits returned to them, they were only too glad to be directed. Lerien sent them back toward the mainland, using Stavel and Ketar to keep off the Pharicians so that his people could cross in safety. Once this was done, he rode back to the causeway, looking for more groups that might be similarly guided through the storm.

But the cause of the storm greeted him instead. Quintar's Company were charging across the causeway, turning the foam red where they passed. They were solid and real and their battle screams could be heard on the breeze. If Lerien remembered his fight with Vorse, if he remembered the Company as dangerous before—well, they had eighteen years of practice under their belts now.

He rode forward to meet them, hailing them in a loud voice. Vorse took one look at Lerien and drew out his whip with a cruel smile.

"I could have killed you once," he said. "Do you call yourself king? We will soon divest you of that illusion."

Lerien had never been so shit-scared in all his life. He saw all the warning signs in Vorse's face, but he didn't dare back down now.

"I am king," he said. "And you are cowards if, instead of helping your kinsmen, you cut them down where they stand. Where is Quintar?"

"We answer to no man, and I'll give you respect on the day you can hold your ground against me, you fat laggard."

The whip shot out and wrapped around his neck. With a jerk, Vorse dislodged the king from his horse and Lerien found himself being dragged toward the slashing hooves of the Snake's warhorse. The sky spun overhead and his legs kicked out and churned the earth as he fought.

He couldn't breathe, much less speak; but even as things were going from bad to worse, he was thinking his intention in four clear words: *Not this time, Vorse.*

THE COMPANY OF GLASS

$\mathcal{I}$star had lost sight of Chyko. He had gone down the path toward the base of the tower with its red crystal, but the surge of the crowd was pushing her up the path, toward Night. She could sense in the mass movement that something had changed. The fixation of the soldiers had weakened; they were no longer so focused, and instead began to look around as if they didn't quite know where they were. The collective will of the army was wavering. Pharician soldiers around her broke off, and the Company chased them back down the spiral. There were dead bodies everywhere, and at the sight of these the men made even greater haste to be gone.

When she looked up the path, through a parting in the crowd she saw the Sekk and Tarquin. The two were wrapped around one another like lovers, making an unlikely tableau against the shards of the crystal. She pressed toward them. They resembled statues, but Istar knew that their balance was a result of strength matched against equal strength, will against equal will. Their muscles trembled and they were breathing hard.

Istar looked around again for Chyko, but she could no longer see any of the Company, and now the massed soldiers had begun to move decisively down the path. Tarquin must be winning. Then Night wrapped a leg around Tarquin and unbalanced him, and the two went down in a tangle.

Tarquin was on top of the Sekk, but he was dripping with sweat and his hands slipped off its throat. Night needed no further invitation to slither away and rise, unhurt and apparently unwearied. Tarquin was on his knees, breathing hard, furious but exhausted. The Sekk put out one finger and touched Tarquin's face, and Tarquin seemed to go limp. His eyes closed.

The face of the Master was grave and beautiful as it bent over Tarquin like a raven. Its black hands slipped down the warrior's cheeks, thumbs resting gently on each eyelid, and Tarquin tilted his head back to offer his throat. The Sekk made a sound like dark velvet deep in its chest.

Istar didn't know what to do. The Company had raged down into the bottom of the city; the army was fleeing; but the Sekk still had the Glass, and she was standing in the center of Jai Pendu while Tarquin fought for control.

Then Pallo came limping up the spiral, covered in blood, his bow strung on his back and knocking against his legs. "Hello," he said with a weary smile. "I had a hunch I'd find you up here."

Istar pointed to the Glass held by the Sekk. "We have to get it away from them," she said. The two figures were nearly on the edge of the pathway. Below, the spiral looped turn upon turn; a fall would be fatal.

Pallo inched a little closer.

"Be careful," Istar said. "They could go over the edge."

One of the Sekk's palms covered Tarquin's eyes. There was a moment of quiet, and then Tarquin started to struggle again. The two wrestled on their feet, breathing hard and trembling with exertion. The Sekk, although slight, appeared to match Tarquin's strength so exactly that the two balanced against one another almost without moving.

Pallo crept closer.

"Cut it out, Pallo!" Istar shouted. She had visions of the foolish Pharician pitching right over the edge of the pathway if one of the combatants moved suddenly. Almost as if sensing and responding to her fear, the Sekk suddenly dropped against Tarquin and scooped its arms around his legs, seeking to upset him. Tarquin took a long step back and balanced himself, but in the movement a small vial fell from around his neck, its thong broken. Pallo scurried over and snatched it up before it could roll over the edge.

Istar hesitated. She was wondering whether she could jump on the Sekk's back and slit its throat, but now Tarquin was thrashing again and the figures slid a few yards down the spiral, skidding on broken pieces of red crystal.

Pallo was studying the vial. It reminded Istar of the kind her father had used for his poisons; Mhani had saved all his possessions even if she was afraid to use them. Pallo brought it to his nose.

"This is *not* the time," she cautioned. "For once could you not do something stupid."

"I know what this is!" he cried. "It's Freeze! Wait!"

He poured a little of the stuff over the tip of an arrow and then shot the Sekk in the leg from point-blank range.

"Pallo, you stupid *idiot!*"

Tarquin stumbled as Night suddenly stopped resisting him. The Glass fell from the Sekk's slack hand; Istar leaped forward and caught it as it was about to fall over the edge of the path. She glanced once at Tarquin—who was on his hands and knees, utterly spent, shaking his head and saying no—before turning and running back down the spiral.

TARQUIN NEVER TOOK his eyes off Night while he was recovering his strength. True to the reputed powers of Freeze, Night didn't move. At length, Tarquin got to his feet and brought out his sword. He was alone now.

He had sworn he would kill it.

He *would* kill it. He would kill Night.

It stood motionless, breathing lightly, hands relaxed at its sides. He already knew it couldn't see—but what might be happening in its mind? How had it acquired the power to put him in a trance? And where was *she* coming from? The memory of the garden lingered in his mind. He had been unaware of struggling with Night. He had only known he was with her, and that it was quiet in the garden where things were growing as they should. But thanks to Freeze he was back in Jai Pendu, where nothing ever happened as it should. It was his obligation to kill this creature and then to go control his men.

He didn't want to control his men. They had been wronged; it seemed easy enough to understand that they should go on a rampage now, finding themselves freed from the nightmare they had endured all this time. He didn't want to restrain them any more than he would want to stop a starving predator from hunting. And—speaking of predators—it was time to kill Night.

This was the thought that made him sweat.

He made himself walk up to it and look at it closely. Its face was absolute black, the nose and mouth mere suggestions of features and the teeth so white they could never have touched food or wine. There were vague hollows where the eyes would have been, but no brows, no visible veins, no blemish of any kind. It was like a doll's face, Tarquin thought. It did not possess much glamour—certainly it was not individual enough to be beautiful. Strange that Night should have proven so powerful, when up close it looked like a rather badly formed Sekk. He pressed the naked blade to its throat. If it had been the most attractive of Sekk, he would have been able to kill it. He had been trained to do so by long practice.

But he no longer thought of it as a Sekk. It was more mysterious than that. It was Night, his nemesis.

He liked having the edge of his sword pressed against its throat. He liked it that Night was still and he could move. But it was not so easy to draw that blade across the white skin when the enemy was not even struggling.

Count to ten, he told himself. *Then do it.*

He counted slowly, softly, whispering the words to himself. At *three* he thought briefly of Mhani and whether she would still want Chyko in this condition. At *seven* he thought of Keras. *It sounds as if it will be your doom,* she said. At *nine* he thought of the heavy texture of the red hair where it spilled over his face, and for an instant, he flashed the curious sensation of cupping his hands over her swollen belly, and he wondered what that meant between *nine* and *ten*. On *ten* he jerked the sword violently to slit Night's throat.

But Freeze didn't last as long as he thought.

Night was quicker than any animal he had ever seen. It removed itself from his sword range effortlessly and glided down the path, leaving Tarquin to follow clumsily, cursing himself for whatever hesitation had come over him. He couldn't catch up with it, and it slid through into the place of Three Doors undeterred by anyone—all the army either had been beaten back by the Company themselves or had followed Istar with the Glass when she and Pallo left him winded and confused with Night.

Ice was still there. Half-hidden in the darkness, he seemed semidimensional until Tarquin actually touched him. There was no sign of Night. Tarquin glanced at the door marked by the Eye symbol, and uncharacteristically said a quick prayer to the Animal protectors that Night had returned to its watery beginnings, now that its mission here had failed. Then he leaped on Ice's back. There was still the matter of the Company, and he was torn about what to do. He could bring them into line, he was sure. He could probably bring them back to Jai Khalar in triumph, and then the day would have been won.

He would not have gone to his doom, as Keras said.

He would not lose.

But there would still be an Artifact called the Company of Glass, and they would still be connected to it, somehow. It would be even more fodder for the Scholars.

Ice tossed his silvery mane and carried him down into the fray.

WITH PALLO AT her heels, Istar raced back the way she had come, leaping over dead bodies all the while. The Company were still on the loose and killing as she loped across the bridge. The wind was blowing hard. The day had almost passed. The army was fleeing across the last island like a cluster of iron filings when a magnet is placed near, with the Company following in a rage. The horses of the Company charged over and through bodies without regard for affiliation. Men threw down their weapons and fled for the next island in droves. To her shock, she glimpsed Lerien's blond head in the clash, and she saw Clansmen attempting to organize, but the tide was against them. Istar tried to bend her will into the Glass, to control the Company, but she couldn't even effect a scratch.

"Damn it, Pallo!" she cried. "What good is this thing? I can't use it!"

Pallo's call of warning reached her a split second before someone's fighting stick caught her across the side of the head and she reeled, wishing to stay out of trouble—but there was nowhere to run. Everywhere was carnage and destruction. Unexpectedly she spotted Xiriel. For a second she mistook him for one of the Company. He was fighting like nothing she'd ever seen. He had picked up a Pharician spear and was ruthlessly hamstringing anything he could get near, then rushing in and stabbing for the kill. She watched him dispatch four or five men this way, startled by both his strength and his sudden, focused hostility.

She gazed at the Glass in her hands, wishing she knew how to focus her will the way a Seer might. The Company were out of control. The army had broken ranks completely, its members looking for cover or fleeing as the Slaving spell shattered and left them in an unfamiliar place, no longer gripped with the need to fight. The same could not be said of Tarquin's men: they continued to slaughter anything in their path. They were relentless in their energy and indiscriminate in their approach. Istar could think of no way to stop them.

She was being swept along, dodging Pharician arrows and feeling wholly out of her depth, when Tarquin appeared out of the infantry, mounted on the extraordinary horse. She was marveling at the sight when a Wolf Clan soldier came at her and Istar was hard put to use her sword and hold on to the Glass at the same time. She got a cut in across his legs and was ducking one of his axes when Tarquin reached her.

"Give me the Glass," he called, and ripped into the Wolf who stood between them as though hacking down a tree with his sword. The Wolf crashed into Istar and she fell. Blood gushed over her. Tarquin was standing over her, the horse splashed with black gore and wearing not an ounce of leather waiting just beyond his shoulder. She passed him the Glass wordlessly. It was slimy and red. His fist closed around it and suddenly he grinned at her with broken teeth.

"You're not the worst fighter I've ever seen," he said. Then he vaulted onto the horse and shouted her father's name.

Istar stumbled after Tarquin's horse. The top of the island was a wreck of bodies from edge to edge. Most of the men she saw were Clan, freed but still compelled by circumstances to fight. The Company moved among them on horseback to devastating effect. Lerien's horse was running loose. The king had pulled one of the Company to the ground and had him in a hold that would break his neck in a moment. But an arrow flew out of the melée and pierced Lerien's right eye. Chyko came riding in after, laughing as the king crumpled to the ground. The Snake that he'd saved threw open his arms and the two embraced on the field. Then Tarquin arrived, clocked Chyko on the head with his sword hilt, and leaped back as the Wasp whirled to face him. Annoyance changed to joy on Chyko's face.

"Quintar, you son of—"

"Go back," Tarquin said. "You are being used. You must go back."

The two men were astonished. "Go back? You must be mad!"

"No!" Istar stumbled toward them, dodging a thrown ax and climbing over a dead horse. A Pharician took a swing at her, but some nearby Seahawk interposed himself and took the Pharician out of her way. Istar pressed on, hardly noticing her surroundings, though the sounds of battle were tapering off. "Don't send them back, please. . . ."

Chyko looked at her curiously. "It's the boy," he said. "The one inside the red crystal. Come, boy, and—"

"Back to your horses," Tarquin commanded, stepping between Chyko and Istar. "Go back. The time for killing is over."

"I wish it could be," said the other warrior, but Chyko was still trying to peer around Tarquin, who blocked the Wasp's view of his daughter. The rest of the Company had begun to gather, witnessing the exchange.

"Go back," said Tarquin to all of them. As they stood there together, Istar saw many things in their faces, which she would ponder for years to come. Their faces were not like any men she had ever seen. Their eyes were as old and as innocent as animals' eyes. One or two continued to pick off stray Pharicians with their arrows as if for sport.

"*Move!*" Tarquin suddenly roared, apopleptic. Chyko mounted and motioned to the others. The Company began to stir, fierce and hard as diamonds, their skins mingling dark and pale, throbbing with what seemed a collective heartbeat. Chyko at their head whirled his right arm in a signal and they all spurred their horses after him, toward the causeway back to Jai Pendu.

"No," Istar murmured. "Don't let them go." She didn't care whom they killed or what they did. She knew Tarquin could control them if he wanted to, but instead he had sent them away. And now he was going after them on the murderous horse, still holding the Glass. They pounded over the causeway. Istar began running after the Company, but she kept colliding with dazed Clansmen. The wounded with their endless crying distracted her. Then she almost fell across Lerien, who was huddled on the ground, gushing blood. He had ripped the arrow out of his own eye and now sat, jamming his fist into the socket and gnashing his teeth. Istar paused, wondering what, if anything, she could do.

"Xiriel!" she screamed, looking around in distress. She couldn't see him or Pallo. She knelt by Lerien's side.

"I don't care if you're friend or foe," Lerien gasped. "Just don't let them all die."

"It's over," Istar said, and turned her head longingly after the retreating riders. The scene was a complicated, accidental dance of men and horses as the commanders tried to stop the fighting and round up their bemused and exhausted men. The Company were passing over the causeway and into Jai Pendu.

With the last of her strength, Istar picked herself up and ran out onto the causeway. Out of the corner of her eye, she noticed someone following her, but she paid attention only to the vision of Jai Pendu. The tide was coming in. The sun was going down. Her father had recognized her—or would have recognized her if only Tarquin had not been in the way. Bloody damned Tarquin. Istar ran out as far as she could, but the waves were rising fast. She halted. The Company were ranged at the top of the causeway, looking back toward land.

"Chyko . . ." Istar bit her fist.

The light was low. Tarquin's white horse was standing on the far side of the causeway, facing Jai Pendu. A lone figure stood opposing the horse, white-robed, diminutive beside the stallion. It held out a hand to Tarquin and he dismounted.

Oh, no, Istar thought. Whatever she felt about him, she did not want to see Tarquin caught by the Sekk again. Yet she was sure he intended to follow his Company out of the world.

"Tarquin, don't!" she screamed—but she knew he couldn't hear her over the roar of the surf.

The waves drew back. Istar saw Tarquin throw the Glass on the causeway. Then, raising his sword in both hands over his head like an executioner, he brought it down. The Glass shattered and the pieces fell in the sea. The Sekk could do nothing. It was Night's turn to stand motionless, impotent. Slowly, like a sunset, its robes turned black.

"You are as Free as I am now," Tarquin cried up to his men. But

already the Company were being swept away with the floating city. The
sun was going down and the moon was coming up, and through the
transparency of Jai Pendu, two lights at once shone on the spiral path
around the red crystal flower. The riders began to ascend and disappear,
one by one and in twos and threes, into the damaged facets of the crystal
where it intersected the path.

A huge wave was approaching. The causeway was swept under; Tarquin and the Sekk vanished in white and gray water. Istar was swept back
toward the last island and found her feet, standing up to her waist now in
the ebb between waves. She strained her eyes after the Company. She saw
the white horse leap off the edge of Jai Pendu and into the waves, but the
Company were gone within Jai Pendu as it withdrew from the world.

The next wave knocked her down. Her mouth filled with water and
the tide began to pull her away from the submerged causeway. Her head
came up, but too late she realized she didn't have the strength to swim
weighed down against the tide. She had been running on pure will for
some time; now there was nothing left that she could do, except survive—and for that, she had not an ounce of motivation left in her entire
body.

She heard her name among the shouts from the landward side of the
causeway, but her eyes were blurred with saltwater and she couldn't easily
see over the waves, anyway.

A black-braided head came up a few yards away. A figure began pulling toward her. His face came out of the water, and she recognized
Pentar. She was coughing and gasping and angry—for she now realized
that he had been shadowing her since she had crossed the causeway
carrying the Company of Glass. But when his arm fastened across her
shoulders and he began dragging her toward shore, she dug her fingers
into it and hung on for all she was worth. Pallo helped drag them both
out of the water as the waves mounted higher. Pentar half carried her
into the tunnel that led back under the Floating Lands, while others ran
alongside encouraging them. Istar hung on to Pentar without really understanding what was going on. When they got to a safe point, he
stopped to catch his breath. In the confusion that followed the final
breaking of the spell, Clansmen and Pharicians alike were dashing to and
fro.

Pentar was exultant. "Was I glad to see you in that mob! I couldn't
stand it if I had lost you after we made it so far."

She pushed herself away from him, staggering against the wall of the
passage. The realization had taken some time to hit.

"You're not dead!" The words came out a whisper.

Pentar gave a huge smile. "We hid in the equipment and fell in with the army. There were other Clan soldiers, and the Pharicians were not much better than Slaves for their wit, anyway, so no one really noticed. Then later, of course, we had to cut our way out—"

But she wasn't listening.

"*Kassien!*" Her voice cracked on the shriek, just as the familiar figure pushed his way down the crowded passage, minus his bearskin cloak. He smiled at her and waved, and she pushed toward him, no longer tired.

"I-I-I saw your cloak," she stammered. "You were chopped to pieces."

"A Pharician ripped the cloak off me in the stampede. I chopped *him* to bits, Star—get your facts straight." He grinned. "Didn't really want to wear the cloak after that—would you?"

She threw her arms around him, tears streaming down her face.

Pentar's face fell.

"It's a cruel world," Pallo remarked, slapping the Seahawk on the back.

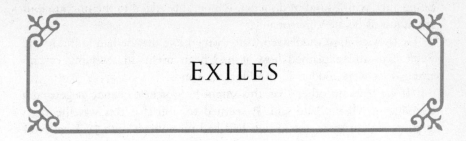
Xiriel was feeling just fine when the sun came up. He had been traipsing back and forth across the Floating Lands freely, for all the bridges had been extended by Night. It gave Xiriel enormous satisfaction to move easily over terrain that had tied his brain in such knots only the day before. But he was perplexed by the idea that the Sekk had brought a whole army through these islands, when he with all his Knowledge had barely brought four others with him. Whatever it was that Night had known, Xiriel was determined to find out for himself. There was much to learn here; he wished he were at liberty to explore it all.

Jai Pendu had gone in the night, leaving great chaos in its wake. The battle between Pharice and the Clans had been quieted, and each side attended to its wounded while trying to leave the other alone. The leaders of the Pharician army were being briefed by Lerien's men, who had so far managed to maintain an uneasy truce with their neighbors. Pharician horsemen were sent off to Jundun with messages while the majority of the army remained scattered across the Floating Lands.

Lerien had been given a powerful Pharician drug, and he was virtually unconscious. Stavel and Taro were acting for him, but they stepped back half a pace when Xiriel approached them to offer his services. Everyone reacted differently to Xiriel now that he was a Snake, even strangers like these two. He was not able to perceive the aura of danger that still clung to him in the wake of the fight with the constrictor; he couldn't even remember the details of that fight, except that he was pretty sure he had lost and had been devoured. As a result, he approached the very fact of being alive with a kind of disbelief, which only added to the unconscious mystique of his new persona.

He showed Taro the flawed, half-formed Eye that he had found in the Sekk cave and explained how it had been useful in revealing certain things that were hidden in the Floating Lands.

"If we have no other Eye, this might be our best chance at getting a message to Mhani," he said. It seemed to him that this was the most urgent of their tasks, for Lerien had had no contact with Jai Khalar for many weeks.

The half-formed Eye did work, but when they found Jai Khalar through it, Mhani was not there, and the Seer who was minding the Eye Tower looked nervous and uncomfortable at the summons. He stammered and the link wavered several times before a new correspondent addressed them. A dark, feral face gazed back at them, rendered slightly convex by the globe. It reacted like a wild creature, jerking back in sudden fright. The Seer Soren murmured something. Tentatively the man crept back into the radius of the Eye. He scrutinized them, and when he recognized Stavel, fear changed to comprehension, and then to satisfaction.

"Ah, my subjects!" Tash gloated. "Greetings from Jai Khalar. You have been annexed. Welcome to the Pharician Empire."

IT WAS ALL that the de facto leaders could do to move their men off the Floating Lands and onto the sea plateau, where they established a base of operations separate from the barely tolerant Pharicians nearby. Except for the ongoing recovery of the dead, the Floating Lands were abandoned.

Istar was sitting on the ruins of one of the emptier islands, picking dried blood out from beneath her nails and humming Chyko's battle song when Kassien brought her the news from the mainland. He had lost weight and his cheekbones stood out sharply, but his eyes on her were soft.

She could scarcely breathe. "What about Mhani?"

"I don't know. Lerien demanded to speak to her, but the Pharicians say they don't know who she is, and Soren just looks scared. It could mean she escaped. It could mean anything."

"It could mean they killed her." Istar focused her eyes on the heel of her own boot where it rested on the crumbling stone. She could hear seagulls, and the smell of woodsmoke reached her, mixed with salt air. When she glanced up, Pentar caught her eye. He was standing ten yards away, which was the distance Istar had thrown his gear and told him to stay away from her, the first night after Jai Pendu had gone. Even so, she was sure he'd overheard. Any impulse to cry that she might have had was quashed by the sight of the pity on his face, and replaced with angry determination.

Kassien was trying to reassure her.

"This warlord Tash—I don't think he's a liar. He's not the type to deny having killed somebody. I think if he wanted Mhani dead, he would have cut off her head and displayed it. Remember, your mother would be valuable to him. He doesn't understand the Water of Glass, and she does. No, I think she escaped. Maybe Hanji's got her stowed away in a wine cellar somewhere."

"And they're both getting really drunk right now," Istar added, laughing and sniffling at the same time. She wiped her eyes. "I hope so, Kass."

"Come on, Istar. Get off your hindbones and come with me to talk to Lerien. What are you doing out here on the Floating Lands, anyway? Don't you know they're dangerous and impassable?"

"I had heard that, yeah. . . ."

The bad news spread quickly through the Clan camp. The Clans reacted as they had done since time immemorial: they began to argue and accuse each other. Kassien and Istar broke up a few scuffles on their way to Lerien's fire. Istar was surprised at the respect tendered her. As an Honorary, she was used to being regarded as a nuisance. When she remarked on this to Kassien, he laughed.

"We're heroes, did you know?"

"It's Pallo who Froze the Sekk so we could get the Glass," Istar said, rising. "Where's he got to?"

"Still asleep," Kassien answered. "He wakes only at the smell of food."

"Some things never change." She raised her voice, calling over her shoulder. "Come on, Pentar. Hurry up."

"WE DON'T HAVE much time," Kassien told Lerien's men. "These Pharicians don't know of Tash's actions, and they probably don't even know that Hezene has declared war on us. We must win them over to our side quickly, or we will find ourselves racing against them to reach Jai Khalar."

"How can we go back to Jai Khalar?" Taro asked, incredulous. "Tash holds it."

Kassien's denial was loud and clear, and it brought several within earshot to their feet. "Tash doesn't scare us! We have saved our people from an enemy that would shrink Tash's balls to walnuts if he knew it. Let him enjoy possessing Jai Khalar—see how he feels after a few weeks of losing his men and his own bed. Anyway, he cannot hold the whole valley without support from Hezene, who will have every reason to reassert his friendship with us once he realizes it is our efforts that have kept his Ristale guard from being swallowed by the Sekk."

Stavel laughed. "How refreshing is the idealism of youth. Kassien, you do not understand politics if you think Hezene will thank you for any of this. If we want to take Everien back, we are going to have to do it ourselves."

"Then we will," Istar stated, animated by conviction. "We have to."

"This is no time to back down," Pentar added quietly from behind her.

"We have little choice but to back down," said Urutar, one of the commanders who had been Enslaved. "That doesn't mean we have to give up. We know our own land well. The Pharicians do not. We should return to the hills as quickly as possible and fight them from the heights, just as the Sekk have always fought us."

"Yes," agreed Stavel. "Why should we spend ourselves trying to re-capture Jai Khalar? Let them wear themselves out trying to hold it. We can go back to old-style campaigning."

"And what of Lerien?" Ketar asked. "He is gravely ill."

"He is still the king," Taro said.

"We shall see," murmured Kassien. "If you will not stand against Tash, then we should leave this place at once. The Pharicians have lost many men to the Company of Glass. They will be looking for someone to take it out on."

"Where will we go?"

Istar said, "We will return to our land—but as Urutar said, we must do so in secret. There will be a way to win back Everien, but until that way is found, we will be exiles in our own country."

Kassien grunted his approval. For once he agreed with her.

Two Months Later

Summer was almost over, and there was a noise of singing in the house of the youngest blacksmith of the Deer Clan at A-vi-Khalar. Two voices tried unsuccessfully to blend: one young and sweet, the other quavering, sometimes dropping the beat or going flat, uncertain. The blacksmith's wife paused in her scrubbing and called, "Enzi, I had better not find out you were pestering your auntie when you are supposed to be washing carrots."

A brown head popped around the corner of the kitchen door, flashed a mischievous smile, and retreated, leaving a trail of giggles.

"I think she is better today," the child's voice rang, echoing down the hall. "She keeps asking to go to the Fire Houses."

"Yes, and I keep asking to go to the Harvest Ball, but does it happen?" muttered the blacksmith's wife, and wiped sweat off her forehead with the back of her arm. "Come in here, Enzi! You will wear her out with your endless questions. Children are so exhausting. I don't know why I have you."

"Auntie Mhani says that children are the ultimate aggravation. I think when I am grown I shall keep goats." Enzi wandered into the kitchen, trailing a finger along the white wall and leaving a gray stain behind. "I'm going to help you now."

"Are you? Good."

Enzi picked up a generous handful of carrots and dunked them in water.

"Auntie Mhani says that having daughters is better than having sons," she confided, "because you can talk to the daughters and they listen to you, and they don't ride off like the sons do and maybe get killed like their fathers—or worse."

"Auntie Mhani says many things. You must not take her too seriously."

"What did she mean by 'worse'? What could be worse than getting killed? Does she mean the Slaving?"

"Perhaps. Or she might be talking about Jai Pendu. But she is not in her right mind, Enzi. Don't let her talk to you of terrors. You will have nightmares."

"But I feel sorry for her," Enzi said. "She has no man, and her own children belong to a different Clan, and one of them never returned from the battle of Jai Pendu. I think she is lonely, Mother. That's why I keep her company—not to pester her."

The blacksmith's wife smiled at her youngest child, who had turned large, sensitive eyes on her. "Of course you mean well, Enzi. Just don't wear her out. She is ill, remember."

"Yes, I know. But she is a great lady, and maybe one day she will get better."

"It is possible." She didn't add, *but I doubt it.*

The child picked up the tune again, humming as she rinsed carrots and pulled off the tops. Only a few minutes had passed when there was a rattle of hooves on the paving stones outside. Enzi's head suddenly came up. "A horse!" she cried, and dropped the carrots in the sink. "Got to go! Sorry, Mother."

"Get back here, Enzi! It might be a Pharician."

But Enzi was too quick for her, darting out of the kitchen and into the passageway that led to the street. Standing in the kitchen doorway, she drew breath to call her daughter back when Bazi, her son, came down the alley and calmly said, "It's not a Pharician, Mother. Or a murderer! Enzi is all right."

"Any excuse to avoid the kitchen," grumbled Enzi's mother, flapping her apron to cover her fear. The Pharicians had not yet made any drastic changes since they had taken over at Jai Khalar, but when you lived in the village that owned the Fire Houses, you had to expect that there would be trouble sooner or later.

She returned to work, but she could hear both of her children talking to the new arrival. The horse's hooves clopped past on the way to the yard and she heard laughter outside. Then a voice she hadn't heard in a long time called, "Halloo? Anybody home?"

The warrior who appeared in the doorway was dressed as a man, hair braided Seahawk-style, hands tough and brown and one arm bandaged. Yet few men would have been so short and none so wide-hipped, and anyway without armor it was apparent that the warrior was female, for her shirt was half-open in the summer heat, and the glass vial that she wore on a thong around her neck was nestled within cleavage that Enzi gazed at enviously.

"Is there anything to eat?" the newcomer asked in a low-pitched voice. She leaned against the lintel, feigning exhaustion. "I've been riding all morning, and I'm starving."

EPILOGUE

The sky opened its starry wings above Tarquin as he grappled the waves. They pitched him skyward the way a father might toss a child; except the father would be playing and the ocean was not. The deep was indifferent to Tarquin as he lay on its back like a leaf. It did not care that his throat was full of water, that his chest was tight, or that he was chilled to the bone. The shine and glory of Jai Pendu had vanished long ago, and the waves were too tall to offer any view of land. He had no idea which way to go, and doubted he could withstand the current anyway. His only hope was to keep his head above water and stay conscious even though the cold fed on his life. Were it not for the horse he might have given up.

Once or twice he glimpsed Ice, who looked like a stylized wave with his proud, arching neck and flowing mane, untroubled by the cold swells. Twice he managed to grab hold of Ice's tail and was dragged until the rough waters separated them again. Then he tried to follow the horse. By the time light began to grow and he learned which way was east, Tarquin was too far gone to profit from the information. He was all but witless, thinking only of the bottom of the sea, convinced he was about to go there.

Something had changed in the night. The dawn sky was heavily clouded, tinged with thunder-green. The waves became tepid and calmer, revealing a shoreline of verdant mountains buried in cloud. A warm, humid breeze began to blow. The surge carried him landward, toward a set of sharp, bald cliffs of red clay; when the waves struck they made a sound like deep breathing.

Eventually he managed to gain a handhold, but he hadn't the strength to pull himself out of the water. He dragged himself along the cliff until he came to a low outcropping, where he tried to climb out. His muscles felt gelatinous and foreign. He closed his eyes.

A viselike hand gripped his upper arm and began to tug with considerable strength. Surprised, he kicked against the stone and came out of the water like a seal, scraping himself on the red rock. He looked up at a skinny, white-haired boy with dark brown skin.

"Who the fuck are you?" Tarquin demanded, startled and disbelieving. His savior drew back a pace and regarded him through coal dark eyes. His lips were black but when he smiled, his teeth were paper white. They seemed larger than usual, and they swelled the contours of his face even when his mouth was shut. His nose was curved and fleshy, and he had enormous hands with slender fingers and knobby knuckles. He wore no Clan paint, and he was too weedy to be Pharician; too ugly to be Sekk; too tall to be Wild; too delicate for an islander. . . . Tarquin had traveled for many years, but no. There was no tribe of people that looked anything like this boy.

"Who are you?" he repeated in a faint voice.

"She couldn't give me a name," the boy answered. "There wasn't time. Nemelir said I was to be fed to Ice at birth, and everyone knows the naming day is ten days after that."

Tarquin blinked saltwater from his eyes and tried to make sense of what the boy was saying. *Nemelir?* Wasn't that the name of Keras's trainer?

"It was the craziest deal I ever cut," she said.

"Come on," urged the boy. "I haven't been on my own two feet in ages. Let's explore!"

ACKNOWLEDGMENTS

When I started writing this story, Russ Galen was my imaginary reader, and he is probably wrapped up with the text in ways I don't begin to understand. But I did understand the Talisker, and the view, and one or two other things.

Mic, during this book you saved my life so many times I'm starting to count on divine intervention at regular intervals. In particular, thanks for Cornwall, and my first cigarette, and the words I needed to hear that no one but you knew how to tell me; and thanks for introducing me to China Miéville. (Chi, I hope you like the monsters. They're for you.)

Caroline Oakley and Anne Lesley Groell both did yeomen's work, especially in editing the first draft; as always, I'm grateful for their criticism and understanding in equal parts, and their vast patience above all. I also appreciate the support of Sky Nonhoff and Danny Baror.

Finally, I would like to thank my dear friends Lisa and Caroline, for sage and advice.

ABOUT THE AUTHOR

VALERY LEITH is an expatriate American living in England and practicing martial arts while working on the next Everien novel.